Winner of the Spur Award for Best Western Historical Novel

"[Captures] with grace and passion that agonizing point in history when the opening of the Western frontier spelled demise for the Indian civilization. Cooke deftly weaves its many layers around births, deaths, love affairs, visions awaited, dreams interpreted, battles avoided and begun . . . a lovely chronicle of a changing world."

—*The Philadelphia Inquirer*

"*The Snowblind Moon* can justly be called an epic tale of the struggle between the Indians and whites for control of the Plains in the 1870s. Cooke's prose can be lyrically beautiful . . . And his research is comprehensive . . . an admirable drama."

—*Los Angeles Times*

"Engaging . . . informative . . . The battle scenes are vivid, and everyday life is depicted in authentic, fascinating detail."

—*The New York Times Book Review*

"A giant-sized record of the 'civilizing' of the West."

—*Library Journal*

"An enormous and vital story, resoundingly told. The struggle for the Plains—the last great conflict between whites and Indians—requires a book of great expeditionary detail and length to do justice to the . . . ways of life that met there, and Cooke's novel succeeds with honors."

—*Publishers Weekly*

THE SNOWBLIND MOON by John Byrne Cooke

PART ONE: BETWEEN THE WORLDS
PART TWO: THE PIPE CARRIERS
PART THREE: HOOP OF THE NATION

THE PIPE CARRIERS

THE SNOWBLIND MOON

JOHN BYRNE COOKE

TOR
A TOM DOHERTY ASSOCIATES BOOK

THE SNOWBLIND MOON PART TWO: THE PIPE CARRIERS

Reprinted by arrangement with Simon and Schuster

First Tor printing: August 1986

A TOR Book

Published by Tom Doherty Associates
49 West 24 Street
New York, N.Y. 10010

ISBN: 0-812-58152-0
CAN. ED.: 0-812-58153-9

Library of Congress Catalog Card Number: 84-14009

Printed in the United States

0 9 8 7 6 5 4 3 2 1

For my father, who helped to instill in me a love of books, which was easy, and of history, which took somewhat longer.

When I was a boy the Sioux owned the world; the sun rose and set in their lands; they sent ten thousand horsemen to battle. Where are the warriors today? Who slew them? Where are our lands? Who owns them?

—SITTING BULL

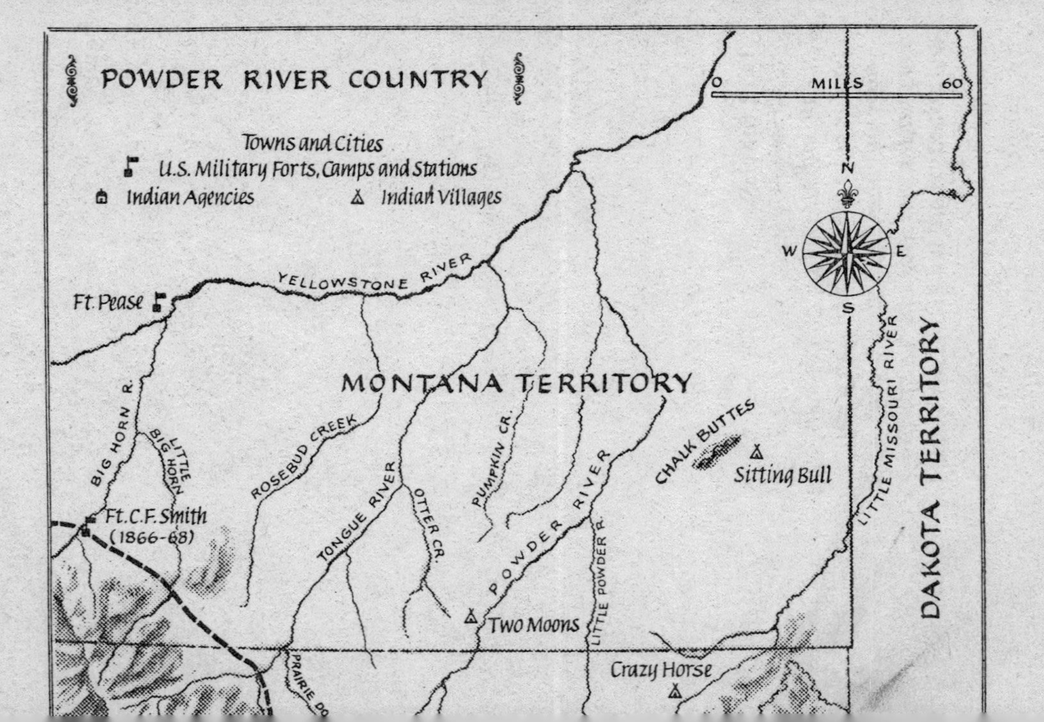
POWDER RIVER COUNTRY
Towns and Cities
U.S. Military Forts, Camps and Stations
Indian Agencies
Indian Villages
0
MILES
60
N
W
E
S
YELLOWSTONE RIVER
Ft. Pease
MONTANA TERRITORY
DAKOTA TERRITORY
LITTLE MISSOURI RIVER
BIG HORN R.
LITTLE BIG HORN
Ft. C.F. Smith
(1866-68)
ROSEBUD CREEK
TONGUE RIVER
OTTER CR.
PUMPKIN CR.
POWDER RIVER
LITTLE POWDER R.
CHALK BUTTES
Sitting Bull
Two Moons
Crazy Horse

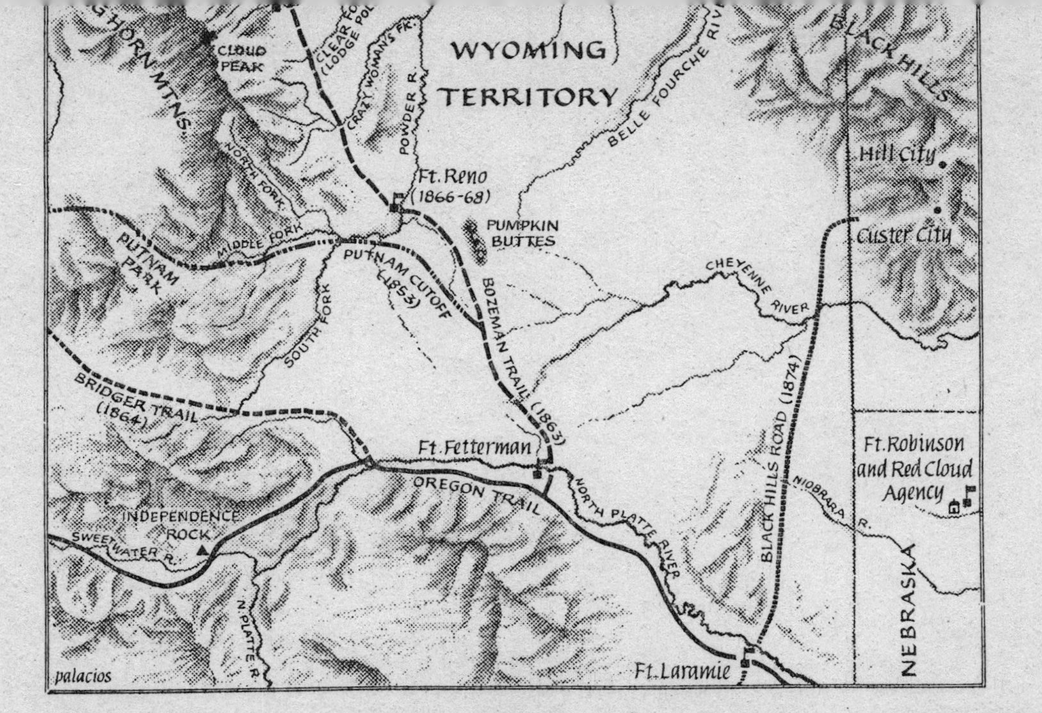
WYOMING
TERRITORY
BLACK HILLS
Hill City
Custer City
CLOUD PEAK
CRAZY WOMAN'S FK.
POWDER R.
BELLE FOURCHE RIV
Ft. Reno (1866-68)
PUMPKIN BUTTES
NORTH FORK
MIDDLE FORK
PUTNAM PARK
PUTNAM CUTOFF (1853)
SOUTH FORK
BOZEMAN TRAIL (1863)
CHEYENNE RIVER
BLACK HILLS ROAD (1874)
BRIDGER TRAIL (1864)
Ft. Fetterman
OREGON TRAIL
NORTH PLATTE RIVER
NIOBRARA R.
Ft. Robinson and Red Cloud Agency
INDEPENDENCE ROCK
SWEETWATER R.
N. PLATTE R.
NEBRASKA
Ft. Laramie
palacios

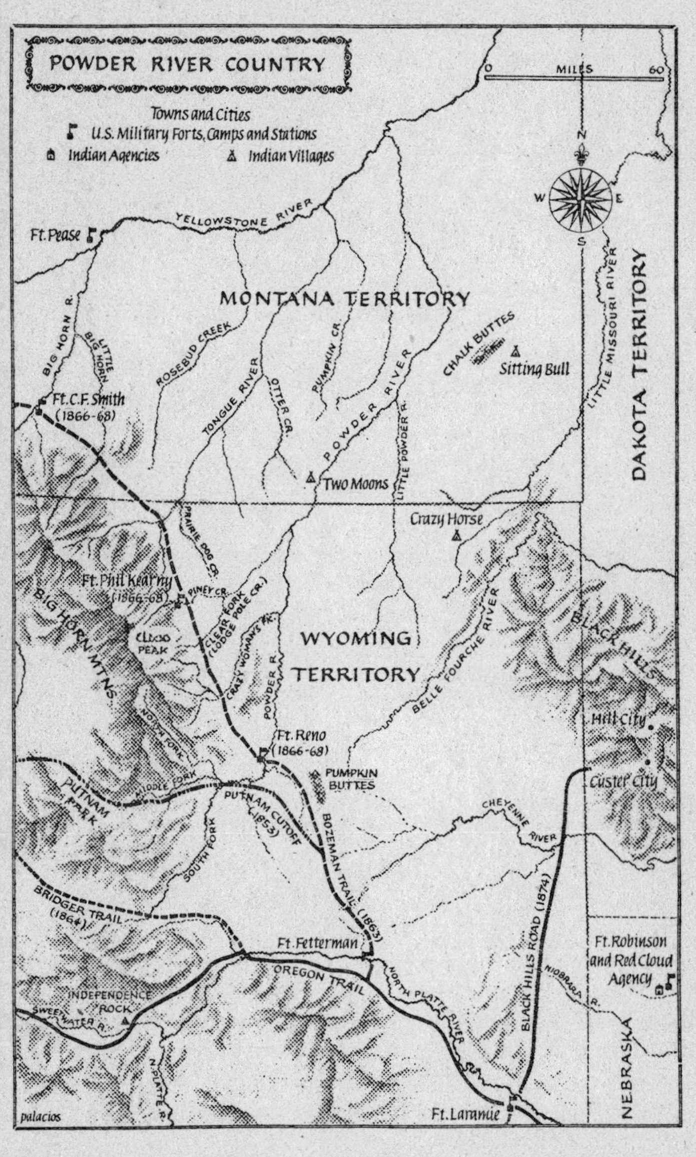
POWDER RIVER COUNTRY
Towns and Cities
U.S. Military Forts, Camps and Stations
Indian Agencies
Indian Villages
0 MILES 60
N
W
E
S
YELLOWSTONE RIVER
Ft. Pease
MONTANA TERRITORY
DAKOTA TERRITORY
BIG HORN R.
LITTLE BIG HORN
ROSEBUD CREEK
TONGUE RIVER
OTTER CR.
PUMPKIN CR.
POWDER RIVER
LITTLE POWDER R.
CHALK BUTTES
Sitting Bull
LITTLE MISSOURI RIVER
Ft. C.F. Smith
(1866-68)
Two Moons
Crazy Horse
PRAIRIE DOG CR.
Ft. Phil Kearny
(1866-68)
PINEY CR.
CLEAR FORK (LODGE POLE CR.)
CRAZY WOMAN'S FK.
POWDER R.
BIG HORN MTNS
CLOUD PEAK
WYOMING
TERRITORY
BELLE FOURCHE RIVER
BLACK HILLS
Hill City
Custer City
NORTH FORK
Ft. Reno
(1866-68)
PUMPKIN BUTTES
MIDDLE FORK
PUTNAM PARK
PUTNAM CUTOFF (1853)
SOUTH FORK
BOZEMAN TRAIL (1863)
CHEYENNE RIVER
BRIDGER TRAIL
(1864)
Ft. Fetterman
BLACK HILLS ROAD (1874)
Ft. Robinson
and Red Cloud
Agency
OREGON TRAIL
NORTH PLATTE RIVER
NIOBRARA R.
INDEPENDENCE ROCK
SWEETWATER R.
N. PLATTE R.
NEBRASKA
palacios
Ft. Laramie

What has gone before in *Between the Worlds*, Part One of *The Snowblind Moon* . . .

In the winter of 1876, war clouds are gathering over the Powder River country of Wyoming Territory. By treaty, this land belongs to the Sioux, but the government is determined to confine the last free-roaming bands on the Dakota reservation. As General George Crook and eight hundred soldiers start north from Fort Fetterman, two riders precede them into the troubled region; they are Chris Hardeman, a former army scout, and Johnny Smoker, a young man who was taken from a wagon train when he was an infant and was raised by the Cheyenne. His life was saved by Hardeman at the Battle of the Washita, where Johnny's Indian parents were killed, and they have been together for the seven years since then. With Crook's blessing they have come in hopes of heading off a new Indian war by persuading Sun Horse, a Sioux peace chief, to surrender, and thereby to influence other hostile headmen to give in without fighting. Johnny's Indian father was Sioux, not Cheyenne, and he was Sun Horse's eldest son. Hardeman too knows Sun Horse, indirectly: as a youth, Hardeman was trained in scouting by Jedediah Putnam, a former mountain man who later settled in the

Big Horn foothills and has turned to raising cattle. Jed and Sun Horse have long been friends; Jed's brother Bat married Sun Horse's daughter and lives with the Sioux. (Like all the western bands, Sun Horse's people call themselves Lakota. Sioux is a name their enemies gave them.) The Sun Band, as Sun Horse's people are known, winters just a few miles from Putnam's Park, where Jed's settlement is located. Hardeman hopes Jed will help persuade Sun Horse to surrender.

But when Hardeman and Johnny arrive in Putnam's Park they learn that Jed Putnam died six months ago and the little ranch is now in the hands of his daughter Lisa, a woman in her early thirties, and his black partner Julius Ingram, a former slave and cavalryman. The news of the approaching army shocks Lisa. She is concerned for Sun Horse's safety and wants to help him remain free, but as she leads Hardeman and Johnny to the Indian village, she can see no choice for the Sioux but the one Hardeman brings: fight or surrender.

Johnny's appearance has a profound effect on Sun Horse, who believed the boy had died with his parents at the Washita. He sees in Johnny's coming a turning point for the Sun Band. Old Hears Twice, the band's prophet, has recently foretold the coming of a power that can help the people, or destroy them. "It comes from the meeting of two people," Hears Twice told the headman. Sun Horse is certain Johnny is one of the two, but who is the other? Since he became leader of the band, Sun Horse's goal has been to understand the whites and lead his people to live in peace beside them, thus fulfilling a promise of power given to him in a medicine dream. He seeks a way to delay in replying to Crook's ultimatum, hoping against hope that he will see how he can keep his people free, without fighting, without surrender. But if there is no other choice, he will surrender, for he knows that to fight the whites is to fight the whirlwind.

Hardeman and Lisa return to Putnam's Park but Johnny stays with his adopted grandfather as the band's council meets to decide what to do. For Johnny, this reunion with

Sun Horse is difficult. When the youth was eight, his Indian parents took him to meet Sun Horse. There Johnny had a dream, a powerful medicine dream not usually given to one so young. In it, he was told by a white buffalo cow—a potent spirit for the Sioux—that in time he would be returned to the world of his birth, but he would not fully belong to the whites. When he was about to become a man, the buffalo said, he would have to choose for good between the Indian and white worlds. Sun Horse interpreted the dream for Johnny and gave him his name—He Stands Between the Worlds—and made him promise that when the time came for him to choose, he would tell Sun Horse of his choice. Now Johnny has chosen. He is white and he will remain in the white world. But being in an Indian village again unsettles him and he delays telling Sun Horse of his decision.

When the council meets, Sun Horse is silent, unable to find an alternative to surrender, and reluctantly the councillors decide to accept Crook's offer of meat and blankets for the people and grain for their horses, in exchange for surrender.

In Putnam's Park, Hardeman waits for Sun Horse to bring his decision and he worries about Johnny. He has given no thought to what effect returning among the Indians might have on the youth. What if Johnny chooses to stay with Sun Horse? What if the war begins despite Hardeman's efforts? What will Sun Horse do?

The waiting is brought to an end by the arrival in the park of something so unexpected that those in the settlement are struck speechless when they see it: up the wagon road come the wagons of a traveling circus. En route to the mining towns of Montana, they have lost their way. Hachaliah Tatum, the show's owner, asks Lisa if he and his people may camp overnight before retracing their steps back to the main trail. At this moment a group of Indians appears—Sun Horse and some of his men, come to give Hardeman their decision. The circus men panic and open fire, but a tragedy is averted by Lisa, Julius and Hardeman, who draw on the circus men and force them to put down their arms.

To help ease the lingering tension, a clown steps out of the crowd and makes whites and Indians alike laugh at his antics. He slips and falls, and when Johnny Smoker helps him up, the clown's cap falls off, revealing long brown hair. It is not a man at all, but a young woman. Johnny is smitten, and his reaction is observed by Sun Horse, who feels a chill of power in this meeting. These are the two the prophet heard! But will their power help or hurt the Sun Band? Sun Horse doesn't know, but he is suddenly full of hope. He must delay giving in to the whites; he must have time to understand this power. And now he sees how to delay. He will send pipes of peace to his cousin Sitting Bull, the most famous of the war leaders, and to General Crook, asking both to keep the peace. If Sitting Bull will restrain his young men and if Crook will leave the country now, Sun Horse will speak to the hostile headmen when the grass is green, urging peace. He will send Bat Putnam and Hardeman with the pipe carriers; two white men to speak to the white general. But Hardeman will not know the full message to Sitting Bull: Sun Horse will ask his cousin to call for a great gathering of the bands in summertime, so the people can decide for themselves the momentous issues of peace and war. Surely, thinks Sun Horse, all the Lakotas gathered together are strong enough to make a true peace, one that might include some of the Powder River hunting country? Perhaps there can be peace after all, without surrender!

THE PIPE CARRIERS

CHAPTER ONE

Music and dancers swirled around Bat Putnam. He smiled as he watched the couples spin by, noting the lip rouge and powder on the circus women, their brightly colored clothing, their high spirits. On the makeshift bandstand at the far end of the room, Hutch sat surrounded by musicians from the circus and flailed at his banjo as if his life depended on it, his eyes returning often to a young girl his own age, one of a family of Italian acrobats and aerial gymnasts, who was dancing near at hand with her father. Bat's smile broadened and he sipped again from the glass he held in his hand, taking a special pleasure in the taste of the fiery corn liquor. He danced by himself in a backwater, shuffling a small step suited to a drunken man on rough ground around a Rendezvous campfire, but he wasn't half drunk, not yet. The unlikely arrival of Tatum's Combined Equestrian and Animal Shows offered a natural opportunity for a man to get respectably wall-eyed and Bat intended to make the best of it. He'd already had enough to send most men to their beds, but he was just now oiled and primed for whatever was to follow. Around him, the saloon rang with laughter and life, and the ghosts were banished.

Whooee, some doin's, he thought, but he kept his glee to himself instead of shouting it out as he might have done. He contained it just as he contained the joy he had felt ever since that afternoon, savoring it as a starving man might savor the liver of a fresh-killed deer. There would be time enough later on for shouting out his triumph, if Sun Horse's plan worked. For now he would keep his hopes to himself.

Back this afternoon things had got a mite touchy there for a bit, but he had seen worse happen when a bunch of greenhorns decided that shooting was what you did first off when you set eyes on Indians. Lisa hadn't taken kindly to the shooting. For his own part, Bat felt that burning a little powder had livened up what had been a quiet winter so far and set everyone up just right for tonight's shindig. There was nothing like dancing to work off a hair-raising fright.

The Lakota were gone now. Sun Horse knew that Indians and whites and whiskey were a bad mix. Before they left, the warriors had walked among the circus wagons for a look at the strange animals. Bat and Sun Horse had joined them there when Sun Horse was done talking with Hardeman. They had marveled at the buffalo from Ceylon and the spotted leopard from Africa, the same land the elephant came from. *Igmú gleshka* they called the leopard—spotted cat. There was much excited talk when they saw the bear and the wolves, animals well known to them. A Lakota called Wolf Talker had lingered for a time with the wolves, but they were some foreign kind of wolf and he couldn't understand their language. A small group of the more courageous circus folk had accompanied the Indians on their tour, the mahout Chatur among them, and the Lakota had puzzled for a time over the dark-skinned man when they learned he was also called Indian but came from a faraway land. They seemed satisfied when they learned that this *India* whence he came was ruled by Grandmother England, the same woman who ruled Grandmother Land, which was just six or seven days' hard ride to the north, up beyond the Yellowstone. Several of them had been to Grandmother Land. "Grandmother England, she treats her Injuns pretty good," Standing Eagle had offered.

It had been quite a day for the circus folk too. With the Indians gone, each had his story to tell about the arrival in Putnam's Park and the first sight of wild Indians, and the stories had grown fanciful in the retelling once the strong drink began to flow. Even now, at a nearby table, Chatur was surrounded by circus women eager to hear it all again from the dark little man who spoke in a strangely accented British English. "Oh, I should say, I was most terrified," he was saying. "But Rama was ready for battle!" The women urged him on as Bat moved away to be closer to the music. He would have his own stories to tell about this day.

Lisa had done Jed proud on short notice today. She had put on a feed and a flingding ánd a celebration that came waist-high to the real thing all those years ago in the Rendezvous camps. After a meal of meat and potatoes and corn pudding and tinned tomatoes and fancy fixings Bat hadn't seen in a dozen years, topped off with pies and breads that little Ling had been the whole afternoon baking, the circus folk had flocked back to the bar for something to wash down the last of their food. And after that there was another glass to wash down the first and before long even the faces of the wagon drivers were downright jolly. From out of the wagons musical instruments were soon fetched, for anyone but a complete fool knows he'd best play for his supper if he's able, and young Hutch had run to get his banjo. It was a fair little band, with some big brass instruments Bat hadn't seen since his Boston youth.

Just now a fat German with nimble fingers stood at the front of the bandstand, which had been made in ten minutes from the bed of an old wagon turned upside down. He played a rollicking polka on an accordion with sweat running down his face. After each song he downed a glass of beer in the time most men took just to draw a breath. Beside him, Hutch kept looking at the man playing the tuba like he might look at a three-legged rooster that had learned how to run. He wasn't quite sure how it did what it did, but you could see by his expression that it tickled him pink.

Bat moved across the floor more quickly now, making his way among the twirling couples as easily as an ermine slipping through a patch of winter willows and feeling just as invisible, for few took notice of him. The quadrilles and reels of earlier in the evening had given way to exuberant polkas and gallops and schottisches, and dancers had their eyes on their partners. The men and women on the floor were breathing hard and sweating freely, their recent hardships forgotten, and Bat could feel the excitement rising around him. The circus folk knew how to enjoy themselves when they found shelter on the trail, that was truth. And if they shouted and laughed and told ribald jokes in French and German and Italian as well as English, that wasn't so different from the old days when the trapper camps heard French on all sides, together with English and Arapaho and Snake and Cheyenne and Lakota.

There had been a time when any chance that brought men together in large numbers had been cause for a boisterous celebration where introductions performed over liberal draughts of forty-rod whiskey led in a short while to oaths of lasting comradeship if affinity was apparent, or mutual avoidance thereafter if it was not. When there were only a few white men in the mountains, it was best to know your comrades well, for your life would certainly depend on them when something set the badger loose. But times had changed. Anymore, the process of getting to know a stranger was slow, from what little Bat knew of current practices in civilized diggin's. The frontier had developed a reserve it lowered so gradually that except in cases of real liking, two parties might meet and talk and go off their own ways with scarcely an inkling about the true nature of the other.

"Wagh!" Bat snorted in disgust at a world where men had so little need to know other men and make a friend where they could. A woman turned, startled by the sound, and shrank back from the mountain man in his greasy leather clothes. Bat saw the rising mounds of her breasts above a low-cut bodice of green satin. He smiled in appreciation and passed on.

Lisa had done her daddy proud, all right, rest his bones. Jed was a mountain man at heart and he had kept to the old ways, even after he planted his stick for good in this valley. Celebrations had been a natural consequence of the arrival in Putnam's Park of any large group, red or white, and today Lisa had put on the show by herself, without Jed at the helm.

Bat saw her now by the kitchen door, looking solemn, and he sidled up close, but she didn't notice him. He slapped her lightly on the rump, then rubbed the spot he had patted, taking an uncle's pride in the shape and feel of his niece.

"Uncle Bat!"

"Won't have you lookin' like that. Not tonight. Don't see a sour puss in this bunch, do you?"

She smiled then and showed her delight. "It's nice, isn't it?"

"What's troublin' you, then?"

"Him."

Bat followed her gaze. Across the room Hardeman was leaning against the wall, watching the dancers. He was wearing the buckskins he had worn all day, but his hair was freshly combed. Johnny Smoker stood beside him. The youth had donned a bright red flannel shirt. A clean bandanna, this one a dark green, was tied loosely around his neck.

"Well?"

"Too close with himself, Father would have said."

"Mebbe."

"What will he do?"

"Don't rightly know. He'll go along for now, I'm thinkin'."

"Will he?"

"It's a chance for peace, honey child. If Sun Horse talks to the war chiefs come summertime, might be we'll all come out ahead."

"It's too good to be true. And it's not what he wants. He said over and over again the peace has to be made now or there will be a war." She watched Hardeman through the happy dancers. He stood outside the celebration, watching but not taking part. "I wish I knew what sort of man he really is."

"This nigger knows that fur. Tough like a badger. Don't let much get to him." Bat put an arm around his niece and held her close to comfort her, as he had often done when she was a child. "Happen you come up on his right side, you'd have a longtime friend, I'm thinkin'."

"I'm not so certain."

Bat grinned and released her. "You ain't, but this critter knows. I been told by the bear!" And he danced away with himself, his feet shuffling as gracefully as the dying grizzly bear had shuffled with poor Toussaint. This was the step he danced this evening, not the whiskey stagger of Rendezvous but the bear's dance that had welcomed him into the mountain life, feeling the bear power alive inside him again. Now as then the chance for new life opened before him, at least for a time. New hope was born, given birth by the words Sun Horse had spoken that afternoon.

When Sun Horse returned from his solitary ponderings beyond the wagon road, Hardeman and Johnny had walked to the corner of the porch, near where Bat and Standing Eagle sat their mounts. Sun Horse had joined them there. He spoke in Lakota and Bat translated, and Hardeman listened quietly, never interrupting. Bat had almost laughed aloud to express his glee when he heard Sun Horse's new plan. Like the headman, he had been silent in the council on the previous day, not wanting to urge his brethren to surrender but unable to suggest another course, and now Sun Horse had found one. Bat had been even more elated when Hardeman agreed to go with the pipe carriers, and even Standing Eagle seemed pleased with the scheme.

Why Johnny had picked that moment to tell Sun Horse that he had decided to stay in the white folks' world, Bat didn't know, but even that news hadn't dampened all of the headman's hopes, as if he knew it was coming sooner or later. And when Hardeman and the boy had gone off, and Standing Eagle went to join the other Lakota men among the circus wagons, Sun Horse had motioned Bat to stay behind, and it was then that he had asked Bat to accompany the pipe carriers. Bat had readily agreed. Sending two white men to plead the headman's plan with Crook might just do the trick, but Bat wasn't so sure about having Standing Eagle along. "My brother Standing Eagle does not always keep his temper around the *washíchun*," he had said. "Three Stars will see that he does not want this peace." Sun Horse had nodded. "Three Stars will see, and he will believe all the more in what the pipe tells him. The *washíchun* hear the word of a war leader."

It was true, although from what Bat had heard of George Crook, he knew the difference between a war leader and a headman. Some officers, the best ones, took the trouble to learn the ways of Indian leadership and they saw that a war leader had power only in war, while it was the headmen and the councils that decided the terms for peace, but most soldiers had the arrogance of their kind and figured that a treaty should bear the marks of the warriors. Back in '68 the Oglala had been forced to make Red Cloud a treaty chief because the whites had insisted that the Laramie treaty would be no good until the mighty Red Cloud signed. And so Red Cloud, who was only a war leader of one band, had been given the power to touch the pen at Laramie, but just for that one time.

Bat grinned at the foolishness of the whites. Sun Horse was no fool. He had covered his bets both ways, sending a war leader to carry the proposal of a headman. And the wise old Lakota had remembered best of all the lesson Bat and Jed Putnam had taught him long ago: "Don't treat a white man any different from a Crow or a Pawnee. Don't answer him yes or no. Make him deal."

Sun Horse had found a way to deal; he had found a way to gain some time for the Sun Band, and Bat had hope that the plan might work. In Sun Horse's manner he had seen new confidence, and from that moment Bat's spirits had risen until now he could scarcely contain them. If Crook accepted the terms, there was hope. If Sun Horse could play the peacemaker among the warlike bands, there was hope. Best of all, the summer council might find a way to make a lasting peace and still keep some of the Powder River country, and if that hope was realized, there was hope for Bat to live out his days with the Sioux.

Of course, Sun Horse had said nothing to Hardeman about the call for a summer gathering of the bands; the whites feared any such gathering, sure it could mean only war. "But he may learn of the great council when we give the pipe to Sitting Bull," Bat had said, suddenly concerned. "Perhaps," Sun Horse had replied. "But by then he will have traveled with the pipe carriers for many days and nights. He will eat with you and sleep with you; he will sit in council with my cousin Sitting Bull and he will see that even the famous war leader wishes only to protect his people and save some of his country. Perhaps then the white scout will see that talk of the summer council should be kept from Three Stars." When Crook finally heard of the gathering he might believe he had been tricked, but by then the councillors would have decided what to do; if they offered peace, the offer would be impressive, coming from such an assemblage; if they chose war, it would not matter what Crook thought.

Bat saw Hardeman now, standing on the fringes of the dancing and gaiety. Bat danced the dance of the bear and he saw with the eyes of the bear. Hardeman was a creature of the wild, though perhaps a bit dulled at the edges by too much time in the towns. He moved his eyes like something wild when caught in a crowd like this one, and Bat felt once more a kinship with the scout. He remembered the way Hardeman was at ease on the trail to the Sun Band's village, and he understood the true wisdom of Sun Horse's plan. Together Bat and Hardeman would go to find Crook, and away from this press of people Hardeman would be at ease and they would come to know each other. Bat wondered if Hardeman had ever traveled with Indians in their own country before or if he had always been with white soldiers, ranging out in front of the column, looking for the Indians as enemies. Who was to say what changes might take place in such a man on a journey down the Powder? Who was to say what might happen if such a man should feel in himself the beginnings of kinship with Bat Putnam, or even with the Sioux?

What might be accomplished by a man who had the trust of both sides, a man who could speak for the Sioux as well as the whites?

"Hooraw fer the mountains!" Bat said softly under his breath. He made his way to the bar, where he held out his glass and caught Julius's eye. When the glass was full once more, he moved along, dancing all the while.

The music filled the room and the floor trembled under the rhythmic tread of the dancers. This was the heart of the evening and Bat wanted to share it with his wife. He wanted to hold her in his arms and kick up his heels. They would dance as they had danced when they were young, to celebrate his hope. She wouldn't want to come amongst so many raucous whites, but he would bring her anyway. She was safe with him.

He turned toward the kitchen door to go fetch her from the lodge, but there was no need. There she stood, talking with Lisa, laughing now. Penelope did not often come into the Big House, never having grown accustomed to white men's lodgings or customs, but sometimes she and Lisa sought each other out just for the sake of the hilarity their talk always engendered.

Bat danced close and hooked his arm through his wife's, taking her by surprise, and he swirled her away to the strains of the polka.

Lisa smiled and watched them go, marveling at how well Penelope knew the white man's dance steps.

"We're done cleaning up, ma'am. I'll help to tend the bar, if you like."

She turned to find the circus cook addressing her. He had found her in the kitchen that afternoon not long after the sudden gunplay had ended. Lisa had been wondering how to begin when he had appeared with two women and an angular man named Monty at his side. "Name's Joe Kitchen," he had said. "I'm the cookie." He was round from eating well and short by nature, a white man's counterpart to Harry Wo, and without him the celebration now in full swing around them would have been a poorer thing.

Lisa had not thought twice about how she intended to welcome Tatum's people to Putnam's Park. It was only how to go about it that had stymied her for a time as she struggled to grasp the quantities of food to be prepared; but Joe Kitchen was used to such problems and needed only to know how best to help out, and with his appearance Lisa's uncertainty had vanished. She ordered dusty jugs of whiskey and gin brought from the cellar, and before the afternoon light had turned gray, the bar glasses were wiped clean and a fire made in the stove and the saloon was open for business. And then from Lisa's scanty stores and the circus supply wagons the meal was assembled. Joe Kitchen provided fresh meat the drivers had brought down three days before when the wagons came on a group of winter-poor antelope, and beer to go with the whiskey and gin, and tins of corned beef, even oysters for those that liked them and deviled ham for those that didn't, and together with what Putnam House had to offer from shelves and root cellar the thing was done. The kitchen had grown hot from the heat of two stoves, and fires had been built outside as well, over which the cooking pots of the circus were hung, and before the cries for food grew too loud the platters had been paraded into the saloon where they were greeted with cheers. Through it all Joe Kitchen's sharp tongue and brash manner with the women had enlivened the cooking. He had a way both familiar and respectful, and by the time she finally sat down to eat, Lisa felt she had a new friend.

"You've done enough for one day," she said now. "You deserve to enjoy yourself."

"Oh, I'll have a dance or two later on, right enough. It looks like a run at the watering trough just now."

At the bar a throng of men and women were all clamoring for attention.

"It does, doesn't it. We'll both go, then."

They joined Julius and a gangling roustabout called Ben Long, who were hastening to keep up with the demands for drink. The circus folk were free with their money, and the ring of silver and gold on the worn wood of the bartop was a continuous accompaniment to the music from the band. Lisa filled her glasses and collected coins and half expected to find that her father had joined them behind the bar, so much did the hubbub in the saloon remind her of days gone by.

"What can I get for you?" Lisa asked the question as she turned. She was taken aback to find herself facing a man who rose fully two feet above her head. It was the giant whose bulk had provided shelter for the clown that afternoon. He was no longer wearing his purple cape but he still cut an imposing figure. His hair floated about his head like a mane of straw.

"Well, now. Whatever you think appropriate, I imagine."

He was English, and his manner was anything but imposing. He was diffident, almost shy. Lisa searched her memory for a British drink. Perhaps he would like one of the mixtures her father had learned to make in the British colonies in Asia. "Perhaps a gin and bitters? A Singapore Sling? Or we make a frontier drink called a hailstorm. It's whiskey on crushed ice. It's supposed to have fresh mint too, but we have none, I'm afraid."

"To be quite honest, I have had an astonishing array of concoctions since coming to your country. I think this evening perhaps just some whiskey, if you don't mind." As Lisa poured he offered hesitantly, "This must be a burden for you, being closed for the season as you were."

"I'm very glad to have you, and I wish we were closed only for the season."

"I don't understand. This is a country inn, is it not?"

Lisa laughed. "I have never heard it called that before." She set his glass before him. "My father established himself here to serve the emigrants, but now most travelers take the railroad. Those going to Montana get off at the Salt Lake and go north from there. We're quite off the beaten track now, and most people are afraid of the Indians."

"Ah. I see," he said, not seeing at all. He sampled the

whiskey. "Good Lord!" he gasped, and nearly choked. He recovered himself and said, "To quote the monster Caliban, 'I'll swear upon that bottle to be thy true servant, for the liquor is not earthly.' "

Lisa laughed again, liking this huge Englishman very much. "Some call it tanglefoot. I must say, I didn't expect to hear Shakespeare from a circus strongman, even an English one. You are the strongman, aren't you?"

"By an accident of stature, I am. Chalmers. Alfred Chalmers; your humble servant, Miss Putnam." He drank again and appraised the taste thoughtfully. His manner reminded Lisa of the fathers of her Boston friends sampling a glass of new Madeira. She refilled his glass.

"This one is on the house. A courtesy for our foreign guests."

Chalmers raised the glass to her before sipping again, still testing the waters cautiously. He smiled and seemed to relax a little. " 'Thou mak'st me merry; I am full of pleasure.' "

"You're an actor, then."

"Would that I could pursue a theatrical career. But there are few roles for one of my, ah, shall we say my standing?" They laughed together and Chalmers drank less cautiously. "I have performed Lear and Macbeth, and once essayed Richard the Third. May I?" His glass was empty. His reticent manner was gone, replaced by a garrulous friendliness. As Lisa poured he grew expansive. "I was consigned to roles, ah, larger than life. But I wished to play them all, Iago and Hamlet and little Puck, and the managers would hear none of it. So I left them to their own devices. Such was the theater's loss. Perhaps in America I shall have better fortune." He drank off half the whiskey in his generous glass and struck a pose, one hand upon the breast. " 'Whether 'tis nobler in the mind to suffer the slings and arrows of outrageous fortune,' or to take drink against a sea of troubles, and so in drowning, end them." He chuckled deep within himself and tossed off the remaining liquid. "With apologies to the Bard. And with apologies to our cousins the Scots, I believe a man might grow accustomed to your corn whiskey. It is certainly less spartan than theirs, and—''

He was interrupted by a sudden commotion on the dance floor. An area of quiet spread like a ripple in all directions as eyes sought the cause. Men rose from their seats, others turned, and then all were still.

Lisa reached beneath the bar and found the short-barrel shotgun that was kept there. She brought it up and set it on the bartop, her eyes searching the room. Across from the bar, in the corner farthest from the musicians, a game of cards was in progress, and she saw now that the one-armed man, the one Hardeman had wounded that afternoon, had joined the game. His arm was supported in a sling that Julius had made for him after he had bandaged the man's wrist. The wrist had been sprained by the shock of Hardeman's bullet snatching the Winchester from the man's hand, but no bones were broken and the flesh wound caused by the splintering gunstock was trifling. A young boy from the circus held the one-armed man's cards for him. The man was looking toward the center of the room, but he kept his seat.

On the dance floor, Bat Putnam faced one of the circus men, and when he spoke, his voice threatened violence. ''What was it you said, mule driver?''

''I said that squaw's kind of cute and I reckoned to get me a dance.'' The speaker was no mule driver at all, but the wagon guide Fisk, the man who had led the circus off the beaten track into the wilds. Bearded, florid of face and unsteady of foot, he faced Bat and Penelope across a six-foot clearing of bare planks.

''You're speakin' of my wife, mule driver.'' Bat had recognized the man, of course, but he would not sully the profession of scouting by including Fisk in its ranks.

''Your wife is it? Jesus Christ, first it's niggers and Injuns, now it's a squaw man!'' Fisk's shoulders were muscular and rounded, his eyes dark. Like a badger he moved slowly, but when cornered he was capable of surprising speed. His body was half turned away from Bat as he spoke, one hand groping at his waist. The hand found the haft of a knife and even as the last words left his mouth, Fisk moved, hoping to take the old man off guard. But he failed as others had failed long before him. His knife hand was seized as it came forward, in a grip that threatened to crush his bones, and by means of a movement he could not comprehend even later, when he pondered it long and hard, he found himself spun around and wrapped in the clutch of the old man's arm, while a long skinning knife appeared at his throat.

"That's a loose tongue you got, mule driver. I'm thinkin' you might ought to apologize to my wife."

In the crowd, one of the teamsters, a wiry Ohioan named Morton, his hair prematurely gray, drew a pistol half out of its holster. He was called "Redeye" by the others because of his fondness for forty-rod whiskey, and he had already taken on a respectable load of the cheapest spirits offered by Putnam House, but even drunk he was cautious. He hesitated now, unsure if he should take part, and before he could make up his mind, the decision was made for him.

He felt something cold touch his neck and heard the click of a pistol's hammer being drawn back to full cock. A voice said, "There's a time for saloon fighting and there's a time for gunplay. You want to survive in this country, you'd do well to learn the difference."

Morton let his own gun fall back into place. The cold object left his neck. He turned to see the man called Hardeman, the one whose shot had lifted Henry Kinnean out of his saddle and dumped him in the snow that afternoon, already turning away from him. Hardeman's revolver had found its way back into his belt, where he kept it stuffed like a farmer. So confident was he that his warning would be obeyed, he did not bother to look back. Morton flushed red with anger and once again his hand found the butt of his pistol, but the tall Negro, who had been serving at the bar until a moment ago, was nearby in the crowd and his eyes were on Morton. Morton let his hand drop. Even without the colored man's presence, he would have thought twice before drawing again near

Hardeman. A short time ago he had been standing by the card table, watching the play. When Kinnean arrived, one of the drivers had remarked that he was lucky to get off with a sprained wrist, but Kinnean had silenced the man with a black look. "Luck was no part of it," Kinnean had said. "He'd of meant to kill me, he'd of done it." His tone allowed for no further treatment of the matter and it had come to rest there. Was it possible that Hardeman had hit what he aimed for, that in the midst of such chaos he had intended all the time to knock the Winchester from Kinnean's hand? Thaddeus Morton would not be the one to find out.

"Say you're sorry, there's a nice fella," Bat Putnam said now. The skinning knife pricked the skin below Fisk's Adam's apple.

"I'm . . . sorry."

"Drop the knife."

The knife fell. Bat released Fisk and picked it up. Without seeming to look where he threw it, he tossed it to Julius. Then he met Julius's eyes and grinned. "You're movin' kind of slow today, ain't you?"

"Didn't want to spoil your fun," Julius said.

And so it ended; no blood had been spilled, not a blow struck. The silence crumbled, then broke asunder as those in the saloon returned to libations and conversations abandoned in mid-glass or midstream, glad of an end to the tension, eager to put behind them the awkward moment that had arisen so suddenly. The band struck up a tune, and in the space of a few measures the floor was filled once again with twirling couples.

Julius found Hardeman in the crowd. "I'm obliged to you for taking a hand," the Negro said.

Hardeman shrugged. "It seemed like you had it under control, you and Bat and Miss Putnam." He nodded toward the bar, where Lisa was replacing the short shotgun beneath the counter. "I didn't mean to step on any toes."

"You didn't. Seems like you've got a way of steppin' in and takin' up the slack no one else sees. I'll stand you to a whiskey, if you're agreeable."

Hardeman nodded, and relaxed enough to favor Julius with a trace of a smile. "I'm agreeable." Together they crossed the room to the bar, where Julius held up two fingers to Lisa.

She nodded in response to the request, but as she reached for a jug of whiskey, part of her attention was still on Alfred Chalmers. The giant had followed Julius to the center of the room when the trouble broke out. Would he have supported Fisk if the fighting had gone further? She had noticed that the men of the troupe—those dressed as performers, not the rough-clad teamsters—had looked in his direction, as if awaiting his move, but he had made none. He was joined now by a rotund woman wearing a silk scarf around her neck, a sash at her waist, a billowing blouse and a skirt that reached to the floor, all in bright colors. She greeted him warmly, but as he spoke to her her expression became serious and she looked darkly at Fisk and the teamsters, now grouped around the card table. She accompanied Chalmers when he returned to the bar and remained by his side. The giant's face was solemn, displaying none of the easy humor the whiskey had brought out in him only moments earlier.

"In Mr. Tatum's absence," he said, addressing Lisa, "I must apologize on behalf of one and all. Such behavior ill repays your hospitality."

"Such things happen, Mr. Chalmers," Lisa said, glad to know where Chalmers stood in the matter. "No real harm was done. Thank you for your concern."

"You are very kind."

Lisa set out two more glasses and poured one half full; before pouring in the last one she raised her eyebrows inquiringly, looking at the brightly clothed woman. The woman's skin was swarthy and her eyes were black and sharp. Her face was framed by dense black curls that fell in ringlets.

"Oh, I beg your pardon," Chalmers exclaimed, putting an arm around the woman and drawing her close. "Forgive me, my dear. Miss Putnam, may I present Lydia Kaslov."

The two women exchanged expressions of greeting and Lydia nodded shyly when Lisa renewed the offer of a drink. Chalmers drank off half of his whiskey in a swallow and addressed Lisa again, keeping his voice low.

"I feel I should warn you, the drivers are rough men, and just now are under scant restraint. The unfortunate Mr. Kinnean showed an uncommon ability to make them mind their behavior, but he is powerless for the time being."

"Kinnean?" Hardeman said.

"The one-armed gentleman with whom you crossed swords, so to speak, this afternoon. He was formerly an army officer, but lost an arm in your recent war, I am told. Mr. Tatum found him in the Black Hills, gambling and down on his luck. He took him on to control the drivers, many of whom were also hired there after our old drivers ran off to try their luck at gold mining. He takes naturally to command and the drivers respect him; but I am afraid a one-armed man with an injured wrist exerts little real authority."

"Might be worth havin' a word with Tatum," Julius said. "Another one of them fellers looks crosseyed at Bat, Tatum won't be leavin' here with all his drivers alive."

As if on cue, the door beyond the bar opened and Hachaliah Tatum stepped into the saloon. Like a child arriving late for school, he became the center of attention for those close at hand. He wore a frock coat and starched collar and a silk brocade vest, and the lights of the lamps shone like fireflies in the polished sheen of his boots. His dark hair was precisely parted and brushed back; at the nape of his neck it formed a series of small ringlets. He paused for a moment in the doorway and then stood aside to let the girl who stood behind him enter. He closed the door and ushered her forward, smiling at Lisa.

"Miss Putnam, may I present Miss Amanda Spencer. You know her better as Joey the Clown."

The girl took Lisa's hand briefly with a touch that could barely be felt before she let go.

"I'm pleased to meet you, Amanda." Lisa smiled. "I must admit I had no idea you were a girl until you lost your hat. It's been years since I have seen a clown. It was a great surprise for all of us.''

The girl smiled shyly and said nothing. Her hair was combed straight to her shoulders and was held back at the sides with ivory clasps. She wore a simple fawn-colored dress with understated frills at the bodice and cuffs and hem. It's silk, Lisa realized with a start. A real silk dress on a child. How old can she be? Eighteen? Twenty? And so beautiful. ''What a lovely dress,'' she said.

''Thank you. Hachaliah gave it to me.'' Amanda's voice was as soft and smooth as the fabric of the dress.

''Are your parents with the circus too?''

Amanda dropped her eyes. ''My parents are dead.''

''A tragic fire,'' Tatum said, placing a comforting hand on Amanda's shoulder. ''It was some years ago. Amanda was just eight at the time. My wife perished in the same fire. We were thrown together by tragedy, you see. It was only natural that I should care for her.'' A shadow passed across his face, like the remembrance of some nearly forgotten pain, but then he smiled at the girl, regarding her fondly. ''She has rewarded me for her care many times over by becoming the star of the show.''

Across the room the band ended its breakneck tune, and above the rising rush of voices a man called out: ''Amanda!'' He waved to her from the bandstand, holding a fiddle above his head.

Lydia smiled at the girl. ''You will play for us? Your friends are impatient. Many have requested that you play.'' She gave her *r*'s a Romany roll.

The fiddler approached them, making his way through the crowd, fiddle in hand. ''Come on, now,'' he said when he reached them. ''We've held the fort long enough.''

Amanda glanced at Tatum and received an encouraging nod and a smile in reply. She took the violin from the fiddler's hand and was gone, skipping through the crowd like a child turned out to play.

Standing alone in the throng, Johnny Smoker had watched the girl ever since she entered the room. Now, as she passed nearby, she saw him and gave him a hint of a smile. The rhythm of her feather-light steps missed a beat, as if she might stop to say a word, but she passed on.

Amanda. That was what the fiddle player had called out. Amanda. Johnny said the name over in his mind until it fit the girl, who now stood on the bandstand holding the fiddle cocked to her ear as she thumbed the strings one by one and made small adjustments to the pegs. That afternoon he had been struck dumb to discover that the clown was a girl. He could still feel the touch of her hand in his own, the quick squeeze she gave before letting go. Amanda. The name and its owner had entered his life for the first time today, and he would never be the same.

With a nod to the band, Amanda set the fiddle under her chin and began to play. At the end of the first measure, the other musicians joined in and around the room men quickly found partners for the polka.

At the bar, Tatum bowed to Lisa. "May I have the honor?" He held her with authority and led her effortlessly among the dancers until they were close to the bandstand. There was a special quality in the music now and Lisa realized that it came from Amanda. The other fiddler had been content to blend with the band, following rather than leading, but there could be no doubt where the direction of the music came from once the slight girl took the bow in her hand. The others looked to her, and when she nodded to one or the other he stepped forward and took his turn at playing his best. As he stepped back, the sound of the fiddle would rise again smoothly, urging the band onward.

Lisa was flushed and her heart was pounding. How long had it been since a gentleman held her in his arms and guided her through the steps of a polka?

"I want to apologize again for the misunderstanding this afternoon," Tatum said. "Naturally, I had no way of knowing the Indians were peaceful. I must say, you and your man—your partner, Mr. Ingram, took matters in hand very well."

"I'm afraid there was very nearly more trouble this evening, just before you came in. One of your men attacked my uncle. He had made advances toward my uncle's wife." She indicated Bat and Penelope, who were dancing nearby.

Tatum's expression revealed an irritation quickly controlled. "It seems I must apologize again. My men are a rough breed, but such men are necessary in the wilderness. Many of them are veterans of the war; they are familiar with firearms and violence. Mr. Kinnean, the man Mr. Hardeman shot, has organized them for the defense of the circus, should that be necessary. I shall have to take it on myself to control them until his wound is healed."

"I shouldn't like to see any more of your men hurt while you're here."

Tatum seemed about to say something more when the tempo of the dance increased and he gave all his attention to guiding her safely among the careening couples. On the wagon box, Amanda nodded to Hutch and he earned a cheer from musicians and dancers alike as his banjo sang out the melody and moved the polka to a ringing conclusion.

Tatum bowed. "I hope you will honor me with another dance later on. If you will excuse me now, I'll have a word with my men."

Lisa was left alone near the bandstand, where now Julius joined the other musicians, his own fiddle in his hand. Amanda stepped back, yielding the front of the stage, but he declined the offer. "You play whatever you like," he said. "I'll try to find my way."

"Play that waltz," suggested the bassist.

"That's the ticket," said another man. "The one you made up."

The band remained silent as Amanda began a lovely melody in slow waltz time and couples started to move about the floor. As the others joined in softly behind the fiddle, Lisa saw Chalmers making his way towards her, his eyes on her alone as he broached the crowd like a plow horse moving effortlessly through a field of corn, but before he reached her she felt a light touch at her elbow.

"Miss Putnam?"

It was Johnny Smoker. Concealing her surprise, Lisa took the hand he offered and rested her other one on his shoulder as his arm went around her waist. She smiled at Chalmers as they moved away, and nodded when he silently asked, The next one then? She felt like the belle of the ball, sought after from all sides. It was a heady feeling and very pleasant.

She had resolved to take whatever pleasure she could from the circus's unexpected visit. Her success at controlling the crowd this afternoon, her sudden decisiveness when danger threatened, had bolstered her confidence. "Meet trouble when it comes along and don't fret about it beforehand," her father had said. So it would be. She had stood and fought when the moment called for it, and she had put on a meal and an evening's entertainment for a crowd of nearly a hundred on a moment's notice. She would stand and fight again if necessary, for Sun Horse and Putnam's Park, but Sun Horse's plan to send pipes to General Crook and Sitting Bull gave her a breathing space. Tonight she would savor the almost forgotten joy of an evening like this one and tomorrow she would be prepared to face whatever came.

With something close to astonishment, she became aware of the skill with which Johnny was guiding her across the floor. He did not tramp out the beat as many a novice waltzer would do, but glided along with only the gentlest shifting of head and foot and pressure at the small of her back to match the two of them to the lilting rhythm of the dance. And his limp was gone. Lisa's astonishment grew. His gait was perfectly even as he moved to one side and then the other. It was as if the music had effected a miraculous cure. He moved as gracefully as any partner she had ever known. If she closed her eyes she could be back in Boston, at the ball where she had first danced the waltz in public. In school she and the other girls had practiced the forbidden step in secret as soon as one of their number had learned it, but it had taken the daring of an eccentric Boston dowager to bring the waltz into its own in that conservative town. Whatever did they fear? "Too stimulating for young ladies," they warned. And they were right. Waltzing now in her own saloon, Lisa felt the thrill of her first waltz all over again and she hoped the dance would go on forever.

Yet something was missing. Despite Johnny's expert grace, he was not entirely with her. She saw as they turned about the floor that his eyes were often on the bandstand. He is dancing with her music, she realized suddenly. In his mind he was really embracing the notes that Amanda played, as if she were playing just for him.

And then she saw that Amanda's eyes found Johnny too, although they never stayed on him for long. Each pretends not to be entranced by the other, she thought. No wonder young people take so long to find each other. Neither sees the other's feelings.

Tatum passed by the bandstand with one of the circus women in his arms and he smiled at Amanda. Her eyes moved from Tatum to Johnny and back again, but Tatum did not notice. He doesn't see it either, Lisa realized. Why? Because he too has a blindness. He thinks she is still a child.

"May I ask where you learned to waltz so beautifully?" she inquired.

"Oh, it seemed like something worth learning from the white man," Johnny said, a little embarrassed. "Dancing, I mean. I lived in St. Louis for a time. Chris thought I needed a proper home. The man was the brother of an officer Chris knew. His wife taught dancing to young ladies. She used me as a dancing partner for just about every young lady in St. Louis."

"I envy them," she said, and he blushed. "Why ever did you leave?"

"I stayed through the winter. They were good people. In the springtime it just didn't seem right to be in a place like that, all crowded streets and noise day and night. Chris was in Utah Territory, hunting meat for the track crews. I found him there."

So Hardeman had sought a home for the boy, and it had been Johnny's choice to leave that home and rejoin Hardeman in the wandering life. Lisa added this information to what little else she knew of Johnny's companion and protector. He was a puzzling man, but she would leave the solving of the puzzle for another time. She was enjoying herself too much just now to worry about anything. She put her thoughts aside and surrendered completely to the waltz.

On the bandstand, Julius set the fiddle against his chest and moved his fingers silently on the strings, feeling the music. When he was sure of the melody he joined in softly. Amanda heard and turned to face him. She played the tune through with him once from start to finish, and the two fiddles playing the same notes together produced a richness of tone that suffused the room and urged the dancers on.

Joining the waltz late, Bat and Penelope moved onto the floor now, their heads held high, and the onlookers fell back to make more room. They gazed in amusement at the spectacle of the short, bronzed woman and her gaunt mountain man, his otter-wrapped braids swaying in time with the music, as they negotiated the steps of the dance with the confidence of the Astors.

As the melody began again, Amanda moved her fingers up the neck of her fiddle, playing a third above Julius, and together the fiddles sang in harmony. Amanda and Julius faced each other, the bows dancing in their hands as the room danced around them.

At the bar, Hardeman sipped sparingly from a glass of whiskey as he leaned back against the bartop and watched the dancers. It was his second drink of the evening. He had rationed himself carefully, going against a wish to drink until the whiskey overcame his reticence and propelled him onto the floor to dance with Lisa Putnam or any other woman who caught his fancy. Drink when they don't expect it and don't drink when they do; for now he would remain unpredictable. He felt like celebrating as much as anyone in the saloon, but he hadn't given in to it; he had guarded his feelings. He would keep his wits about him and do what he could to strengthen his hand, now that he knew Johnny would be out of the line of fire if trouble came.

Lisa and Johnny were dancing nearby. She moved lightly in the young man's arms, her toes scarcely seeming to touch the floor. Hardeman had tried several times during the evening to screw up his courage to ask her to dance, but each time he had drawn back. The ballroom was not a place in which he felt at home. He lacked the natural grace displayed by Johnny and the circus master Tatum, who had been the first to take Lisa onto the dance floor. He could perform the steps in a workmanlike manner, but he always felt ill at ease. He half wished he had taken up Johnny's offer to give him lessons, made in jest this past winter in Ellsworth.

The waltz ended and Johnny and Lisa parted. Johnny looked about, spied Hardeman, and picked his way through the crowd.

"Buy you something to wet your whistle?" Hardeman suggested when the youth reached his side.

"A beer maybe." Johnny was flushed from the dancing and breathing hard. He used a corner of his green bandanna to wipe the sweat from his brow.

Hardeman raised a hand to Joe Kitchen. "A beer for a thirsty man."

As Joe delivered the beer, a group of circus men hove up to the bar all in a cluster, calling for a round of drinks. Morton was among them. He glanced down the bar at Hardeman and looked quickly away.

Hardeman raised his glass to Johnny. "When a young man decides to step out on his own, I guess that calls for a toast. Here's to your independence."

A little self-consciously, Johnny touched his glass to Hardeman's and they drank together. Hardeman savored the familiar warmth of the whiskey, but he was pleasantly relaxed without the liquor's assistance. He felt foolish for ever having doubted the boy. Maybe Johnny had sensed his doubts and that was why he had told Sun Horse of his decision this afternoon, in front of Hardeman, there on the porch. When Sun Horse was done laying out his idea about the pipes for Crook and Sitting Bull, and when Hardeman had said he would go along, the boy had waited until it looked like the talk was done and then he had made signs to Sun Horse. *Grandfather,* he had signed without preamble, *I have chosen between the worlds. I am a white man. I will stay with the whites.*

Hardeman had found himself taking a deep breath and letting it out slowly. He felt that half his cares had left him in that moment.

Johnny's words had plainly set Sun Horse back a step or two, but he had nodded, smiling slightly, and his hands said *I know. That is what you came to tell me.* Sun Horse had maneuvered his horse close to the edge of the porch and he reached out and took Johnny's hand. It had seemed to Hardeman that he was bidding his grandson farewell. He didn't shake the boy's hand; he just held it. When he let go at last, he had made more signs. *The whiteman's life is always new, always changing. The Lakota life will no longer be the life my father and grandfather knew. It will not be the life you knew as a boy.*

Johnny had stood there awkwardly for a few moments, not knowing what else to say. Finally he made as if to leave, but then he hesitated and turned back. *I am glad you are sending the pipes to Three Stars,* he signed. *I am glad you and your people will remain here, in your own country. I do not want you to go to the reservation.*

Sun Horse had looked at Hardeman as he replied. *My friend has agreed to help us,* he signed. *Together the whiteman and the Lakota will make a peace.*

Hardeman hadn't been sure whether Sun Horse meant himself and one white man together, or all the Sioux and all the whites. Either way, he hoped the old man was right.

He and Johnny had left Bat and the Indians then, and when they were alone, Johnny had said he was glad Hardeman would go with the pipe carriers to see Crook.

"It seems like it gives the Sun Band a better chance, with you there too. At least General Crook will listen to you."

Hardeman had kept his misgivings to himself. When the Indians took their leave he had chosen to stay behind, preferring to spend a last night in Putnam's Park before setting out on what could prove to be a more dangerous journey than Johnny had any reason to imagine. Hardeman intended to give Sun Horse's pipes every chance to work their medicine, but his own plans were still held in reserve. Tomorrow he and Bat Putnam would go to the Indian village, where they would no doubt be obliged to bide their time a while longer. There would be another council to hear about the pipes, then ceremonies to get the pipes ready. All in all another day or two would pass before he could be away and on the trail with the pipe carriers, where actions and choices came easily to him and he wasted no time in fruitless imaginings.

Johnny was sipping his beer as slowly as Hardeman sipped his whiskey, and Hardeman saw how the boy looked over the rim of the glass as he drank, his eyes returning again and again to the bandstand and the girl playing the fiddle.

"Some doings, the circus and all," Hardeman observed.

Johnny smiled, a little embarrassed, as if one of his secrets had been found out.

"They're dead set on moving along tomorrow," Hardeman continued blandly. "They got big doings ahead, up Montana way, then Salt Lake and California. We always said we'd get to California, you and me."

"I heard them talking," Johnny said. "The big Englishman and a couple of the others. They want a guide to show them out of the mountains and on to the Bridger road. They don't trust that Fisk to find his own boots on a clear day."

Hardeman seemed to ponder this for a moment, but he had heard the same talk. "Well, I've got to be going off with the pipe carriers in a day or two, whenever Sun Horse is ready with the pipes. But you could get them on their way easy enough." He said it as if it were a brand-new idea.

Johnny smiled, suddenly pleased with himself. "Well, I guess I could do that, couldn't I?"

Hardeman was reminded once again of himself when he

was much younger, and how Jed Putnam had set him off on his own. He would try to do as good a job for Johnny, and he would do it with a will, now that Johnny was staying in the white man's world for sure. Maybe Johnny would keep on going with the circus and see California. If the two of them had to go their separate ways, now was as good a time as any, and Hardeman would be left here alone to do what he had to do.

"Maybe I'll have a word with Tatum," Johnny said, and then as if Hardeman had spoken his thoughts aloud, he added, "I'd come back up once I got them to where they knew the trail. I'd be here when you get back. I could spend some time with Sun Horse."

Hardeman nodded, showing no surprise. He should have known the boy wouldn't go off for good, not knowing his grandfather's fate. With luck it might all be over before Johnny got back, but Hardeman was still troubled by the memory of Sun Horse's manner, all confident and cocksure like a young man, when he explained to Hardeman about the pipes that afternoon. He had been too confident, maybe, as if he had kept some secret to himself, but Hardeman had looked for a trap in the plan and found none. His mind had worked quickly, and he had agreed to go with the pipe carriers for one reason—Sun Horse's willingness to talk directly with the hostile headmen and plead for peace. He remembered what Lisa Putnam had told him about Sun Horse earlier that same day. *A vision brought him here, to avoid the hostilities. His power is to understand the white men and make a lasting peace.* If that was true, it was a powerful reason for Sun Horse to work hard for surrender. To an Indian, a vision wasn't an assurance of what would be, but a glimpse of what was possible, with all the burden for making the vision come true falling on the one who had it.

Sun Horse's plan was better than sending messengers to the hostiles, and it increased the chance of bringing them all in without trickery. But it meant stalling for time, and that was risky now that the campaign had begun. Custer and Gibbon might both be out by now, and while troops were on the prowl, the war could start at any moment and blow the chance for a truce to smithereens. If Custer came within striking distance of the Indians, there would be hell to pay. And even if Hardeman found Crook and Crook agreed to Sun Horse's offer, there would still be risk; it would take time to send word to the other commanders in the field.

The risks loomed larger in Hardeman's mind now, but a general peace would be worth all the risks if it could be brought about. And if Crook would not accept the pipe, there would still be time to bring him here, with the pipe carriers taken hostage to assure the good behavior of the Sun Band, and even then the peace might be preserved, despite the deception and betrayal.

Hardeman drank the rest of the whiskey down in a gulp and set the glass on the bar. He felt the rush of the liquor rise to his face and the Dutch courage growing strong inside him, but he would drink no more this evening. From now until he and the pipe carriers returned from their journey, he would have to depend on his own inner resources, not the helping hand of John Barleycorn.

The musicians ended their tune and Johnny drained off the last of his beer.

"If you don't have the sense to dance with a pretty woman, I sure do," he said. He grinned at Hardeman and slipped away to reach Lisa's side before any other man could beat him to it. Hardeman saw Lisa smile and nod, accepting the young man's invitation, and as he looked around the room he saw the pleasure in the face of each woman as a man presented himself to her. By asking a woman to dance you paid her a compliment, and the compliment was all the more welcome if you were the one who had been watched as only a woman could watch, never looking directly, but always knowing the whereabouts of the man whose attentions she wished for most of all.

Hardeman leaned back against the bar and tapped his foot to the polka, keeping his eyes on Johnny and Lisa as they circled the floor. She was enjoying herself as if she hadn't a care in the world.

When the band slowed and the dance drew to an end, the couple moved closer until they stood before him. They parted and Lisa curtsied. "Mr. Smoker, sir, I haven't enjoyed myself so much in years."

Johnny inclined his head in a small bow and moved off, flashing a quick smile at Hardeman, as if he had brought Lisa here intentionally. She looked at Hardeman and he stepped forward.

"Miss Putnam? I'm not as good as Johnny, I'm afraid, but if it's not too fast—"

"Never apologize for asking a lady to dance, Mr. Hardeman." She smiled, and Hardeman was surprised to see the light of pleasure in her eyes. The band began a waltz and Hardeman started off. Left lead, right lead, *one*-two-three. It really wasn't so hard. If he could make a horse change leads at will, he could certainly manage it himself.

Lisa accommodated herself to his movements effortlessly, even when his balance or timing threatened to desert him. She fit perfectly in his arms, and after a time he had mastered the rhythm of the dance sufficiently to notice that the back of her waist felt firm beneath his palm, not soft like most women. He could feel her muscles move as she leaned back against his hand and he realized now that she was looking at him, and she was smiling.

"Mr. Hardeman—"

"Miss Putnam—"

They spoke at the same instant and the coincidence forced them to laugh. She moved a little closer and held his shoulder more firmly.

"I wanted to speak to you," she said. "To thank you for agreeing to the peace pipes, and to speak to General Crook for Sun Horse. I feel that we are allies now."

His first impulse was to warn her not to count her chickens, but he restrained it. She saw his hesitation.

"You do think there is a chance for peace?"

He nodded. "If Crook will hold off now and come back

in summer. And if Sitting Bull will agree. With the pipe, and the word of a war chief and a peace chief, Crook might be able to persuade Sheridan to stop the campaign, at least for a while. If the War Department will go along; and if Crook thinks it's a good idea in the first place. That's a lot of ifs."

"But if he does, surely his word will carry weight. He is the commander of the Department of the Platte."

"He answers to Sheridan and Sherman. And there's more to it than just the Platte, Miss Putnam. There's an army reduction bill going up to Congress soon, and a bill to give control of the reservations to the army. Sheridan wants to show that he needs the troops and can keep the Indians in line if he has them."

"I see." She considered this soberly for a time, never missing a step of the waltz. "But surely in Congress there are some who favor fair dealing with the Indians. Senator Schurz—"

"It's in the army's hands now. If they want to bring this thing to a close, they'll do it, and they'll take the scalps back and nail them on the wall while Congress is still talking."

"And if General Crook will not accept the pipe?"

"We've got to plan for that, too."

"You sound as if we were truly allies, Mr. Hardeman."

His reply was cautious. "We can be. If Crook won't take the pipe, there'll be just one choice left for Sun Horse. I've already told him he'll have to fight or go in. If you ask him to surrender, he might listen to you. He trusts you."

She drew back. "I have already advised him not to go in."

"So has Johnny. Or at least he told Sun Horse he's glad he found a way to stay out." That surprised her. "It's advice from the gut, not the head, Miss Putnam, if you don't mind my putting it that way. And either one of you can change your mind. Both of you together might be enough to convince him, if it comes down to it."

"I have seen the reservations, Mr. Hardeman. Have you?" Her voice was hard now.

Hardeman nodded. "So has Johnny. And Sun Horse knows what's there. But if it's put to him right, he's smart enough to pick the . . . drawbacks of living on a reservation to a war that might destroy his people."

"Drawbacks? Is that what you call a life barren of all hope?"

"On the reservation they'll still be alive, Miss Putnam. As long as they're alive, they can find a reason to live."

She was silent and very serious for a time, but finally she met his eyes again. "Yes. I believe that."

They danced in silence. Hardeman saw Harry Wo and Ling watching them from where they stood near the kitchen door, smiling in evident approval. Bat Putnam and his Sioux wife danced nearby and he too smiled, as if it mattered not a whit to him that Hardeman and Lisa seemed always to succeed at making each other uncomfortable, or that they ran out of things to say. Hardeman sought a way to raise Lisa's spirits again and bring back the look of pleasure in her eyes, but before he could think of one the dance ended and she curtsied quickly and silently before disappearing into the crowd.

Lisa Putnam's Journal

Saturday, March 4th. 6:45 a.m.

Usually my early mornings with this journal are spent in silence, but today I can hear the circus folk up and about, animals being fed, some wagons already moving into line. The stars shone brightly all night and I believe it will be a fair day for the departure of these guests who have brightened our lives so unexpectedly.

Mr. Chalmers ate breakfast in the kitchen this morning, where we fed the early risers in the midst of the preparations to feed the rest of our guests. He was accompanied by Lydia, whom I met only in passing yesterday evening. She is a Gypsy, of "noble" blood, she claims, and my, didn't Hutch's eyes open wide when he saw her bracelets and earrings and lip rouge and her imposing girth. Next to any person of normal stature she would have to be considered a large woman, but next to Mr. Chalmers she manages to appear almost delicate. Each of them put away enough porridge, pork chops and eggs for two workingmen. What an odd couple they are, and what good company. They always seem to be laughing about one thing or another. They are not married, but I do not deceive myself into believing they are merely friends, and so I conclude that not all the tales told of traveling performers, whether in the theater or a circus such as this one, are fanciful or slanderous. And yet while the morals of these folk may not be those professed (if not always practiced) by polite society, and while they take no pains to conceal their informal liaisons, *in the short time that I have known the men and women of Mr. Tatum's circus I have found among them some who are as trustworthy and honest as any upright citizen on Beacon Street or Broadway. Certainly morals are one of the standards by which we judge one another; we wish nothing to do with those who lack them entirely; but a breach of common morality, in itself, is not sufficient reason for rejecting someone outright. Such has long been the wisdom of the frontier, where persons are judged according to more universal standards. (Forgive me. Tomorrow is Sunday and I shall keep any further sermons to myself until then. Sometimes I find myself defending our life here, which is difficult to understand in some respects unless one has been forced to live it. I am always mindful of future generations that may read these pages, and I try to set forth the standards by which we judge ourselves, for their standards will surely be different. Today I find myself defending Alfred and Lydia, for whom I have much respect and affection after knowing them for less than a dozen hours.)*

Mr. Chalmers thinks it will be mid-morning before the caravan is formed and on its way. He sees in his fellow troupers a reluctance to leave this place of festivity and rest. Usually, he says, they are all up and about before the sun without complaint, and off to the next town or city.

Johnny Smoker will guide the circus out to the plains and south to Mr. Bridger's trail. He will be gone perhaps as long as a week or more. Although it is pure guesswork on my part, I imagine that his feelings for young Amanda played some part in his decision to undertake this job. Last evening they finally did get a dance and a chance to exchange a word or two. Johnny was waiting near the stage when she put her violin aside, and as the rest of the band played on, he gave her a waltz that would have pleased Terpsichore herself. When it was over, Amanda was off like a shot. I fancied I knew something of what she was feeling. How many times did I allow myself to be friendly with some young man passing by and stopping for the night? I might favor him with a dance or two, knowing all the while that in the morning we should part, never to see each other again. Perhaps because of just such knowledge, Amanda gave Johnny little encouragement. Now they will be in company together for some days, but when the train of colorful wagons is safely on its way to Montana, he will retrace his steps to Putnam's Park.

Before the evening was over last night, he asked me most politely if he might remain here while Mr. Hardeman is off with the pipe carriers, and of course I agreed. "I'll lend a hand around the place," he said. "If there's something that needs doing, just point me to it." I am sure he will do more than his share. But during our short conversation I also learned something about him that caused me to alter my first impression of him. When Mr. Hardeman told me Johnny had chosen to remain among white people, I accepted this as only natural. After all, he has been with Mr. Hardeman for seven years and more, and I imagined he wished nothing more from life than to follow Mr. Hardeman wherever he might chance to go. But it seems that when Mr. Hardeman has returned, the two of them will part soon after leaving here. Johnny takes it as a consequence of his choice that he should set out on his own, making his way as a man, looking after himself. He informed me of this very simply, as if it were no more than natural, but to me that decision reveals much courage and independence of mind, and I will see him in a new light from now on.

As for Mr. Hardeman, there too I have learned something new. He came to breakfast this morning just as I was leaving the kitchen, and I saw in his expression an eagerness to be on his way, and something more, something I felt I should recognize. I realize now that I saw that same look on my father's face, many years ago in my childhood, when we lived in Massachusetts. My relatives saw it too, and hadn't the faintest idea what it was. They considered him a good-for-nothing who would drag my "poor suffering mother" to an early grave. But we knew better, she and I. He sought a life that was complete; a home in a place he loved and an active life suited to that place and to his perception of the world at large; this is what he found in Putnam's Park. When my mother and I disembarked at St. Louis and saw him there waiting for us, the searching look was gone, replaced by one of real contentment. Mr. Hardeman's quest is similar, of that I am sure. When his journey on behalf of Sun Horse is done, he will move along and keep moving until he finds what he is looking for. I hope for his sake that he finds his own Putnam's Park, and I regret the somewhat hostile face I have shown him on more than one occasion. Whatever danger he may have brought with him, the government's actions with regard to the Indians are not his doing, and I believe he is motivated by peaceful intentions. Certainly the horrors of the Washita must have had a deep effect on him, to make him leave the service of the army and take under his wing an orphaned boy. Soon he and Uncle Bat will leave here for Sun Horse's village, there to await the preparation of the pipes and the departure of the pipe carriers. I wish him Godspeed.

Ling used the meal gong to summon the circus folk to breakfast. In recent years we have used it only in summer, when the hands may be far from the house as mealtimes approach. I enjoyed the familiar clanging. It sounded a short time ago, and judging by the noise from the saloon, breakfast is in full swing. I must prepare Mr. Tatum's account.

CHAPTER TWO

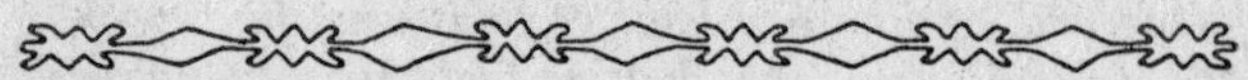

Bat Putnam stepped out onto the kitchen stoop and paused to let his eyes adjust to the brilliant sunshine. In his hand he held a small sack of coffee he had wheedled out of Ling in exchange for a promise of fresh meat when next he made a raise, once he got back. Today Bat needed coffee to keep him alive, and it would be welcome on the trail.

He looked distastefully at the meal gong, hanging from the tree closest to the stoop. It was a three-quarter section of iron wagon-wheel rim, suspended by a rope. Ling had set to thrashing it with her hammer just as Bat staggered towards the house from his tipi that morning, and she had had the gall to laugh when she saw how he cringed and stopped his ears against the noise.

He looked around the yard, savoring the peaceful silence now that the circus wagons had pulled out. The day was clear and warm and the glare of the sunlight off the snow was blinding. He had rubbed some stove soot on his cheekbones to cut the glare, but still the light made his head throb painfully.

In the blacksmith shed, Harry was firing up his forge. There would be clanging and banging from that quarter before long. Bat cast a quick glance in the direction of the sun, squinting hard. It was nearing midday, and high time to be getting along.

Beyond the barn, Penelope had struck the lodge. He could see her packing the last of their belongings onto the pony drags that were lashed to the four sturdy Indian ponies. While the pipe carriers were gone she would live in the circle of her people.

"It won't be the same here without you and Penelope," Lisa said, coming out of the door. She had on her gum boots and she had thrown her mountain goatskin coat over her dress. She was hatless; the light breeze ruffled her hair, which glistened in the sunlight.

"Oh, we'll be back soon enough, one way or t'other," Bat said. He saw the worry in her face and his tone grew stern. "Now don't you set to frettin'. We'll do what we can."

She smiled. "I know you will." She linked her arm in his and they started off together.

Across the yard, Hardeman emerged from the double doors of the barn, leading his saddled horse. Bat felt Lisa hesitate, and saw how she looked in the scout's direction. He patted her rump gently.

"You go on now, and remember what I told you. Come up on his right side."

"I can't seem to find it," she said, but she left him and strode off toward the barn with long steps, lifting her boots high in the soft snow that had been turned to mush by wagon wheels and hooves and booted feet.

"You're not leaving without a word, Mr. Hardeman?" she said as she reached him.

"Just coming now to find you, Miss Putnam."

"I wanted to wish you luck."

Hardeman thought to tell her that it would take more than luck, but he saw that she was full of hope and he had no wish to dampen her spirits. Johnny had said the same thing not long before, shaking Hardeman's hand and wishing him luck as the circus wagons began to roll off down the road.

He looked down the valley and saw that the caravan had just reached the clump of pines where the road made its last turn to the settlement. Johnny was somewhere in the long string of wagons and animals, but he would come back before long. "Well, I'll see you soon, then" was all Hardeman had said as the caravan started off. He didn't care for goodbyes.

Lisa had followed his gaze. "It will seem empty here without them," she said.

He heard the loneliness in her voice and turned to look at her, remembering the feel of her lithe body in his arms as he danced with her, and suddenly he wanted to take her in his arms to comfort her. She would permit it; he could see it in her eyes. But the eyes did not ask, as some women's did. They did not invite him. She kept her wants concealed.

"You 'bout set, Christopher?" Bat called. He sat astride his bay mare beyond the yard fence, with Penelope beside him on her paint and the four pack horses in train behind her.

"All set," he called back. "Well, you take care, Miss Putnam." He swung up into the saddle and started off.

"And you, Mr. Hardeman," he heard her say.

When he reached the gate that would let him out of the yard he looked back as he leaned down to open the latch, and he saw that she was still standing there. Maybe when he returned . . .

Such thoughts were useless. He latched the gate carefully from the other side. "Hyup!" he said to his horse, kicking it into a trot to overtake Bat and the Indian woman, who had started on ahead. Today both of Hardeman's rifles were in their scabbards and all his essential belongings were packed in the saddlebags and bedroll. He would come back for Johnny Smoker if he could, but for now he was on his own, self-contained and self-sufficient.

It felt good to be on the move again.

Down in the meadow, Hutch and Julius stopped working to watch the circus pass by a hundred yards away. Hutch spied Johnny Smoker riding beside the wagons and they exchanged waves.

"Never seen the like of it in this valley before," Julius said. "Won't see it again if I live to be a hundred."

Other hands were raised in farewell from some of the wagons. Johnny was riding beside a wagon driven by Chalmers, the English giant, and beside him on the seat Hutch imagined he could make out the much smaller figure of Amanda, the clown girl. He envied Johnny his few additional years and the independence they gave him. The quiet youth was more than a little sweet on Amanda, Hutch was fairly certain, and now he would have at least a few days to get to know her better. All Hutch knew about the acrobat's daughter he had watched throughout the evening, until her father had sent her off to bed, was that her name was Maria Abbruzzi. She was nineteen years old, he had learned from one of the musicians, and the one time she had looked him right in the eye and smiled, Hutch's heart had turned over inside him. But she was gone now, along with the rest of them. He recalled a line from a song he knew, and he hummed it softly, thinking the words without saying them—*There's more pretty girls than one, there's more pretty girls than one*. Just now it didn't seem possible.

"Watch that fork," Julius said. They had begun to feed the cattle again to quiet their bawling, and Hutch had pitched a forkful of hay dangerously close past the colored man's arm.

"Sorry."

From up the valley came a high-pitched cry and they both turned, Hutch a little apprehensive, wondering what crisis might have arisen. Julius saw his worried look and smiled.

"Nothin' to fret about. That's just Lisa moving cattle. Looks like she and Harry are taking the heifers in to the calving lot." The squat outline of Harry Wo was unmistakable at a distance, all the more so when he was on horseback. The heifers had been fed first in the pasture close to the settlement, on the far side of the river, and Lisa and Harry were gathering them now to move them into the lot beside the barn. It was another of Jed's customs, bringing the first-time mothers in to be watched during calving. Dairymen did it, and beef-cattle breeders too, in more settled countries. First births were often difficult and there was no need to lose any more calves than would be lost anyway in the natural course of things, so Jed had reasoned.

"Hooo!" came the cry again. The taller of the two riders raised a hand in the direction of the hay sled, and Julius and Hutch waved in reply.

To Lisa, the two men looked like miniature figures on a toy sled, dwarfed by the vastness of the broad meadows all white with snow and the empty sky above. "Hooo!" she shouted, urging the heifers along. She was glad to be outside and on horseback where she could vent her feelings freely. She wore the smoked goggles her father had used in the springtime to ward off snowblindness. Her goatskin coat hung open and she could smell the scent of pine on the air. The willows were budding already; spring would remain a tantalizing suggestion for another month or more, but the hope was there, and Lisa felt her spirits improving.

After Hardeman and Bat had left, she had thought to help Ling strip the bed linens. Joe Kitchen and his helpers had cleared away the remains of breakfast and left the kitchen spick-and-span before stacking their own pots and pans in the large boxes fixed to the sideboards of the supply wagons. All that was left for Ling and Lisa was to air the rooms and sweep the saloon and wash the linens, but Lisa had been unable to face the suddenly empty house. On an impulse she had decided to move the heifers today. After sending Harry to saddle the horses she had changed her clothes in a moment, and on her way back outside she had told Ling to leave the washing for later.

It's not as if I were shirking, she told herself now, turning her horse aside to bring along a trio of heifers that hoped to avoid the roundup. There is always other work to be done if you don't like one job, and we should have brought the heifers in before now. There's the calving shed to be prepared too. There's always plenty of work to take your mind off other things.

But the other thoughts remained with her, demanding to be heard, as they had been doing ever since Bat and Penelope and Chris Hardeman rode off up the creek trail, and Lisa turned inward to face them now, to get it over with. She felt abandoned, and the feeling brought to mind the summer she had turned twenty-five, when the cavalry lieutenant with the tired eyes rode out of Putnam's Park for the last time. He had been stationed at Fort Reno during the first year of Red Cloud's War, and when he could get away he would ride up to Putnam's Park alone, pitting the bravado of his love against the eyesight of the Sioux. Lisa had returned his love, but when he had asked her to marry him and live the life of a frontier cavalry wife, she had hesitated, and lost him. There, at least, the feelings had been freely spoken and the choice had been clear: choose between Putnam's Park and life in the most tightly bound society west of Chicago. Paradoxically, the officer caste imitated most closely the customs and habits of the very social set that so disdained the army—the proper, inbred, educated classes of the East, the same people from whom Lisa had fled in haste once her schooling was completed. But when the young lieutenant first rode into the park with his troop behind him, such thoughts were far from Lisa's mind. There had been little reasoning involved, only an outrush of feeling that swept them both up and brought him time and again to her door, through the autumn and the winter and on into another summer. She had sensed a hurt in him, a wound the Civil War had caused not in his body but his spirit, and she had done her best to heal him. On a day as perfect as this one in the second summer of their courtship, he had asked her to marry him, and without giving him an answer she had set aside with scarcely any hesitation the virtue she had sternly guarded in the face of advances made in eastern cities. Afterward, when he pressed her for an answer, she had delayed, silencing him with kisses, but from that moment, reasoning and realities had replaced the tide of feelings. In the end, Lisa had been unable to leave her home, although she might have left it safely then in her father's hands. Daughters married and became a part of their husbands' worlds, and fathers were left behind to pass on the estates to their sons. But Jed Putnam had no sons, and he had fed his love of the mountains to his only child; she had consumed his passion as if it were ice cream served on a hot August afternoon on one of the neatly mown lawns her mother's relations maintained around their country homes in the East. She had stayed in Putnam's Park, and it had been her own doing.

There were no other hands to receive it now. In any event, Lisa had made her choice. She would remain. Someday, perhaps, if her tenure here endured, a man would choose to remain with her, to become part of her life and make his own mark here as Jed Putnam had done; as his daughter would do, given time.

"Hooo!" she shouted, louder than was necessary to move the fifteen heifers along. They were in a bunch now, nearing the buildings of the settlement.

Where was it written that she must be drawn only to men who threatened the very fabric of her life? A cavalry lieutenant sent to provoke an Indian war; a scout sent to herald the end of countless centuries of Indian dominion over these lands. The image of Chris Hardeman rose in her mind and she recalled the calm words she had written about him that morning in her journal. As usual, she had kept her feelings veiled, as far as the written record was concerned. In her heart she wished him Godspeed not only to convey him safely through a hazardous journey, not only in the hope that he and the others might succeed in turning back General Crook's expedition against the hostiles, but also to bring him back to Putnam's Park and to her.

A skittish heifer bolted from the bunch suddenly and tried for a third time to return to the meadow, but Harry was there to head her off. He berated her loudly in Chinese, which he was sure would frighten her far worse than anything he might say in English, and Lisa couldn't help smiling at the sight of the stout blacksmith shaking his finger at the wide-eyed bovine. Harry wore a broad-brimmed hat pulled low over his eyes to protect himself against the glare. He was a good enough rider, and always dependable when moving cattle, but he bounced in the saddle. His legs were simply not long enough to grip the horse properly. He was the shortest, fattest cow-boy Lisa had ever seen.

"Hooooop!" she shouted, feeling better. She always felt better when she confronted her fears. For now she would place her fears for the pipe carriers in the part of her mind that was reserved for events whose outcome she could not affect. "If you can't change it, let it be," her father had been fond of saying, and she would try to do just that. Hardeman would return or he would not. If he did . . . He seemed to be as reluctant to show his feelings as she was to reveal her own, but things might be different when he returned. Things were always different when two people parted and came together again.

Meanwhile, there was work to keep her busy. It was always so; others came and went from Putnam's Park, but Lisa remained. The park remained, the work remained, and it sustained her.

The heifers were entering the yard between the house and the barn. They trotted in a contented group now, only occasionally casting a glance back at the two horseback figures behind them. Patches of hay remained here and there where the circus animals had been fed before dawn. Lisa had made a tidy sum on the hay she had sold to Tatum, and still she had more than enough to last out a cold spring, if that were in store. One of the heifers stopped to steal a mouthful of hay and Lisa rode her horse up behind the browsing animal.

"Boo," she said suddenly and the heifer ran to rejoin her companions.

Harry had the gate open and the first heifers were ambling into the buck-fenced lot. Lisa reined her horse aside to recover two animals that were drifting off toward the barn and the bull pasture beyond, and then she saw the cancer-eye cow. She had been cut out and brought to the calving lot two days earlier, when Lisa and Hardeman rode through the meadows to look over the cows. She was standing still and peculiar in the middle of the lot. Her vulva was protruding and her tail was partially raised. She hobbled around in a circle, her back humped up. Two tiny hooves stuck out from beneath her tail.

"Harry! We've got a calf to pull!" Lisa called. She hazed the two heifers toward the gate and left them for Harry to gather in while she hitched her horse to the fence and ran to the barn for the rope and tackle that were sometimes used to pull a backwards calf from inside its mother. Without help the cow would die, and the calf, if it were ever born at all, would be born dead. The calving supplies should have been seen to and put in the calving shed days ago, but she had put it off. First because I was lost in a winter of mourning and reflection that I believed would go on forever, she thought. And then I let the circus distract me. You can't do that when these animals need you.

When she returned from the barn, Harry was already off his horse and in the lot, moving this way and that with his surprisingly quick rolling trot, trying to turn the cow into the calving shed, but she didn't want to go into that dark place. Her nature was to stay outside and give birth in the mud and snow of the corral.

"Come on, mama cow," Lisa said as she climbed the fence, holding the calf tackle in her free hand. "Be a good girl instead of a contrary beast. We're only trying to help."

There was a sound like distant thunder and Lisa looked at the sky all around, but there was not a single cloud. She had removed her goggles in the barn and it took a moment for her eyes to adjust to the glare. In the meadow she made out the hay sled, almost empty now. Julius and Hutch seemed to have heard something too, for they were motionless on the rack. At the foot of the valley the circus wagons were gone from sight. A small white cloud that Lisa hadn't noticed before hung over the river canyon.

* * *

Amanda waved for a last time as the circus caravan left the hay sled behind. "I wish we could stay longer," she said. "I'd like to learn all those Negro dance songs Julius knows. Oh, look!"

She pointed suddenly. On the far side of the river a moose and her calf lumbered out of a thicket and headed across the meadow, legs jerking high above the snow. The calf followed in its mother's tracks. As they reached the split-rail fence at the edge of the meadow, the mother paused, then jumped and cleared the top rail with ungainly ease. The calf hesitated before making its way between two of the rails with a lurching leap.

"What are they?" Amanda asked in a hushed voice.

"Moose, I believe," Chalmers offered, glancing to Johnny for corroboration. The youth was riding close beside Chalmers' wagon.

"That's right."

The three of them watched as the two dark forms disappeared into the trees.

"I must say, I wish I had time for some hunting hereabouts," Chalmers mused. "Moose is quite good eating, I believe."

"It's all right," Johnny said. "Elk is better, and buffalo is best of all."

"Ah. Then I have already had the best," Chalmers said, pleased with himself. "At Delmonico's, of all places. I had a bison steak. Not at all the same as cooking the fresh-killed beast over a fire in the bush, though. Still, it was excellent."

"I think mooses look as if their hind legs were put on backwards by mistake," Amanda said.

"The plural of moose is moose, dear," Chalmers corrected her.

"That's ridiculous," she said, but she seemed pleased with this bit of information, however odd, just as she seemed pleased with the fine day and everything around her. Ever since the wagons left the settlement she had kept up a bright chatter, asking questions and looking all about. She took a childish delight in the smallest thing, the flight of a raven or the sound of a bull in the bull pasture calling out his springtime feelings to the cows.

"Mr. Springer! Keep up with the rest, if you please!" Hachaliah Tatum had left his place at the head of the caravan to stop by the trailside, and now he called out to a lagging wagon in the middle of the caravan. Chalmers' wagon was fifth in line and the Springer wagon was several more to the rear.

The circus caravan had been late getting off, and Tatum had been in a bad humor by the time the wagons were finally all in line; his farewell to Lisa Putnam and the settlement had been brief. The delay was caused by many small things—packing the cooking pots, capturing half a dozen draft horses that had escaped their pasture during the night to join the cattle in the meadow—but most of all by the general reluctance of one and all to leave Putnam's Park, where they had been welcomed so warmly.

"Everything in order, Mr. Chalmers?" Tatum inquired as Chalmers' wagon drew even with the circus master. Tatum reined his horse in beside Johnny's and rode in tandem with the young man.

"Quite in order, Mr. Tatum," Chalmers replied. "The spirits of the performing artists are excellent. No difficulties of any sort." Chalmers was the unofficial spokesman for the performers; when Tatum wished to convey any general directions to his artists, he spoke to Chalmers and the strongman passed the orders along.

"Very well," said Tatum now. "Be sure to keep up the pace."

"Oh, Hachaliah, that's ridiculous! We can't go any faster than the wagon in front of us!" Amanda smiled to take the sting out of her words.

A small window opened behind Chalmers' head and Lydia's round face appeared.

"Lydia." Tatum tipped his silk hat to the Gypsy woman, then touched his heels to the white stallion's flanks and trotted ahead to resume his place in the lead.

"You mustn't tweak his nose just for the fun of it, my

dear,'' Lydia cautioned Amanda once Tatum was out of hearing.

Amanda smiled, seeming pleased with herself. For a time she was quiet, looking about her at the valley and the snow-covered hills that loomed ahead of the caravan as it approached the river trail.

"What will you do when Mr. Hardeman comes back?" she asked suddenly, speaking to Johnny. "I mean when you leave here."

The question took Johnny by surprise. "I don't know," he said. The uncertainty didn't concern him. He would figure out what to do when the time came. Amanda knew that he would be going off on his own once he and Chris left Putnam's Park; he had told her the night before, when he danced with her, just as he had told Lisa Putnam. Telling others of his plans made them all the more real, and it strengthened his resolve, although his resolve had been in fine shape ever since he had returned to Putnam's Park. Of course knowing Sun Horse was safe for the time being had helped some. At first, the council's decision to surrender had seemed like the only thing for them to do, and Johnny had realized then that he wasn't really standing between the worlds at all. The Indian life was changing, and he no longer had the chance to go back to the life he had known in his boyhood. And then, when he had stood on the porch beside Chris and heard Sun Horse set out his startling new plan, Johnny had seen fresh hope for his grandfather, but the free life that hope might gain belonged to Sun Horse and his band, not to Johnny. Back in the park, seeing the circus and finding himself among white men and women again, the worries he had felt in the Lakota camp had seemed suddenly trifling, and his confidence in his choice had returned. The presence of the circus in the park was a perfect example of the surprises and sudden possibilities that sprang up in the white world when you least expected them, like the job offer from the Chicago cattle buyer, and once again it seemed unthinkable to abandon this world and the freedom it offered. And so when Chris and Sun Horse were through speaking,

Johnny had told his grandfather of his decision then, more certain than ever that he was doing the right thing.

Sure, he was a little frightened by the idea of being on his own and not having Chris to depend on, but he knew the rewards to be gained by standing on his own two feet and setting out to get what he wanted. He had done it once before, when he left the Wheelers' home in St. Louis and crossed three states and the whole of Wyoming Territory before he found Chris at last in Utah. After just one winter with the Wheelers he knew he wanted something more from life than growing up as a merchant's ward in St. Louis, and he knew he was too young to find it on his own. Chris Hardeman was a man who could help him find what he was after, if Chris was willing, and so Johnny had set out to ask him. The odd thing was how few folks thought it strange that a boy so young should be going all that way on his lonesome. "I'm goin' to find my pa," Johnny had told them. He hadn't said that Chris wasn't his real pa, or that he had lived with the Cheyenne Indians until five months before, and folks had taken him at his word. A lot of them had helped him along his way with a meal or some company on the trail or just a kind word of encouragement. Here and there some of them had offered him a job, and looking back on it now, Johnny saw how even then the white man's world had been reaching out to show him what it had to offer.

He breathed deeply of the cool clean air with its scent of pine and suggestion of spring, and his life opened before him. He was old enough now to find what he wanted on his own, and the time had come to do it. Looking back over his years with Chris, it seemed that Chris might have been preparing him for this moment all the while, making him ready to stand on his own, starting with the bargain they had struck back in the beginning: whenever one of them wanted to move on, they went. In such matters Johnny's wishes had carried as much weight as Chris's, and time after time Chris had forced him to make up his own mind about one thing or another. To hang back now would be to throw away all the lessons Chris had taught him. When he had found what he was looking for, he and Chris could hook up again, and that would suit Johnny just fine, but for now he had some looking around to do. Opportunities were everywhere; all he had to do was pick among them. Why, in just the past few days new ones had arisen. Hadn't Amanda said that Tatum's Combined Shows would be in San Francisco all summer? And hadn't he and Chris always said they would go to California someday? What was to say he couldn't go alone? The job training racehorses in Chicago had slipped by him, but who was to say what chances might come his way if he found himself in San Francisco?

Johnny suddenly wished he could hurry the circus along at a faster clip, and hurry himself back here, and hurry the pipe carriers on to General Crook—where the general would surely listen to reason and grant Sun Horse's request because Chris Hardeman was the one who brought the pipe to him—and hurry Chris back to Putnam's Park, all so Johnny could start off on the adventure that lay before him and find what he was looking for, and hook up with Chris again just so Chris would be proud of him and he could stand beside his old friend as an equal.

But if General Crook accepted Sun Horse's offer to meet with the hostile chiefs in summer after Sun Horse had talked with them, Johnny would remain near his grandfather until then. He owed the old man that much.

For the first time in his life he felt a duty that threatened to keep him from what he really wanted to do.

"Look how solemn he is," Amanda said, and Johnny saw that she was watching him. She nudged Chalmers and imitated Johnny, slumping in her seat until she was a pitiful figure to behold. She passed one hand up before her face and straightened at the same time, revealing a bright and happy expression. She passed the hand back down and once again assumed the sorrowful face of tragedy, but then she smiled. "Those are the two faces of a clown. You have to be able to change from one to the other in a moment."

Johnny smiled. "Sun Horse says you have *heyoka* power."

"What kind of power?"

"*Heyoka*. It's what the Sioux call a clown."

Amanda was puzzled. "What do they know about clowns?"

"They have clowns of their own. The *heyokas* make the people laugh in hard times, and when times are good they act sad to remind the people that hard times are never far away."

"That's what we do!" Amanda said, delighted.

"*Heyokas* are a good bit different from white clowns, I guess," Johnny said. He had seen a real clown show only once, in St. Louis. "The *heyokas* are sacred beings. They control the power of the west. They dress in ragged clothes, and they're painted all over with sacred symbols. There's more to them than just clowning."

"Do they paint their faces?" Amanda asked. "Like Indians, I mean?"

"*Heyokas* paint their faces in special ways only *heyokas* can use, with lightning and hailstones."

"I wish I could see them!" the girl exclaimed. She looked around at the valley and the mountains. "I wish we could stay here longer. When we're gone all this will seem like a dream. It's already like a dream. No one will believe us when we tell them about the Indians." She was filled with sudden despair and Johnny looked about for anything that might distract her from the thought of leaving Putnam's Park.

The caravan was entering the river canyon, where the air was cooler. The canyon descended directly toward the south, and the late morning sun had just cleared the high cliff across the river on the eastern side. Its rays touched the wagon road for only a short time each day, and the ground here was frozen hard. To the right, bathed in sunlight, rose a steep hillside that ascended for a thousand feet or more to a broken rimrock crowned with smooth cornices of snow sculpted by the winter winds. Close beside the trail the brush grew thicker where it received the runoff from the slope.

"Look there." Johnny pointed to a clump of sagebrush.

"What?" Amanda looked and saw nothing. Chalmers too was peering at the brush.

"It's a snowshoe rabbit. See his tracks? Follow them until they stop."

"Oh! He's beautiful!" Amanda said in a voice that was barely louder than a whisper.

The creature, actually a hare, but called a rabbit throughout the West, crouched motionless in the shadow of a bush, still white in its winter coat, its ears flat against its head. They watched it until they had passed beyond and out of sight.

Four wagons to the rear another pair of eyes spied the tracks, and then the hare against the snow. "Look there." Kinnean gestured with his injured arm, confined in its sling. The driver beside him wrapped his reins around the brake lever and reached slowly for the shotgun that lay at his feet. Just as slowly, he raised the gun to his shoulder.

"Better than chicken, if you ask me." He sighted and fired.

The driver's name was Johansen. He was pale-eyed and blond, a lanky man in his twenties. At home he had shot rabbits and quail and partridges for his mother's table, and at the age of ten he had watched his home burned and both his parents killed in the Sioux uprising of 1862. He had come west to the Black Hills from Minnesota in the autumn and throughout the winter he had kept his shotgun loaded with buckshot against the chance of being surprised by Indians at close range. He fired at the hare instinctively, without thinking to change his load, and reduced the animal to a bloody swatch in the snow.

"Damn," he said unemotionally as he realized his error.

The booming roar of the shotgun rose from the base of the canyon, gaining strength as it echoed between the hillside and the rock face of the cliff across the way. As the echoes rolled away there came another sound.

Up and down the string of wagons, men and women looked to see who had fired. At the head of the column, Tatum looked up. At first he saw nothing more than what seemed to be a small cloud at the base of the rimrock, but it increased rapidly in size and took form as the snow at the top of the slope began to move.

"Avalanche!" someone shouted.

"Turn the wagons!" Tatum cried out. All along the caravan, people shouted in alarm, and in seconds the scene became one of pandemonium.

Three wagons had already reached the narrowest part of the trail, where there was no hope of turning, but still the drivers whipped and shouted at their teams, heaving on reins and cursing in an effort to back or turn the teams in the impossible space. These were supply wagons with broad wheels, hauled by slow-witted oxen, and always placed in the front of the train to make a trail for the rest.

"Jump!" Tatum shouted at the frantic men. "Get away!" He was at the fourth wagon, where he seized the bridle of the lead Clydesdale. He kicked his own horse and heaved the draft horse around, managing to double the team back and pull the wagon in a tight turn. One wheel slipped over the edge of the embankment that fell sharply to the river, but Tatum's urging kept the team pulling and the wheel found purchase on the frozen ground and rolled, bouncing over snow-covered rocks, back to the road surface.

"Hah! Get up!" the driver shouted and the wagon jumped forward as the team hauled in unison. It careened past other wagons still trying to turn, only to find its way blocked fifty yards beyond by a tangle of men and horses and wagons that would take long minutes to undo.

"Amanda!" Johnny shouted. The noise from the animals and wagons and the people of the circus was almost deafening. He kicked his horse close to Chalmers' wagon and reached out as Amanda turned and saw him. She had sat paralyzed throughout the first moments of the growing chaos around her. Now she moved into Johnny's arms without thinking. He lifted her from the seat and placed her before him on the horse as he shouted to Chalmers to get down from the wagon. At the same moment, the back door of the gaily painted little house burst open and Lydia jumped out, screaming. Johnny looked back as he spurred his horse to safety and he saw the avalanche gaining speed close above the road. The road was covered with milling, panicked horses.

The horse herd had been driven in front of the wagons to break a way through the recent snow. At the first shout the wranglers had looked up. They were frontiersmen and did not need to be warned twice of an impending avalanche. They saw the moving snow and without hesitation they reined their horses around and fled back the way they had come, all but Jack Fisk. Fisk was ahead of the horses, leading the way. He too looked up, and even as he grasped the meaning of what he saw, he waved his free arm and shouted "Hyahhh!" to spook the lead horses and turn them back. The herd wheeled and some of the animals bolted, taking their direction from the fleeing wranglers, but the shouts and confusion surrounding the lead wagons checked their flight. They caught the panic of the struggling oxen and refused to pass. As the driver of the first wagon leaped from his seat and ran for safety, the oxen felt the slackening of the reins and lumbered forward, scattering and dividing the horse herd. Those on the side of the trail close to the hillside saw an opening there and took flight back along the line of wagons, but the remaining horses fled in the opposite direction, given impetus by the bellowing oxen and the clatter of the wagon. Once decided on their purpose, the riderless horses flew like thistles on a storm wind, those in the rear overtaking and passing the clumsy wagon and moving now among the leaders, a single rider swept along in their midst.

Back in the tangled caravan the horses that had found the way to safety there ran the length of the train, shying from men and women on foot, conveying their fear to the other animals, even those well out of danger. The mules pulling Joe Kitchen's cookwagon bucked in the harness, kicking out at the air.

"Whoa, now!" Joe hauled on the reins with all his might to keep the mules in line. The leader reared as a panicked horse swerved away from a running man and bumped against the pitching mule; the mule kicked out and the horse kicked back, striking the mule in the hindquarters. The leader lunged into his harness with a force that threw Joe Kitchen off-balance and sent him sprawling to the seat, grabbing for a handhold. The reins slipped from his hands and the team was off and running, careening between Chalmers' abandoned wagon and the hillside.

None but Joe himself had seen the events that caused this sudden flight. Each person in the caravan had his own jumbled impressions of the unnatural moments that followed the first warning shout. Feet seemed weighted down with lead. No action was quick enough to respond to the white danger that gathered force and hurtled down the slope with heart-stopping speed. But soon most saw that they were well beyond the path of the avalanche; they stopped running and turned to watch the spectacle.

The billowing cloud was huge and high above the slope, rising from the leading edge of the avalanche like steam from a rift in the roof of Hell. It bore down on the road with express-train velocity, but as the horrified spectators looked on with mouths agape, the cookwagon raced with equal speed to meet it.

"Jump, Joe!"

"Jump for your life!"

Cookwagon and mules and driver were lost in the rolling cloud of snow as the avalanche poured over the road and into the river beyond, blocking half the stream. A cold gray mist spread to the knot of watchers and beyond, cutting off the sun.

"Joe!"

"He's gone."

"Gott im Himmel."

"I saw him jump!"

"Quiet!" Tatum held up a hand for silence. "Joe! Joe Kitchen!"

They listened. Men and women shivered and hugged themselves and stamped their feet against the sudden chill, but already the sunlight filtered through as the mist settled, like the miraculous clearing of the sky in the middle of a winter storm. The flakes continued to fall, becoming finer and finer and sparkling in the sunlight to lend a numbed enchantment to the scene; the air over the roadway cleared, and the hushed group of onlookers could see where the lead wagons had been. One remained on the trail. There was no trace of the cookwagon.

"There! Look there!"

A figure moved, crawling from beneath the wagon that had been spared. The figure stood and walked toward the onlookers. It was a man, short and round.

"Joe?"

"By Christ, it's him!"

Joe Kitchen wore a strangely satisfied look as he approached them, and to their surprise they could hear him laughing to himself.

"He's come unhinged."

"Like hell I have!" he shouted. "I'm just taking what satisfaction I can from knowing I won't have to fight those muleheaded sonofabitches anymore." He stopped and pointed at those watching him, laughing even harder now. "By God, look at you. You're a bunch of snowmen!"

They looked at one another and saw that he was right. As the snowy mist settled it had covered them all with a layer of white that clung to hair and hats and coats, even to eyebrows and mustaches and beards. They looked like minions of Jack Frost, or a gathering of ghosts. They laughed at themselves, grateful to be alive.

"He's quite right, you know," Chalmers boomed, laughing with the rest. "Look at us all." He slapped the snow off himself and Lydia and clapped Joe Kitchen on the back as the cook joined them.

Amanda and Johnny Smoker still sat astride Johnny's horse a short distance away. Johnny's arms were around the girl, holding her close against him as they stared in awe at the mound of snow that covered the road to five times the height of a wagon.

Others returned their attention to the avalanche now.

"Where is Jack Fisk?" Tatum demanded of the crowd at large.

"He was out in front," someone said.

A wrangler rode toward the jumbled mass of snow and

rocks. A horse caught in the soft snow at the edge of the mound struggled to get up but repeatedly slipped and fell, denied the use of its broken leg.

"I saw him," the man said to no one in particular. "He took out the other way." He drew a revolver and shot the horse neatly through the brain, then raised the gun and fired twice more into the air. "Fisk!" he called.

"Stop that, you fool!" Tatum was livid. He cast a worried glance up the slope. "You'll bring down the whole mountain!"

"Seems to me it's already done fell on us. Fisk!" The call echoed in the canyon but there was no reply.

CHAPTER THREE

On the fifth day of March the snow began before dawn and continued throughout the morning, coming from the northeast. The troopers pulled their caps down low and their collars high and turned their faces westward to avoid the stinging pellets that threatened to blind them.

The countryside was dreary, growing rougher as the expedition approached the Powder. The rolling, barren prairie had given way to rills and gullies that had deepened into ravines and arroyos. Whitcomb was amused by the proliferation of terms used by the troopers and packers to describe all the varieties of little canyons that cut the frozen countryside. Thus far, he was certain only that a swale had a rounded bottom, often grass-covered, and a coulee had steep sides. As the soldiers descended the Dry Fork of the Powder they were flanked by treeless bluffs of dull slate and sandstone, occasionally colored by streaks of yellow clay. The Big Horns, which they had first seen two days earlier resplendent in their snow-capped majesty, loomed nearer, gray and forbidding now when the clouds thinned and rose high enough to reveal the presence of the mountain chain. Off to the right, Pumpkin Buttes watched the column's progress like four massive sentinels.

Squads of flankers rode always within sight of the column, usually within a hundred yards. The day before, under a brilliant sun, the flankers had been three hundred yards to the sides and the scouts six hundred or more to the front; now Colonel Stanton kept his scouts in pairs, each in sight of the next as they ranged back and forth in advance of the column. They were the eyes of the expedition, watching for sign, peering into ravines, searching for a footprint or a force of lurking Indians.

Since the night attack on the camp there had been abundant evidence that the hostiles were aware of the column's every movement. Until today the sun had shone almost constantly on the expedition, cheering the men and making it easier to bear the wind that blew steadily in their faces, but the clear air had aided the hostiles as well; looking-glass signals had flashed often from the right flank and once a dark column of smoke had risen from a butte on the northern horizon. Today such signals were made impossible by the storm, but already the column had crossed the tracks left by several small parties of Indians and the troopers had caught their first glimpse of the savage warriors. Several times during the morning horsemen had revealed themselves to the soldiers singly or in small groups, never more than half a dozen, sitting out of rifle shot, watching, first from the right and then from the left, first from the front and then from the rear. The company commanders were under orders to observe these vedettes but under no account to give chase. Nor did the scouts follow any of the trails they saw. The risk of ambuscade was too great and General Crook wanted to conserve the strength of the horses. By his steady progress northward and his refusal to engage small groups such as these, he hoped to confuse the hostiles, so he had told the company commanders. Confusion was his only weapon now; any hope of surprise was futile, thanks to the watchfulness of the Indians.

"Sir, there's another one!" Corporal Atherton called out, raising his voice just enough to carry up the column to Lieutenant Corwin. E Troop was at the tail of the line today; since the night attack one company of cavalry had been placed behind the pack train to guard the expedition's rear. Whitcomb and Corwin were riding together at the head of the troop. They reined aside now to look where Atherton was pointing. Seventy or eighty yards away First Sergeant Dupré and his three flankers had come to a halt. Dupré was pointing to the southeast. Whitcomb slipped off his green goggles and dropped them around his neck and now he saw the Indians, half a mile beyond the flankers, nearly invisible in the thin snow that had stopped falling only twice all morning. There were four. Or five. Or four men with five horses. He shook his head and shielded his eyes with both hands. The movement of the snow made seeing details at long distances nearly impossible.

"Are they always the same ones, first in one place and then the next?" he wondered aloud.

"There's no way of knowing," Corwin said. They watched the Indians for a few moments longer and then Corwin trotted on to regain his place in the column. Whitcomb followed close behind. For three days now, ever since the incident with the beef herd, he had been kept under Corwin's constant supervision. For any job that required the least responsibility, Corwin called on Dupré or one of the other non-commissioned officers. Only when a chore was devoid of any risk did he call on Ham Whitcomb.

Two officers were riding back along the column. They touched their caps as they reached Corwin and turned to ride alongside him.

"Good day, Major," said Lieutenant Bourke, Crook's aide. He smiled at Whitcomb. "Lieutenant Whitcomb."

Whitcomb smiled in reply. "Lieutenant Bourke." He recognized the other man as Charles Morton, Colonel Reynolds' adjutant, a second lieutenant like Whitcomb and Bourke. Colonel Joseph J. Reynolds was nominally in charge of the troops, but officers and men alike knew full well that Crook himself was actually giving the orders. Reynolds had been a major general of U.S. Volunteers during the Civil War, and he preferred to be addressed as "General." He had been the commanding officer of the Third Cavalry for the past six years, but while serving as commander of the Department of Texas he had been tainted by some vague scandal and relieved of that duty. The general opinion within the expedition was that Crook had taken Reynolds under his wing and would watch him closely.

"Sir, General Reynolds' compliments," said Morton, addressing Corwin, "and he asks if you will kindly put out two more sets of flankers to the east."

Corwin nodded and turned to Whitcomb. "Mr. Whitcomb, you will go to the rear and relieve Sergeant Polachek as file closer. Instruct him to put out two more sets of flankers to the east and lead one himself."

"Yes, sir." Whitcomb reined around and trotted back along the line, cursing silently. Surely he could be trusted to lead a set of flankers! The Indians were plainly taunting the column and had no intention of attacking! What could be the harm in giving him something to do for once?

When he reached Polachek he passed along Corwin's orders and then took over the tedious chore of "file closer," the man charged with seeing that the end of the column kept closed up. The wind gusted, lashing snow in his face; he put his goggles back in place to protect his eyes and stretched his mouth wide to flex his face against the cold. He felt a small pain and then a chill as a drop of blood oozed from a new crevice in his lower lip. His lips were cracked from drinking the brackish alkali water that was all the country offered. He cursed his forgetfulness and dabbed the blood away with a glove.

Ahead, Morton and Bourke parted company with Corwin. As Morton cantered off to rejoin the front of the column, Bourke rode toward the rear. He raised a hand in greeting as he neared Whitcomb.

Whitcomb had made it a point to learn as much as he could about John Bourke since their meetings at Fetterman. Bourke had enlisted in the Union Army when he was only sixteen and had served throughout the war as a private with the Fifteenth Pennsylvania, winning a Medal of Honor before he was twenty. After the war he had attended West Point and then served for some years in Arizona Territory. He had been Crook's aide for five years now, commencing shortly after Crook took command of the Department of Arizona. Next to the general's striker, Andrew Peiser, it was said that Bourke knew the general better than any other man. Three years ago, for reasons unknown, he had turned down a brevet promotion to captain.

"Well, Mr. Whitcomb," Bourke greeted him cheerily, "how are you enjoying our little jaunt? Being from the South, you must feel the cold more than most." Bourke's beard, begun at the start of the campaign to augment his full mustache, already covered his jaw completely. Whitcomb's own sparse chin hairs were an embarrassment to him and afforded no significant shelter from the weather.

"I am more stiff than cold," Whitcomb replied. "I've been saved by an impulsive purchase at Fetterman. The trader sold me a set of underwear made from merino wool sewn to perforated buckskin. He said they were the last pair in my size, and indispensable to a winter campaign. When I was fifty yards from the store I almost went back to demand my money. But I kept them. And glad of it, I must admit."

Bourke nodded. "I have some myself."

"You do? You wouldn't humor me?"

"On my honor. I wouldn't be without them."

Whitcomb smiled, relieved. "I very nearly left them in my saddlebags. I was embarrassed to be seen putting them on. But that second night, after we lost the beef herd, I braved the cold. That was the hardest part, stripping down to put them on."

"I wouldn't worry. You'll probably wear them for the rest of the campaign, and when you see the fort again, they'll stand on their own." The two men laughed together.

"You seem in very good spirits," Whitcomb ventured.

"I am always in good spirits on campaign, Mr. Whitcomb. If my spirits lag, I grow careless and fail to note a change in the wind, or the direction a rabbit is facing; then before I know it, General Crook has wished aloud to know just such a thing and my ignorance is revealed." He smiled.

"The general has a consuming interest in many things, I understand."

"In all things!" Bourke laughed again, and Whitcomb felt the cold less than he had a few moments before. "For example, yesterday when that dust cloud was sighted, it was Little Bat who first saw it and came riding to report to Colonel Stanton. The colonel was riding with General Crook at the time, and the general wanted to know not only the size of the cloud, but also its drift, direction and speed, the color of the dust and a few details I have forgotten. No piece of information is too small to escape his curiosity. And believe me, once he learns something, he never forgets it. He knows more about scouting and signs than Grouard or any of the rest. When he asks you something, half the time he already knows the answer, and you had better be prepared to answer him thoroughly."

"You have been with him some time. Since he took command of the Department of Arizona, I believe."

Bourke looked at Whitcomb more closely. "Well, I was warned. I had been told that our Mr. Reb was something of a student of the western campaigns, but I had no idea that study included the histories of each general's aides."

Whitcomb stiffened at the use of a name he had hoped not to hear again, and Bourke noticed. "Oh, no offense, none at all, I give you my word. I didn't mean to let it out. It seems you have acquired a nickname. An admiring one at that, at least in part."

"It is hardly admiring to be called a rebel," Whitcomb said coldly.

"Please believe me, Ham— Do they call you Ham or Hamilton?"

"My friends call me Ham."

"And I would be pleased to count myself among your friends. You must believe me when I tell you that having a nickname is a good omen. It's the first step in being accepted by the men. I am afraid Southerners will be called Johnny Rebs for some time to come, and no amount of indignation can change that, but like Yankee or Jayhawker or Paddy, it can be either pejorative or admiring, depending on the use. I've heard the name Patlander a few times, as you can imagine."

"But you're not . . . Well, not like the others."

"D' yez mean Oi've lost the brogue? Arrah! Oi'm iz Oirish iz inny man in the column." Bourke grinned and dropped the broad accent he had learned from the enlisted men. "My people merely came well ahead of the tide. Even I say 'Irish' meaning the more recent immigrants."

"You said my nickname was admiring only in part."

"Well, the men admired your spunk, going off on your own. What remains to be seen is whether you are brave or merely foolish."

They laughed, and Whitcomb put a glove to his mouth. He inspected a new spot of blood. "Here," Bourke offered, and he pulled a small jar from the pocket of his overcoat. He unscrewed the top clumsily with his gloved hands and extended the jar to Whitcomb. It was filled with a greasy substance. "It's beef tallow. I got it from Colonel Stanton's cook. Rub a little on your lips."

Whitcomb clamped one glove under the other arm and slipped his hand free, quickly dipping a finger in the tallow and applying it to his lips. He rubbed them together to work the tallow into the cracks. At once the chapped skin felt better. "Thanks," he said as he restored his hand to the bulky muskrat gauntlet. In less than a minute he had almost lost the feeling in his fingers, but the temporary discomfort was worth it. How many more bits of lore were there still to learn about staying comfortable in a cold climate? Hundreds, certainly. He would never learn them all.

"May I ask you something?" he inquired of Bourke. "I've heard several of the men refer to Major Corwin as 'Boots.' You said it yourself, back at Fetterman. Do you know how he got the nickname?"

"The men will tell you it's short for 'Boots and Saddles,' because he's army through and through, but the real origin is more interesting." He hesitated a moment, glancing at Whitcomb, and then said, "He was taken prisoner during the Rebellion. Did you know that?"

Whitcomb nodded. "That much and little more."

"The day he was captured the Rebels took his boots. From then until he was exchanged, he had only rags to cover his feet. His boots mean more to him than most of us. He always has an extra pair in his kit."

"He sleeps with his boots on too."

"How are you getting along, or shouldn't I ask?"

Whitcomb was about to say something of his treatment at Corwin's hands, but he thought better of it. In the army no one liked a complainer, and complaints about a superior officer were always suspect. "Well enough," he said. "But I must say I find it a little discouraging to see him still in first lieutenant's bars after all his years in the army." He flushed suddenly, realizing Bourke might take this personally. "I'm sorry. I understand you could be a captain now if you'd wanted."

Bourke shrugged. "In the war a brevet rank was good for something in the way of command responsibility, but no longer. I decided I would have a permanent promotion or none at all. Advancement is slow nowadays."

"I'm afraid I'll be old and gray before I ever command a troop."

"Oh, I wouldn't be so sure. You have already come to General Crook's attention. The headquarters staff is tickled pink by that chase after the beef herd."

Whitcomb felt the blood rise to his face again. "That's an incident I would just as soon have forgotten, as you can imagine."

"Let me tell you something," Bourke said in a tone that did not carry far. "That dressing down you got from Boots

Corwin is nothing compared to what you would have received from the general if you had succeeded in turning the herd."

Whitcomb frowned. "I don't understand."

"Good Lord, man, you don't imagine Crook wanted that herd along for the whole campaign? If Sheridan had agreed, we never would have had the first steer on this march. The staff officers are joking that Crook himself hired those Indians to run them off."

"You can't be serious!"

"He only brought them because he was ordered to! That raid suited him perfectly!" Bourke was gleeful, his eyes twinkling, although his walrus mustache hid most of his grin. "Cattle always slow you down and they could have been stampeded by a wolf or an Indian on some other night, under much worse circumstances. As it is, they ran off when they still had a chance of getting back to Fetterman and the general is grateful. We're going to cover some ground now, you mark my words."

"We don't seem to be in any great rush just yet."

"He likes to give the men and animals a few days to condition themselves. Before long we'll leave the wagons behind and then you'll see us move right along. The general wants us on an equal footing with the Indians except for one thing—the condition of our horses."

Ahead of them the column was slowing and now they heard the command, passed down the line: "Dismount! Walk your horses." For fifteen minutes of each hour the cavalry walked to warm themselves and give their horses some rest.

"Well, if I listen closely, I can hear my duty calling," Bourke said as Whitcomb reined his horse to a stop. "I had better get back up front. Perhaps I'll see you when we make camp tonight."

He rode off leaving Whitcomb feeling pleased with himself, as if he had done General Crook a personal favor by failing to recover the cattle. I might emerge from this campaign with flying colors after all, he thought, if that chase is not to be held against me.

* * *

At mid-afternoon, the column halted suddenly.

Corwin turned to Whitcomb, who was once more riding beside him. After a few hours of file closing he had been relieved by Corporal McCaslin. "Go to the front, Mr. Whitcomb, and find out why we have stopped. If the men can dismount, let me know."

Even as Whitcomb gratefully spurred his horse into a warming canter, the call to dismount was relayed down the column, and he was doubly glad. His orders took him from Corwin's stifling presence, at least for a time, and now there was no reason for him to return quickly.

The reason for the halt was apparent when he reached the head of the column, where officers and scouts were inspecting a trail that had recently been traveled by a large body of Indians crossing the path of the army's advance. A few of the scouts walked along the trail for a few dozen yards to be clear of the gathering and there they examined the tracks closely. Whitcomb saw John Bourke with Generals Crook and Reynolds, who were listening intently to the reports of several scouts. Reynolds was white-haired, with muttonchop whiskers, and he alone of all the officers kept his chin clean-shaven on the march. Whitcomb dismounted and moved a little nearer. It was the closest he had been to the colorful scouts since the start of the expedition. They were dressed for the most part in furs, buckskins and leggings, high boots or moccasins, and hats and caps of every variety. The one man Whitcomb knew by sight was the swarthy Frank Grouard, who was speaking to Crook now, gesturing at the trail. Grouard was a hulking figure standing over six feet tall; his past was a mystery, and the subject of much speculation in the command. Some said he was half Sioux and half Negro, while others maintained that he had been born in the South Seas. All agreed that he had been held captive for some years among the Sioux, in the camp of Crazy Horse himself, it was said. Whitcomb had heard a rumor that Grouard's loyalty to the white man was suspect, and that General Crook had instructed Big Bat and Little Bat—the scouts

Pourier and Garnier—to drop Grouard in his tracks if he showed the first sign of betraying the column to the hostiles.

"Mr. Whitcomb, isn't it?"

Whitcomb turned to see Captain Anson Mills addressing him. The twelve companies in the command had been divided at the start into six battalions of two troops each; Mills was commander of the battalion that comprised his own Company M, Third Cavalry, and Corwin's E Company. Mills carried a long-barreled shotgun in the crook of his arm. Many of the officers bore personal weapons instead of the cavalry carbines; Winchester repeaters were a favorite but Mills touted the virtues of double-ought buckshot for dispatching Indians at close quarters.

"Yes, sir." Whitcomb saluted.

"Have you been sent here by Major Corwin?" Mills was always punctilious about referring to Corwin by his brevet rank, a courtesy he himself expected in return. He had been brevetted lieutenant colonel for gallantry in the battle of Nashville, Tennessee. He had black hair, black eyes, a mustache and goatee. His speech was abrupt and his manner excitable, which always made Whitcomb nervous in his presence.

"I'm to find out why we've stopped, sir. Major Corwin wished to know if there was to be a long delay."

"I imagine we'll move along soon," Mills replied. "Quite a trail, this one." He jabbed a hand at the tracks.

The overlapping prints of unshod horses and moccasins of all sizes were plain to see, but Whitcomb was puzzled by the long striations that scored the ground where the Indians had passed. He pointed at the marks. "What makes those tracks, sir?"

Mills looked at him as if he had asked how many legs were to be found on the average horse. "Lodgepoles," he said, and Whitcomb blushed violently, feeling the perfect fool. He knew very well that the Indians transported their belongings on travois, or pony drags, made by crossing two tipi poles across a horse's back and lashing a small framework across the lower ends of the poles to bear whatever might be required, whether the lodge covering, household belongings, or a wounded man. Yet he had not put this knowledge together with the strange marks before him. All his life had been spent in the white man's world, where there were foot and hoof and wheel prints, but nothing such as this.

As he rode back along the column he glanced at the newest mules in the pack train, young animals with their manes roached and tails bobbed short so the packers could tell at a glance which were the inexperienced beasts most likely to cause trouble. No wonder the troopers called fresh young second lieutenants "shavetails." Graduates of the military academy, they were educated men, but they knew nothing at all in the areas that mattered most. It seemed that acquiring knowledge was not enough. Like a new tool, knowledge must be used over and over again until its application became second nature. Whitcomb resolved that before the campaign was over, he would be a shavetail no longer.

As the afternoon wore on the snow gradually stopped. Two more vedettes of hostiles were sighted and duly ignored as they attempted to entice a foolish pursuit. Later, shots boomed out far in front and set the column on alert, but one of the scouts returned with the welcome news that his comrades had brought down two buffalo bulls. More shots sounded as the head of the column drew near the wooded valley of the Powder, and again game was the cause of the shooting, antelope this time. The guides chose a crossing through a patch of sluggish, milky water rather than risk the wagons on the treacherous alkali ice; the river bottom was quaggy and the horses lurched about, unhappy not to be able to see their footing, but the crossing was made without incident and as E Troop arrived at the far bank they saw that the companies from the head of the line were already encamped for the night and the men were gathered around the cookfires, watching the butchering of bison and antelope with unconcealed interest.

The valley was broad, more than a mile wide near the crossing, and well timbered with cottonwood. But despite a generous growth of lowland grasses, the horses and mules were picketed in lines together and fed grain from the wagons, and the command was camped near the stream, well removed from the densest stands of trees and any other cover that might provide an avenue of approach for infiltrating Indians.

Visible on higher ground beyond the river bottom were a few jagged timbers and a fragment of a palisade wall.

"Old Fort Reno, I imagine," Whitcomb observed to McCaslin as they dismounted.

"Indayd, sorr. Major Corwin was stationed here once upon a time, durin' Red Cloud's War."

"Oh?"

"Yes, sorr. For him it must be like comin' home to a graveyard."

McCaslin crossed himself, but Whitcomb did not need that sign of the Catholic faith to give him the feeling that there were ghosts about. Fort Reno was ninety miles from Fetterman, and it was the southernmost of the three forts built ten years before to guard the Bozeman Trail. It had been abandoned in 1868 when the Laramie treaty was signed, and before the last trooper was out of sight the gleeful savages had set it alight. This was the first military expedition into the Powder River country since then and suddenly Whitcomb felt that even this bustling camp of eight hundred men was small and trifling compared with the vastness of the terrain they sought to pacify.

By now the matter of making camp had become routine. Major Coates posted his infantry sentries, animals were picketed and fed, tents were erected in rows by company, and the evening meal was prepared. Whitcomb performed his duties and set out his bedroll and when he was done he sauntered in the direction of the headquarters tents, where he found John Bourke writing in a small leatherbound book. Nearby, a gathering of company officers and scouts was just breaking up, the scouts already mounting their horses and starting off to the north to survey the surrounding country.

Bourke closed his book and replaced it in a pocket of his greatcoat. "There. If I don't write in my diary each day when we make camp, I don't get it done at all.'' He stood up and gestured about the campsite. ''Well, this is all right, isn't it? Lots of firewood, at least. I swear, I can feel the cold in my bones. Come along over here; we've a good fire going.''

''Rank hath its privileges,'' Whitcomb muttered, eyeing the commodious tents for the staff officers and the tables set here and there.

''What? Oh, I see, the luxuries of the headquarters mess.'' Bourke's tone was sarcastic. ''Look here, you see the general?'' He nodded toward a tent not far away. With the staff meeting over, General Crook was reclining on a buffalo robe outside the tent, his arms crossed beneath his head, gazing skyward as if relaxing on a warm spring day. ''That is where he sleeps,'' Bourke continued. ''You see that fellow there? That's his striker, Andy Peiser. He's been with the general as long as I have.'' Beyond Crook, an enlisted man of fair complexion and middling height sat in a folding canvas chair, reading a small Bible. When Crook shifted position, resting his head on one hand, Peiser looked up, and returned to his reading only when it was clear that Crook required nothing of him. Many officers had strikers, enlisted men hired as personal servants, and many troopers sought the job, for it could earn them something beyond a private soldier's thirteen dollars a month.

''Why does the commanding general sleep on the ground, you ask?'' Bourke grinned. ''He's got a striker to make his bed for him, you think. He could sleep on a cot, swaddled in a stack of buffalo robes like some traveling British lord. Well, he sleeps like that because he prefers it that way, and once we're clear of the wagons the rest of us will have it no better. You won't find another man on the campaign who can do with fewer comforts or keep up the pace better than George Crook. He's uncanny, boyo, you mind what I say. Once down in Arizona we had marched for twenty-six hours straight, and when we finally stopped, we all fell to the ground like tenpins. Not him. He strolled off to the marsh nearby and shot a dozen reed ducks for the men's supper. Oh, here's a man you should meet." Nearby, an officer was hanging a mercury thermometer from the pole of the medical tent. "Your life may depend on him, although I earnestly hope not. Dr. Munn," Bourke addressed the man, drawing near, "may I present Lieutenant Whitcomb. Lieutenant, Assistant Surgeon Munn, our ranking medical officer. Dr. Munn is preparing to measure the degree of our discomfort."

Whitcomb and Munn shook hands and exchanged pleasantries and the doctor nodded at the thermometer. "Back in Washington they love bits of intelligence such as this. I tell them what temperatures we encountered and they write in their reports that the troops were perfectly comfortable at thus and such a temperature in standard field issue. God help us if anyone believes that. No frostbite in your troop, I trust, Mr. Whitcomb?"

"No, sir, none at all." All the officers in the command had been warned to be on the alert for the first signs of frostbite among the men, and to see that no one exposed himself carelessly to that crippling affliction.

The light on the scene, which until then had been dim and growing steadily dimmer as night approached, now changed dramatically. The camp was illuminated suddenly by a brilliant orange glow and the three men turned to see that the sun had emerged from beneath the clouds, its lower edge already touching the horizon. To the east the slopes of the benches and hills descending to the river were painted in gold and scarlet and for a brief time the camp was almost silent as everywhere men stopped to regard the unexpected beauty.

"Fat lot of good he does us now," Bourke observed irreverently as the fiery sphere slipped below the western hills and left the camp in a gloom that thickened quickly. "I could have used a glimpse of old Sol about noontime today." He moved a few steps closer to the large fire in the middle of the headquarters camp. "If it clears tonight it will be damn cold."

"Mr. Bourke!" A man Whitcomb did not know was approaching, waving to get Bourke's attention. "I have been looking for you. Oh, I don't know your friend. Perhaps you would introduce—''

Shots sounded from the edge of camp, first one and then two more; all were the familiar reports of the infantry's Springfield rifles. Close on the heels of the shots came derisive shouts demanding to know how many trees had been injured. ''More jittery nerves,'' Whitcomb said, joining Bourke and the other man by the fire. Since the first attack on camp there had been some shooting each night, directed at anything that resembled the shape of a man in the uncertain light. At dawn, most of these ''Indians'' had proved to be stumps or rocks. The night before, three flesh-and-blood Indians had crept up through the brush in the hope of stealing a few horses, but they had been sent running with a brisk flight of lead compliments.

A ragged stuttering of sharp explosions broke out from two sides now, and a bullet passed not far overhead.

''More than nerves, I think,'' Bourke said, looking around. Men were running toward the edges of camp and a few shouts from the officers were attempting to put order in the soldiers' response to the shooting. A ball struck the fire, sending up a cloud of sparks and causing the three men to jump back. ''You might want to join your troop,'' Bourke observed, and he walked calmly away.

Whitcomb lost no time in following Bourke's suggestion and he reached the tents of E Troop just as Corwin came running through the growing confusion. Ignoring Whitcomb, he addressed Sergeant Dupré.

''Form up the men on foot, Sergeant. General Crook expects the hostiles to go for the horse herd; we're to help protect it.''

''Yes, sair.'' Dupré began to move among the men, passing Corwin's orders along to the other non-commissioned officers and speaking calmly to steady the excited soldiers.

''Mr. Whitcomb.'' Corwin turned to his second-in-command. ''Take Sergeant Duggan and ten men and assist Major Coates.''

''Yes, *sir!*'' He found Duggan, a lanky Irishman, among the milling troopers and in a few moments they had assembled a squad of ten men, armed with carbines. As he led the way at double time toward the sound of the firing, Whitcomb was smiling. The real brunt of the attack might well come in the vicinity of the horse herd—if the hostiles could put the cavalry afoot they would have won the campaign with a single well-timed stroke—but Corwin hadn't been able to isolate Whitcomb from the fighting entirely. From the sound of it, a lively exchange was in progress between Coates's infantry and a considerable band of concealed attackers.

The cookfires had been kicked to smithereens within minutes of the first shots and the camp was in a dim twilight now, coming in part from the west, where a small orange glow lingered, and in part from the dull gray clouds overhead, lit by the unseen half-moon. Whitcomb nearly bumped into a running man, excused himself, and suddenly found himself among the infantry, who had taken sheltered positions in hastily improvised rifle pits. "Put the men where they'll do the most good, Sergeant," he instructed Duggan, and then worked his way toward the edge of the perimeter to survey the state of affairs.

Muzzle flashes sparked in the dense cluster of cottonwoods immediately to the front and the troopers responded at once, firing at the flashes. Whitcomb discerned the reports of cavalry carbines among those of the infantry's rifles. Good man, Duggan, he thought. The E Troop men were already in position. The return fire was disciplined and brief. The men reloaded quickly to wait for the next flash that would reveal some lurking Indian's position. The trees were sharply silhouetted against the somewhat lighter sky, but no detail at all was visible in the foreground.

Whitcomb found a place behind a stump and drew his revolver. A pistol would be as much use as a carbine here; more use, if the attackers got up their courage to charge.

More shots came from the cottonwoods and there was a cry of pain close in front of Whitcomb. "Ye haythen bastards!" the wounded man shouted. His voice was strangely muffled, as if he spoke with his mouth full of food. A figure rose ten yards beyond and fired at the woods. It was an infantryman; Whitcomb could make out the long shape of the man's rifle. The figure struggled to push another round into the trapdoor breech, but he paused and raised a hand to his head, then slowly toppled to the ground. He fell near the remains of one of the cookfires and the glow from the coals illuminated his still form sufficiently well for the attackers to see; shots began to sound from the cottonwoods and bullets kicked up gouts of dirt near the fallen soldier.

Without forethought, Whitcomb scrambled across the intervening distance, pistol in hand, ignoring the sound of two balls that passed close by, one on either side of him.

"Careful, boys, there's a man to the front!" The return fire from the troopers was lively and Whitcomb was glad to hear the cautionary warning. The voice was calm and forceful, and from those few words Whitcomb recognized a fellow Virginian. Who could it be? He hadn't been aware that there was another Virginian on the campaign. He had reached the wounded man now and he dropped to his knees beside him. The man had been shot through the face. A ragged hole gaped in his left cheek. Small wonder that his voice sounded odd, Whitcomb thought. He holstered his pistol and grabbed the man by the armpits, dragging him quickly away from the fire as more shots struck the ground nearby. He paused in the shelter of a large rock and ducked as a ball struck the boulder and sprayed the two men with flying chips. The wounded soldier groaned.

"It's all right," Whitcomb said, and he wondered if everyone mouthed such platitudes at times like this.

"Covering fire, boys!" came the same voice that had called the warning just moments before. The troopers' Springfields set up a barrage and the muskets in the woods fell silent. Whitcomb heaved on the wounded man and dragged him across the final yards to the troopers' lines. Two men jumped up to help him.

"That were a fine piece o' work, friend. Let's us truck 'im to the doc. Oh, 'scuse me, sir."

How in the devil did the man recognize me? Whitcomb wondered. Is my face known to every man in the command? He looked closely at the soldier who had spoken and he recognized him as one of the privates from his own company. What was his name? Dowdy, that was it. "Thank you, Dowdy. He's out cold, I'm afraid."

"Donnelly here, sir," said the second figure. "If you two lay aholt of his shoulders, I can tote his feet."

Together they carried the unconscious man like some awkward piece of broken-down machinery and found their way to the surgeon's tent.

"What have we here?" Surgeon Munn examined the man quickly by the dim light of a veiled lamp. "Well, it's messy, but not too bad, I think. The ball missed the jawbone but it took out three teeth. It must have given him quite a blow."

"He'd of got more'n that, if Mr. Whitcomb hadn't of pulled his bacon out'n the fire," Donnelly said.

"The ball knocked him out, sir," Whitcomb said quickly. "But he got off a shot at them first. He stood up and let them have it."

"I'm amazed he could stand. Well, I'll patch him up as best I can."

As the three men returned to the line the fire was lessening. Whitcomb found Sergeant Duggan and familiarized himself with the positions of the E Company troopers in case he should need them for some further action, but a silence fell on the encampment and as it lengthened it became apparent that the invisible attackers had withdrawn. After half an hour the cookfires were rekindled, and, with a double guard keeping watch, the troopers finally had their supper. It wasn't until Whitcomb had seated himself on a cottonwood log with a tin plate in his lap that he realized he had come through the brief skirmish without a moment's confusion. From start to finish he had obeyed his orders and done the right thing almost by second nature. He held out a hand and saw it was steady. Perhaps he was born to be a soldier after all.

He was examining this notion with some curiosity when he was approached by the same man who had just joined him and Lieutenant Bourke when the attack began.

"Lieutenant Whitcomb?" Whitcomb nodded. "May I sit down?" Whitcomb nodded again, still trying to force down the last piece of leathery bull meat. The man removed a glove and extended his hand as he seated himself beside Whitcomb on the log. "Bob Strahorn, *Rocky Mountain News*."

Whitcomb had heard of Robert Strahorn, the only civilian on the campaign, and he realized now that he had seen the man from time to time without knowing who he was. He usually kept close to General Crook and Whitcomb had assumed he was another of the staff officers, for he was clothed like all the rest. He was tall and lean and had straight black hair. The two men shook hands.

"Well," Strahorn said, "you were certainly in the thick of it this evening. I hope you won't mind if I corroborate a few facts?"

"I don't mind." Whitcomb was both flattered and wary at being approached by a member of the press. His wariness was compounded by the professional soldier's reserve in the face of civilian inquiry. Newspapers were seldom kind to the frontier army, but the dispatches Whitcomb had seen in several papers on his journey west all spoke admiringly of General Crook. Strahorn's own paper, the Denver *Rocky Mountain News*, in its February 22 edition, had offered the opinion that General Crook, on his imminent campaign, would " 'go through' the Indian country after his usual fashion and will leave things in better shape than he finds them." For all Whitcomb knew, Strahorn might have written the flattering piece himself. Still, he would have to be cautious until he had taken the measure of the man.

"I understand you have been on active duty just a short time." Strahorn's manner was open and curious.

"That's right. I reported to Fort Fetterman on February twenty-ninth. My father has been ill and I was allowed to spend some time at home." Careful. Answer the question; don't volunteer information.

"This was a more serious attack than the others, wouldn't

you say? General Crook believes the hostiles wanted to run off our horses."

"The horses are under guard, sir, well within the camp boundaries, and will remain so."

"That's true enough. But once we leave the wagons behind and proceed on our own, it will be necessary to tether the horses individually so they can forage for themselves at least for a few hours each evening."

Whitcomb hesitated. Clearly the man knew a good deal about the workings of a cavalry campaign. Perhaps more than himself. "I don't presume to anticipate the orders of my superiors," he said.

"That was a brave thing you did this evening. Major Coates is grateful for your help in saving Corporal Slavey."

"Who was it?"

"Corporal Slavey, of Captain Ferris's company."

"Well, I was closest to him when he was hit. Anyone else would have done the same thing."

"Perhaps. Your modesty becomes you. Please don't think I am trying to draw you into any boastful statement, Mr. Whitcomb. I am simply trying to get to know you. After all, you have occasioned some notice on the campaign so far, what with your single-handed attempt to retrieve the cattle, and all."

"Oh, Lord, don't write about that, I beg you."

"It may not reflect too badly on your spirit, I should think."

Whitcomb recalled Bourke's comment on that event, and the question of whether it had been brave or merely foolhardy. How would this evening's actions reflect on him? To his benefit, he earnestly hoped. Several of his own men had said a word or two to him as the camp returned to normal, praising him for helping the wounded man. Lieutenant Corwin had distinguished himself by his silence on the matter, although Whitcomb was sure his superior had heard of it by now. Why should a word of encouragement from Corwin be so important to him? He didn't know, but he wished for it still. E Troop's commander was a "foine son of a bitch" indeed, and a harsh judge, unwilling to mete out praise when it was deserved.

"I understand you have a nickname," Strahorn was saying. "I overheard some of the men referring to you as Mr. Reb."

"I wish I had never heard the name."

"Why, you're a young man. The Rebellion was not your responsibility."

"It is not an easy responsibility to set aside."

"Yes, I know life has been hard in the Southern states," Strahorn offered, misunderstanding him. "Many families were ruined. I hope yours was not among them."

"We still have our land, and the British insist on their Virginia tobacco." Whitcomb did not elaborate on the difficulties of Reconstruction, or the great changes the defeat of the Southern cause had imposed on the plantation system of growing tobacco.

"May I ask if your relatives took up arms for the Confederacy?"

"Yes, sir, they did." Whitcomb drew himself up. "My father and uncles fought with the Army of Northern Virginia, as I would have done, had I been old enough. A man must fight when his homeland is threatened."

"True enough. Even now the Indians are fighting for theirs, but they'll lose in the end, of course. I must say I don't see too much future for this country here. There might be some farming in the river bottoms, I suppose, and the scouts say the land is less arid farther north. We have seen several outcroppings of coal, though. That alone may be reason enough to open it up."

"And there's the Black Hills gold. That's why we're here, indirectly."

Whitcomb was scarcely aware of how skillfully Strahorn drew him out. The man was friendly and encouraging, and for his part, Whitcomb was glad of a chance to talk with someone who was neither superior nor inferior in rank, with the attendant difficulties that impeded free expression in those cases. First with Bourke and now with Strahorn, today had offered him his first opportunities to speak freely since the campaign began. The two men sat for a time, discovering common interests and chatting of many things, and before long Strahorn steered the talk back to Whitcomb's family and background. By the time they parted to go to their beds, the newspaperman could have written a concise biography of Second Lieutenant Hamilton Whitcomb and given a thumbnail sketch of his closest relatives.

After bidding Strahorn good night, Whitcomb took a short walk among the sleeping men of Company E, a habit he had already developed as part of his routine before retiring. Corwin was awake, preparing his own bedroll, but he said nothing beyond a curt reply to Whitcomb's good night. Whitcomb could feel Corwin's eyes follow him as he walked along the row of tents. He's always watching me, he thought. Why? To catch me in a mistake.

A figure rose from the ground as he approached his bedroll and he recognized one of the men from Sergeant Duggan's squad, but he didn't know the man's name. The soldier was older than most of the other privates in the company, with graying hair and beard. He was of Whitcomb's height but more solidly built. He stood ramrod straight, almost at attention, as he came to a stop before the young officer.

"Mr. Whitcomb, sir."

He was the Virginian! By those few words, Whitcomb recognized the voice that had called out a warning to protect Whitcomb as he helped the wounded soldier.

"Private—?"

"Gray, sir. John Gray. It's a little joke on the Yankees. I was formerly Captain John Wesley of the Army of Northern Virginia. I knew your uncle Reuben, sir. I just wanted to say it is an honor to serve under you."

The man's complete sincerity moved Whitcomb deeply and for a moment he had trouble finding his voice. Private John Gray, formerly Captain John Wesley of the Army of Northern Virginia. How many other former Confederate officers were to be found in the ranks of the United States Army, enlisted under assumed names, the only way they could continue in uniform? And why had Gray waited until now to present himself? Because of what Whitcomb had done for a fellow soldier this evening? Until he was sure of the young officer whom he himself should be commanding? Whatever the reason, he had come forward now, and Whitcomb felt he had been given rare praise indeed.

"Thank you, Private Gray," he said at last. "The honor is mine." Without thinking, he extended his hand. Gray hesitated, then took it, and they shook hands firmly. "Well, good night," Whitcomb offered, not knowing what else to say.

Private Gray smiled. "Good night, Mr. Reb." He winked one eye almost imperceptibly, then saluted quickly and went off to his bed of buffalo robes.

The command was on the march again shortly after dawn, passing by the ruins of old Fort Reno on the benchland above the river. Little remained of the once proud post: a few chimneys, part of an adobe wall, a fragment of one small building. The site was littered with broken gun carriages, axles, old stoves and other metal debris. Two hundred yards north of the fort there stood a dozen broken and falling headboards to mark the cemetery.

"Eyes right!" Lieutenant Corwin ordered as E Troop passed near the graves, and he held a salute as he rode by.

Once again the column advanced directly against the force of the storm, which had returned before first light to dispel any hope that the glimpse of sun on the previous evening might presage a pleasant day to follow. The men huddled deep within their coverings of fur. Scarves and bandannas were tied across their faces leaving only the eyes exposed. Those who had them wore the green Arizona goggles. The snow descended in a succession of squalls that whipped up the fresh flakes from the ground and enveloped the column in sudden whiteouts, sometimes limiting visibility to less than a hundred yards. In between these intense assaults, patches of blue sky and tantalizing periods of sunshine intervened. At these times the countryside far on all sides was revealed, along with new evidence of hostile eyes watching. No horsemen appeared today but several columns of smoke rose in silent conversation far to the north and looking-glass signals flashed nearer at hand until the clouds returned.

The landscape to the north and west of the Powder River Crossing was a divide of numbing monotony, an alternation of ridge and gulch barren of vegetation, save for an occasional low mesa with a decorative fringe of bunchgrass. For twenty-seven miles the mounted troopers shivered in their saddles or led their horses while flankers and scouts kept watch. As always, the infantry marched the entire way, and both infantryman and cavalryman thought the other had the best of it. As dusk approached they gratefully made camp by Crazy Woman's Fork, the most pleasant stream they had yet encountered. There was ample brush for firewood and sheltered campsites, and the water ran sweet and clear beneath a solid foot of ice. The halfbreed scouts said that the stream took its colorful name from a Sioux squaw who was not content to sport in her sleeping robes with her husband alone, but took herself to two or three other tipis as well while camped on these very banks. Women of the Sioux were expected to be chaste and modest, the scouts said, and the tribe considered such flagrant behavior to be truly demented.

In the morning there was no order to get under way. The soldiers stayed close to the cookfires and ate all that was offered. At midday the storm ceased abruptly, the wind dropped and the sky cleared; the troopers took to strolling beyond the limits of camp to survey the countryside, while keeping an eye on the headquarters tents. They noticed the scouts coming and going from the north, over the next divide.

As the sun dropped below the mountains, which rose stark and majestic fifteen miles to the west, the company officers were gathered in a semicircle around General Crook and Colonel Reynolds. Boots Corwin found a seat beside his friend Teddy Egan, captain of Company K, Second Cavalry.

James Egan, called "Teddy" by his friends for reasons that were lost in the past, had served with Corwin in the Second Cavalry during the Rebellion, and like Corwin he had risen from the ranks. Unlike Corwin he had not been captured by the enemy. He had emerged from the war a first lieutenant and was commissioned captain three years later. In his service on the frontier he had already distinguished himself. He seemed to have a knack for being in the thick of trouble. At the peace conference with the Sioux in the previous autumn there had been a tense moment when one of the chiefs who favored war rather than selling the Black Hills had harangued his fellow tribesmen, saying there was no time like the present to start the fighting. Egan had drawn up his troop between the Indians and the commissioners, with carbines at the ready. Faced by this silent, motionless line of determined men, the Indians, who outnumbered the soldiers ten to one, had backed down.

"A dollar says Reynolds never opens his mouth," Egan said now, too softly for anyone but Corwin to hear.

"Thanks, I'll keep my money."

"Gentlemen," said Crook, calling the meeting to order, "I had thought to bring the wagons a bit farther with us, but General Reynolds and I have decided to return them to Fort Reno to await us there." Reynolds kept his eyes on Crook, and he seemed content to let his superior do the talking. "The many signs of Indians hereabouts have convinced us that we must move quickly if we wish to regain the initiative." A light breeze lifted the twin tails of Crook's beard where they rested against his greatcoat.

The officers glanced at one another. There would be no more crushed-cork mattresses, no extra robes and overgarments thrown into a wagon during the day to be recovered at night when the mercury fell. But their expectations of hardships to come were tempered by a quickening of the blood. At last the real campaign was to begin. The marches had lengthened steadily each day, building endurance in livestock and men, until the limit of the wagon train's capability had been reached.

"We will carry no excess baggage," Crook continued. "Each man, officer and trooper alike, will carry only the clothing he can wear, and one buffalo robe or two blankets. There will be no tents. Officers will mess with the men. Staff officers and others who may be unattached—Mr. Strahorn, that will include yourself—will mess with the pack train. We will expect to remain in the field for fifteen days. Our provisions will be hardtack and coffee, half rations of bacon, and whatever the country may provide. For the horses, one-sixth rations of grain.'' He paused and looked around the gathering. ''Look to your animals, gentlemen, and your men. By now each officer has been informed by Assistant Surgeon Munn regarding the measures necessary to prevent frostbite. Thus far we have had none and I intend that we shall have none. A man with frostbite might as well have been wounded by the enemy.'' He paused again to let his words take effect before issuing his final pronouncement. ''Gentlemen, insofar as it is possible for half a thousand men and horses to disappear, it is my intention that we should do just that. For the next several days we will march only at night, or under cover of the weather.''

He opened his greatcoat, revealing a glimpse of red flannel lining, and pulled out a plain Waltham watch of the kind called a ''turnip'' by the troopers, for its shape and size. He consulted the watch for a moment, then put it away. ''We leave at dark. Be prepared for a march of more than thirty miles.''

Corwin and Egan walked together back toward their companies when the meeting disbanded. ''It's about time!'' Egan exclaimed when they were beyond the headquarters area. Corwin shared his friend's enthusiasm and hoped he might have a bit of Egan's fabled luck. He was well aware that both Crook and Reynolds regarded Egan as an up-and-coming officer destined for further promotions. He resented neither Egan's rank nor his achievements, but he earnestly wished for similar opportunities.

''How are your men bearing up?'' he asked as they prepared to part.

''Ready to whip their weight in bears. How's your new lieutenant coming along?''

''I'm keeping him on a tight rein.''

Egan smiled. "Up to your old tricks?"

"Something like that."

An hour later the cavalrymen bid farewell to the supply train and the infantry, which would escort the wagons back to Fort Reno and remain there to guard them, and set out under clear skies and a gibbous moon that bathed the country in an eerie silver light. The rough prairie soon gave way to sharper bluffs and rising foothills, and the column was compelled to climb steeper and steeper grades. Before long they traveled in a column of twos instead of the standard four abreast. When they reached the divide where the Clear Fork of the Powder originated, they saw that the terrain around them had become thoroughly mountainous. To their left, the Big Horns stood silent and grand in the moonlight.

As the tail of Company E reached the crest of the trail and began the descent into the valley of the Clear Fork, Ham Whitcomb, the troop's file closer once more, found John Bourke sitting his horse beside the trail and he reined aside to join him.

"You look like Hannibal's sentinel," he greeted his friend.

"By God, look at us, Ham!" Bourke whispered in awe. "It's like some monstrous snake." He was almost chuckling from the exhilaration and grandeur of the scene, and Whitcomb saw the aptness of the image at once. The chain of mounted men and pack mules could easily have been a tremendous serpent slithering over the crest of the divide and down the other side in search of a mythic prey. It was an image out of the Arabian Nights, all the more so for being seen by moon and starlight. The creak and slap of leather and steel were the sounds of the reptile's scales, and the glint from burnished holsters and the shining metal of bridles and carbines flashing along the column in the cold light only heightened the impression of sinuous movement. The frosted breath from the mouths of animals and men became puffs of steam or smoke, evidence of the fire within. The serpent had only to open its mouth and tongues of flame would burst forth.

"We better get along before you're missed," Bourke said, breaking the spell.

"There's not much danger of that," said Whitcomb, but as they overtook E Troop he saw Corwin riding in the rear, beside Sergeant Duggan.

"I'll see you later," he muttered to Bourke, and slipped into his place in line.

"Were you lost, Mr. Reb?" Corwin demanded coldly.

"No, sir. I had the troop in sight all the time." He would not defend himself. He had done nothing really wrong, after all.

Corwin said nothing further, but he rode alongside for a time before finally touching his spurs to his horse and moving off toward the head of the troop.

"It's a grand view, sir," observed Sergeant Duggan when Corwin was out of earshot. "Well worth a little stop."

"You'll see nothing like it in Ireland, eh, Sergeant?" Whitcomb had been told that Virginia in the springtime, with its multihued carpets of green, brought some men to mind of the Emerald Isle.

"Oh, no, sir. To be sure."

"You're not suggesting that Mr. Whitcomb stopped merely to take in the countryside?" came the measured tones of Private John Gray, riding near the rear of the troop.

"He were seein' the general's aide 'bout our full rations of bacon, ain't that right, sir?" The moonlight fell on the smiling face of Private Peter Dowdy. "The general knows there ain't no troop in the command what fights like the Foreign Legion, so he's givin' us full rations to keep our strength up. Ain't that right, sir?"

"Quiet in the ranks. You know the orders," said Whitcomb. On a calm night a voice could carry unexpectedly far and the officers had been cautioned to keep their men silent, but his tone softened the mild rebuke. By their words of support, Duggan and the others had confirmed what Whitcomb already had dared to hope—he had made a start at winning the trust of the men. They were coming to like him. They were silent now, but he could feel their high spirits, equal to his own, and he was proud to be in such company. Everywhere along the line heads were up and looking about and there were soft exclamations of wonder, even from the unlettered among them, at the strangely beautiful landscape. For more than a week now these men had endured constant discomfort, but not of a constant nature; with every change in the weather, with each diurnal change from light to dark, they had had to alter their response to the demands placed upon them; yet if anything they were now a more cohesive force, strengthened by the hardships of the march and the probing of the enemy, more sure of their mission. Equal to any force in the world.

Equal or superior? Given birth by a higher culture than that of the Indians and engaged on the grand enterprise of the white race, they should be more than a match for the barbarous foe, but Whitcomb found a lingering uncertainty within himself. So far from all physical evidence of the "higher culture," the cavalrymen were mounted warriors much like the hostiles. The frontier army and the Indians alike were scattered in small groups across a harsh land, occasionally venturing forth to do combat. He remembered his talk with Strahorn then, and what he himself had said about men defending their homeland, and a few lines from Macaulay's *Lays of Ancient Rome* came to him:

For how can man die better
Than facing fearful odds,
For the ashes of his fathers
And the temples of his Gods?

At the age of ten he had felt a boyish determination to fight and die, if necessary, to prevent the conquest of the South by the Yankee invaders. The Indians were fighting now to protect hunting grounds and loved ones and the burial places of their fathers. Could it be that they too felt a similar resolve? Perhaps any man, high or low, gained an added measure of strength when he fought for his home.

They were equal, then, the two sides. Save for the condition of the horses.

Could it really be reduced to that? he wondered. Equal save for a few handfuls of grain?

Equal save for the use of the wheel. Wagons had transported the grain and so the cavalry horses remained fit and strong; this was the tactical edge, not any superiority of race.

He thought again of the travois tracks two days before, and was struck by the gulf that separated the red men and the white. How could two such different races ever hope to live in harmony? What could you do or say to be understood by a people who saw the wheel and comprehended its purpose, but rejected its adoption?

Lisa Putnam's Journal

Monday, March 6th. 11:45 a.m.

For the first time since the avalanche I have found a moment to write. There have been no calves born since late yesterday and I came in early to catch my breath before dinner. There has been much to do, what with getting the circus folk settled for a stay of some weeks. Snow has been falling almost continuously since yesterday morning and the foul weather, made worse by wind, has been no help, either in resettling the circus or in keeping an eye on the calves, which now number four.

We who live here are accustomed to the threat of being blocked in the park for a time by an avalanche in winter or a slide in spring or fall whenever the rains are heavy, and I should have warned Mr. Tatum to avoid loud noises in the canyon, but there is no use crying over spilt milk. Harry and I were about to pull a calf when I heard a distant sound. I watched the cloud of snow grow larger and larger over the gap and still I didn't realize what I was seeing until the circus horses came tearing up the valley. Then I was off, and I thought my heart would stop or wear itself out before I reached the river canyon. Harry offered to go with me, of course, but even in that moment of panic I did not wish to lose a calf, and so I left him to tend the cancer-eye cow while I took his horse with me, thinking to pick up Julius on the way. Julius and Hutch had already begun to run towards the river and had very nearly reached the bottom of the valley before I overtook them. When we arrived at the scene we found men and women standing in bunches, staring at what used to be a wagon road, and we soon learned the reason for their benumbed expressions. Jack Fisk and half the circus horses had vanished as the avalanche struck the road; without those animals, many of the most valuable and highly trained performing horses among them, all the planned performances across the western territories and in California were in peril. And then came the miracle. Julius climbed atop the avalanche to survey its extent, when what should he see but a figure coming towards him from the other direction, none other than Jack Fisk, and very much alive. He and all the missing horses, save one that was not quite swift enough to avoid being caught and swept away, had reached safety farther down the road. He had feared that many of those behind him might have suffered a dreadful fate. The reunion was a sight to see. Everyone laughed and embraced, even the usually taciturn teamsters and wranglers. Such was the general relief at seeing Mr. Fisk alive and learning that the horses were well, everyone commenced to tell the others his or her own experiences in the frightening moments as the avalanche tumbled down upon them, and it was not uncommon to see two people relating their individual tales, each to the other, and both speaking at once.

There was just time enough left in the day for Julius to go with Mr. Fisk and two wranglers and drive the stranded horses up over the southern ridge to reenter the park by that route. They would have had hard going in bad weather, but the day remained fair except for the advent of some high clouds, the harbingers of the storm that has been blowing ever since.

I learned that Johnny Smoker had snatched Amanda from Mr. Chalmers' wagon, which he believed to be doomed, and he was generally praised for saving her life, although the wagon survived. Mr. Tatum thanked him most gravely. When I first arrived, Amanda and Johnny were still together on Johnny's horse, but they saw me looking in their direction and Amanda slipped quickly to the ground. How soon the awareness of common proprieties returns once danger is past. Since then they have often been in each other's company, and they, at least, have some reason to welcome this turn of events. When he is not with Amanda, Johnny is helping out with some chore or another. He seems always to know where to lend a hand, and already I think of him as one of the crew. Yesterday morning he went feeding with Julius and Hutch, and Julius says that Johnny handles a team as well as men with twice his age and experience. He suggested it might be possible for Johnny and Hutch to feed alone now and then, freeing Julius to spend more time with the cows and heifers during calving. This may prove to be a great blessing in the weeks to come.

There is no doubt that Mr. Tatum and his wagons are trapped here until warm weather sets in. The avalanche is the worst I can remember. It swept the slope clean. In addition to the mass of snow, which is thirty feet deep in places, the slide is full of rocks and boulders of all sizes. This will make the clearing away very difficult and time-consuming, and there is no sense even beginning until the snow and ice are gone. As we have done before for the worst of these blockages, we shall have to hire men with wagons from Rawlins to help us, and I cannot afford to pay them to haul away ice and snow that will melt of its own accord soon enough. The road is blocked for eighty to one hundred yards and is piled high for most of that distance. The surface is almost too rough for a man on foot, quite unthinkable for a horse. Because of the rocks and earth, which will freeze into the mass as it sets itself and settles, smoothing a way across the top will not be possible, and as my father learned when he first attempted that solution, such a snowy highway becomes treacherous whenever the temperature rises above freezing, and it is unusable in spring until the snow melts away and the rocks are removed.

The circus folk have recovered from the initial shock of finding themselves marooned here and have settled in, apparently determined to use the time to good advantage. Yesterday Mr. Tatum was everywhere, organizing rehearsals and seeing to the animals, Meanwhile, Joe Kitchen and Monty and Ben Long and I went to explore the edge of the avalanche to see what might be saved. We are all grateful that the loss of life and property was not greater, but what was lost has hurt us sorely: in the missing supply wagons was nearly every bit of the circus's food stores. In two hours of hard digging, we salvaged scarcely two crates of tinned goods and felt lucky to find that much. This morning, Joe and I surveyed the contents of cellar, storeroom, pantry and root cellar, and while there are sufficient goods to feed a large group such as the circus for a few days, enough to sustain the park's year-round inhabitants almost indefinitely, there is not enough of anything (except the good Wind River valley potatoes) to feed all these mouths for the month or two the circus will be forced to remain. Beef is our sole resource. We have already butchered old One-Eye and soon we will have to select other cows from the herd; the steers will go first, of course, but they won't last long. Some of the circus animals need meat and I can no more see them starve than I could let these people go hungry. Naturally Mr. Tatum will compensate me, but money cannot immediately restore good mother cows of the same crossed breed, nor their healthy calves. We will lose a calf for every cow that is killed, and we will feel the loss for some time to come.

Today Mr. Tatum has passed the morning in the saloon at a table near the stove, poring over ledgers and notebooks and spending long intervals staring out into the falling snow, according to Ling. Coffee is one thing not in short supply and she came often to refill his cup. When I passed by just now, on my way to come here, he rose and invited me, with his gracious good manners, to eat supper with him this evening. He suggested we might discuss our shared difficulties and perhaps find solutions to some of them, although what more he thinks we can do except wait for spring, I cannot imagine.

The pipe carriers must be well on their way by now. It may be weeks before we learn the outcome of their journey.

CHAPTER FOUR

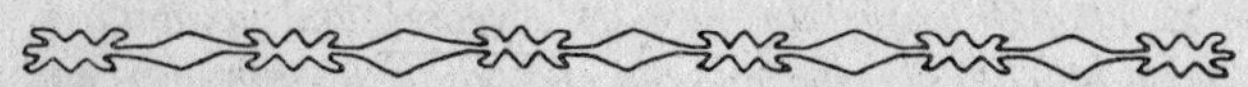

Early in the afternoon the snow stopped, but chill winds kept most of those in the settlement indoors.

Beyond the circus wagons, Hutch and Johnny Smoker and the fat German accordionist pitched hay from a wagon to the circus horses, which had been turned into the fenced pasture with the bulls.

"Good grass you haff here," said the German. He

rolled a handful of hay between his gloved fingers and held it to his nose, nodding approvingly. His name was Gunther Waldheim and he was the circus's riding master. His two sons, Johann and Willy, were the star equestrians of the troupe, expert at acrobatics performed on horseback as well as the spectacular leaps to and from the saddle at full speed that were known as *voltige*. They brought Teutonic enthusiasm to their athletic stunts and they enjoyed the respect of Hachaliah Tatum, to whom they left the more stately art of High School, the ultimate form of equine training, designed to demonstrate perfect accord between horse and rider. Johann and Willy's father was known to everyone in the circus as Papa Waldheim. He no longer performed, but the care and training of the horses remained in his hands.

"Good grass," he said again, letting the dried stalks fall. He pitched a huge forkful of hay over the fence, spreading it out with a practiced flip of the fork as the hay fell. His girth was deceiving, for beneath a protective layer of fat his muscles were as hard as ever, and he could still demonstrate any of the horseback stunts to his sons when he thought they were not performing up to his standards.

"If we're gonna keep this many horses in here all the time we ought to build a hay crib in the pasture," Hutch said, looking at Johnny to see what he thought of the idea. Then he remembered that the circus horses would be here for only six or eight weeks, and he was afraid Johnny might think the notion foolish, but Johnny just nodded soberly.

"Mm hmm. Might be handy, just for the bulls."

Hutch hadn't thought that a crib might be useful even after the circus was gone; he was pleased once again with the way Johnny was making himself part of the outfit, now that he too was here for an indefinite stay. The presence of the circus had deprived Hutch of the friendly mealtime company around the kitchen table; everyone ate in the saloon now, filing past long serving tables and sitting wherever they pleased. Julius and Miss Lisa were still taken up with their own thoughts, which had something to do with Sun Horse and General Crook's march up-country, and it all confused Hutch a good deal, because up until now he had thought you just naturally raised a cheer when the soldiers set out to chase Indians. Hutch and Johnny had taken to eating together, and Hutch was grateful for the older boy's company. From the first, Johnny had shown a willingness to help out without any trace of presumption, even though he had been on the Texas cattle trails and obviously knew a lot more about working a cow outfit than Hutch did, and it had occurred to Hutch that he might learn a thing or two from Johnny. He eyed the rope hanging from Johnny's saddle every time he was in the barn, and before long he hoped to get Johnny to teach him how to rope. That was one skill a man ought to know before he set out to work on a bigger place.

"You reckon we'll have to haul more hay to that elephant today?" Hutch asked Johnny now.

Johnny shook his head. "Chatur said one load a day'll do him."

"I never did see the like of how that critter eats hay," Hutch said. They had taken a wagonload of hay to Rama that morning after they were done feeding the cattle, and Chatur had demonstrated a few of Rama's tricks for Johnny and Hutch.

"Come, Rama," the little brown man had said, smiling at the elephant and making a motion with his staff. "Show the *sahibs* how you are saying hello."

The elephant had raised his trunk above his head and sat up on his haunches like a dog.

The wagon was nearly empty now and Papa Waldheim leaned on his pitchfork while Hutch and Johnny cleaned up the last forkfuls.

"Good job, boys. It vill be enough today."

A shot sounded nearby and the three of them turned to see Hachaliah Tatum standing at the end of the twin line of painted wagons, a pistol in his hand. He took aim and fired again, and a tin can flew off the fence railing fifty feet away. Without lowering the nickel-plated Colt he fired three more times and each shot knocked another can from the fence.

"That's good shooting," Johnny observed.

"Oh, he iss good," Papa Waldheim said. "In the circus he performs mit pistol and rifle, shooting glass balls in the air. Here, see him now."

Tatum drew something from his pocket. With the Colt held in his left hand he tossed a small round object high in the air. With no apparent haste he transferred the gun back to his right hand and fired without seeming to take aim. The glass ball vanished in a puff of shards.

"By golly, he can't miss, can he," Hutch exclaimed.

"It iss not the best he does," Papa Waldheim said. "In performance he shoots mit mirrors, over the shoulder. Many tricks, all very good. Like this, when he practices, it iss because he iss thinking. It helps him to concentrate, he says. The better he shoots, the harder he iss thinking."

Tatum had reloaded his pistol. Holding it in his left hand once more he reached in his pocket again and this time he threw three balls in the air with a single toss. He fired once, twice, and a third time, catching the last ball just before it hit the ground.

A shrill whistle sounded from the opposite direction, coming from the barn.

"Uh oh," Hutch said as he turned. Julius was waving to them from the barn door. "He seen us lollygagging around. Now he'll have another job for us quick."

"So, ve face the music together," Papa Waldheim said. "You haff helped me, now I help you."

Hutch picked up the reins and clucked to Zeke, who was hitched to the wagon alone. When they neared the barn they heard laughter from within, and Julius was smiling.

"Hop down, boys," he said. "We've got us a clown show."

"Ach, I forget!" Papa Waldheim exclaimed, putting a hand to his head. "I am supposed to invite you. Amanda asked special for you," he said to Johnny. "Come, come, come. She vill never forgiff me."

He clambered to the ground and ushered Johnny and

Hutch quickly into the barn, where they were surprised to find nearly everyone in the settlement gathered to watch an impromptu performance.

The barn had been taken over by acrobats and aerialists the day before, and large steamer trunks containing their costumes and equipment stood open in vacant horse stalls. The hayloft had a square opening in the center, so it could be loaded from a wagon driven in the large double doors. Across this opening a tightrope had been strung, and a trapeze hung from one of the roof beams. At the moment, neither of these was in use. The attention of the audience was directed instead to a single improbable figure in the middle of the floor, a gray-haired man dressed as a parody of a British gentleman. He wore a silk top hat and a morning coat with tails so long they trailed on the ground. His formal trousers were baggy and the soles of his shoes were about to part company with the uppers. He stood motionless, or nearly so, yet he managed to give every appearance of being in the final stages of drunkenness, and his efforts to retain both his dignity and his consciousness provoked almost continuous laughter from the audience. His eyes began to droop, his figure to wilt, and in the nick of time he caught himself and stood bolt upright, looking around quickly to see if he had been observed. He clasped his hands atop his ebony walking stick and assumed a dignified pose, but soon he began to lean to one side, and just when he was about to fall he saved himself by taking a step in that direction.

"Ah. Here you are." Alfred Chalmers appeared beside Johnny and Hutch. "Amanda has been saving the best for last. Come along with me; we have a place for you."

He beckoned them to follow him and led them through the crowd to a place near the front rank, where he seated Johnny on a packing crate beside Lisa Putnam. Chatur shifted sideways where he sat cross-legged on the floor and made room for Hutch, smiling a welcome.

Chalmers cleared his throat loudly and waved to Amanda, who was across the way in one of the stalls, dressed in her colorful costume and wearing her makeup. She nodded, waved to Johnny, then clapped her hands twice to signal the man on the floor.

Without turning he raised a hand to acknowledge the signal. The movement overbalanced him to one side; he lurched in that direction and reeled offstage to a round of applause.

"That gentleman is Samuel Higgins, one of Amanda's partners," Chalmers explained to Johnny in a low voice. "You are about to see both of them, and Amanda as well, in a new piece of work they are performing here for the first time."

Amanda was the first to appear. She carried a parasol and she had removed her red clown's cap. Her long brown hair bounced lightly as she strolled along, twirling the parasol, a young lady out taking the air. Now, from opposite sides of the barn, two other figures entered the stage. One was the elderly English gentleman, quite sober now and moving his walking stick jauntily as he stepped along. The other was a French cavalier, a lithe young man scarcely five feet tall, with black hair, pale skin and bright, flashing eyes. He wore a sword at his waist, a huge-brimmed hat adorned with an ostrich feather, and a heavy cape that threatened to envelop him at every stride.

"The young gentleman is Carlos Moro," Chalmers informed Johnny and Lisa. "He is Spanish and he joined us only a year ago. He is quite marvelous. His first training was as an acrobat, but Sam has taken him under his wing and he and Amanda are teaching him the clown's art. I think you'll agree that he is a good pupil."

Both men spied Amanda at the same moment. They approached her from opposite sides and bowed to her. The Englishman inclined slightly at the waist and tipped his silk hat; the cavalier bent almost double and swept his plumed hat across the ground. As they straightened, each eyed the other suspiciously while he endeavored to engage the young lady's attention. Amanda favored first Sam and then Carlos with a smile, a little flustered by all the attention she was receiving. Carlos took her smile as encouragement; he stepped in front of her, giving Sam a gentle shove to one side, at the same time offering his arm to Amanda. Before she could decide whether or not to accept, Sam recovered his balance and stepped hard into Carlos, throwing the small cavalier to one knee. Utterly ignoring the smaller man, Sam tipped his hat to Amanda once more and offered her his own arm. But already Carlos was on his feet again; he placed one booted foot on Sam's posterior and shoved hard, sending the Englishman sprawling facedown on the ground. Carlos smiled to Amanda and bowed low, but Sam was back quick as a flash and he delivered a stinging blow to Carlos's backside with his walking stick. The young cavalier shot upright, his mouth wide in a silent howl of pain. Recovering himself, he advanced on the Englishman, who raised his walking stick in a stern warning. In an instant the cavalier's rapier was drawn, its blade placed across the tip of the walking stick, and still Carlos advanced, forcing the Englishman back.

Now it was Amanda who pleaded for attention. She moved along with the two men, arms outstretched, silently entreating them to stop before the fighting went further, but neither of the men would take his eyes from the other. She touched Carlos's sword arm, tugging at the sleeve, and he glanced at her. With the small man's attention distracted, Sam knocked the cavalier's hat to the ground with a swipe of his walking stick.

There was no restraining Carlos now. He brushed Amanda aside and advanced on the Englishman. His rapier crossed the walking stick once, twice, and then with a flick of the wrist he sent the stick flying, leaving Sam defenseless. The cavalier silently laughed his triumph as he pranced around the Englishman, flicking at him with the rapier. So great was his joy that he spun in a pirouette, whereupon his cape wrapped itself tightly around him, pinning his sword arm against his side.

Seeing his adversary's predicament, the Englishman drew from his morning coat a three-foot length of flexible lath with a handle at one end. Gleefully he struck the cavalier on the backside with a resounding *thwack* that brought a burst of laughter from the crowd and sent Carlos sprawling on the floor, howling silently in pretended pain. As he struggled to his hands and knees the slap-stick fell again, *thwack,* and sent him head over heels in a somersault. *Thwack,* and another somersault, and by expert timing of both blows and somersaults, Sam appeared to be rolling Carlos around the floor like some ungainly ball, to the great delight of the onlookers.

Amanda, meanwhile, was in despair. On her knees, she begged the two men to stop, but they ignored her. Casting about for some way to get their attention, she spied the ladder leading to the hayloft, and now an idea seized her. She sprang to the ladder and scrambled up to the loft, where she put her hands to her mouth and pretended to cry out to the men below. Sam stopped with slap-stick upraised. Carlos untangled himself from his cape and looked up. Amanda stood at the edge of the loft and silently proclaimed her intention of throwing herself into the abyss if they would not stop fighting.

In an instant the two men were on their knees, their animosity forgotten as they begged her to step back from the edge. She took a step back but held up a warning finger. There must be no more fighting. Her suitors' gestures assured her that all was peace and good will between them, and would be forever more.

She smiled, and began to descend the ladder. Sam's attention was all on Amanda, but Carlos had spied the slap-stick, which the Englishman had cast aside. Moving slowly, the cavalier grasped the wide piece of lath, and he struck the kneeling Englishman suddenly from behind without warning, sending Sam in a tumbling somersault.

But Amanda heard the blow, and in a trice she was atop the ladder again. When Carlos saw what he had done he threw the slap-stick aside and begged her to forgive him, but she ignored her suitors now, apparently lost in a profound sorrow. From the floor of the loft she picked up a violin and a bow, and placing the violin beneath her chin she stepped to the edge of the loft. Without hesitation she took another step—onto the tightrope.

Below her, Sam and Carlos placed their hands to their mouths, not daring to make a sound.

As Amanda moved along the rope with measured steps, she began to play a tune that her audience knew well, the lovely waltz that had moved Johnny Smoker to take Lisa Putnam in his arms and glide around the saloon with her on the night of the circus's arrival in Putnam's Park. But the tune had a different quality now. The notes were played lingeringly, in time with Amanda's steps on the tightrope, and the air became plaintive and sad. The clown seemed to be utterly alone, oblivious to her audience. Everything about her attitude and her movements bespoke solitude and loneliness.

Those assembled below watched her progress in utter silence, captivated by the pathos of the scene.

At the edge of the loft, two cats appeared. They looked down at the audience, then at Amanda. The almost feral barn cats had been very little in evidence since their domain had been invaded by the circus folk, keeping instead to the loft and the shadows and the nighttime hours. Encouraged by the stillness and the music, these two ventured forth now to see what was afoot.

When Amanda reached the far end of the rope she stepped lightly to the boards of the loft and turned, sustaining the last note for a long moment before she dropped the bow to her side.

The audience burst out with applause and cheers, but the clown did not acknowledge them. Her attention was on her suitors, and they too were applauding, pausing now to clap each other on the back and embrace, so great was their relief at seeing her complete her journey safely. Eagerly, they beckoned her to come down.

A rope hung from the post to which the end of the tightrope was tied. Setting her fiddle aside, Amanda grasped the rope with hands and feet and slid gently to the barn floor, where her suitors awaited her. They stepped forward, jostling for position, each wishing to have the privilege of greeting her first, and for a moment it seemed that they might resume their hostilities, but Amanda raised a warning finger. At once the gentleman and the cavalier fell all over themselves to protest their innocence; they embraced, bowed to each other, shook hands, and ended by placing their arms across each other's shoulders as evidence of their comradeship. Satisfied, Amanda offered an arm to each of them, which they readily accepted, and together the three clowns walked off the floor in high good spirits, to the cheers of the onlookers.

"Bravo!" Chalmers exclaimed, getting to his feet. Around him the others rose, and as the jubilant trio returned to bow to their public, the audience accorded them a standing ovation.

The clowns bowed several more times, holding hands, evidently quite pleased by their reception. Finally they left the floor as the audience rose from their places to offer individual congratulations or to return to activities that had been set aside when the performance began, but no one was anxious to leave the barn and the festive air the clowns had created.

Hutch spied the blond head of Maria Abbruzzi in the crowd and he moved in her direction as Johnny and Lisa accompanied Alfred Chalmers to the last horse stall at the rear of the barn, which had been provided with a canvas curtain to serve as a makeshift dressing room. Lydia was among the well-wishers there and she had Amanda wrapped in her arms, clutching the girl to her more than ample bosom.

"Ah, how you make me smile, little one. How you lift my spirits."

"Delightful, simply delightful!" Chatur exclaimed, seizing Amanda's hand when Lydia released her, and wringing it between both of his own. "Quite different, and most delightful!"

"Do you really think so?"

"It seems they found it enjoyable," Sam said, standing close beside her. Like Alfred Chalmers, he spoke with an English accent. Carlos kept to the background, smiling and nodding pleasantly.

Amanda noticed Johnny and Lisa now and she smiled, happy to see them.

"You were wonderful," Lisa said, taking the girl by the hands.

"Did you like it, really?" Amanda's eyes moved to Johnny.

"I'm just sorry I didn't get to see the beginning," he said.

"Oh, you can see those routines any time. We'll do them just for you. It was the new piece I wanted you to see. Sam and Carlos and I worked it up ourselves." Amanda seemed more at ease now, comforted by the praise of her friends and colleagues.

"It is quite a novelty, my dear," said another voice. "And quite a surprise to me, as you may imagine."

Hachaliah Tatum stepped through the small crowd around the clowns. Everyone had been so intent on the performance that few had noticed when he entered the barn to join the audience.

Concern replaced Amanda's smile. "But you did like it, though?"

"Since you ask, I think it may stray a bit too close to theatricality, and you know how I feel about that."

"It isn't theatricality!" Amanda's tone was both insistent and pleading. "It's the combination of clowning and pantomime. You've always talked about that and now we've done it. And everyone liked it. I thought you'd be pleased." She turned to Chatur. "You liked it, didn't you, Chatur?"

"Oh, exceedingly, I should say."

"My dear, Chatur is hardly your most exacting critic." Tatum smiled with a trace of condescension.

"Well, Alfred liked it too." She turned to the strongman for support.

"Ah. Well, in fact I did. I found it charming."

"There. You see?" Amanda faced Tatum.

"I must question the ending," he said. "Are we to think the young lady can keep both suitors?"

"Oh, for heaven's sake, Hachaliah, don't be so practical! Now you're looking at it as theater. You're not supposed to see a story. It's only supposed to give you a feeling."

Tatum was still dubious. "Perhaps," he said. "Do you intend to perform it without your cap?"

"Of course. The audience has to see that the clown is a girl."

"You think the public is prepared to accept a female clown?"

Chalmers spoke up, taking Amanda's side. "Ah, I think perhaps they may, Mr. Tatum, especially if this is only revealed near the end of the performance. It makes the scene original in more ways than one, you see. It could be quite a triumph."

Tatum considered this for a moment before he replied, looking at Amanda all the while. "Well, we shall see. But I must insist that before you take the time to rehearse a new work, you consult me first."

"But I wanted to surprise you!" Amanda's eyes glistened with tears.

At once, Tatum was conciliatory. "There now," he said, patting her shoulder. "There is no need to upset yourself. You did surprise me indeed. You go and get washed up now and I will see you after supper. We can talk about it then. All right?"

"All right," she conceded a bit sulkily.

Satisfied, Tatum turned to Lisa. "Miss Putnam. I promised to show you the animals. It is their feeding time soon, if you would care to accompany me?"

Lisa hesitated, then nodded her assent, and with a parting smile to Amanda, she left with the circus master.

"Oh, he infuriates me!" Amanda exclaimed when Tatum was gone. She stamped her foot in outrage. "Why can't he just accept something new?" She took Johnny's arm. "You did like it, really?"

Johnny nodded, blushing with pleasure. "I've only seen one clown show before, but I don't guess I'll ever see a better one."

"Don't worry, little one," Lydia soothed. "Hachaliah

will come around in time. But you mustn't fight him. Charm him instead."

Lisa gave her hair a few finishing strokes and set the silver-handled brush aside before coiling the brown tresses loosely atop her head and fixing the coils in place with two tortoise-shell combs. She stepped back from her dresser to survey the result. She wore her best winter dress of forest-green wool, finely woven on English looms. The neckline revealed the merest hint of bosom. Around her neck was a single strand of perfectly graduated pearls; it had been a gift from her father to her mother, brought from China by his own hand. On the lobe of each ear was another pearl, set in gold. All in all, Lisa was pleased with the effect. She had bought the dress when she was eighteen, before returning to Putnam's Park from Boston, and it still fit her perfectly.

She turned to the window for a look at the sky before going downstairs. Although the sun had peeked through briefly just before it set, the clouds were solid once more as the last light failed, but they were tinged faintly with pink.

Red sky at night, sailor's delight, her father would say. Although he had rejected the seafaring life, he had retained a sailor's eye for the weather, tempered by years of experience in the western mountains.

Lisa hoped the weather would turn fair soon. The circus teamsters had grown restless in just two days of inactivity. They played cards all day and into the evening, and more than once there had been sharp words at the gaming table. In fair weather perhaps they would find something useful to do out of doors. And in fair weather the pipe carriers could travel more quickly and return sooner.

But under clear skies the cavalry would enjoy the same advantage and would more easily spy the telltale smoke from distant lodge fires.

Lisa drew the curtains shut with a jerk, wishing to shut out the world beyond the park as quickly as she shut out the approaching night. The pipe carriers would find General Crook and Sitting Bull and make a peace at least until summer, and they would come safely back. In the meantime, she was safe in her home with Julius and Hutch and Ling and Harry, and her new friends from the circus, Alfred Chalmers and Lydia and Amanda; a gentleman had asked her to dine and he was waiting for her now.

She glanced again in the looking glass on her dressing table and patted a stray strand of hair into place, wondering if she should have dressed more conservatively. She might feel out of place in the saloon, surrounded by so many roughly dressed men.

The devil take them, she thought, turning for the door. I dressed this way for myself, not for them.

She felt elegant and she intended to enjoy herself. She would make the best of this evening and each day that followed, and if unwanted thoughts returned she would banish them with work. There were fences to mend and calves to be helped into the world. She would have another look at the heifers in the lot before going to bed. Tonight they were her responsibility.

"Ah, Miss Putnam." Tatum rose as Lisa entered the saloon. He was dressed as he had been for the celebration on the first night, in tailored trousers and frock coat, polished boots, brocade waistcoat and starched collar. He held out a hand and she hesitated for a moment before realizing what he intended, but she recovered in time and curtsied as he raised her hand to his lips without touching them to her skin. A gentleman did not actually kiss the hand of a young unmarried lady.

"You are the picture of elegance," Tatum said, and Lisa felt her face grow warm. She had found that she enjoyed Hachaliah Tatum's company. He was always the proper gentleman, and although she thought he had been a bit too quick to criticize Amanda that afternoon, he had been very pleasant as he showed Lisa the animals in their barred cages; he knew the needs and moods of each one and his genuine concern for their welfare had impressed her. He seemed to regard them as his children.

He offered her his arm now and to her surprise he led

her out of the saloon and down the hallway to the library, where a greater surprise awaited her. A small table had been set before the fire. Candlelight glinted off polished silverware that gleamed against freshly ironed napery. In the center of the table was a small bouquet of Ling's dried flowers and leaves. When Lisa found her voice she said, "Why, Mr. Tatum. You take my breath away. I hadn't expected a formal dinner."

"Quite informal, I assure you. I hope you like oysters. I'm only sorry that they aren't fresh, but we must make do with tinned." There was a *pop* as the cork flew from a bottle of champagne. He deftly allowed the overflowing bubbles to fall into a waiting glass.

"Oysters and champagne? I am overwhelmed."

"Please, sit down." He held her chair and seated her at the table. At the center of each place setting was a small dish of oysters in a reddish sauce.

He seated himself and raised his glass. "I hope you won't mind if I drink to an early and warm spring."

She laughed. "Not at all." They touched glasses and sipped. "I feel utterly spoiled. Wherever did you find champagne?"

"In my private stores. I felt under the circumstances there was no point in hoarding it. Please, try an oyster. The sauce is horseradish and tomato." He said to*mah*to in the New England manner.

As a child, Lisa had never cared for the slippery texture of oysters, but the sauce was pleasantly tangy and the sheer romance of oysters and champagne was more than enough to make up for the strange taste.

"We should really have a squeeze of lemon to make it perfect," Tatum said. He drew a gold watch from his waistcoat and opened the case. "We have a few moments before the main course arrives. I instructed Joe to begin at seven o'clock sharp. Your Chinawoman helped him prepare the meal. I am afraid I took some liberties with your household."

"You must have a way with Ling," Lisa said. "You

have charmed her into bringing out the very best silver and linen. I haven't seen these things since my mother died."

"I told her it was a special occasion. And I hope you won't mind, but I have changed my mind about one thing. As I told you, I thought you and I might dine together in order that we could discuss matters of our mutual concern—as the proprietor of Tatum's Combined Shows and proprietress of Putnam's Park, if you see my point. But then it occurred to me that what we both need is precisely the opposite: to forget our concerns for a time and enjoy ourselves. And so I propose that we should do just that, although perhaps over coffee I might touch on a few points of mutual interest, if you do not object."

"Not at all."

"More champagne?"

Lisa was surprised to discover that her glass was nearly empty. "Thank you," she said.

"Before we turn to other things, I do have one additional favor to ask," he said as he poured. "You have already done so much for us, I'm glad that what I ask will be only a small imposition, or so I hope. When the weather improves, I trust you would have no objection if we erect our tent? The acts must be rehearsed in a ring to stay in top form, particularly the riding and animal acts. The performers would be grateful for the shelter."

"By all means," Lisa said at once. "Put it up wherever you can find suitable ground. That's no imposition at all." She smiled. "I must tell you I admire the way you make the best of things. You seem to turn disadvantage to advantage." She ate another oyster and sipped her champagne.

"The truth is, this delay will hurt us," Tatum said, "but the damage will not be irreparable. We will surely give up the journey to Montana, and our stay by the Salt Lake will be shortened. The one thing we cannot delay is our arrival in San Francisco." He was silent for a moment. "A month or more before we can expect warmer weather, you said?"

"I'm afraid there is no way to know. It could come tomorrow or not until May."

"Well, there is nothing to do but wait."

Yes, Lisa thought, we are all waiting. You for the arrival of spring, while Sun Horse and I await the return of the pipe carriers to learn if there will be peace or war. For the time being our fates are out of our hands.

She did not like the helpless feeling this realization aroused in her.

"Forgive me," Tatum said, seeing her troubled expression. "I hadn't meant to bother you with my concerns. Ah, here is Joseph."

Tatum beamed as Joe Kitchen entered the library carrying three serving dishes on a tray. He was followed by Ling, and together they astonished Lisa by serving the meal impeccably, each dish presented in turn, first to Lisa and then to Tatum. The main dish was Ling's rabbit fricassee, which Lisa knew well, but she smelled new spices and a hint of wine in the sauce, and she gained a new respect for Joe. Anyone who could convince Ling to alter her recipes was persuasive indeed. Baked potatoes accompanied the fricassee, with thick cream that had just begun to sour, and what must surely have been the last portions of canned asparagus in Putnam's Park.

Joe winked to Lisa as he and Ling withdrew, as silently as they had come.

"I hope you like Hock," Tatum said, magically producing a second bottle of wine with the cork already drawn but reinserted in the neck. He poured the still wine in the second glass that stood beside the champagne glass at each place setting, and as he poured he regarded Lisa so intently that she dropped her gaze and busied herself with tasting the food.

"Forgive me, Miss Putnam. I didn't mean to stare. But you see, as I suspected, you enjoy the finer things in life. I don't mean to offend you by being too personal, but I can't imagine what it would be like to live here all the time, as you do. You must find it . . . well, a bit removed? You must long for news of the outside world."

"Sometimes," she acknowledged. "But on the whole I am accustomed to it. And we are not as cut off as you might think. We do manage to keep abreast of the nation and its doings. There is the occasional traveler, except in winter, and we get newspapers and magazines by mail. Of course, our mail is irregular, but that is actually a blessing. Once we hear of them, things of no more than passing importance have come and gone, while significant events are reduced to the essence and we can see them in perspective. For example, I gather that President Grant is beset almost daily by new scandals and accusations, but from here I see his Administration not so much as a den of thieves but more as the imperfect work of a good man who failed, perhaps because he was not suited to the task. With apologies to General Washington, there is no reason that good generals should make good Presidents."

She sipped the wine and remembered one of her Boston suitors who had told her of a voyage down the Rhine from the wine-making country. He was the heir of a banking family and he had promised to take her there.

"A point well taken," Tatum was saying. "I am surprised that you take such an interest in political matters."

"Women have the vote in this territory, Mr. Tatum. It is our duty to stay informed. But I must admit that I have only voted twice. Election day is no time to be leaving Putnam's Park for a long journey. Winter comes early here."

"And if you could vote in the national elections, do you believe the course of the nation would benefit?"

"Perhaps, but I doubt it." Lisa smiled. "I believe women are no wiser in their judgments, as a group, than you men."

"*Touché.*" Tatum laughed politely and refilled her glass.

"Which is not to say that we shouldn't have the vote all the same," Lisa hastened to add. "We have as much right to express our judgments, however mistaken they may be, as men do."

"You may be right," Tatum conceded, although he didn't sound convinced. "But since you have brought up the subject of our national government, let me tell you of an experience I had not long ago. You may find it interesting. I was in New York City, and whom should I chance to encounter at an elegant soirée than General Custer himself. He was quite the catch for the prominent hostesses this season. At any rate, I had the chance to speak with him briefly and I found him most forceful. You may not know that there is talk he may be nominated by the Democrats.'' Lisa made no immediate reply and he misjudged her silence. ''Here I am talking politics and your plate is almost empty. Let me get you something more.''

He started to rise, but Lisa was out of her chair in an instant. ''I'll get it,'' she said, and he sat back, more at ease being waited upon than doing the serving himself.

''I told Joseph that we would serve ourselves once each course was delivered. They won't disturb us again until dessert.''

Lisa served him and then herself, glad of a chance to marshal her thoughts on a subject about which she felt very strongly.

''I believe General Custer to be ambitious, and therefore dangerous,'' she said as she resumed her seat, taking Tatum off guard. ''To give him his due, I believe he is honest. Like many others he has spoken out to condemn the corruption and mismanagement that plagues Indian affairs. But he is a military man; when he has met the Indians on the battlefield he has dealt with them very harshly, and not always with good reason. Like most people, where elections are concerned I am afraid I would decide the contest on matters of direct interest to me, and there are other men I would prefer to see in charge of Indian affairs. Even last autumn I read rumors that Senator Schurz might propose Governor Hayes, of Ohio, at the convention. I know little of Governor Hayes, but I have read a good deal about Senator Schurz. He is well disposed towards the Indians, and if he were part of a new Administration, I believe their affairs might be better handled.''

''You continue to surprise me,'' Tatum said, and meant

it. "You are not only well informed, but astute. I must admit I know little of the Indian problem. All that is clear to me is that they must surely give way so these vast lands can be used to their best advantage." He left her dismissal of General Custer unchallenged. The last thing he wanted was an open disagreement with her. He had planned this meal down to the last detail for the express purpose of putting himself in her good graces.

"Oh, but they do use these lands, Mr. Tatum," Lisa said. "From this somewhat barren region, the Indians gain everything necessary for life."

"Nevertheless, they are few while we are many, and we cannot let a handful of primitives stand in the way of a great civilization."

"Such is the common wisdom," Lisa acknowledged, and Tatum heard the disapproval in her voice.

"You don't agree?"

She thought for a moment, and then said, "If we are a great people, surely one of the signs of our greatness is the principle we have enshrined in our government and laws, the idea that each man will decide for himself his own destiny. The Sioux are not a people of written laws, but they too hold nothing in higher regard than a man's right to choose for himself in all matters. That belief is sacred to them, in the sense that it must not be infringed. Yet now they are moved about and their lives utterly changed by powers they do not recognize as having any hold over them. We fought a revolution to rid ourselves of just such oppression. Is it any wonder that they fight us? And can we call ourselves truly great as long as we deny free choice to a people who were here long before we came? The Sioux lived on this land, much as they do now, while your forefathers and mine were burning witches and torturing heretics."

Tatum brightened. "You have put your foot in the quicksand, Miss Putnam. They must give way to us precisely because we have advanced ourselves while they have not. You don't deny that the Indians still practice torture? The tales are too well known."

"Yes, they torture, but to test physical courage, not to punish wrong beliefs. All torture is evil, but is it not most evil when the body is used merely as an instrument to torture the mind?"

Tatum sipped his wine. "It would seem we have entered the realm of metaphysics. Not at all what I expected when I asked you to dine."

"I'm sorry if I disappoint you."

"Not at all," he said quickly. "I could ask for no more stimulating company. Please don't misunderstand me. But frankly, I don't feel qualified to judge which form of torture is the greatest sin. In any event, we have left torture behind us, have we not? The Christian peoples?"

"Not entirely," Lisa replied. "I could tell you of some evils committed against the Indians in the name of righteous Christianity that would rival anything permitted by the Inquisition. But that would hardly be fit conversation for such an excellent supper, or for such gracious company. Forgive me, I forgot my manners. I didn't mean to be argumentative."

"Please, no apology is called for. I have heard others voice support for the Indian, but never with such passion. Your view is refreshingly unsentimental. Many in the East still proclaim the Indian to be the 'Noble Savage.' "

"They are neither noble savages nor the savage beasts that many others describe," Lisa said softly, inwardly scolding herself for forcing her views on a man who could scarcely share her concerns. Tatum was her host at this supper and she resolved to bring the subject to a close. "The truth lies somewhere in between. At bottom they are men and women with many of the same feelings we have about home and family, yet they lead a very different life, one that has given them a perspective quite different from our own."

The door opened and Ling Wo put her head in the room. "You ready for dessert now?"

"Yes, Ling, come in." Tatum welcomed the interruption. The arrival of dessert gave him an opportunity to collect himself and prepare for the negotiation he would instigate once the meal was done.

Ling cleared the table and served a steaming peach cobbler, using Lisa's mahogany secretary as a sideboard. The cobbler had a crust of crumbs and butter and brown sugar, and the tinned peaches had been enlivened by a dash of brandy, also from Tatum's private stores. Ling set a small coffeepot by Lisa's right hand, and a pitcher of thick cream for the cobbler, the coffee, or both.

"Well, this smells marvelous," Tatum said. "Thank you, Ling."

Ling gave a small bow, smiling, and left them alone.

"Oh, it *is* marvelous," Lisa exclaimed, tasting the cobbler. Her expression revealed her pleasure, and all her seriousness of a moment before had evaporated.

Tatum was glad that he had kept his own opinion of the Indians to himself, and pleased that Lisa had been the one to apologize. It would put her a little further in his debt and he would need every advantage he could muster if he were to emerge from Putnam's Park unscathed when spring finally came.

There must be something more he could do! He could not simply wait here for a fickle Nature to release him. He must act! But for two days he had examined his predicament from every side and he could find no escape.

The effect of being marooned here was potentially far more serious than he had admitted to Lisa Putnam. True, if the circus could be on its way by the start of May there might be time to play an abbreviated engagement at Salt Lake City, but the shows in Carson City and Virginia City and Reno would have to be canceled along with the Montana tour, and Tatum had been counting on those receipts to fund his summer in San Francisco. Colonel Hyde, his sole investor on the west coast, had insisted that they should share the expense of erecting the building where Tatum's Combined Shows would perform throughout the summer months. There could be no thought of performing in the tent all that time. A permanent building offered better shelter from the cold summer fogs, less chance of fire, better lighting, and the necessary supports for the full array of aerial acrobatics that the show offered since Tatum had bid successfully for the services of the Abbruzzi family. Those services had not come cheaply, and Tatum's future depended on a successful summer engagement. It had taken his last available dollar to finance this tour; if the tour failed, hope would be lost for a triumphant return to the East and the engagements in New York, Philadelphia and Boston that would elevate Tatum's Combined Shows to the top rank in American showmanship, above Bailey, even above the Barnum & Coup spectacle that was attracting so much attention.

Tatum found the recent success of Phineas Taylor Barnum particularly galling. Barnum had built his reputation by exhibiting freaks and human oddities, some of them real and some the grossest frauds, which Barnum had readily admitted after the fact. "The public likes to be fooled," he had said, while counting his ample receipts. Only lately had Barnum allied himself with W. C. Coup and entered the business of the traveling circus. Tatum considered Barnum a Johnny-come-lately, and thought his already considerable success unmerited. But Barnum's name attracted crowds, and he had even experimented briefly with two rings exhibiting different acts at the same time. Happily, he had reverted to a single ring, but rumors continued that he was seeking new ways to expand the size of his show and Tatum knew he must make his move now, while the gap between himself and Barnum might be closed by a single brilliant stroke such as the one he had planned.

But now everything he had planned was imperiled, put at risk by a shot fired at the wrong moment and a hundred tons of snow and rock. He had spent the morning going over his books and he had reached an inescapable conclusion: the cost of remaining here even for a single month would consume the lion's share of his remaining cash and he would be unable to meet his payroll. Already, a few of the drivers had approached him, saying they were thinking of riding out of the valley on horseback and asking to be paid. He had put a quick stop to that kind of talk. Wary of losing more drivers along the way, as had happened in the Black Hills, he had hired the replacement teamsters for a flat wage to be paid upon reaching Salt Lake City, not before, no matter how long the journey took. This morning he had reiterated that condition in no uncertain terms and the drivers had withdrawn to the card table, where they muttered among themselves and cast dark looks in the circus master's direction. If they caused trouble he would have to handle it himself; it would be weeks before Kinnean's wrist regained its strength. And all the time the circus remained in Putnam's Park the teamsters would be idle while Tatum was obliged to pay Lisa Putnam for their board; when he reached the Salt Lake at last, he would be unable to pay them, and when he tried to put them off with promises to pay them out of his first receipts, they would complain loudly. Word that Tatum's Combined Shows was in financial straits would spread, and Colonel Hyde might well back out of the summer arrangement even if Tatum managed to find his share of the funds. But if some way could be found to pay off the teamsters, a highly successful engagement in Salt Lake City could provide just enough capital to meet Colonel Hyde's requirements and assure the success of the San Francisco engagement.

The only possible solution was somehow to reduce the cost of the enforced stay in Putnam's Park. The extravagance of the private dinner he had lavished on his hostess, although it had required no outlay of hard cash except for a gold eagle to the Chinawoman for bringing out the linen and silver, was intended to remove from Lisa Putnam's mind any suspicion that he might fear the expense. He intended to take her entirely unaware, hoping to obtain a reduced rate for boarding his men by offering in return something less vital than money, but so far he had been unable to imagine what he might offer, or what the ranch might need. As he searched for the answer he had grown increasingly frustrated, feeling himself thwarted by forces that were alien to him, trapped in a frozen cul-de-sac where the devices he was accustomed to use in civilized surroundings were useless. Years of experience in the highly competitive world of traveling entertainments had made him adept at bending others to his will, but what use were his persuasive powers against an avalanche? Such a phenomenon confounded him.

"You have hardly touched your dessert," Lisa said, and he saw that hers was half gone.

"I beg your pardon. I'm afraid I was lost in my thoughts."

He took a bite of the cobbler. The crust was crisp and the peaches sweet, but he was unable to enjoy it.

"Will you have coffee now?" Lisa reached for the pot.

"Thank you."

"I hope you'll give Amanda a chance to perform the new act," she said as she poured. "I don't mean to interfere in your business, but it certainly seemed to please everyone today."

"Of course she shall have a chance," Tatum said pleasantly. "She took me by surprise, that's all. We ordinarily work out new scenes together. Sometimes old Sam helps as well. He is from the old school and he knows a good deal. In England today, the circus has become corrupted by theatrical influence. Some presentations are no more than plays on horseback. The scenes given in Astley's palace would make him turn in his grave. He was the first to present equestrian exhibitions in a ring, you know, and horsemanship has always been at the heart of the entertainments we call 'circus' now. The juggling and acrobatics and clowning come from medieval fairs, of course. But the theater is a separate art and I have endeavored to keep its influence out of my shows. I have a very particular sort of clowning in mind for Amanda, and I don't want her to take any wrong steps." He leaned forward, warming to his topic. "You see, there have always been two quite different styles of clowning since the earliest times. The Greeks and the Romans had buffoons and medieval kings had their jesters, and there is much buffoonery in clowning still, what with the mock fights and the swordplay and all the rough-and-tumble. And many of these clowns have talked.

Grimaldi talked and Dan Rice does little else. But I have always believed there could be a combining of the comic aspects with some higher elements of pure pantomime, more in the spirit of the *commedia dell'arte*. There is room for artistry, and pathos too, don't you think? After all, tears and laughter are not so very far apart."

"Certainly if I had not believed so before, I would have after seeing Amanda today. She made us all aware of that."

"Yes. Yes, she did." Tatum knew he had been foolish to challenge Amanda without thinking, foolish to reveal his wounded pride to her. He had suspected that the secretiveness with which she and Sam and Carlos had developed the new work had been deliberately intended to provoke him. And her manner had provoked him as well. So often she seemed to be trying to break away. In makeup, she could be almost defiant. But it was evening now and the makeup would be gone. He would praise the new work and tell her she might include it in the summer performances, and she would be mollified. He would suggest some small changes, of course. It wouldn't do to let her know that she was on the verge of surpassing him with her own inventiveness. If she suspected that, she would soon see that he had no more to teach her, and his hold over her would diminish.

"You should be proud of her achievements," Lisa said. She leaned back in her chair with the coffee cup in her hand. "Life must have been very hard for her after she lost her parents. You have brought her a long way."

Tatum nodded. "This show is her family now, as it was even before her loss. The Spencers were English. They came to this country before Amanda was born, together with Sam Higgins. They knew Alfred Chalmers as well, although he came over later on. Sam and the Spencers came to work for a circus owned by a family named Cooper, where I was assistant manager. My wife was a Cooper, you see. When she died, I took over things as best I could. Amanda and I were both orphaned by that fire, in a manner of speaking, and since then I have looked to her artistic and personal welfare as best I could." His expression was somber as he recalled his loss.

Hachaliah Tatum's parents had been farmers on land adjoining the Cooper property in Dutchess County, New York. Since before the Revolution, Yankee farmers and inkeepers had occasionally exhibited tropical animals to the curious, but the Coopers were among the first to combine their menagerie with circus and equestrian acts and tour the countryside. The family was large and well-to-do, and as a boy, Tatum had worked for them in the stables where their horses and the other animals were kept. There he had met Helena Cooper; she was his own age, and captivatingly pretty. In time, when he had risen to a position of sufficient responsibility to merit her attention, he had courted her and, to his surprise, won her. Like Hachaliah himself, she was willful, ambitious, an excellent rider and a crack shot. Together they performed feats of marksmanship for an admiring public, and Helena took part in the trick-riding act as well, while Hachaliah honed his skill at dressage, of which High School was only a part, and assisted Helena's brother Aaron in managing the show. From the start there had been friction between them. Aaron had a taste for the sensational, and like Barnum he would present anything that might attract the public, no matter how bizarre; Hachaliah favored a circus of almost classical simplicity, with each act presented in its purest form and no oddities or freaks, no theatricalities. The arguments between them had become more and more heated, and the last months of Helena's life were fraught with contention as she tried to keep the peace between her brother and the husband she loved. But the conflagration that consumed the Coopers' permanent exhibition palace in New York City put an end to the arguments. While the ashes were still warm, Aaron had confronted a heartbroken Hachaliah and informed him that the show would be rebuilt according to his dictates, with or without Hachaliah's help; as Aaron's brother-in-law, Hachaliah had received a share in the profits, but that too would come to an end. Though not intended to do anything of the sort, these pronouncements speeded Hachaliah's recovery. His anger at Aaron's cruelty gave him strength and determination, and with Amanda Spencer, Samuel Higgins and a handful of other performers who shared Tatum's views, he had left Aaron Cooper to his own devices and founded Tatum's Combined Shows. Under his careful management the show survived its rocky beginnings and in time it prospered. He had increased its size gradually, and now, as he prepared to stake his claim among the foremost circuses in the land, he was also preparing to take a measure of revenge on his former brother-in-law. Aaron Cooper had recently joined forces with James A. Bailey and they had announced a tour of the Pacific coast to coincide with the nation's centennial. Tatum had kept his own plans quiet, but in California, Colonel Hyde would launch the planned publicity soon. Tatum would beat Cooper and Bailey to the Golden Gate and steal their thunder, but not unless he came to terms with Lisa Putnam now. And yet other than revealing his predicament and throwing himself on her mercy, he could think of no way to broach the subject. He felt himself grasping at straws.

"I tell you what we shall do," he said, pretending a beneficence he did not feel. "Before we leave here we shall give you a proper performance. You shall see Tatum's Combined Shows in all its glory."

"Hmm?" Lisa was taken by surprise. "A performance? What a wonderful idea! I'm afraid I was quite lost in my thoughts. I was trying to remember when the last slide occurred. It has been some years since we had one, and there have been none worse that I know of. It will be quite a job to clear the road."

Tatum's eyebrows shot up. "You have had these before?"

"Of course. And mudslides at other times of year."

Tatum's heart was pounding. "And so you must clear them away?"

Lisa nodded. "Yes. We hire men and wagons from Rawlins to help us, but there's no use bothering until the snow melts."

Tatum shook his head. "What a fool I've been."

"I don't understand," Lisa said, but Tatum rushed on, suddenly leaning across the table toward her.

"You would have to pay to clear the road eventually?"

"Yes," she admitted, taken aback by his intensity.

"And if you could avoid that expense, if you did not actually have to pay money to have it done, that would be greatly to your benefit?"

"Yes, but—"

"Could it be dug away now?" he demanded. "Without waiting for spring?"

"Why, yes, but the work is difficult. The weight of the mass compresses it nearly to the consistency of ice, and it must be blasted apart. It's much easier to wait for the snow and ice to melt. Then all you have to do is haul away the rocks and restore the roadbed if it has been damaged. If I hired men to dig it away now, it would cost more than twice as much."

Tatum was triumphant. "I wasn't thinking of your men, Miss Putnam, but mine. It would cost you no money at all."

"Oh!" Lisa put a hand to her mouth and her eyes grew wide. "I am so accustomed to dealing with this sort of thing in one manner, I hadn't thought that there might be another way!"

Tatum spoke rapidly now. "The cabins in which my people live can be removed from the wagon beds, so you see we have as many flatbed wagons as we need. And more than enough draft animals. But you said the ice must be blasted away?"

"There is plenty of powder! My father always kept some for clearing rocks and stumps, and for emergencies." She did not add that he had also traded powder to Sun Horse's men for hunting—but never enough for war—despite the ban on trading with the Powder River bands.

Tatum thought hard for a moment, then rose and went to the secretary, where Ling had left a decanter of brandy and two small glasses. He poured and returned to the table with the glasses, setting one in front of Lisa as he resumed his seat.

"If my men and I clear that road now, would you contribute shovels and picks and blasting powder?"

"Of course!" Lisa exclaimed. "That's nothing to ask."

He held up a cautionary hand. "I haven't asked everything yet. Would you board my people while we are here in exchange for this labor?"

"It might take you as long to dig through it as it would for it to melt of its own accord."

Tatum replied without hesitation. "Then the digging will go faster as the melting progresses and we shall be away from here all the sooner, and you will have a clear road that cost you nothing but the food to feed us. The main thing is that we will be doing something for ourselves instead of awaiting the whims of the Almighty!"

He could hardly contain himself. He had been the perfect fool not to see that the answer to his problem was close at hand all the time. The avalanche was something so foreign to his experience that it had not occurred to him that other men routinely confronted such obstacles and found ways to remove them. Once Lisa Putnam made him aware of that simple fact, he had seen at once that he could not only put his teamsters to work and save the expense of boarding them, but he might reach Salt Lake City on the date originally planned. The Nevada engagements might be kept after all and the San Francisco plans were out of danger! If she would agree.

"Is it a bargain?" he asked, struggling to remain calm.

Lisa hesitated briefly, making quick calculations in her mind. She could not afford to feed all the circus people for nothing, and her father had taught her never to yield to the first demand in any bargaining. What should her counteroffer be? Until now only Amanda and Tatum and Joe Kitchen had slept in the house, while the performers slept in their wagons and the teamsters in tents. Others might prefer to sleep indoors for such a prolonged stay. She could afford to make them comfortable and she didn't care if the teamsters slept in the hallways now that they would be kept out of mischief by hard work.

"I will board any man that works on the road and I will

give you the rooms in Putnam House as well. You will pay me only to board your performing artists."

"Done!" Tatum said at once, and he raised his glass. "To the success of our endeavors."

Lisa surprised him by tossing down her brandy in a single swallow. The fire was warm on her back and the brandy fueled the rising excitement within her. The true cost of feeding the teamsters might in the end equal or surpass that of paying Rawlins men to clear the road in the spring, but the sooner the circus was gone the fewer of her cows she would have to slaughter, and the value of the lesson she had learned this evening from Hachaliah Tatum would more than cover any small deficit that remained. He had taken charge of his own fate and she must do the same. Like him, she could not be content to await the outcome of events beyond her control. The pipe carriers might succeed and they might not; they might come back safely and they might not. She could no more decree their success and safe return than she could single-handedly change the government in Washington City and establish a more just Indian policy, but by following Tatum's example and acting instead of waiting, she could control her own destiny, and with luck she might help to ensure that Sun Horse, at least, could remain free even if the pipe carriers failed.

LISA PUTNAM'S JOURNAL

Tuesday, March 7th. 5:10 a.m.

Last night I could scarcely get to sleep and this morning I awoke early and came here to sit by the fire and think, and even as I was making the fire I found the answer. I have found a way to help Sun Horse! Whether he will accept my help I cannot say, but I know now that I must tender the offer. I am impatient for dawn to come and for breakfast to be done so I can talk to Julius and seek his approval. I will ask Harry and Hutch to feed the cows this morning, and if Julius agrees to what I intend, we can be on our way up to Sun Horse's village by mid-morning. But until the house is awake, I shall have to bide my time here. How slowly the clock on the mantel seems to tick today!

As I often do when I am excited, I am getting ahead of myself. As I said yesterday, Mr. Tatum invited me to take supper with him. We had a charming meal in the library, all arranged by Mr. Tatum in collusion with Ling and Joe Kitchen. We ate very well and spoke of many things, and then in the time it took us to drink our coffee, Mr. Tatum found the solution to his own dilemma. He and his men will dig away the avalanche! It is the first such attempt since my father's abortive effort years ago. I took heart from Mr. Tatum's determination and resolved once more to attempt some action on behalf of Sun Horse, so he need not merely wait for his emissaries to General Crook to return, but as before, I could not see the way. My father often cautioned me not to worry a problem the way a dog worries a bone. "Set your cares aside," he said, "and look at them again in the morning," and I tried to do just that, with only moderate success.

After supper, Mr. Tatum and I adjourned to the saloon, where he began at once to issue instructions for the digging efforts, which will begin today. I will say more about these as time goes on, when we have had a chance to gauge their chance of success.

There was music in the saloon, not the lively band tunes of three nights before, but the enchanting sound of two violins played together by two magicians, Julius and Amanda. I joined the small group gathered around the stove to hear them, hoping the music would help me to set my cares aside. Johnny Smoker was there, and Hutch. He seems to have caught the eye of a young girl named Maria, and he sat by her for a time. When she was called away by her rather stern papa, I asked Hutch why he didn't get his banjo, but he said he had "played myself out" the other night and wished only to listen to the violinists. Julius and Amanda were playing for each other, all but oblivious to their audience. One would stop in the midst of a song and ask, "Say, do you know this one?" and begin to play a new strain, and whenever they found one they both knew it was something to hear. When Mr. Tatum was done with the wagon drivers he joined us, and before long he took Amanda away. He was very gentle with her and said in front of everyone that he had enjoyed the new work she performed that afternoon. He promised it would have a place in the show this summer, and this made her happy. They spoke for a time at a secluded table while Mr. Tatum had a nightcap, and soon they both went to their rooms.

Once Amanda set her fiddle aside, Hutch did finally get his banjo and he and Julius played a while longer. Then, in between songs, quite out of the blue, he said to Julius, "There's something I've been meaning to ask about old

Sun Horse. If he's a good Injun, like you say, shouldn't he be on some reservation?" Well, Julius thought for a time and then he gave as good an answer as any I could have come up with. "Say a man came to your pa's farm and told him he'd have to sell his house and land. Say he told your pa he couldn't settle where he pleased, but only where this feller said he could. How would you feel about that?" "Well, I wouldn't like it any too well," Hutch replied. "Anyone tried anything like that with my pa, he'd have himself a fight on his hands, I'll tell you what." Well, the minute the words were out of his mouth he saw what Julius was getting at.

Julius went on to tell him about my father's long friendship with Sun Horse and how Sun Horse has always done his best to keep the peace with the whites and sees no reason he should be moved against his will, but what struck me most of all about this exchange was a sudden awareness that until that moment young Hutch had taken the recurrent warfare between ourselves and the Indians as something completely normal, part of the natural state of things, and what is worse, he saw no end for the Indians other than to be shoved aside and left on whatever bits of land we choose to give them. I found myself wondering, if that is the prevalent attitude across the land, how can there ever be peace? This question reminded me of more basic questions, such as: Could all the tragic fighting between ourselves and the Indians have been avoided in the first place? Was it inevitable that the differences between our way of life and theirs should lead to a generation of hostilities and deplorable barbarities on both sides? My father believed that the answers were, first, no, and second, yes. He placed most of the blame on a single characteristic of the white race. Thanks in large part to his teaching, I understand certain things, such as the force of our numbers and the resulting inevitability of our movement to settle this great continent, that are not plain to the Indians. But there is much about the aborigines that is not plain to us, and as one who has had a chance to know them over a period of years, I can only say that while I have always seen in the Indians a desire to learn about the whites, I see in the whites no such curiosity, beyond a passing interest in the savage and bizarre. It is this unwillingness, and the ignorance that has therefore persisted among the majority of settlers in the mountain region, that my father believed was at fault for the conflicts that have brought so much harm to both races.

Still, there is hope. A fair-minded man like General Crook, one who knows the futility of war, may yet make a just settlement. The pipe carriers may increase the chance that for the Sioux the end will be arrived at through discussion rather than fighting, and the white race may redeem some of its failings by making a peace that sets aside for the Sioux some of their ancestral lands. They too deserve a home they love and an active life suited to that place and to their perceptions of the world around them. But last evening's talk reminded me that I cannot trust the wisdom of white men to guarantee Sun Horse the best hope for the future, and this strengthened my resolve to help him. Throughout a restless night I sought the means, and this morning I saw that I hold them in my hands. It was the talk of blasting powder during supper, and the thought of the cows we will save if the circus leaves soon, that gave me the idea. I realize that nothing I can do will assure Sun Horse's survival, but I may increase his chances of saving himself, if he will let me. Should the pipe carriers' mission fail, I am still convinced that the best hope for Sun Horse (and for all the free-roaming bands) lies in remaining free for at least another year, until cooler heads in Washington may prevail. But to stay free, he must be able to move beyond the soldiers' reach. If he accepts my offer and if the gift becomes known, the government will take a harsh view of my action and the title to Putnam's Park may be in jeopardy. Yet I pray that this one time Sun Horse will accept a gift, for the future of his people.

CHAPTER FIVE

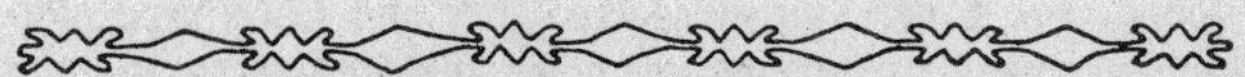

The clouds broke and drifted off to the southeast as the morning progressed and by the time the riders approached the Lakota village the sun stood high above the mountains. They entered the camp two by two, Lisa and Julius in the lead and Johnny and Amanda following close behind. Before leaving the settlement, Lisa had impulsively given Amanda a buffalo coat that had belonged to Eleanor Putnam; the coat fit Amanda perfectly, completely hiding her clown costume, but her red cap and white makeup were plain for all to see and the Indians gathered quickly around the riders; some had heard of the clown girl from those who had been in the white settlement when the circus arrived and they were eager to see her for themselves.

Lisa led the way straight across the camp, making no formal passage around the circle this time. She wanted to give the impression that this was a casual visit undertaken on the spur of the moment. Like the visit, the gift would be casually offered, with no formality, and presented in that way it might be easier for Sun Horse to accept. She had asked Johnny and Amanda to come along because she wanted to miss no opportunity to raise Sun Horse's spirits and increase the chance that he would take what she offered; on the day the circus arrived she had noticed that the old man seemed to be both amused and fascinated by

Amanda, and she knew he would be glad to see his white grandson again. The two young people had jumped at the chance to accompany Lisa and Julius, and Amanda had accepted without question Lisa's suggestion that she might put on her costume and prepare a few tricks to amuse the Indians.

Even before she entered the camp, Lisa had noticed the smell of cooking meat and she saw now that iron pots hung from their three-legged supports in front of several lodges. The Sioux preferred to do most of their cooking outside on all but the worst days. In front of Sun Horse's lodge, Elk Calf, Sings His Daughter and Bat's wife, Penelope, were all cutting meat for the stewpot that hung over the fire there. A small rib roast was already propped up near the flames to cook. The women smiled as Lisa dismounted.

She greeted Elk Calf Woman with deference and said, "We have brought the white girl to visit the camp of Sun Horse. Is your husband within?"

"He is there," Elk Calf said, pointing. "He will be glad to see his white friends."

Lisa looked in the direction the old woman pointed and she saw two figures not far beyond the camp circle, walking slowly side by side as if they were deep in conversation. But they had seen the riders arrive. An arm was raised in greeting and Lisa waved in reply. The figures quickened their pace somewhat, one holding the arm of the other.

A burst of laughter close at hand caused Lisa to turn. Julius, Amanda and Johnny had dismounted and Amanda had removed her buffalo coat. The clown was silently scolding her horse, but Lisa couldn't imagine why this amused the Lakotas so.

Amanda turned and bowed slightly to the Indians and at once the horse pushed her with his head, nearly knocking her to the ground and bringing renewed laughter from the onlookers. Amanda shook an angry finger at the horse; he bared his teeth in a mock laugh. With palm upraised she commanded him to stop, and when the horse resumed his normal expression, she turned and led him along by the reins, as if training him to follow a lead. Again he placed his head against her back and shoved, this time sending her sprawling in the snow. The Indians laughed uproariously, plainly delighted by this unexpected behavior from an animal they thought they knew so well. *Shunka tanka*, the Sioux called a horse—big dog. When they had first encountered the horse some generations earlier, in the hands of their southern neighbors, the strange animal had appeared to be a larger version of a dog, and the Lakota soon saw that the new beast was used for some of the same purposes—carrying loads, and pulling even larger loads on a drag made by crossing poles over his back. But far more astonishing was the discovery that a horse would carry a man, and the Lakota understood at once that the swift creature would afford hunters and warriors far greater mobility than they ever had before. By raiding and trade they soon obtained horses of their own; they came to know the animal's nature and they experienced the thrill of mastering him, and they gave the horse a new name, one that revealed a heightened respect: *shunka wakán* they called him, the mysterious dog.

Obviously enraged, Amanda leaped to her feet and raised a hand as if she might slap the horse, but at once he hung his head abjectly, full of genuine remorse, and the laughter welled up even stronger. Taking pity on the dejected animal, the clown cradled his head in her arms and stroked his velvety nose to comfort him. Finally she turned to bow to the crowd, showing that the little performance was at an end, and immediately the horse nudged her backside with his head and sent her face first into the snow once more, to the uncontrolled delight of the Indians.

Sun Horse had joined the gathering in time to see the horse's final prank, and Lisa recognized the young man who accompanied him. It was the blind holy man Sees Beyond. His brown eyes were clear and bright and nothing about his bearing betrayed his sightlessness except for an unusual tilt of the head, the face slightly raised in the manner of a man who listened intently for a faint sound.

Sun Horse was speaking softly to him, describing Amanda's antics as she got to her feet and scolded the horse again, and Sees Beyond smiled and laughed along with the rest.

"No time like the present, I guess," Julius said to Lisa. "Looks like Amanda's about done."

They handed their reins to two of the young boys who stood nearby, waiting for the privilege of caring for a guest's horse, and together they approached the two *wichasha wakán*.

"*Hau,* Grandfather," Lisa greeted Sun Horse in Lakota. "We have brought you visitors." She turned to Amanda. "Amanda, come and say hello to Sun Horse. You remember him from the other day."

Leaving her horse where he was, Amanda turned a cartwheel in the snow and bounced to a stop in front of Sun Horse and Sees Beyond. She made as if to bow to them, but suddenly she interrupted the motion and straightened, looking apprehensively over her shoulder at the horse and bringing a final swell of laughter from the crowd. The horse stood placidly where she had left him. Confidently now, Amanda bowed low to Sun Horse, removing her red clown's cap and letting her hair fall free as she swept the cap across the snow with the gesture of a courtier. There were murmurs of surprise from the crowd. Not everyone in the village had known that the clown was a girl.

Johnny Smoker came forward, leading his own horse as well as Amanda's, and Sun Horse shook his hand, smiling. "I am always glad to see my grandson," he said in Cheyenne. Then, changing to Lakota, he welcomed the others. "These friends are always welcome in my village. *Hau,* Julius." He shook the black man's hand. "Lisaputnam." As was his habit, he held both of her hands in his own for a long moment. "And this little one is especially welcome." He stretched out a wrinkled hand to Amanda.

Amanda took the hand in her own and curtsied, forgetting she was dressed as a clown.

Sun Horse smiled and returned his eyes to Lisa. "Stay and eat with us. Our hunters have brought in two deer today. The meat has made the people happy, and the white *heyoka* girl has made them happier still."

Lisa knew that the meat of two deer would not go far in a village this size, and she knew it would all be consumed in a single meal. White men might have conserved some of the meat, trying to stretch it out over a few days, but that was not the Lakota way. They believed in eating when meat was on hand and enjoying the pleasure of a full stomach. When there was no meat, that was the time to go hungry.

If Sun Horse would accept what she offered, his people need not be hungry much longer.

"We will stay, Grandfather. But the women are still cutting the meat. Shall we walk together while it is cooking, you and Julius and I?"

Sun Horse nodded, pleased by the suggestion. "I like to walk in the sun. I am an old man now, and I need the warmth of the sun in my bones." He turned to Sees Beyond, who had followed the conversation with his unseeing eyes, always appearing to look directly at the speaker. "Walk with us, my friend." Sees Beyond inclined his head in assent and Sun Horse turned to Johnny Smoker, speaking now in Cheyenne. "And what of my grandson. Will he too walk with us before we eat?"

"Amanda wishes to meet your sacred clowns and learn something about them," Johnny replied in the same language.

Sun Horse motioned to two men, one old and the other young, who stood nearby, waiting. Around them most of the Lakota were going about their business now that they had seen the *heyoka* girl and heard the visitors welcomed. "They too have wished to see her, and they are here," Sun Horse said. Throughout Amanda's performance these two had watched intently, often talking exitedly to each other. Sun Horse motioned them to approach and when Amanda noticed them her eyes grew wide with astonishment.

"Is that them, Johnny? Are they the clowns?" When he

nodded, she said, "Look at them! Don't you see? It's Sam and Carlos. They're just alike!"

And indeed the two were in some respects similar to her companions from the circus. The older man was the taller of the two and he walked with a certain dignified care that recalled the Englishman's gait, while the younger one was compact and wiry, with quick eyes and a smile that flashed now as he saw that the whitefaced clown's attention was on him. Both men were dark-skinned; they had jagged streaks of paint on their foreheads and cheeks and their clothing was in tatters, but taken together they could have been mistaken for the circus clowns, made up for a new and unusual scene in their act.

"They are called Talks Fast and Won't Go Alone," said Sun Horse, indicating first the elder *heyoka* and then the younger. "Talks Fast speaks almost as little as Hears Twice," he added; he and Sees Beyond chuckled softly at the joke. The power of *heyoka* lay in doing everything in a manner contrary to the normal one, and even in his name, Talks Fast represented a notion that was the opposite of his true nature.

Hears Twice had appeared beside Julius as the crowd dispersed and the two of them were speaking together now. Sees Beyond turned in that direction as he laughed, as if he could sense the prophet's presence.

"Won't Go Alone is of the Real People," Sun Horse said to Johnny. "He married Half Moon, the elder daughter of Walks Bent Over. You can talk with him in the tongue of the Real People and translate for the clown girl."

Johnny brightened, and spoke a few words to the young *heyoka*. Equally surprised, Won't Go Alone responded with a torrent of Cheyenne so rapid that Johnny smiled and held up a hand, making signs to say that the young man would have to speak more slowly.

"Tell me what you're saying," Amanda insisted, taking Johnny's arm and looking from one *heyoka* to the other with open curiosity. "I can't stand it when I don't know what people are saying."

"This one is called Won't Go Alone, and he's Cheyenne. I was just telling him it's good to find a Cheyenne here among the Sioux. I asked what band he was from and he said he's northern Cheyenne. His band is led by Little Wolf now; Sun Horse and his people see Little Wolf in the summer, when they go north to hunt."

Sun Horse watched the four of them with benign interest for a few moments, the two *heyoka* and the two young whites, and then he nodded to Lisa and touched Sees Beyond's arm. Sees Beyond took Sun Horse by the elbow and together they started off, Lisa walking with the two Indians. Julius left Hears Twice and joined them as they moved out of the camp circle, following an often-used pathway to the creek.

"I am happy to see that the Sun Band's hunters have brought meat," Lisa said. The presence of fresh meat in the village today was a blessing, she realized now, for it served to remind Sun Horse of the raised spirits and renewed sense of well-being that having meat in camp produced among the people.

"Wolf Talker heard the wolves last night," Sun Horse explained. "They told of a kill the pack had made, and more deer to be found there. Wolf Talker left the village early this morning with Rib Bone and Crooked Horn, and they found two deer near where the wolves had eaten."

"Your hunters might bring in more meat if the horses were strong enough to carry them farther from the village," Lisa said. As soon as the words were out she realized her mistake, but she gave no sign that anything was wrong. To emphasize the usefulness of a gift increased its value and she wanted to do just the opposite. She would have to be more careful. She was careful to keep her tone casual when she continued, as if referring to something of little importance. "My father kept much grain, more than we need. We have brought a little for your horses. And some gunpowder too, for the hunters," she added as if it were an afterthought.

"Always in the past I have traded with your father for

gunpowder," Sun Horse said. "What may I give you in exchange for these things?"

Lisa made a gesture with her hand, politely brushing aside any thought of an exchange. "Sometimes the Lakota make gifts in the name of another," she said. "I have seen you give horses and other things away to honor a brave man, or a boy who has received a new name. Whitemen too make gifts to honor one another. We give gifts to honor a good man who has died." She hoped her father, if he were listening, would forgive her this small lie in a good cause. "Julius and I wish to give you these things to honor my father. He always shared what he had with his friends. The grain and gunpowder are only part of what we bring you today."

They had arrived at a large boulder overlooking the creek. The top of the rock was flat and clear of snow, and nearly twice as large as the kitchen table in Putnam House. Sun Horse placed his foot in a natural step in the side of the rock and clambered to the top. "Come," he said. "Let us sit."

Sees Beyond patted the boulder lightly to orient himself and then without hesitation his foot found the same step and he joined Sun Horse atop the rock. Lisa and Julius sat cross-legged like the Indians, and they discovered that the dark stone was pleasantly warm from the sun.

Once they were settled, Julius brought from a pocket in his heavy corduroy overcoat ten pieces of willow stick, equal in length. The Lakota often used sticks to represent gifts that were too large to be passed easily from one man to another. One by one he set the sticks in a row in front of Sun Horse.

"Each stick represents one of our spotted buffalo," Lisa explained, using the Lakota term *pte gleshka* for the white man's cattle. She said nothing about the value of the cows to the Sun Band, nothing about the poor hunting all winter or the gaunt faces of the men and women who had gathered to watch Amanda perform, nothing of the fact that with these three things, grain, gunpowder and beef, the Sun Band would be strong enough to move whenever they wished.

Sees Beyond reached out a hand, finding the sticks and counting them, but he made no comment.

Julius found that he was breathing easier now that the sticks were out of his hands. He felt almost light-headed, and unaccountably pleased with himself.

The sticks had been his idea, as had the grain. Lisa's first impulse had been to bring the cows along today, and she had planned to offer hay for the ponies. She had looked at the loft in the barn, still half full with winter nearly over, and she knew there were two cribs still full in the west meadow, and she had imagined the Lakota driving their horses over to feed in the park, but Julius had improved on Lisa's ideas and at the same time made it less likely that the circus whites would learn of the help the settlement was offering to the Indians.

From the first, he had been in no doubt about which side his own bread was buttered on, or where the best chance for Putnam's Park lay. Keep the hell out of it, let the army and the Indians work things out between them, and hope when the dust settled that Putnam's Park could go on like before. Sun Horse sending a pipe to Crook had raised his hopes, and when Hardeman had agreed to go along with the pipe carriers and speak to Crook, Julius had figured that wrapped it up; however things turned out, Lisa's deed would have as much chance as ever of withstanding the changes that followed, whether the Indians' title to the Powder River country was reaffirmed or whether they were all removed from the country forever and hauled away to Dakota. But every time he entertained such hopes he had felt mean and small, and last night when Hutch had asked him about Sun Horse he had thought for a time and found that he could give only one answer. After all, if a man lived at peace in his own home, who had the right to move him against his will? Julius Ingram had lived for thirty-nine of his fifty years without the right to his own home or any hope of having it, and now he saw the matter of a man's rights as standing pretty high on the list of things he might fight for. But even so, it was one thing to speak up for Sun Horse and another thing to fight for him, and Julius had hoped he wouldn't have to choose between Putnam's Park and helping the Indians, because he wasn't sure which way he would jump when his own future hung in the balance. And then this morning when Lisa had asked Hutch and Harry to feed the cattle and told Julius she had to talk with him, he had known what was coming, and once again he had found there was only one answer he could give. He knew what Jed's wishes would be and he couldn't go against them, and even leaving Jed and his wishes aside, if that were possible, he couldn't stand against Lisa, not when he saw that her heart was set on helping Sun Horse.

"We have hay and beef and gunpowder," Lisa had said right off, once they were alone in the library. "With those three things Sun Horse and his people can move if they have to. They can go now if they want. Farther north they might find better hunting. The main thing is to keep away from the soldiers."

They had sat in front of the fire holding cups of coffee in their hands and Lisa had clutched hers tightly, as if only the heat from the cup gave her the courage to talk of what she planned to do.

"Not the hay," Julius had said. "That's not the way." He had seen the sudden worry in her expression and he held up a hand to calm her. "We've got plenty of hay, but them Indian ponies will burn all the good they'll get from it just walkin' over the mountain and back, and you start bringin' a bunch o' young bucks into the park with them wagon drivers here, there's gonna be trouble. Besides, if all these folks see us feedin' Injun horses, there's gonna be someone hear of it 'fore long. It ain't that I grudge them the hay," he had added. "It's just that a forty-pound sack of oats is a sight more use to a hungry horse than a forkful of hay. We can tote grain over the mountains easy enough."

They had plenty of grain, stored in tin-lined bins in the hayloft, safe from mice and other rodents, kept for the draft horses in winter and the riding horses in summer; it was a far greater reserve than the little ranch needed, but Jed had kept the bins full ever since the road-ranching days, and the cost of replenishing what they used each year was one he had judged prudent.

Lisa had agreed to the change at once, and then for a while they had worried together about what the circus folk would think if they saw ten cows driven out of the park toward the mountains, but Julius had remembered the gift sticks the Lakota used to transfer horses in naming ceremonies, and that had solved that problem. "There'll be time enough to bring the cows along later," he had said. "We can move 'em into the lot with the heifers and none o' these folks will think twice about it, and the next day when no one's about we can drive 'em up the crick. Do it before breakfast, we'll get out without a soul around."

Together with the cows they would lose to provide meat for the circus even if Tatum and his people stayed for just another month, the herd would be reduced by nearly a third, but Lisa had been quick to point out that they wouldn't have to pay men from Rawlins to clear the road, which meant they would have more cash in the fall when the steer calves were shipped. They might buy another bull, she suggested; they might keep more heifers back too, to expand the herd faster. Somehow they would make it up, if they kept the ranch.

"It will mean we're risking everything," Lisa had said. "You know that. If the government learns we helped a band of hostiles there will be no hope at all that they'll recognize the deed when this is all over."

Julius had shrugged, and he had surprised himself with the simplicity of his answer. "Might be we'd lose it all anyway, if we sit tight. Be a shame to hang on to all we got for no good reason, not if we could help some other folks."

But as they went ahead with their preparations and set out for the Indian village, he couldn't help asking himself what he would have left if he lost Putnam's Park. I'll have my fiddle, he thought, and he had remembered Old Will, the slave who had taught him to play. He remembered as if it were yesterday the first time Will had showed him how to rest the fiddle against his chest and hold the neck with his left hand. "Let you body feel the music," the old man had said. "You body sway, the fiddle she sway too. Tha's the way to make the fiddle sing."

Old Will had died years before the Union major set fire to the plantation. He had lived his life as a slave and his fiddle was all he had ever owned. If Julius had to start over again, he would still have his fiddle and his music, and he would still be a free man. That was more than Old Will ever had, even in his most fanciful dreams.

And the truth was, Julius had his own reason for helping Sun Horse. In four years of working hand in hand with Jed Putnam, talking while they worked, he had learned that everywhere else in the world the white man had enslaved the natives as he spread his empires around the globe, but not in America. In Africa and India and Mexico and South America it had always been the same, but in America Julius and his ancestors had been held in slavery for two hundred years and all that time the Indians had stayed free, those that survived. They had chosen to stay free or die. The whites had brought their own slaves to America because the red men resisted enslavement, and Julius wondered if it might be that he had something to learn from the Indians. He hadn't found the answer to that puzzle yet, and all along the trail from Putnam's Park he had been nagged by the fear that he was risking his life's dream to help folks who could do their own fighting, but here on the boulder beside the stream, as he had set out the ten sticks in a neat row he had felt the fear leave him, and it was as if a great weight had been lifted from his shoulders. He felt like doing a jig.

Sun Horse gazed thoughtfully at the sticks, but he did not touch them. Finally he smiled at Lisa. "It is good to honor the dead. And it is true that the Lakota make gifts to honor a good man, but in time there are other gifts that follow, and the circle is complete. The things you bring are of great value to the Lakota. We would give you something in return, but we have little to offer."

Lisa felt a surge of hope. She imagined that she sensed

in Sun Horse a desire to accept the gifts. Was he bargaining with her? He spoke of gifts returned in time . . .

"When you return in the fall you can bring us some meat from the hunt," she said, feeling her heart pounding in her breast. Like the notion of making the gifts to honor her father, this one had come to her at the last moment.

It was Sees Beyond who spoke now. "*Wakán Tanka* has given the *pte* to the Lakota to provide us with meat and covering for our lodges, and many other things. Like the Lakota, the *pte* roam the prairie, going where they wish. We do not keep animals for meat. When we need meat, we hunt. This is the Lakota way."

"The *washíchun* keep the spotted *pte* so that when hunting is bad there will still be meat," Lisa said, hoping to turn the holy man's argument back on him. "It is our custom to share what we have with our friends, just as it is yours. Today we will eat the deer your hunters have brought; tomorrow you will eat the meat from my cattle; in the fall you will bring us meat from the hunt and we too will share the strength of *pte*."

Sees Beyond shook his head. "Our strength is in the Lakota way. If we change our way of life, if we eat the meat of the whiteman's spotted buffalo, we are Lakota no longer."

"And if the soldiers come here and take you to Dakota, to the reservation, will you be Lakota then?"

Sees Beyond shrugged. "It may be that the Lakota life is not strong enough to stand against the *washíchun*."

"But if you take the meat and grain, your people and your horses will be strong enough to travel, and you can stay away from the soldiers." Lisa threw caution to the winds, speaking the value of the gift out loud. They must find a way to accept!

"And yet it will be the strength of the *washíchun* that allows us to move on, and the people will see this," Sees Beyond said, his sharp eyes fixed on Lisa. She could not escape the power of that sightless stare and she looked away.

"No spotted buffalo then," Julius said suddenly in his

crude Lakota. He had not understood everything that was said, but he caught enough of the words to follow the conversation. Both Sun Horse and Sees Beyond spoke more distinctly when talking with Lisa, and that was a help. He too had seen that the Lakota were bargaining. "Take grain, take gunpowder," he said. "Lakota hunt. With strong horses, maybe find meat. Hunt in Lakota way, live in Lakota way. Grain makes horses strong; meat makes people strong. If hunting is good, you can move when soldiers come."

Sun Horse knew that what the black whiteman said was true, and he knew just as surely that he could not accept. The Sun Band used iron pots and steel sewing needles and glass beads; they used flintlock and percussion rifles, and the newer guns that took metal cartridges, when they could get them; but each of these things replaced something that the Lakota had used previously, something that served the same purpose; none had changed the Lakota life in a fundamental way. And never had they accepted outright gifts from the whites. To do so would make them no better than the Loaf-Around-the-Forts. As always, Sees Beyond had reminded Sun Horse of a vital principle at the proper moment. It was to preserve the Lakota way of life that he had led his people here to this wintering place; that way of life could not be abandoned carelessly now to protect the band against a danger that might or might not come. If the pipe carriers succeeded, there would be no need to move until the grass was up. But if they failed . . .

"Still it will be the gifts that give us strength," Sun Horse said. "If the hunting is bad in the warm moons, we will have no way to repay you."

"Then take the grain and gunpowder and hunt now, and hunt for us as well!" Lisa said, speaking the thought as soon as it exploded in her mind. It took all her will to remain calm. "We will hunt with you! *Washíchun* and Lakota will hunt together. Take the grain and gunpowder to honor my father, and as long as we hunt we will bring you more. In return, share your knowledge with us. The Lakota are great hunters and great trackers. Lead us and we will follow. We will share the hunting and we will share the meat!" Her mind was racing. Perhaps some of the circus men could hunt too! The teamsters were busy with their digging, but if some of the performers could join the hunt and bring in meat, that would further reduce Tatum's costs and he would certainly give his consent.

She picked up the ten willow sticks in her gloved hand and held them up triumphantly for Sun Horse to see. "This is another gift you make to us. These cows are mothers. There is new life within them. To honor my father I would kill them for you, and to feed the people in my valley I will kill some anyway, but if you will hunt with us they may live; for every deer we bring in, for every elk, a cow will live and her calf will grow strong. This is something of great value to me, a gift far greater than anything I offer you in return, but I ask it all the same. Say you will accept the grain and gunpowder, and say you will hunt with us."

Sees Beyond turned to Sun Horse, his head held at its habitual upraised angle, his eyes on Sun Horse's face and the fleeing hint of a smile playing about his lips. "The coming together of two people," he said. "It can bring strength to each one."

Lisa did not know what the younger holy man meant by these words, but Sun Horse seemed to consider them very seriously. Finally he nodded.

"To honor my friend Jedediah we accept the grain and the gunpowder. The hunters of the Sun Band will lead the white hunters; we will share the hunt and we will share the meat."

As they walked back toward the circle of lodges Sun Horse was at peace with himself. His white grandson and the clown girl had brought their power to the village today, and he was certain now that it was a power to benefit the people. *It may help us or destroy us,* Hears Twice had said, but seeing the meeting between Johnny Smoker and the clown girl had given Sun Horse the idea of sending the pipes, and now yet another choice opened for the Sun Band; for a time, at least, the horses would eat grain from the white settlement, and if the hunt succeeded, the people would have meat. If war threatened, the village could move. Much had changed in just a few days, and no longer was it necessary to choose only between fighting or surrender.

He had been puzzled for a time, when he realized that the clown girl would be leaving right away with the rest of the Strange-Animal People. How could the power grow if she and Johnny Smoker were apart? he had wondered. He had delayed sending the pipe carriers on their way, pondering this mystery, and then had come the news of the avalanche. Blackbird and three other boys had been off hunting and they had tried to pass through the river canyon below the white settlement. They had returned to say that the road was blocked by a huge snowslide and the Strange-Animal People were trapped in the park, and Sun Horse's hopes had soared once more. The bright sun had shone on the hillside above the river, the snow had fallen to block the trail, and the clown girl would stay. So simple. *Okaga*, the power of the south, had done this, and *Okaga* was a life-giving power; the color of the south was yellow because the warm summer sun was yellow, and the sun was the power that nurtured all life. Thus the life-giving power had worked to reaffirm the promise that *wamblí* had made, by blocking the road and assuring that the clown girl would remain.

And here today, Sun Horse had understood something more: the meeting Hears Twice had predicted was not only the meeting of two individuals, but the coming together of two peoples, the Lakota and the *washíchun*. The presence of his white grandson and the clown girl in the village, the way they had sought out the *heyoka*, the way the people accepted them, these were the signs that had alerted Sun Horse to the truth; when Lisaputnam proposed the hunt, showing how the two races could work together for the benefit of both, he was sure. These were but the first steps to a wider coming together, and a wider peace.

Within the camp circle a performance by the *heyoka* was in progress, and once more some of the people had gathered to watch. Won't Go Alone was seated on the ground, furiously working a firebow while Talks Fast heaped snow instead of tinder around the base of the spinning stick on its hardwood base. Amanda knelt beside them, blowing hard to encourage an imaginary spark into flame. The performance was well known to the people; they enjoyed the seriousness with which the *heyoka* applied themselves to this futile effort, and the natural way the clown girl had taken part.

Won't Go Alone stopped spinning the firebow now, greatly saddened by his failure. Amanda hung her head, out of breath and exhausted. But then she brightened as if she had a sudden idea. She motioned Johnny Smoker to join her and she took a small box from his hands. With more motions she instructed him to shield the mound of snow with his hands. She took a sulphur match from the box and lit it, then held it carefully against the snow. She blew gently at first, then harder and harder, and the match went out. The expression of drop-jawed disbelief that she assumed at this new failure brought a burst of laughter from the onlookers. She lit another match and shielded it even more carefully with her own hands and Johnny's, and she blew it out even sooner. By now even the two *heyoka* were laughing.

LISA PUTNAM'S JOURNAL

Wednesday, March 8th. 6:25 p.m.

We got back from Sun Horse's village a little before one o'clock today, having accepted an invitation to spend the night. I have never liked making that ride twice in one day, although it can be done. It seems like a proper journey, and when you reach journey's end you want to stay a while. And so we did. There was dancing after the feast and it was a sight to see, the whole village gathered around an enormous bonfire in the center of camp under the much colder light of a brilliant three-quarter moon. Amanda was worn out after a long day by the time the dancing started, but Sun Horse provided her with a good buffalo robe and she sat by his side, swaddled to her chin in her coat and robe, and she stayed awake through the dancing. She liked the buffalo dancers best of all; she listened with interest as Johnny translated Sun Horse's explanation of the meaning—all about invoking the power of the buffalo for the hunt—but it was the dancer's uncanny buffalo-like movements that really fascinated her. She insists she is going to try to learn them and to use them somehow in the circus act. When the dancing was over we all slept in Uncle Bat's lodge and Penelope was glad of our company. The pipe carriers only left the village on Monday, but she already misses her husband as if he had been gone a long time. I assured her he would come safely back to her, and didn't show my own concern.

By this morning the snow was falling again and our ride home was not as pleasant as the ride over yesterday. We arrived here to find Mr. Tatum in a proper state. When we left yesterday, he was off with his men surveying the avalanche, planning their attack; I left word with Alfred Chalmers that Amanda had gone with us and would be well looked-after. Well, you would think we had abducted her by force and delivered her into the hands of Barbary pirates. How he carried on! He scolded us the minute we showed our faces in the saloon, it being midday and everyone being there for dinner, and later he took me aside to apologize for his tone, but then he scolded me all over again. "Had your father not known them for years, and did not your uncle live among them, they might have killed you all," he said darkly, and then he added, "or worse." There it is again, the supposed ever-present threat of unmentionable outrages against white womanhood. That fear seems to grow in the minds of our people like a weed. There have been such cases, of course; the tribulations of Mrs. Kelly and Mrs. Eubanks are well known. When the Indians outrage a white woman the newspapers call them "brutal savages," as if they were less than human, and men gather in the taprooms to talk of bloody revenge. But is this not just one more way we incite ourselves to hate against a people whose land we covet, whose way of life seems strange to us and therefore hateful? We point at the crime all good people abhor and using it as an excuse we attack the red men wherever we find them. I am a woman, and therefore vulnerable to the violence of men, but everyone speaks of the Indians as if they were the only ones guilty of such abominations. Should I not fear the same thing if I were a Frenchwoman in the Prussians' path? And how did Southern ladies feel when they saw General Sherman's armies bearing down on them? In every war to rend the heart of Europe or England or America such outrages have occurred. Among the aboriginal people of this continent these acts are expected, even accepted, when female captives are taken. It is the way of things here. The Indians are in a primitive state and act in accord with their harsh beliefs, but "Christian" people profess a higher standard, and our own savageries carry the added burden of hypocrisy.

I contained myself and did not loose this outburst on Mr. Tatum, nor did I intend to set it down here, but I feel better for having done so. I reminded Mr. Tatum that my father did know Sun Horse for Years and that Uncle Bat does live with the band, and I assured him there was never the slightest danger. He made me promise not to take Amanda off again without speaking to him first.

The circus tent was erected while we were gone! It is a gay affair, the alternating sections of canvas painted white and red and the whole of it waterproofed with paraffin. Other work was done as well. Several of the circus cabins rest on the ground now, while the wagons are used to help clear the road. More on this as the work progresses.

This afternoon the bulls broke out of their pasture and raced down to pay their respects to the cows; we drove them back quickly enough, but I am afraid there may be one or two early calves next year. Harry and Hutch and Johnny Smoker spent the rest of the afternoon repairing the fence, work they will carry ahead in coming days. It has been too long neglected.

The best news of all is that Alfred Chalmers tells me several of the men among the performers have experience with sporting arms; the Waldheims have hunted at home in Bavaria, and Alfred assures me that we can mount competent hunting parties to do our part. We are going to hunt with the Sun Band! I offered Sun Horse beef and grain and gunpowder, and to put the outcome in a nutshell, he refused the beef but accepted the grain and gunpowder on the condition that we hunt together. I don't have the time now to set forth how we arrived at this plan; I will save that for tomorrow morning when I am a bit more collected. Now I will only say that I am full of hope. We may save a few cows, but the hunt has far greater importance for Sun Horse and his people. With meat and strong horses, they can flee to safety if danger threatens. Julius shares my excitement and tomorrow he will lead the first party of hunters from the settlement. They will meet the Lakotas atop the ridge and set out from there in smaller groups.

Good hunting to us all!

CHAPTER SIX

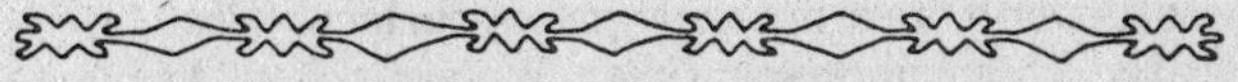

The scout watched the approaching rider for a time to be sure he was white. The scout's name was Speed Stagner and he had been the post guide at Fort Fetterman for several years; he had been detailed to remain behind with Major Coates and the supply train when General Crook and the cavalry left them the previous evening and now he was leading the wagons back to old Fort Reno. Falling snow obscured all detail in the landscape beyond a quarter mile, and he had experienced the eerie feeling of seeing the rider appear out of nothing. There was something sinister about the way someone could approach the small column of wagons and infantry so closely without being seen. In clear weather the rider would have been spotted when he first appeared on the horizon and his coming could have been prepared for. Stagner knew all the scouts on Crook's present expedition and most of the other men who had scouted for the army of the Platte in recent years, but he did not recognize this man. He reined his horse around and rode back toward the wagons at a brisk canter.

Major Coates was the first to spy the returning scout and he raised a hand to halt the column. His own company of Fourth Infantry led the way, followed by the supply wagons; Captain Ferris's company brought up the rear. Without any further sign from Coates, three squads of his company fanned out ahead and to the sides of the column. These were their standing orders, and he knew that other squads were taking positions to guard the column's flanks and rear. The knowledge comforted him but did not entirely quell a feeling of vulnerability. They were a much smaller force since the cavalry had left them.

Coates was from New York. He had fought through the whole of the Civil War, including the Battles of the Wilderness, where Grant's and Lee's armies had stumbled about in dense forests and infantrymen had fared far better than cavalry. He had been on the frontier since '69, but he had never grown used to the exposed feeling that always came over him on the empty intermountain plains.

The encampment on Crazy Woman's Fork had been filled with murmured farewells the evening before as the cavalry made ready to depart, and when the last rider was out of sight the campsite had seemed deserted. Coates had drawn his companies into a tight defensive perimeter with their backs to the stream, using the wagons as barricades, but the night had stayed calm and quiet and the men not on guard had slept peacefully. It was mid-morning now, and they had made six miles back toward Fort Reno when Coates last checked the odometer on the lead wagon.

"One man coming up the road, Major," Stagner said as he joined Coates. "White man. I make him to be a guide. Don't know him, though."

"Not one of ours?"

"I ha'n't set eyes on him, best I can make out."

They were joined by Captain Ferris and Lieutenant Mason and the four men watched together as the rider came into sight at an unhurried trot and drew near. The man raised a hand to the soldiers who covered his approach with rifles at the ready, and rode through their lines.

Hardeman glanced at the length of the column, noting the absence of cavalry. He dismounted when he reached the officers, looking for rank insignia and seeing none. He looked at the man standing slightly in front of the others.

"Are you the officer in command?"

"Major E. M. Coates, Fourth Infantry." Coates took in the man's field boots, and the buckskin beneath his St. Paul coat.

"Christopher Hardeman, Major. I'm a special scout for General Crook, sent on ahead of the expedition. It's urgent that I find the general."

"General Crook is not here."

"I see that, sir." Hardeman heard the wariness in the major's voice and he tried to curb his impatience. He was out of practice at talking to a man who considered himself a scout's superior. "I have a message for the general from Sun Horse, the Sioux peace chief."

"I have not heard your name before in connection with this command, Mr. . . . Hartman, is it?"

"Hardeman, Major. I saw the general in Cheyenne and he sent me to find Sun Horse. If you'll just tell me where you left the general, I'll be on my way."

Coates mulled this over for a time, searching his memory. "Hardeman. Christopher Hardeman. No, the name is unknown to me. At what fort are you employed?"

"I haven't scouted for the army in some years, not since I was at the Washita with General Custer."

Coates's eyebrows raised slightly. "Indeed. Did you know Major Joel Elliott?"

Hardeman nodded. "I led his troop to its attack position."

"But you did not remain with him during the battle?"

"When the battle started I was scouting off beyond the village. Once I got back it was every man for himself." As this Major Coates knew very well. He knew too that scouts were often not expected to take part in the fighting. With army officers the questions were always the same: Did you know Elliott? Could Custer have saved him?

During the battle, Elliott and seventeen men had pursued some escaping Cheyenne out of sight of the village and they had never returned. Custer had made one halfhearted attempt to learn Elliott's whereabouts, sending a scout and a few men to search for him, but that party had been met two miles from the village and driven back by bands of Kiowa and Arapaho coming from the villages downstream to help their Cheyenne friends. More than a week later, Custer had returned to the battleground with Phil Sheridan and only then had the bodies of Elliott and his men been found, all horribly mutilated. Hardeman had not known Elliott well, but he believed him to have been a decent man, and the news of his death had only served to raise Hardeman's suspicions about George A. Custer's trustworthiness as a field commander.

"Why is it you need to find General Crook so urgently, Mr. Hardeman?" Coates wished to know.

"There's a chance to end this war without a fight, Major. But I'll have to find the general as soon as I can."

"Do you believe it should be ended without a fight?"

"If it's possible. Yes, I do." Hardeman met Coates's eyes straight on as he said this. He gathered his reins and made ready to mount. He really didn't need the major's help to find Crook. The wagons would be easy to backtrack even in the storm, and the trail would lead to the place where Crook had parted company with his supply train. What Hardeman really wanted to know from Coates was how long ago that had been. Was it yesterday? The day before? If it was last night or this morning, Crook was less than a day ahead, but each additional day the wagons had been returning south doubled the distance between Hardeman and the cavalry and made overtaking Crook all the more difficult.

The pipe carriers had left the Sun Band's village two days before, not as soon as Hardeman would have liked, but you couldn't hurry the endless palaver in an Indian council lodge. The Sun Band's councillors had taken nearly an entire day to work out all the fine points of the pipe carriers' mission, and then there had been another day and a half of ceremonies to prepare the pipes. Hardeman hadn't been invited to attend the council and Bat Putnam had told him little about it, except to say that some of the talk had to do with whether the pipe carriers should try to find Crook or Sitting Bull first, and that they had settled on Crook. They knew the soldier chief was more likely to agree to leave the country now if Sitting Bull's participation in the peace plan were already assured, but they were even more certain that the Hunkpapa headman would never consent to remain peaceful until summer unless he first received Crook's promise to withdraw from the Powder River country. His young men were hot for war and he could not go against them without a strong hand. So the pipe carriers would find Crook, and if he were sympathetic to Sun Horse's proposal he would remain where he was while the Sun Band's messengers went on to find Sitting Bull and return with his answer. It was a sound plan and it might work, but Hardeman was anxious to overtake the cavalry before they stumbled on some village and started a war that might be prevented.

"I'll have to move along if I want to catch up with the general today," he said now, hoping to elicit some response that would tell him of Crook's whereabouts. He put one foot in the stirrup. One of the other officers opened his mouth to say something, but Major Coates spoke quickly to keep him quiet.

"A moment, Mr. Hardeman. It occurs to me that some might think it peculiar to find a solitary white man roaming free in a countryside crawling with hostiles."

"The country's big enough. A man keeps out of sight if he knows his way."

"But there might be another explanation. If the man were known to the Indians, he would be allowed to come and go as he pleased. Especially if the Indians knew he was friendly to them."

"What are you saying, Major? Speak plain."

"I am saying that a number of renegade whites are known to be living with the Sioux. Some have been observed fighting against our troops."

"You think I'm such a man?"

"Perhaps. Perhaps not. I am simply saying that such a man who fell into my hands would not be likely to reach a post stockade alive. Just so we understand each other, Mr. Hardeman. I would be most unwise to permit such a man to tell the Indians that General Crook has detached his supply train and is moving up-country with only a mounted column."

"And if I'm telling the truth, Major, you would be unwise to keep me here." He dropped his foot back to the ground. The horse was between himself and the cluster of troops who were listening to the conversation from a short distance away, but the outlying squads were behind him.

"Nevertheless, I would prefer we talk a while longer before I make a final decision about what to do with you," Coates said. "Captain Ferris, will you get Mr. Hardeman's weapons and search him for a side arm?"

Hardeman sighed inwardly. He had prepared himself for this eventuality long since. Why was it that soldiers were so bad at hiding their intentions? They were used to facing the enemy in a bunch; they didn't know how to handle a man who might be either friend or foe. Even this major, who probably had years of service on the frontier, was as open as a book. It took living in the mountains, a man on his own, to read such things, but once you knew the signs they were plain enough. Hardeman had guessed what Coates would do even before the major himself was settled on his course, and as Coates spoke, Hardeman was moving. He dropped the reins and his pistol appeared in his hand as he covered the three steps to the side of the nearest officer. He placed the gun in the man's side. "What's your name?" he demanded.

"Mason, Mr. Hardeman. Lieutenant Mason."

Good man; not too nervous. Forty years old if he was a day, and still a lieutenant. Well, that wasn't so unusual. The man Coates had addressed as Captain Ferris was only now opening his holster, too late.

"Mr. Mason and I will be leaving together, Major," Hardeman said. "I'll turn him loose half a mile from the road. You just hold your water a bit and you'll have him back."

"You men! Cover this man!" Captain Ferris barked. He drew his Remington Army .44 and aimed it uncertainly in Hardeman's direction, but Coates put out a restraining hand.

"Easy, Captain. It seems we have a stalemate, Mr. Hardeman." Several soldiers on both sides of Hardeman had him covered.

"I don't think so, Major. You might get me, but you'll lose Lieutenant Mason here, and I don't think you'll risk that. I'm sorry I don't have more time for talk, but you just say my name to the general when you see him and he'll set you straight. We'll be getting along now, Lieutenant." He reached out to recover his horse's reins and prodded Mason with the pistol to start him moving. It wouldn't do to give anyone much time to think.

"Hardeman! Wait now, just a moment." Coates held out a hand as if to pull Hardeman back, but the scout kept going. "Look here, if I am wrong, I apologize. Surely you can understand my concern." He hoped to detain Hardeman with conversation while he tried to decide what to do.

"I understand, Major, but I have concerns of my own, and staying here half the day to satisfy you isn't one of them." The two men continued on, through the scattering of pickets surrounding the column, Mason in the lead with Hardeman close behind him and the horse coming last to shield them.

Coates raised a reluctant hand to indicate that the scout and his hostage should be allowed to pass unhindered.

"Major, you can't let him leave!" Ferris brandished his pistol again but Coates forced his arm down. "He'll kill Mason himself if he's a renegade!" Ferris protested.

"Then his death will be on Mr. Hardeman's hands." Coates raised his voice so Hardeman would be sure to hear.

Hardeman and Mason walked steadily away from the supply column until it disappeared behind them. Hardeman kept up the pace for perhaps another five minutes and then brought his hostage to a halt.

"Sorry to inconvenience you, Lieutenant." He took Mason's pistol from its holster and removed the percussion caps from their nipples. The gun was a Remington, like Ferris's. Apparently the infantry had a low priority for the new metal-cartridge Colts. Hardeman had bought his own three years ago when they first appeared. The cavalry would certainly have the Colts by now. He threw the caps into the snow, which was deepening among the sparse stubble of the prairie grass. Until this storm, the ground here had been almost bare.

"Can you find your way back to the wagons?"

"Yes, sir," Mason replied. "I'll just follow our tracks."

Hardeman mounted his horse.

"Excuse me, Mr. Hardeman. Was that the truth about a chance to stop the war without a fight?"

"I hope so."

"You may not believe this, but I wish you luck."

Hardeman raised a hand in thanks and started off, but he reined in almost at once and called back to Mason. "It will help me if I know where you left General Crook."

"I'm sorry; I shouldn't tell you that. In case I am wrong about you."

Hardeman nodded and kicked his horse into a canter. He had led Mason straight away from the wagon road, due west, and he continued in that direction now. When he looked back a few moments later, Mason was barely visible, already walking back toward the wagons. Once the dim figure was gone from sight, Hardeman reined to the right, turning north to circle around and regain the road a mile or two beyond, where Bat and the others would be waiting for him. Despite his impatience he allowed the horse to slow to a trot. There was no sense wearing out the roan now; he might have a long journey ahead of him. Since leaving the Sun Band's village two days ago, the pipe carriers had not made good time, and they had lost more ground by coming out onto the plain to the Bozeman road only to find that Crook had already come and gone.

Hardeman's horse and Bat Putnam's could have made twice the distance they were covering each day; the bay mare had eaten grain all winter in Putnam's Park and Hardeman's roan had been similarly pampered for four days, and more grain had been in their saddlebags when they left the settlement, forced on them by Lisa as a parting gift. But the Indian horses were weak, although the pipe carriers had been given the strongest mounts in the Sun Band's herd. The grain was gone now, the last of it doled out this morning to the Indian ponies to fortify them for a long day's ride over barren lands with little or no natural forage and no time to stop for browsing what there was. From now on all of the pipe carriers' horses would have to live off the land.

"We might ought t' ride all night, if Three Stars's got more'n a day start on us," Bat said once Hardeman had found the little band and told them that he had learned nothing, save that Crook and his cavalry had left the supply train behind and could move across the country now as fast as an Indian war party. In recent moments the wind had strengthened. Bat peered into the storm from within the heavy blanket hood of his Hudson's Bay capote. He wore a trade blanket outside the capote, belted at the waist. The Indians too wore their robes and blankets belted against the cold, and fur coverings on their heads, from which the feet and heads of the former owners dangled. Standing Eagle's winter cape of grizzly-bear fur was pulled up high and held in place at the neck by a rawhide thong, permitting it to serve as both cap and cloak. All the men but Hardeman wore winter moccasins made of buffalo hide, laced to the knee.

"Horses ain't up to night ridin'," Standing Eagle said. He looked about at the sky, which told him nothing. "We best make tracks while we can." He led off with Little Hand beside him. Standing Eagle was the leader of the group because he was war leader of the Sun Band, although he carried no weapons now. The bearer of a peace pipe could not touch a weapon until the pipe was accepted by the one for whom it was intended, and Standing Eagle carried the pipe for General Crook. Nor was Little Hand armed, for he was related in a roundabout manner to Sitting Bull and carried the pipe for the Hunkpapa holy man.

The others moved off behind the leaders. They were six in all and they rode two by two here on the wagon road. Blackbird followed close behind Standing Eagle; beside him rode his *hunká*-father, Hawk Chaser, a middle-aged warrior whose hair was just beginning to gray. Hawk Chaser's exploits in battle were unequaled in the Sun Band. His eyes, set on either side of a nose as straight and sharp as an arrowhead, were constantly on the move, taking in everything. It was Hawk Chaser who had seen the army scout before the whiteman could spy the pipe carriers. He smiled now as Blackbird fell in beside him. The bond between the warrior and his son-by-choice was strong. The boy was silent most of the time but his eyes shone with pride at having been picked to go along. It was Hawk Chaser who had put forth his name, and Sun Horse had agreed. Blackbird was the moccasin carrier; to him fell the responsibility for looking after the bundles of spare moccasins and winter garments for the men, holding their horses when they stopped, caring for the single pack horse, gathering firewood and making the sleeping shelter for the night, and more. It was an important position, and a large step toward manhood for a boy who did his duty without unnecessary talk and performed bravely if the opportunity arose.

Hardeman and Bat brought up the rear, willing to let the Indians lead the way. A man found his natural companions on the trail, Hardeman had learned in his years as a scout. The man you were comfortable riding next to all day usually proved to be the man you could count on in a fight, or when the trail grew difficult. At the Sun Band's village Hardeman had slept in Bat's lodge, and he felt a growing liking for this mountain man who had lived so long with the Sioux. The old man's humor masked a sharp mind; the jokes and mountain tales were the means by which that mind stayed limber and showed its enjoyment of life, but the jokes and tales had been few since they had been on the trail. *You are quiet today*, Bat had signed to Hardeman the day before. Hardeman had merely nodded in reply, causing Bat to break his silence. "Good thing to keep shut on the trail. I'm becoming a gabby cuss in my old age," he had said, after which he was quiet again.

In other circumstances they could have been friends. But friends told one another something of what they guarded in the secret places of the mind, or at least they revealed such things in time even if they said nothing in words, and it seemed to Hardeman, judging by the cautious way he and Bat talked on the rare occasions when the silence of their journey was broken, that both of them were keeping back things they could not reveal, at least not until the pipe was delivered to General Crook and the outcome of Sun Horse's proposal was known.

But even at the start, Bat had been allied with Hardeman against Standing Eagle. What with the delay in getting off, Hardeman had argued for striking north as fast as they could travel once they reached the foothills, and sending just one man out to look for wagon tracks on the Bozeman road. Bat had supported Hardeman, seeing that as the best way to overtake Crook if he had already passed by or to head him off if he had not yet come this far. But Standing Eagle had said that the bluecoats always moved slowly, especially with wagons; the pipe carriers would go east to the wagon road, he insisted, and if they found no tracks there, as seemed likely, they would turn south to await Three Stars at Fort Reno and the Powder River Crossing. The war leader had shown no remorse when he learned that he had underestimated the white soldier chief. He had merely grunted and turned north, following the tracks until the army scout was seen and Hardeman rode forward alone.

Now the six horsemen pressed forward into the strengthening storm and for the rest of the afternoon they had no rest and no food except a few pieces of jerky from the bundles each man packed behind his saddle. As the light dimmed, giving the first indication of approaching night, they arrived at Crazy Woman's Fork and discovered the soldiers' campground. A short examination revealed that the wagon tracks went no farther.

"The cavalry left here before today," Hardeman said, looking at the faint tracks. "Yesterday, maybe. Can't be sure." Three inches of new snow covered the tracks.

Standing Eagle broke a stout branch from a clump of willows and dug in the remains of one of the campfires. When he had excavated a few inches into the ground beneath the ashes he felt the earth with his bare hand and then spoke in Lakota to Little Hand and Hawk Chaser, gesturing about the campsite.

"He says the wagons left here this morning," Bat translated for Hardeman. "He don't know how long they were here. Might be one day, might be more." Bat had examined the campsite for himself, as each of the others had done while Blackbird held the horses. Now the mountain man walked away from the frozen stream to one of the fire pits farthest from the bank, and he brushed the ashes aside to feel the ground. "These fires here are a mite older," he observed. "Ground's plumb frozen. Let's say the pony soldiers left yestiddy and the wagons stayed the night. That puts the cavalry a day ahead of us."

"Or more," Hardeman added.

Bat nodded, looking in the direction the cavalry had taken.

Standing Eagle had been talking with Little Hand and now he switched to trapper's English in midstream. "Ain't much light left. We'll cache here for the night. This child's got a powerful hunger." He pointed to the grass that grew thick beyond the campsite. "Pony sojers kept their horses in close." He grinned. "Must be 'feared o' wild Injuns. Our critters'll eat good tonight."

Hardeman looked at the gloomy sky. "There's an hour of light, maybe more. We might go on a way."

Bat shook his head. "Eagle's right. We best stay put. The country up yonder's rough goin'. No forage and less water. 'Sides," he added, giving Hardeman a wink, "old

Eagle feels his belly rappin' on his backbone, he cain't think of nothin' else. 'Bout as much use as powder with no flint till he gets hisself fed.'' He gave Standing Eagle a hard look then. ''Come first light, we'll move along right smart.''

Standing Eagle's expression revealed nothing as he led his horse away to look for the best grass. Blackbird was already gathering firewood without a word said.

Hardeman too led his own horse away, apparently willing to accept Bat's judgment in the matter. Bat rummaged in his saddlebags for his hobbles. He would picket his mare on a long tether of braided rawhide so she could eat well. A horse was like a tipi, with a hide covering and a fire inside; if you wanted to keep her warm in winter, you had to build a bigger fire. Grass was the fuel, and here on the banks of the Crazy Woman it stood thick and tall above the thin layer of snow.

As he went about the tasks of seeing to his horse and making camp, Bat mulled over a growing certainty that Standing Eagle was dragging his feet every chance he got. First that notion to go east to the Bozeman road, now the solicitous care he lavished on the horses every step of the way. That his brother-in-law was right about the horses' need to eat didn't lessen Bat's suspicions. Eagle was an admirer of good horseflesh, but he would push a pony until it dropped if he had a good enough reason for covering ground. He's holding back, Bat thought. Wants Crook to find a village and set the badger loose. Standing Eagle was as inflexible as a dried beaver hide when it came to seeking any accommodation with the whites and he would rather die than surrender. He had said so in the council.

The Sun Band's councillors had agreed quickly enough to Sun Horse's plan, and then the talk had turned to what would be done if Three Stars would not accept the pipe. Most of the men reaffirmed their earlier decision to go to the Dakota agencies rather than fight. They would permit Crook to escort the band if he still offered that choice, or they would go as best they could if left to their own devices.

"I will not go to that place!" Standing Eagle had interrupted, nearly shouting, and his bad manners had not set well with the councillors, but he had bulled ahead. "I will go to my cousin Sitting Bull and I will fight the *washíchun* by his side! I have seen the agencies. The people there fight among themselves and wait outside the agent's lodge for food like soldier mules sniffing for a few grains of corn! They are no longer Lakota! A Lakota fights for what is his and he lets no man tell him where to go or where to stop!"

"The war leader forgets his first duty!" Walks Bent Over had said with some heat. "Think of the helpless ones!" It was an unprecedented rebuke from the misshapen, thoughtful man who was the head scout of the band. The first duty of a war leader was to protect the helpless ones, the women and children and the elderly, and it had seemed to Bat, as it must have seemed to Walks Bent Over, that Standing Eagle was thinking only of the glory of war and his own honors, but the war leader had defended himself with impassioned eloquence.

"I do think of them!" he had thrown back at his accuser. "They are helpless in war but I am not!" He had brought himself under control then, and as he continued he had looked around the council, demanding with his eyes that his listeners hear the truth of what he said. "If we go to the agencies and place ourselves in the hands of the whites, we will all be helpless. Last year in the cold moons hunting was bad, as it is now, but life was bad at the agencies too. You have heard the tales told by our relatives there. There was not enough food, and only one blanket for three Lakota. Only the robes brought in from the hunting bands saved many from freezing. Tell me, my friends, if all the hunting bands surrender, who then will see to the good of the people? The *washíchun?* Will you place your trust in the *washíchun?* I will not. I will fight now, for the helpless ones, for as long as I have the strength. I will die before I will surrender!"

His reasoning had swayed some of the councillors but even so they had held to their decision to send the pipes.

Sun Horse had recommended a course of action and it must be given a chance. There was time enough to think and talk about what to do later.

Standing Eagle had come close to refusing the pipe for Three Stars, but when he saw that he stood alone he had offered his participation in the venture as a conciliating gesture. "It is right that the people should decide these things. All the people, gathered together. If Three Stars will receive the pipe my father sends, there will be peace until the hoop of the nation is raised in the Moon of Fat Calves. Then the Lakota nation will decide on peace or war. My father will speak for peace and I will listen. But I will speak for war."

He had said this calmly and with the dignity a man was expected to show in council, and there had been a few soft *hau*'s of approval for the way he spoke his change of heart. But Bat knew his wife's brother better than most. Standing Eagle might have swallowed his pride, but he hadn't swallowed it whole. He would carry out the wishes of the council, but if Three Stars should happen to stay out ahead of the pipe carriers and find some small village in the Tongue River bottom before they caught him, that was out of the war leader's hands.

Bat watched Standing Eagle now as the man tethered his horse. He had chosen his best hunter for the journey and the animal hardly seemed tired at all after what had been a pretty good day's ride. The other horses too were growing accustomed to the trail. A horse could be a contrary animal sometimes; you let him run free all winter without asking too much of him, and he wasn't in a hurry to submit to saddle and rein, but if you kept after him for a few days and made him mind his manners, pretty soon he'd put his whole heart into whatever you asked of him. Standing Eagle was right about one thing: the horses would eat well tonight. Come morning they might not be up to grain-fed mounts, but they'd be fit to travel and Standing Eagle would have one less reason to go slow.

The wind was stiffening and night was coming on fast. The men helped Blackbird build the sleeping shelter and in no time it was done. The night before, they had slept wrapped in their blankets under a bright gibbous moon, but tonight a shelter was needed. It was much the same as a small sweat lodge; willow poles were bent over and lashed together to form a low oval frame, then blankets and robes were spread over it and tied down for a covering, leaving a small smoke hole. A man had to get on his knees to enter and it was impossible to sit fully upright, but the fire was quickly started with one of Hardeman's sulphur matches and in no time the shelter was warm. He had brought the matches out the first night on the trail, when he saw Little Hand begin the slow process of striking flint and steel into a small handful of tinder. None of the Lakota had objected to using the white man's way of making fire.

"Snug as a trader in his lodge," Bat said now, wiping at his watering eyes. There were no flaps to control the venting and when the wind gusted it was smoky inside the shelter, but it was a comforting place for a cold night.

The men chewed slowly on pieces of jerky as they watched Blackbird break small pieces of the trail food the Lakota called *wasná* into a horn bowl filled with water. As moccasin carrier, it was the boy's job to do the cooking. He dropped small hot stones from the fire pit into the bowl and the water began to warm. The cavalry had chopped through the foot-thick ice on the stream to get water for their horses and the thin new ice on the holes had been easy to break. Blackbird added a handful of dried wild onions to the water, then shredded bits of jerky and more *wasná*. Pemmican, the whites called it, using a word from an eastern tribe. It was made from dried meat, usually buffalo, pounded together with dried chokecherries or serviceberries and mixed with tallow. The mixture was sealed in lengths of intestine, with more tallow poured over it to keep out the air, and was carried on hunting and war parties as well as when the village itself was on the move. A man could live indefinitely on *wasná* and the pipe carriers had been given a supply sufficient to last them until the next moon grew horns and lingered in the western sky after the sun had set.

Blackbird removed cool stones and added hot ones and the water began to steam. He patiently stirred the mixture with a wooden spoon and when he judged it ready the bowl was passed from man to man until the weak stew was all gone and the bowl wiped clean with fingers, leaving no scrap behind.

In what seemed like no time at all, Standing Eagle and Little Hand were in their blankets and fast asleep, feet to the fire. Standing Eagle's slumber was marked by a rhythmic snoring. Hawk Chaser took out a pipe and smoked it, speaking low to Blackbird, who never lay down until the last of the men was asleep. The warrior told tales of other journeys he had been on as boy and man, and Blackbird listened with rapt attention, his eyes bright with excitement. It seemed to him that each breath he took was charged with the power of manhood.

Bat followed Hawk Chaser's example and took out his own pipe for casual smoking, a Missouri corncob he had bought the summer before from a trader who had defied the ban on trading in the Powder River country. The man had brought gunpowder too. Bat stoked the pipe with a generous pinch of Lakota smoking mixture and lit it, smoking just one pinch at a time in the Lakota manner. Outside the shelter the storm blew, buffeting the thin covering.

"Well, you reckon we'll get Crook to swallow the bargain?" Bat's question took Hardeman unaware.

"The bargain?"

"Let the Sun Band be now, in exchange for Sun Horse talking to the other chiefs come summer?"

"I don't know. Washington wants it settled now," Hardeman said. The government's impatience might be cooled for a while if Crook would plead Sun Horse's cause, but at best the hope was precarious. Back in the Sun Band's village, Hardeman had talked to Sun Horse before the council, with Bat translating, trying one last time to make the headman say yes or no and settle it all now, but Sun Horse had merely smiled and shaken his head.

"I have heard what Three Stars wishes," the old chief had said. "Now he will hear what I wish for my people and all the Lakota. Often men must talk for a time before they can agree, and when Lakota talks with *washíchun*, they must talk for a long time."

"I can bring Three Stars here," Hardeman had offered, taking an enormous risk by planting that possibility in Sun Horse's mind. "You can speak with him yourself. If you believe he's a truthful man, take your people to the reservation. Then you can ride to speak to the hostiles when the grass is up."

But Sun Horse had shaken his head again. "It is not good to travel in the Snowblind Moon. Tell Three Stars that if my cousin Sitting Bull agrees, the Lakota will remain at peace until the grass is green and then we will meet to talk. Say that to Three Stars, and give him the pipe so he will know the words are true."

Sun Horse had been subdued, as if he himself might have doubts about the plan's chance for success, and strangely, he had been in no great hurry to send the pipe carriers on their way. Even Bat had commented that the headman seemed to be stalling for time. "Been time enough to prepare a dozen pipes," the mountain man grumped on Hardeman's second evening in Bat and Penelope's lodge. But then the next day there had come the news of the avalanche, and the change in Sun Horse had been remarkable to see. He looked as if someone had just handed him title to the whole of the Powder River country, signed by President Grant himself, and then he had produced the pipes at last and given leave for the emissaries to go, sending them on their way with a hail and farewell after a series of trivial delays had kept them in the village for another half day when they should already have been off and gone.

Recalling the scene now made Hardeman uneasy. The old man had stood there in his ratty robe, waving goodbye in evident high spirits, and somehow Hardeman had been left with the feeling that Sun Horse was one up on him. Since then he had found no way to explain the headman's singular changes of mood, but neither had he found any room for deception in the pipe carriers' mission. Besides, Sun Horse was Johnny's grandfather; it was unlikely that he would betray the boy's trust. What was more, he was a peace man with a vision of bringing an end to the conflict with the whites, and Hardeman had come to feel a commonness of purpose with the old man. *My friend has agreed to help us,* Sun Horse had told Johnny. *Together the whiteman and the Lakota will make peace.* The words had reminded Hardeman that his own efforts to make peace over the years had all come about because Jed Putnam had taught him long ago that it was possible to be friends with the Indians, even while both red man and white kept to his own nature and his own ways. If he and Sun Horse could act in good faith, like true friends, they might just pull it off.

"Them politicians are in an all-fired hurry to get this thing settled," Bat said now, setting another pinch of smoke in his pipe. He said the word "politicians" like a curse. "They done got it settled already, three times. I went with Sun Horse in '68, down at Laramie. Him and a hundred more made their marks on the paper that give 'em this country here forever."

"The government needs gold," Hardeman replied. "Needs gold and wants land."

"Hell, the Injuns don't want the gold. Let the politicians have the gold." Bat spat into the fire as if to rid his mouth of the distasteful word. "I'll tell you what, gold's one o' the things got the Injuns plumb convinced that we're all as crazy as a bunch o' loons. That first blackrobe in the country here, the one called De Smet? Wasn't half crazy, him. He told all the Injuns he preached at never to let on to a white man that they knew where there was a drop of gold. Forget you seen it, he says, it makes white men crazy." He lit the pipe with a glowing stick and puffed twice. "Let 'em have the gold. What these boys want is the *Paha Sapa*. The Black Hills is the spirit center of the nation. That's the place the souls of the young men fly with the eagles." He looked at Hardeman. "I made the vision quest myself. When I was forty-five years old. Don't imagine you can know what that's like."

Hardeman shook his head.

"Big medicine. Heap big. White man laughs at the red man's medicine and calls him a superstitious heathen. Might as well laugh at a tree. It's something that exists. Stands right there as tall as a mountain, real as a rock, and they laugh at it. It don't pay to mess with Lakota medicine." Again he stoked his pipe and relit it, and Hardeman waited, sensing that the mountain man was working up to something.

"Sun Horse, he figgers there's medicine in Johnny Smoker," Bat continued once the pipe was going. "They call him Stands Between the Worlds, but that ain't all. He's got a heap o' names. The Boy with Many Names, they say. Buffalo Dreamer's one o' them." He watched Hardeman closely and saw no reaction. "Seems like you might not know that part of it. The boy dreamed of White Buffalo Cow Woman. *Ptésanwin,* we call her." He said the name with an unmistakable reverence. "It ain't every boy dreams of *Ptésanwin.*"

Hardeman had heard of the White Buffalo Cow Woman. Legend said that she had brought the sacred pipe to the Sioux and instructed them in its use, and to this day a white buffalo was among the most sacred of animals to the tribe. But Johnny had never mentioned *Ptésanwin*.

" 'Course that don't mean nothin' now, seein' as the boy picked the white man's trail. That like to took the stuffin' out o' Sun Horse." Bat was staring into the fire, but now he turned again to Hardeman and fixed the scout with his gaze. "See, Sun Horse figgered if'n the boy picked the Injun life, he'd come back to the Lakotas, his pa's folks, not the Cheyenne. *Ptésanwin*, she belongs to the Lakota myths." He used his pipe to make a sign close to his head, indicating matters of the spirit world. "She brought the ceremonies and the ceremonies are the life of the people. They're the heart of the Lakota way, you might say. A buffalo dreamer comin' to the Sun Band would bring life to the people; might even bring the power to save them in troubled times." Bat sucked hard on the pipe, but it was out. He took it from his mouth and held it in both hands, his eyes still on Hardeman. "Young Johnny don't know none o' this. Sun Horse never told him. Reckoned the boy oughta make his choice free and clear, for his own reasons."

The mountain man fell silent. With slow care he scraped the bowl of the pipe clean and dropped the ashes into the fire before returning the pipe to the elkskin sack he had carried slung from his shoulder since leaving the village. A "possibles sack" the fur trappers had called it, and most had carried one. They kept therein their smallest and most essential belongings.

"Big medicine in dreams," Bat said. "Reckon I'll catch me some. We can use all the medicine we got."

He curled in his robe like a bear settling in for the winter, and pulled it over his face. In a short time his breathing slowed and fell into rhythm with the other sleepers.

Hardeman lay back on his bedroll and stretched out, listening to the wind and Standing Eagle's soft snoring, remembering other nights on the trail. The shelter reminded him a good deal of the Cheyenne hunting shelters Johnny had often built for the two of them when they traveled in bad weather; this one was not much bigger, although it held six.

He thought of Sun Horse then, and he realized that he owed him a great debt of gratitude. No wonder it had been a blow to the old man when Johnny told him he had picked the white world! It meant the loss of any spirit power the boy might have brought to the Sun Band. And yet when the boy had the dream, Sun Horse had kept the full import from him, leaving Johnny free to choose. Hardeman wondered if he himself could have kept from trying to influence the boy's decision if he believed the survival of his people might depend on it.

In the end, Johnny had picked the white world and that was that. Back in Putnam's Park on the day they had parted, Johnny had sat astride his horse next to Alfred Chalmers' wagon and Amanda Spencer was there on the driver's seat next to the Englishman, smiling down at

Johnny. Johnny had returned her smile before leaning down to shake Chris's hand and wish him good luck, and there had been something in Johnny's expression that Hardeman hadn't seen before, as if the youth had lately discovered one of life's great secrets, the kind that seemed so obvious once you got hold of it, and you felt like a blind man for not seeing it sooner. He was set on his path, and neither his Cheyenne childhood nor Sun Horse's failed hopes for the boy and his dream would affect the outcome now.

Hardeman removed his buckskin coat and spread it over the blankets and the oilskin before crawling into the bedroll. What mattered now was to get on and find Crook, and see if he would risk as much as Sun Horse to make a lasting peace.

Hardeman lay back with his head on his hands. The cavalry was pushing northward, leaving the Sun Band's village farther behind each day, and he was secretly glad. There could be no thought any longer of leading Crook to Sun Horse. Even if the pipe carriers overtook the expedition tomorrow, Crook would not want to turn back and retrace his steps, not while there were other troops in the field and a hostile village perhaps around the next bend in the river. If he would not accept the pipe . . . Hardeman would cross that bridge when he came to it. But from now on he would sleep easier knowing that the Sun Band, and the people in Putnam's Park, were out of immediate danger.

Hawk Chaser and Blackbird were readying themselves for sleep. As Hawk Chaser wrapped himself in his robe, he cast a glance at Hardeman and it struck the scout that there had been more than a few times in the past two days when he had caught the warrior keeping an eye on him, but there was nothing so unusual in that. In a small group traveling together each man liked to know what the others were doing, especially when one was a stranger. Hardeman gave it no more thought and dropped quickly into a sound slumber.

* * *

In the morning the pipe carriers were on their way as soon as the light permitted, moving once more into the face of the storm. Throughout the day the trail left by the cavalry grew fainter as the snow filled in the tracks. When nightfall forced the men to camp once more, in a shallow ravine with no water near, they had not found the soldiers' next stopping place.

CHAPTER SEVEN

"Jesus H. Christ and twenty-three names of Lucifer! Will yez look at my bleeding bacon! It's frozen harder than a corporal's heart!"

Boots Corwin was wakened by the cursing of the cook. Huddled deep within his robes with even his face covered, he was almost warm enough. He lifted the corner of the robe and sniffed the air. No hint of breakfast greeted him but a gust of snow blew in his face. He dropped the robe and settled back in his lair. Whether or not the command moved today, there would be no orders before breakfast.

They were only five miles from where they had first made camp the day before, after the exhilarating thirty-mile night march. The going had become dangerous at times as the trail wound around steep rock faces where a bad fall awaited any misstep, but no obstacle had seemed to daunt men or beasts and the brilliant moonlight had guided all hands to safety. At five o'clock in the morning of the eighth of March the command had made camp on the Clear Fork of the Powder and had turned into their robes for some much needed rest. Three hours later they woke to find that the clear skies had vanished behind new onslaughts of clouds, and snow was falling again harder than ever, propelled by renewed winds from the north. With black looks at the sky and much cursing, the column had been formed and put under way, but just five miles down the broad valley they had come on this sheltered cove and here they had passed the rest of the day. The men had improvised added protection from the weather as best they could, making crude lean-tos from the abundant willow and cottonwood brush, and they had sought what humor there was to be found in their own discomfort.

Corwin had seen General Crook walking through the encampment more than once and he had noted the concern on the commander's face. The reason was not hard to imagine. The men were just over a week away from Fetterman, scarcely three days from the supply wagons. The campaign was still high adventure. Neither the real danger nor the real fatigue had yet been felt. How would the men hold up?

As evening fell, the storm had not slackened, although the temperature dropped sharply, approaching zero on Dr. Munn's thermometer. A blanket was ordered to be placed on each of the horses, and the men had slept stacked like cordwood, sharing every scrap of available covering.

Corwin raised the corner of his robe again. "Mr. Whitcomb!" he called out.

"Yes, Major?" came an immediate reply from close at hand. The voice had the habitual tone of good spirits Corwin had come to expect from his second lieutenant. The boy rebounded quickly from any disappointment.

Corwin threw the robe off his head and shoulders and squinted against the driving snow. Whitcomb stood a few yards away, cloaked in fur hat and buffalo coat and bulky overboots. He looked entirely comfortable. Beyond the young officer the cook continued to swear inventively as he tried to cut up the frozen bacon with a hand axe. By now the cooks had learned that if they did not want to be hindered in their endeavors by men clustering around the cookfires, they must provide some alternative source of warmth. Some had adopted the practice of building large bonfires for the men, and such a blaze was burning now in Company E's bivouac, but even so, nearly half the troop was gathered around the cook, offering words of advice and encouragement.

"The God damn bacon! Will yez look at that? The God damn bacon broke my axe!" The angry cook pointed to a fresh chip in the blade.

"It ain't the bacon's fault, cookie," said Sergeant Rossi. "The cold makes the steel brittle, see? You could chip it on the ice, even on a log." Rossi spoke American like a native New Yorker. He had been born in Italy but brought to the New World as an infant. He knew more about everything than the next man and had a cheerful way of telling him so.

"All I know is the God damn bacon broke my axe. Give me some room to work here, boys." The cook turned to his small fire and tried to encourage it to more vigorous life. He propped the slab of bacon close to the flames and set the axe beside it.

"Are there any orders yet, Mr. Whitcomb?" Corwin pushed the robe aside and rose to a sitting position. Except for his overcoat, which he had removed and placed atop himself beneath his robe, he had slept fully clothed.

"Nothing yet, sir. It doesn't seem to be snowing quite so hard today."

Corwin looked about at the snow, which flew nearly horizontally across the stream and swirled thickly in the recesses of the cove. It seemed to him that Boreas had returned with new vitality, but he said nothing.

Around him the camp was fully awake, although the light was still dim. As usual, he was among the last up. It was a bad example for the men, but he hated getting up in the morning when he hadn't slept well. It was the one failing as a commander that he recognized in himself, but fifteen years of army life hadn't changed his habits.

Sergeant Rossi suddenly left the group at the cookfire and walked quickly toward Corwin, looking over his shoulder. "Sir, Dr. Munn is making his morning rounds and General Crook is with him."

"Thanks, Rossi." Corwin arose quickly and was folding his robe into a tight roll when the surgeon reached E Troop's bivouac. In addition to Crook, he was accompanied by Lieutenant Bourke and the correspondent Strahorn. Corwin greeted them.

"Good morning, General. Dr. Munn. Mr. Bourke." There were nods and perfunctory salutes all around. Each man's gestures were reduced by the cold to the minimum necessary motions.

"No frostbite, I trust, Lieutenant?" Munn inquired of Corwin. "Everyone can feel his toes this morning?" The surgeon had become more visible each day as the weather turned colder and more severe, keeping watch for frostbite and pneumonitic ailments.

Corwin hesitated. He should already have made his own morning rounds, looking for the telltale white spots on noses or ears or fingers. He didn't want to be caught in an incorrect report.

"Sir, I have inspected the troop on Major Corwin's orders. There is no sign of frostbite." Whitcomb gave this intelligence looking straight ahead, standing nearly at attention in the expedition commander's presence, although Crook did not require such formalities on campaign.

"Excellent," said Munn.

Corwin had given no such orders, but if his subaltern had the initiative to perform routine chores without instruction, he would not protest.

"You certainly have the weather you wanted, General," Strahorn observed. He swung his arms in circles to warm himself, looking somewhat like an ungainly bird attempting flight.

"I think the general might have settled for a less severe blizzard than this one, Mr. Strahorn," said Bourke with a wink at Whitcomb.

"Oh, this will serve nicely, Mr. Bourke," said Crook.

His beard twitched as he repressed a smile. Since the moment of his arrival he had occupied himself in looking about the campsite, where at last the smell of bacon was beginning to make itself known. The men watched the cook like a pack of hungry coyotes. Icicles hung from mustaches and beards and droplets of ice had formed even on their eyebrows. Collars grew misted with rime as breath froze to the fur. But if they were well fed and kept in tight discipline they would do well enough, Corwin thought. He no longer grew nervous when General Crook took an occasion to inspect E Company. Crook observed everything and he forgot nothing, but he rarely meddled in the responsibilities of his subordinates and never reprimanded his officers in the presence of others except under extreme provocation.

"I don't believe the men will benefit from another day of idleness, Major," Crook said to Corwin. "We will take advantage of the weather to move along under its protection once the men have eaten."

"Yes, sir. As you see, General, there is some delay here. It seems the bacon was frozen too hard to cut."

"All the cooks are having the same problem," Surgeon Munn put in. "Warn the men that forks and spoons should be run through hot water or ashes before using them, or the flesh will freeze to the metal."

"The same precaution applies to the horses' bits; they must be warmed before bridling," Crook added, with a farewell wave of his hand.

With the bacon finally thawed and the men fed, the command formed up and started off, turning west from the Clear Fork and ascending Piney Creek, a small tributary.

"What is the hour, Mr. Reb?" Corwin inquired once they were under way. His horse was tossing its head and prancing a little, urging a faster pace, but Corwin held him in.

With a motion that had become almost second nature by now, Whitcomb ungloved his right hand and reached through the opening of his buffalo greatcoat and then the hip-length coat of Minnesota blanket beneath and brought forth his pocket watch. The case was gold and the inside of the cover bore a miniature portrait of the family mansion in Virginia. By a miracle, both the watch and the ancestral home had survived the war.

"A quarter to seven, sir." He snapped the cover closed and replaced the watch in its interior pocket, surprised at the early hour. All his instincts told him that they were traveling a far northern country in the dead of winter, but the equinox was less than two weeks away and the days were steadily lengthening.

Before long the column left the small watercourse and entered broken country that rapidly grew rougher as it ascended the southern slopes of the next divide. The ground was covered with six inches or more of new snow and on the lee side of the ridges it was drifted as deep as a horse's belly. Once atop the divide the column made its way across an enormous plateau, moving northeast toward the valley of the Tongue River. Ravines cut the trail every hundred yards or so, and the difficulties encountered in descending and ascending the steep and slippery banks of these obstacles slowed the command's advance to the pace of a slow walk. As each troop and each division of pack mules reached the edge of a ravine, that entire section of the column would halt while the horses or mules crossed one by one until they were reassembled on the other side. E Troop was once more serving as rear guard and its progress was painfully slow as the head of the column stretched out farther and farther ahead of it.

At mid-morning, while the troop was halted waiting for the last division of pack mules to cross a particularly deep ravine, word was passed back along the column instructing each company commander to bring his flankers in to a distance of fifty yards. The scouts had found buffalo droppings and recent Indian sign.

"Sergeant Polachek!" Corwin called out above the sound of the wind and the braying of the mules nearby, "you bring in the squads to the east; I'll take the west side! Mr. Reb, you see to crossing the troop. And keep the line closed up as best you can."

"Yes, sir." Whitcomb's disappointment at being passed over yet again for the more hazardous duty was only somewhat mollified by the knowledge that crossing the ravine posed a certain degree of danger to horse and rider and the responsibility for getting the troop safely across now rested with him. The ravine was made by runoff at the edge of the plateau and one mule had already been killed that morning when it panicked at the bottom of a ravine and bolted down the gully and over a cliff.

"A'right now, thet's his turn, y' blackguard!" There was a sudden commotion among the mule packers at the edge of the chasm, and a shifting away from three of the men, two of them holding a single mule and glaring at a lone packer who held another of the beasts. The mules had their ears laid back and they were shifting about nervously.

"That's 'ank 'ewitt, sir," said Corporal Atherton, the only non-commissioned officer remaining at the head of the troop. He was a stocky Englishman with bad teeth. "The man with 'im is Yank Bartlett. ''ank 'n' Yank,' they call 'em. They're like two peas in a pod, always together. The other man is called Chileno John. Watch his left 'and, on the knife."

"*Lo siento mucho, viejo cabrón,*" the Spanish American said with elaborate hostility, one hand grasping the haft of his large skinning knife. For the moment, the blade remained in its scabbard at his belt. "*Tu te equivocas, sin duda a causa de tu edad avanzada*. It is my turn!"

"Call me an old goat, y' Papist beaner? Why, I'll slit yer from gut t' gullet soon 's look at yer!"

"Try it, *gringo!*"

The packers, all of whom had served with General Crook in Arizona before being brought north at his insistence for the present campaign, were a disparate lot, the two largest contingents being Yankee forty-niners who had learned their trade by packing their own supplies into the California foothills during the gold rush and Mexicans who had grown tired of being drafted to pack arms and ammunition for every revolutionary bandit king that fancied the

Mexican presidency. They were separated now into two groups, backing their respective champions.

Whatever the cause of the quarrel, Whitcomb's immediate concern was to end it and resume the chore of crossing the ravine. He dismounted and led his horse forward as Chileno John whacked his mule with a heavy glove and shouted, "*Vaya,* Pinto Jim!"

Yank Bartlett grabbed Pinto Jim's halter and held the mule back. "This animule waits his turn or he's deader'n thet mush you call brains. Keno goes first this time!"

Chileno John's knife began to rise in its scabbard, but Whitcomb stepped quickly in front of the irate Mexican. "Gentlemen," he pleaded with all the firmness of tone he could muster. "I beg you, stand not on the order of your going, but go!"

"Cain't do it, General," said Hank Hewitt, brevetting Whitcomb six grades in rank. "Thar's a double eagle on this here deal. Each mule got to go on his lonesome, 'n the one t' make the crossin' gets the gold."

"Thet's God's truth, General," Yank agreed, and his face brightened with an idea. "Now ef'n you'd be the jedge, why I reckon we c'd be off an' runnin' 'fore y' c'd say 'Old Jack Long's dead 'n' gone.' "

"Corporal Atherton? You know more of this sort of thing than I do."

"Forgive me, sir. I would sooner carry both their packs to the Yellowstone than get in a dispute between Keno and Pinto Jim."

By now most of E Troop was gathered at the edge of the ravine, waiting to see what Whitcomb would do. He took a deep breath and turned back to the packers. "Very well, gentlemen, if you will accept me as sole judge you must also agree that my decision is final and not subject to argument. Understood?" There were no objections. "Very well. How are we to decide who goes first?"

Another of the Mexican packers drew a silver dollar from a pocket and flipped it to the young officer. "*Qué dices, Juan,*" the man said to Chileno John. "*Cabeza o culo?*"

"*Culo,*" Chileno John replied at once, smiling broadly. "*Culo para mi amigo Hank!*" The other Spanish-speaking packers roared, and even the Americans laughed.

"That means 'e picks tails, sir," Atherton explained. "Well, it don't exactly mean tails. It's an impolite term, sir, if you take my meaning."

Whitcomb flipped the coin and caught it, and slapped it atop his other hand. "Heads," he announced.

Hank 'n' Yank smiled, pleased at this small victory, and together they led Keno to the edge of the ravine. Hank patted the mule's neck and stroked his long ears and then he spoke in tones usually reserved for expressing the fondest feelings close to the ear of a loved one. "Y'r a miserable bastard," he began, " 'n' some day when I'm starvin' 'n' cold I'll shoot yer dead 'n' feast on yer meat, 'n' when I'm done I'll sleep tight in thet moth-eaten coat y' call yer skin. But fer now, you jest slip down here slick as a beaver, 'n' there'll be oats on yer *sudera* tonight." He hit the mule a sudden blow on the rump and shouted, "Now *git,* y' wuthless hunk o' meat."

As if the blow had been no more than a fleabite, Keno sauntered forth and cocked his head to look at the trail. Without more than a moment's hesitation he stepped down the slope, made slick by the passage of nine companies of cavalry and all the other mules that had already crossed ahead of him. His front feet began to slide, and at once he set his hind legs in a half crouch, keeping his back and his load level as he coasted calmly to the bottom, where he recommenced walking as soon as he had come to a stop, and quickly scrambled up the far slope.

A cheer went up from the onlookers, but Chileno John shrugged. Removing one glove he reached deep into a pocket of his overcoat. He withdrew his hand and offered something to Pinto Jim. The mule flapped his lips greedily and ate the offering, nudging the Mexican's coat for more, but Chileno John shook his head. He pointed at the ravine. "*Ande, pues,*" he said simply.

If a mule can look disappointed, such was the look Pinto Jim gave his master before setting off down the icy slope, but he turned to his business willingly enough and displayed his own preferred method of navigating the obstacle. Disdaining Keno's caution, he kept walking even after the footing became treacherous, slipping and sliding and resigning himself to coasting only when he appeared likely to lose his control entirely and roll headlong to the bottom. Before he came to a stop he leaped for the upslope, giving a small crowhop and a kick of his heels, and lurched to the top as surefooted as a mountain goat, though scarcely as gracefully. No sooner had he reached level ground among the crowd waiting there than he stopped, planted his feet, raised his tail and broke wind loudly, looking back over his shoulder at his master.

The onlookers went wild, packers and troopers alike slapping one another on the back and pointing across the way at the insolent mule. Gradually the cheers subsided and all eyes came to rest on the young lieutenant, awaiting his decision. Whitcomb noted that Chileno John still had his hand on the haft of his knife, and he realized that his own hands were sweating within his heavy muskrat gloves.

"Gentlemen," he began, "mine has not been an easy task. But I have been given a duty, and as an officer in the service of our country, I will never shirk a duty." This brought a derisive cheer from the soldiers, many of them welcoming the chance to add insulting comments about the officer class from within the anonymity of the crowd. Whitcomb feigned not to hear them. When it was quiet again, he continued. "It is my decision that in the matter of *style,* Keno is clearly the winner—"

At this, Hank 'n' Yank let out whoops of victory and began to do a jig on the frozen ground to the cheers of a small group of supporters while Chileno John and the Mexicans raised an even louder cry of protest. Chileno John advanced on Whitcomb, but he stopped as the officer raised a hand for silence.

"Quiet, please, gentlemen!" When he had their attention once again, he said, "As I was about to say, I have not been called solely to judge style. I have been asked to judge *mules*. And gentlemen, if ever I have seen behavior more mulish than Pinto Jim's, I can't remember the occasion. I declare Pinto Jim the winner!"

The uproar was deafening now, and even Hank 'n' Yank and their supporters could find no fault with the judge's ruling, although they made token protests for form's sake.

There was a sudden lessening of the general merriment and Whitcomb turned to see Lieutenant Corwin making his way through the gathering on horseback. Behind him were four groups of flankers led by Sergeants Dupré, Duggan and Rossi and Corporal Stiegler.

"Did you order the men to break formation and dismount, Mr. Whitcomb?"

"Not exactly, sir. The packers were having a dispute and we've just now got it settled." Whitcomb noticed that someone had thought to post a few pickets, men with carbines at the ready who were watching the troop's flanks and rear.

"I leave you in charge of the troop for a quarter of an hour and you have let yourself become separated from the command. God help you if the Indians attack while you're cut off like this."

The snow had thinned somewhat and Whitcomb saw that the rest of the column had already crossed the next ravine a quarter of a mile away.

"Sergeant Dupré!" Corwin called out to the first sergeant. "Let's get the men across quickly and get after the column. Mr. Reb, you will bring up the rear with Corporal McCaslin. When you reach the other side you will join me at the head of the troop."

From the moment of Corwin's appearance the packers had become very busy getting the remaining mules across the ravine and on their way, and the trail was clear now for E Troop to cross. Corwin dismounted and led the way, followed by Sergeant Dupré. In what seemed a short time, after the delay for mule judging, Whitcomb and McCaslin were following the last of the men down the icy trail.

"I don't know whom I have to thank for putting out the pickets while I was occupied with those mules," Whitcomb said. "I am grateful to whomever thought of it."

"Routine precaution, sorr. No need for yez to concern yerself. The boys had themselves a good laugh. Does 'em a world o' good, 'specially when they see an officer joinin' in the spirit o' things."

"I'm afraid I got another black mark in Major Corwin's book."

"Don't concern yerself, sorr. Y'r learnin', that's what counts. We all begin like babes in the woods; it's how quick we learn that matters."

As they remounted their horses on level ground, Whitcomb turned to McCaslin again. "By the way, what was it that Chileno John fed his mule back there?"

"That's how he gets his name, sorr. That mule's favorite treat is pinto beans."

Smiling to himself, Whitcomb cantered past the troop, which was moving along at a brisk trot, and took his place beside Corwin in the lead, ready to receive the further reprimand he was certain was coming. But Corwin remained silent until the company had crossed the next ravine and overtaken the rest of the column, and when he did speak his tone was pleasant, as if the morning had passed without incident.

"Look at those mules, Mr. Whitcomb," he said, waving a hand to take in the pack train ahead of them. "Look at the size of those packs. The army says a mule will carry one hundred and seventy-five pounds. At that rate, our train could carry enough to keep us on maneuvers for just seven or eight days, but we're out for fifteen. Our mules carry three hundred and twenty pounds on the average, and they can march twice as far as any other mules in the army on a standard ration of feed. Those pack cushions are called *aparejos,* and every *aparejo* in this train has been made especially for one particular mule, so he can carry a heavy load in comfort. There isn't a department commander west of the Missouri who wouldn't kill General Crook in his sleep if he thought he could make off with this pack train."

He paused for a moment to let this information sink in. "Now look at the men. There are men in this troop, in all the troops, who have started out on winter campaigns where only the officers wore fur coats, while the soldiers were dressed in army blue. But these men are dressed as well as you and I. They're ready to carry a load as well. Before the campaign is over they will have hardships to bear, and they'll carry on because that's their duty." Again he paused, glancing at Whitcomb. "Officers are prepared to carry something called the burden of command, Mr. Whitcomb. In an expedition led by George Crook that responsibility bears an added weight. Just as the mules and the men are expected to carry their loads, so are you. You're not here to entertain the men, or to wipe their noses, or to hold their hands. You're here to lead and command. The more intimate you become with them, the harder that job will be. If you remember nothing else, remember that."

Even this last injunction was said without rancor. It was passed along in much the same manner as Whitcomb's own father had sometimes passed along useful observations about life in general to young Ham, back before the war.

The command encamped that night beside Prairie Dog Creek, having made just fourteen miles from the Clear Fork in a long day of hard marching. During the evening meal the men remained unusually quiet and once they had eaten most went soon to their blankets and robes and little shelters instead of spending the usual time around the cookfires for warmth and conversation. It seemed a somber camp, as if the weather had succeeded at last in smothering the good cheer of the men even as it smothered the landscape in a layer of deadening white, but as Whitcomb climbed into his robes, one of the last to do so, he heard a voice raised from a bedroll nearby to address the troop at large. He thought at first it was McCaslin, but the voice was younger and it gave a sardonic lilt to the words.

"Oh, this soldierin' under Gineral Crook is mighty foine, boys. No odds how hard we tramp over this blasted country all day, when we come to camp at night we get all the comforts and convaniences the land affords. Jist think of it—hardtack and coffee for supper, picket pine for mattresses and lariats for coverin', an' the fun of it is, the gineral gets it all the same!"

Whitcomb thought of what Corwin had said that day, about the provisions made for the comfort of the mules and men, and he saw that Corwin was right. The men knew that Crook had outfitted them well and would ask nothing of them that he would not endure himself, and so they would carry an extra burden willingly. But he felt that Corwin was wrong too; such mutual trust and respect need not be put in jeopardy by a moment's man-to-man contact between officer and enlisted men, especially if such moments bred a camaraderie that transcended rank. Until the incident with the wounded trooper during the second attack on camp, Whitcomb had felt like an outsider, and he had begun to despair of ever being accepted. But that moment had proved to be a turning point. John Bourke had said that chasing after the cattle had shown he had pluck; perhaps rescuing the wounded corporal in the fight at the Powder had proved that he had something more than a fool's courage. And if the mule judging today helped to show that he could be a regular fellow, what harm was there in that? None of his actions had been planned to impress the enlisted men, but their attitude toward him had changed nevertheless. Now he felt that he belonged. Such a feeling could benefit both himself and the troop, for it strengthened the bonds between them. The men needed to know that their officers were able and took their welfare to heart. It was as simple as that. Secure in that knowledge they would do anything asked of them. There must be respect for one's superiors, of course, but that did not rule out companionship, even a kind of friendship as well. He understood that, even if Corwin did not. Perhaps it was Corwin and not he who was truly the outsider.

The next day, in the face of continued snow and a persistent wind that lashed the stinging crystals into the faces of the men, the command moved down Prairie Dog Creek toward its confluence with the Tongue River. The animals that gave the stream its name were very much in evidence, running hither and yon on ground and snowbank, perching by the entrances of their burrows to give their shrill warning chatter, unperturbed by the storm. Finally, in late afternoon the strength of the winds dropped and blue skies appeared to the west. As camp was made for the night a party of guides returned from a scout of several days, which had taken them through the country to the north and west, to the banks of the Rosebud. They had killed three deer on the return journey and this venison was quickly distributed to the grateful cooks. Around the fires there was laughter and even a few songs.

Some of the men had adopted the custom of General Crook and the packers, beginning preparations for their beds as soon as the column halted. When the horses had been seen to, each man who followed this method brushed a flat area of ground clear of snow and started a small fire that he would maintain throughout supper and the post-prandial conversations around the cookfires. Then, shortly before going to sleep he would sweep away the last coals of his private fire and spread his robes, wherein he would sleep warm and comfortable all night on the heat stored by the ground beneath him. Tonight, with the clouds evaporating, the air took on a threatening chill, and as night fell and the moon rose, nearly full, scores of these bed-ground fires twinkled throughout the encampment, as if in answer to the more austere and distant sparkling of the stars overhead.

Before supper the company officers were called to the headquarters fire to hear the reports of the scouts, and once again Boots Corwin and Teddy Egan sought each other out.

"The damn Indians have skedaddled, Boots," Egan said in greeting. "I got it from Louis Richaud. Lots of villages, plenty of sign, and not a live one in a hundred miles. I'm beginning to catch the odor of wild geese."

And indeed, the first piece of intelligence the scouts reported was the discovery of an abandoned village of sixty tipis. They had found every indication that the Indians who had lived there were well supplied with all the necessities of life.

"They strip cottonwood bark, plenty bark, General. Horses strong, I bet," said Frank Grouard, his dark skin emphasizing the whiteness of his eyes in the firelight. The scouts and officers were gathered in a circle around the fire. Some of the men squatted on their hams while others sat cross-legged on robes or India-rubber ponchos. Corwin was struck by how much the gathering resembled an Indian council. "People strong too," Grouard continued. "Plenty meat. More game close to the Yellowstone. Deer, I think. Elk too, maybe buffalo. Good hunting. We find this in a tree, hung up." He nodded to one of the other guides and the man dropped something at Crook's feet. The general turned it over with the toe of his boot and those around the fire could see that it was the body of a young dog, with the cord that had been used to strangle it still tied around its neck.

Crook looked at the small body curiously, without surprise. "What does it mean, Frank?"

Grouard shrugged and looked at Big Bat Pourier and Little Bat Garnier, who squatted beside him. "Me, I reckon some squaw fixin' dog to eat."

Big Bat spoke up. He was not significantly larger than Little Bat, although he was several years older than the younger man, who was perhaps twenty-two. "They use dogs in ceremonies, General. 'Specially ceremonies for war."

"Plenty Crows in that country," Little Bat put in. "Sioux got their horses in corral. I think they worry about Crows come steal their horses, General. Mebbe make war on Crows." Garnier was half Sioux himself, his skin darker than a white man's, but without the tropical features and duskiness that distinguished Grouard.

"Could be," said Grouard with another shrug. "Could be it's just dog stew. That village they move quick, but not scared, General. These people strong."

"And the other village you found," Crook wanted to know, "that one had been abandoned how long?"

"Hard to say." It was Big Bat who answered. The scouts had been divided into two groups in order to cover more country; his group had found the second village. "Everything's froze up pretty good. Might be a couple weeks back, in the thaw. They was Oglala, General. Maybe went over to the Powder, maybe in to the agency. Might be they got the word and went in peaceful, like they're supposed to."

"Sir, isn't it possible that the large village also decided to go in?" The speaker was Captain Alexander Moore, brevet colonel, commander of the Fifth Battalion. "Isn't it even possible that there was a general movement to the agencies in the good weather? After all, the order was perfectly clear about what would happen to those who remained here."

"It's possible, Colonel," said Crook. He did not sound as if he thought it likely. "Frank, what do you think?"

"Sioux don't go to the reservation when he got good hunting," Grouard said. "I reckon they go over Powder River."

"But there were no Hunkpapa among them? No sign of Sitting Bull?"

"No Hunkpapa. Small village Oglala. Maybe Crazy Horse."

"Too small for Crazy Horse," said Big Bat, and Little Bat nodded.

"Big medicine, Crazy Horse. He's getting plenty strong, General. Lots of lodges in his village, I'll bet."

Crook digested these differences of opinion as he did all information that his guides or officers brought to him—as worthy of consideration, something to be thought on seriously. He nodded slowly, looking into the fire, and Corwin glanced around the circle of faces gathered there. Colonel Reynolds and his adjutant, Lieutenant Morton, sat beside Crook, and it seemed to Corwin that Reynolds awaited Crook's decision about their immediate course with some trepidation.

He's worried about the beef herd still, Corwin thought. That incident had reflected badly on Reynolds. It was his responsibility to post adequate guards and he had failed to do so. Rumor had it that Crook was sympathetic toward

Reynolds, who had once commanded the Department of Texas. He had been relieved of that post and returned to his regiment after a small scandal involving irregularities in military supply contracts, and rumors of bribery. Lieutenant Bourke had told Lieutenant Sibley, who had told Lieutenant Rawolle, who had mentioned it to Corwin, that Crook hoped this campaign would help to restore Reynolds' good reputation. The loss of the beef herd, which had actually hurt the campaign very little, was an error that would easily be overlooked if Reynolds later distinguished himself. But if Reynolds made further mistakes, the running off of the herd would be seen as the first in a series of events for which he would be called to account.

Crook cleared his throat and looked up like a man who had been lost in his own thoughts and suddenly realized that others were awaiting his words. "We will continue down the Tongue, gentlemen. If General Terry and Colonel Gibbon are in the field we should rendezvous with them near the Yellowstone. Are there any questions?"

"General?" It was Reynolds.

"General Reynolds?"

"Mightn't it be best to cross to the Powder now and follow its course to the Yellowstone? It would seem that there must be some hostiles there. Any major village will do, as you yourself have said. A swift defeat, and the spirit of resistance broken?"

"Perhaps," Crook replied, "but if there are any hostiles remaining on the Tongue, it wouldn't do to have them at our backs when we turn east. If we find them here we can pivot to the right and force them towards Dakota even if the first engagement is not successful. But we need not go all the way to the Yellowstone ourselves. In a few more days we can send the scouts ahead and if they find no hostiles, and no sign of General Terry, I will gladly turn towards the Powder then." He looked around patiently, but there were no further questions. Corwin expected the council to end then, but Crook addressed them again.

"Gentlemen, battle is part of a soldier's life, but his job is to end battle. This is the inherent paradox of our calling.

We steel ourselves for the charge; our hearts beat faster and our excitement grows until we actually look forward to the release that battle provides. But we must not forget that our job here is to enforce a peace on this region. If it can be made without bloodshed, the peace will come faster and will sit easier on the shoulders of both peoples. As many of you know, in Arizona we pursued a vigorous campaign against the Apaches until their headmen showed a willingness to sit down and speak peacefully with us. And since that time that region has enjoyed the fruits of peace. In time there will be peace here too, but whether won with quiet words or by the sword remains to be seen. The difference between the two methods is the amount of blood that may be shed in the meantime and the nature of the peace that follows, whether full of a lingering hatred or blessed by a growing mutual understanding. Without the bitterness of a battlefield defeat in their hearts, the Sioux will learn all the sooner that their future lies in living peacefully beside the white men and adopting the industrious ways of the higher civilization.'' He looked up and his calm blue-gray eyes swept the circle. ''And so, as we prepared for war, I sent out an emissary of peace. If he is successful, we may obtain the surrender of Sitting Bull and Crazy Horse without bloodshed.''

There was a rustling of small movements around the circle as the men shifted about and glanced at one another.

''Four bits says that's news to Reynolds,'' Corwin said to Egan under his breath.

''Thanks, I'll keep my money.''

''Perhaps there are indeed no villages remaining on the Tongue,'' Crook continued. ''But by taking the militarily sound course of completing our sweep to the Yellowstone and assuring that there is no danger to our rear, we may delay the first encounter for a day or two and give my man a little more time to find us if he has been successful. But make no mistake, gentlemen. If we come upon the hostiles before he finds us, we will not hesitate. If a military solution presents itself, that is the course we will follow. We are soldiers, after all. The choice will have been made for us by fate and we will do our duty as soldiers, knowing we did our best to win over the enemy by entreaty and persuasion."

Crook stood and the others rose with him. The officers dispersed quietly, but when they reached their own bivouacs they gathered in small knots to talk over the general's surprising news. Corwin got his dinner from the cook and ate by himself, shocked by what he had heard. Crook was deliberately slowing the pace of the campaign! If the mysterious peace emissary were successful, the fact would reflect more honor on the reputation of General George Crook, but the officers and men who had gone hunting wild geese through the bitter blasts of a northern winter would be no more than motes in the residual dust of history. Nor would their participation be recognized by the bureaucrats who inscribed and filed the army's records in Washington City, and Corwin would have lost yet another chance for further promotion, the one thing he wanted most of all. He had a good record, but the pages were yellowing with age. The deeds that shone brightest were in the time of the Rebellion, before his capture and imprisonment. Ever since his release from prison he had felt the need to prove himself again. He was young enough to have another ten years of service ahead of him, but he did not want to serve out his days as a lieutenant. Advancement won in the closing days of the Sioux wars would assure him posts of increasing responsibility and opportunities that would stand him in good stead when he retired.

He had had other opportunities in his lifetime, but he had passed them by for the sake of the army.

As a youth he had wanted to go to sea in a whaling ship. His father, a textile worker in the burgeoning mill town of Lawrence, Massachusetts, had given his consent, and young Francis had been apprenticed to a firm of New Bedford whaling merchants. But one voyage had been enough to reveal the folly of his dream, for he was seasick the whole time. On his return to port he learned that the guns of rebellion were being unlimbered in the South, and he enlisted in the army after being assured he would be required to serve only on dry land. He had learned his new trade quickly and shown an aptitude for leadership, and he had been rewarded beyond his expectations with decorations and rapid promotion. After the war he had spent the last months of his recovery at home, where he saw the new mills lining the river. There was opportunity there, but his mother urged him not to stay. "Look at yer father, Frankie," she said to him one night when the rest of the household was asleep. "He's forty-five years old and his health is gone. Maybe in the army ye can make somethin' better for yerself." Young Boots Corwin was already an officer, and therefore a gentleman, and so he had stayed in uniform.

A few years later, on the frontier, he had met a girl for whom he might have turned his back on the army if he had been wiser and less ambitious. They could make a life together, she said, but not in the army. The Indian wars had been in full swing and Boots had his sights set on captain's bars, and so he had passed that fork in the road without turning aside. Not long after that he had met another girl, one more willing to suffer the hardships of an army wife, and he had married her. With the northern plains temporarily quieted he was transferred to Arizona and she followed him there, where their daughter Elizabeth was born. And then in a move from one post to another the ambulance carrying his wife and daughter had failed to arrive. When their bodies were found, Boots was not permitted to see them.

He had survived by rededicating himself to his profession, at first for no other reason than to take revenge on the savages who had shattered his life, but when he had occasion to view the bodies of some Apache women and children, he found that he had no taste for revenge. He put his hatred aside and his tragedy behind him, and neither he nor those who knew him had spoken of it since. Occasionally he could forget for days at a time that it was something real, something that had happened to him.

He wondered now if he had made the wrong choices at every step of the way. There were fewer opportunities left to him now, and less time, and still the greatest chance for success seemed to him to lie on the path he had chosen.

How great was the probability that Crook's peace mission would succeed? One man, alone? Not much, he thought, and found himself impatient for the dawn, when the command would be on the march again downriver, down to the Tongue and north toward the Yellowstone to scour the country there and find a village if there was one, and if not, to turn to the Powder. When they reached the Powder they would go south, upriver, in a flanking movement that would turn east again toward the Black Hills until the whole country was swept clean, or until it was clear that the hostiles had abandoned their defiance and had scurried off to Dakota when they heard that soldiers were in their country in the dead of winter.

They couldn't all be gone, could they? The memory of the scouts' reports fueled his hope. A strong enemy, well supplied and feeling their oats, that was the enemy Corwin wanted to face. And by a daring winter stroke the plains Indian wars would be won with a bang, not a whimper. The campaign would be studied at West Point and Boots Corwin would be a part of it.

Give me the opportunity and I'll come out of it a captain. That's all I ask.

Fleeting clouds scudded across the face of a round moon that lit the landscape brilliantly when it shone freely. Corwin returned his plate to the cook and the snow creaked beneath his overboots like the flooring in an old house as he made his way to his bedroll. The skin on his face was drawn up tight from the cold and he was grateful for the thick growth of beard he had acquired during ten days of marching. As he settled himself in his robe he noticed the slight figure of Lieutenant Whitcomb moving among the sleeping forms of E Troop's men as placidly as if it were a summer night. He always seemed to prowl about the camp before he went to sleep.

Whitcomb showed promise of becoming a competent officer, but it was far too early to lessen the pressure on him. High spirits and a benign nature were poor armor for the Indian wars. The young officer was too familiar with the men and he needed to acquire a modicum of caution in all things, a suspicion that the world did not mean him well. So far, he had shown himself capable of bearing up under strict discipline and harsh conditions, but he had not yet faced the test of battle, where his good nature would have to be set aside.

CHAPTER EIGHT

Once again the pipe carriers examined a place where the cavalry had spent the night, this one on the Clear Fork of the Powder. The morning was not yet half gone and they had already come ten miles since dawn. It was their fifth day on the trail and the third day of the storm, which was blowing still as if it meant to blow forever. By Hardeman's calculation it was the tenth of March, and with every hour that Crook moved northward the risk of war increased.

The valley of the Clear Fork was several hundred yards wide at this point, the bottomland stretching broad and flat to the west of the river. Low peaked hills rose on either side, displaying an occasional streak of reddish clay; the vivid color was startling in the otherwise uniform grayness the storm imposed on the landscape. There were growths of cottonwood and willow along the course of the stream, the first trees the pipe carriers had seen since the Big Horn foothills and the first willow brush since Crazy Woman's Fork. As they moved north the land was becoming less arid. The river bottom was grassy, and Blackbird permitted the horses to crop what they might while the men examined the bluecoats' camp for signs.

Hardeman had looked at the campsite only briefly. He stood now with Blackbird and the horses, waiting for the others to satisfy themselves. As he waited he worked out times and distances, trying to force the cavalry closer by willpower. The signs said the cavalry had been here longer ago than one night. If they were ahead of the pipe carriers by two days, it might as well be two weeks. Crook was moving his troops up-country with a speed Hardeman would not have believed possible under such trying conditions; if he kept up the pace, the pipe carriers would never catch him. Unless Hardeman pushed on alone while his roan was still strong.

"Let's get moving," he said curtly, and the other men paused in their searching to look at him. "They were here and now they're gone. What else do you need to know?" He climbed aboard his horse. "The trail goes downstream." He started off without waiting to see if they would come now or waste more time.

Standing Eagle and Little Hand exchanged a glance. Many of the northern bands were said to be on the lower Powder. If the bluecoat chief descended the Clear Fork to the larger stream, he might mean to continue on the Powder all the way to the Yellowstone, and before long he would come on one village or another. The two men mounted their horses and moved off behind Hardeman, with Bat and Hawk Chaser and Blackbird close on their heels.

The soldiers' trail was easy to follow in the relative shelter of the river bottom, and in what seemed to Hardeman an impossibly short time, certainly it was less than two hours, he came upon a small cove where there were many fire pits and evidence of some cooking.

"They laid over," he said to Bat as he dismounted. He led his horse down the bank into the cove and looked about, his spirits rising. "Must have spent all day here, or a long night, waiting out the storm. They might be just a day ahead." He remounted and gave the horse a sharp tap with his bootheels, urging the roan up the bank to where Bat was waiting. The mountain man had not bothered to dismount.

"Could be we're gettin' lucky," Bat said. "We'll press on. Eagle! Quit yer dawdlin' and climb onto that piece o' wolf meat y' call a horse!"

Standing Eagle insisted on digging in the largest of the fire pits, but the earth was frozen hard and yielded nothing.

Almost at once the cavalry's trail left the Clear Fork and turned to the northwest, following a smaller stream that flowed down from that direction. The stream led into rougher country and finally petered out on the lee slope of a rugged divide. From atop the ridge, squinting against the full force of the wind and snow, the pipe carriers looked across a broad plateau to the valley of the Tongue River.

"Looks like Three Stars ain't goin' down the Powder after all," Bat remarked, and got a sour look from Standing Eagle.

Through the middle part of the day the riders made good time, despite the steady resistance of the storm. The going was hard in the broken country of the divide, but the unshod Indian horses were nimble-footed and Hardeman's roan seemed at home in any terrain; he negotiated ravines and steep hillsides without complaint. The going was easier when the cavalry's trail descended to a stream Bat believed to be Prairie Dog Creek, and at mid-afternoon the pipe carriers found the soldiers' next night camp.

The riders dismounted from their grateful horses, which Blackbird led to a thick patch of grass close at hand. The stalks of last year's growth rose through the thin covering of snow everywhere hereabouts, carpeting the land even far from the watercourses.

The men chewed jerky and *wasná* as they poked about the camp and here it was Hardeman who dug in one of the fire pits. Six inches down, the earth was still warm. He grinned in triumph, feeling a growing excitement. "Bat!" he called. "They were here last night."

"Still a ways ahead and movin' quick," Bat said, stooping to press his bare hand to the warm earth. "We'll move on a bit, but we best find some shelter and some feed for the ponies afore dark."

Hardeman nodded, knowing Bat was right. The horses had eaten poorly the night before, and the strength they had gained back at Crazy Woman was gone now. Much as he would have liked to forge on through the night, hoping to close on Crook by dawn or soon thereafter, he knew such a course was foolhardy. The trail might easily be lost in the storm, and it was reckless to chance stumbling on the cavalry in the dark, possibly provoking a deadly reaction from the sentries before Hardeman could identify himself. The little band would have to find a good place to camp and start out again at first light. With luck they would catch Crook tomorrow.

"We ain't makin' tracks settin' here," Bat said, rising to his feet and moving toward the horses. In the last two days the mountain man had taken a controlling hand in deciding the pace of the march. There had been some grumbling from Standing Eagle but no open opposition, and Bat and Hardeman often rode in the lead now.

Bat's horse started and shied sideways as he mounted, throwing her head and rolling her eyes, her nostrils flaring. The mare made a soft *huh-huh-huh* and her ears flicked this way and that. "Grizzly, maybe," Bat said, calming the horse and looking about. "Early yet, less'n he went to bed hungry."

The others mounted up and drew closer together as their eyes looked all about, trying to penetrate the ever-shifting clouds of snow.

"Might be nothin', or could be she seen a spook," Standing Eagle said, but his own eyes kept moving.

"It was sump'n," Bat said. The wind covered all sounds a man could hear, but the other horses showed signs of nervousness now, snorting the air and turning their heads as if they were as anxious as the men to know what lay beyond the obscuring snowfall.

"There," Hardeman said softly.

"I see 'im," said Bat.

A single rider materialized in the snow and drew near, a lance held ready, his mount moving at a cautious walk.

"*Kanghí wichasha,*" hissed Little Hand, and Bat muttered "He's a Crow," to Hardeman. *Absaroka* the Crows called themselves in their own language; they were the Children of the Raven, but the white men came from the east, where crows were more common than ravens, and the mistranslation had stuck.

Blackbird kicked his horse to move closer to his father. He reached for one of his boyish arrows that hung in the quiver at his shoulder, but Standing Eagle made a curt motion and the boy dropped his hand.

More horsemen appeared now, all in a line abreast, walking slowly. They stopped when they were a dozen paces behind the lone man in the lead. There were eighteen of them all told.

"Here's wet powder and no fire to dry it," Bat said for Hardeman's ears alone, and he withdrew his Leman rifle from the fringed and beaded case that rested in his lap. Still the Lakota sat silently on their horses and still the Crow rider in the center made no motion, spoke no word.

He's sizing us up, Hardeman thought. Doesn't know what to make of Sioux and white men traveling together in these parts. He wondered whether to clear the way to his pistol. It would be pistol against bow and lance at this distance. Bat might get off a shot but there would be no time for reloading, and none of the Lakotas carried firearms. Apart from Blackbird, only Hawk Chaser was armed at all. He had both lance and bow, but the bow was slung across his back with his quiver and he had only the lance in his hand. Christ, Standing Eagle must feel as naked as a babe about now, Hardeman thought. Eighteen against six. This bunch isn't up to a fight with eighteen Crows. He thought of Johnny Smoker, who, like the two men carrying the pipes, did not go armed, and hadn't done for seven years now, and he missed having Johnny to keep an eye on his back when a fight was in the offing.

He unfastened three buttons on the St. Paul coat, moving slowly. Winter was a poor time for fighting; the clothing got in the way.

Now Standing Eagle raised a hand, moving slowly. He moved the hand in broad sweeps, making the-signs-that-are-seen-across-a-distance, so all the Crows could understand him. *You are far from the camps of the Crow.*

The lone rider responded. *We have come to hunt. The four-leggeds are few in the country of the Crow.*

The four-leggeds have left the Lakota as well, signed Standing Eagle.

You are not hunters, the Crow said.

"And he's a lyin' Injun," Bat said softly. "Ain't no eighteen Crows out huntin' this far south o' the Yellowstone. Them's young bloods out huntin' coup."

I am Standing Eagle, war leader of Sun Horse's band, signed Standing Eagle. *Today I carry a pipe of peace to the white soldier chief Three Stars.*

This statement caused a stir among the other Crows and there was some brief talk among them. The leader listened for a time before returning his attention to the party in front of him. He motioned at the campfires and the tracks leading away to the north. *There have been many horse soldiers here,* he signed.

Standing Eagle nodded. *They are led by Three Stars. We follow their trail.*

The Crow smiled. *The horse soldiers do not come to the land of the Crow. We are at peace with our white brothers.*

Standing Eagle's expression did not change, but his motions became more emphatic. *We will live at peace with the whites when they leave our land and let us live like men!* He made the last motion sharply, the index finger of his right hand thrust erect before him, like the erect organ of a virile man.

The Crow leader's face grew dark at the insult and from the others there were a few angry words, but the leader cut them off with a quick sign.

Hardeman changed his mind about the pistol. Moving no more purposefully than he might have done to scratch his ear, he slipped the Winchester out of its scabbard and rested it across his lap, in the same position as Bat's muzzle-loader. The pistol would be more use if the Crows decided to fight, but they didn't even know he had a pistol yet, and they feared the reputation of the many-shots-fast lever gun.

The Crow leader noted the motion, and the way the six riders sat quietly before him, their eyes meeting his. *Does it take four Lakota and two whitemen to carry one pipe?* he asked.

We have two pipes, Standing Eagle signed. *This man, Little Hand, carries a pipe to my cousin, who winters nearby.* He did not name Sitting Bull, who was a bitter enemy of the *Kanghí,* but he hoped that the Crow might temper their bravado with caution if they thought there were more Lakota close at hand. *The old whiteman is my brother,* he signed. *The other carries a message for Three Stars from Sun Horse, my father.*

"Old man! I oughta pin yer ears back for ye," Bat muttered. "If'n I live long enough."

There was more talk among the Crows and this time the leader was not quick to end it. Finally he turned back to the Lakotas and whites. *The Crow do not make war on those who carry pipes of peace,* he signed. *We will go now: Another day we will meet again.*

As silently as they had appeared, the Crows turned and rode away, quickly disappearing in the snow.

"I'll be dogged," Bat breathed. "I give it to ye, Eagle, you done that slicker'n dog shit on a wet rock."

Standing Eagle grunted and favored his brother-in-law with a rare smile. "Felt nekkid as a child, and that's truth. Figgered us for gone beaver."

"Oh, I'd of thrown that nigger cold, all right," Bat grinned. "It war the others I worried on. But I reckoned Christopher here and old Hawk and young Blackbird was up to Crow today."

"I will fight the Crow," Blackbird said, and grinned at Hardeman. "But I would rather fight *washíchun.*"

Hardeman did not entirely conceal his surprise. It seemed every member of Sun Horse's male line had been studying on the English tongue.

"You notice he speaks a mite better'n Eagle here," Bat

observed. "I'm teachin' him different. Figger when he's full growed there won't be many left that savvy trapper talk."

He laughed, joined by Blackbird and Standing Eagle, and Hardeman laughed too, enjoying the high spirits that followed a brush with danger, but he wondered if Blackbird would have time to get full grown. He was Standing Eagle's son, there was no mistaking that. The boy watched his father closely and imitated him in many small mannerisms and gestures. He wanted to be just like his father, and Hardeman wondered how much chance he would have. If war came, Bat had said that Standing Eagle and Little Hand would take their families and join the fighting bands. Blackbird could easily find himself confronting army troops before the month was out. But his initial hostility toward Hardeman had given way in the course of five days together to guarded curiosity. Probably he had never had much chance to see a white man close up over a period of time, except for Bat Putnam, his uncle Lodgepole. Hardeman had noted the respect with which the boy always addressed Bat and the considerate good humor Bat bestowed on Blackbird.

"We better put some country between us and those bucks before they change their minds and decide to raise a little hair after all," Hardeman said.

Bat nodded. "We'll move on till dark. Won't be easy to cut trail tonight. I reckon we'll shake 'em."

But even before nightfall the sky cleared rapidly from the west. As the clouds receded toward the eastern horizon the moon rose above them, its rounded face a welcome sight after so many stormy nights. The air turned frigid and the pipe carriers kept a close watch on their back trail, with an eye always to the front as well, searching there for the glow of campfires or a glimpse of moonlit smoke that might betray the presence of the army camp ahead. The valley of the Prairie Dog widened gradually until it grew as large as the Clear Fork had been, where the trail had left that stream. As the moon rose higher its light grew brilliant; the Big Horns, all cloaked in snow, loomed so close in the west that it seemed the men might reach out and touch them. Finally, with no sign of pursuit and the horses breathing hard, unwilling to go faster than a slow trot, the riders stopped in a grove of cottonwoods by the creekbank. They stripped bark from the trees by moonlight and fed it to the horses and tethered them, hobbled, amidst what grass there was, close by the shelter they built for themselves against the numbing cold.

As he drifted toward sleep Hardeman could hear the regular working of the horses' jaws, and he felt pleasantly contented. The rich grass would restore the animals' strength somewhat, and a few hours of sleep would restore the men. Tomorrow they would catch Crook for certain. They couldn't be far behind him now. Hardeman was almost sorry the pipe carriers' solitary journey was nearing an end. How long was it since he had been this far from any settlement, moving through the country with a small band of companions who knew the land and had the skills needed for any emergency? When he set out from Kansas with Johnny he had never imagined for a moment that he would end up traveling with Sioux warriors and an old mountain man who had gone Injun years before. The Indians smelled different, from the animal grease they rubbed in their hair and from the leathers they wore, brain-tanned and cured in the smoke of many lodge fires, but he had been with white men who smelled worse.

His mind went back to the encounter with the Crows and he almost smiled. How many whites would meet a group of their enemies and look them over and say, "It's not a good day to fight. We'll meet again another time." If it had been a squad of Crook's cavalry instead of Crows, they would have fired first and maybe not even bothered to ask questions later. The Indians didn't practice war the way the white men did, relentlessly. And so in the end the Indians would lose.

He awoke suddenly, with no idea how long he might have slept. It was still night, but from somewhere came enough light for him to make out the painted face of a

Crow warrior inches from his own. The man was smiling broadly and Hardeman recognized the leader of the Crow war party.

A knife rested against Hardeman's throat. He could feel the razor-sharp blade and the pounding of his heart. Beneath his blankets his hand closed around the Colt but he dared not cock the weapon for fear the Crow would sense the movement. Ever so slowly, the Crow drew the knife across Hardeman's throat, the touch feather-light. Hardeman felt a drop of blood run down his skin to the collar of his wool shirt. The Crow removed the knife blade and tapped it lightly on Hardeman's forehead, taking his coup gleefully. A man's honor was greatest of all if he moved close among his enemies, to touch them without doing harm and escape with his own life.

Fairly certain now that the Crow did not intend to harm him immediately, Hardeman's awareness expanded. He saw that the lashings holding down the covers of the shelter had been cut, the robes raised on one side, admitting the moonlight. The moon was still high. He heard the stamping of horses and their soft snorting. The sound came from too far away. Blackbird had gone to sleep as he did each night, with his own pony's lead rope tied to his wrist and passing out beneath the coverings of the shelter. As far as Hardeman could tell, the boy and everyone else in the shelter were still asleep. He heard the horses again, still farther away. Most likely that was what the Crows wanted. Steal the horses and count coup on the sleeping men they had left afoot. A good joke on the little party of Sioux and whites.

Because of the encounter with the Crows that day, Hardeman had brought both his rifles into the shelter for the night. They lay beside him now. The Crow picked up the Winchester and admired it briefly, then passed it to a second warrior standing outside the shelter. The leader whispered something to the other man, who nodded and disappeared from sight. The Crow picked up the Sharps then and prodded the sleeping form of Bat Putnam with the muzzle of the buffalo gun. Bat rolled over, his eyes opening. The Crow rested the barrel of the Sharps on Bat's forehead. Bat's eyes widened.

Hardeman waited no longer. With the Colt's trigger pulled back to disengage the hammer from the sear, he thumbed back the hammer and fired from beneath his blankets, hoping the layers of bedding wouldn't deflect the bullet. The two-hundred-grain lead projectile struck the Crow in the side, lifting him from his knees and dropping him dead across Bat Putnam. The muffled roar of the Colt broke the soft night sounds and released a bedlam of reactions within the small shelter.

"Christ almighty, Christopher!"

"He's not alone! They've got the horses!"

Standing Eagle leaped to his feet, stumbled, and fell against the side of the shelter, pulling away the last of the covering and most of the supporting poles. Bat threw off the dead Crow and stood up as Hawk Chaser and Little Hand struggled to free themselves from their robes.

As Blackbird jerked awake he reached instinctively for his bow even as he pulled on the buffalo-hair rein tied to his wrist. The moccasin carrier was the horse guard, and no duty was more important than that one. To his horror he found that his rein had been cut, leaving only a short piece attached to his arm. The horses were neighing now, somewhere off among the cottonwoods. In an instant, Blackbird was on his feet and running, bow in hand, racing for the trees without stopping to see if anyone followed. The theft of the horses was his fault; he would rather die alone trying to get them back than live with the shame of letting the hated *Kanghí* put the pipe carriers afoot.

He was among the trees now and the sounds of the horses were nearer. If only the other *Kanghí* would wait for their companion!

There! Two men were mounting, trying to control the excited animals. He saw no others. Had there been just three of the enemy? He heard his father call his name from somewhere behind him, but the men would not reach the horses in time. He was closest.

He ran silently, bending low so the *Kanghí* would not see him until he was upon them. The moonlight made it easy to avoid the obstacles in his path. How could they not see him now?

Each of the enemy held four horses. The brazen *Kanghí* had ridden or led their own mounts right up to the pipe carriers' tethered animals! They had them all, even the pack horse. If they got away . . .

One man started off downstream, leading his four horses, but the other was having trouble with Lodgepole's little bay mare. She crossed behind the *Kanghí,* pulling him around by the arm that held the lead ropes, twisting him in the saddle. He tried to shift the mare's rope to his other hand, the one that held his own rein, but the mare's rope slipped from his grasp. He grabbed for it, missed, and in that moment Blackbird leaped at the man and knocked him from his horse.

They landed on the ground and rolled apart, but the stocky Crow was quick, already reaching for the lithe boy and seizing him by the ankle, the other hand raising a knife. The Crow's horse reared, whinnying and pawing the air as the two men struggled on the ground at his feet. The Crow looked up and Blackbird struck out wildly with his bow, catching the Crow on the side of the head and stunning him, making him lose his hold. In an instant Blackbird was on his feet. He seized the horse's rein and vaulted into the saddle, urging the frightened animal into flight. Ahead of him, three of the remaining horses were running downstream after the fleeing *Kanghí* and the horses he led, but Lodgepole's mare was circling and slowing. The men would catch her easily enough, and they would deal with the remaining *Kanghí,* who was alone and horseless now. Blackbird was concerned with only one thing, the horses that were getting away. They were gone from sight now around a curve in the riverbed. He leaned low over his mount's neck, using his bow as a quirt, straining to hear any sound beyond the clatter of the horse's hooves on the gravel and ice of the river bottom. What if the rest of the *Kanghí* awaited the horse-stealing party nearby? What could one boy do against the entire war party?

He could die.

The thought chilled Blackbird but it also hardened his determination. He was the only one with a chance to recover the stolen horses. If the pipe carriers were left afoot they could never catch Three Stars and it would be Blackbird's fault.

The moonlight illuminated the valley and low hills around him with cold white light, every feature standing out stark and motionless. As Blackbird rounded the bend in the river the stream ran straight before him; there too everything was still and for a heart-stopping moment he feared he had lost the enemy, but then . . . Yes! There was the *Kanghí* now, emerging from behind a clump of cottonwoods, still leading the four horses and followed by the other three.

At once Blackbird slowed his own mount and looked at the ground ahead carefully, trying to match his pace to that of the *Kanghí wichasha* so the man would not hear him.

Now the Crow turned aside, leaving the valley bottom and ascending a gentle slope to the west. Blackbird reined in within the shadow of a low bluff until the man had crested the rise and was gone from sight. The loose horses continued down the stream and slowed to a trot. They could be found later. This was Blackbird's chance to overtake and surprise the *Kanghí*.

He kicked his mount and raced up the slope where the Crow had gone, fitting an arrow to his bowstring as he rode. He counted on the softer ground, covered with grass and barely a dusting of snow, to muffle the sounds of his approach. He raced headlong now, over the low crest and down a grassy swale, and then he was upon the enemy.

The arrow was in flight as the Crow turned and saw Blackbird for the first time, but his turn protected his body and the iron-tipped shaft pierced the flesh of his underarm through his fur cape and winter shirt. He seized the shaft and ripped it away, keeping his grip on the captured horses all the while. He reined to a stop and turned to face Blackbird, who pulled his horse around to return to the attack.

"Come, Lakotah boy! Shoot again!" the Crow called out in crude Lakota, and Blackbird saw that the man was laughing at him. In a fury he kicked his horse, urging him into a reckless charge, and as he controlled the animal with his knees he let fly a second arrow just before he swerved aside. The *Kanghí* leaned calmly away from the arrow and it flew past him harmlessly as the man laughed aloud.

Blackbird wheeled again and drove in between the Crow and the four horses, determined to break them free. He swung his bow with all his strength at the man's head but hit his shoulder instead. The Crow grabbed the bow and pulled sharply, drawing Blackbird closer. A knife flashed in the moonlight as the *Kanghí*'s free hand swung down and Blackbird felt a deep pain in his thigh, followed by a warm rush as the blood poured down his leg. With a wrench of his arm the Crow jerked Blackbird from his horse and jumped off his own mount to land on top of the boy, knocking the wind out of him.

"You brave Lakotah boy. Die brave now." The man straddled Blackbird, gripping his hair. He reached out with his knife and placed it at Blackbird's temple.

Blackbird closed his eyes and clenched his teeth, determined not to make any sound as the blade circled his head to free the edges of the scalp. He felt the knife begin to move, the man taking his time, in no hurry now, and then suddenly there was a sharp tug at his hair and the weight of the *Kanghí* left him, as if he had been jerked away by unseen hands. As Blackbird opened his eyes he heard a booming explosion that came from far away, and yet it filled the air around him. He sat up, struggling to regain his breath. Far off on the last rise, well beyond bowshot, he saw a man wearing a *washíchun* hat, mounting a horse.

Where was the *Kanghí?* Blackbird turned and saw his enemy lying still, just out of reach. A dark stain was spreading slowly on the man's shirt. Blackbird picked up his bow and struck a blow on the *Kanghí*'s body with all his might, taking his coup, but the effort seemed to exhaust him and the bow slipped from his fingers. He put out a hand to steady himself as his head reeled. He heard hoofbeats and turned to see a rider close at hand, and he recognized the *washíchun* Hardeman, holding a long-shooting buffalo gun in his hand.

Blackbird tried to stand but his legs buckled before he was upright and he fell back to the ground, which felt strangely soft as he struck it. Why did his leg hurt so? He seemed unable to raise his head now, or even to keep his eyes open. He heard the *washíchun*'s voice as if from a great distance, and someone touched him, but then he knew nothing more.

"Watch out, he's hurt bad." Hardeman lowered Blackbird's unconscious form to the waiting hands. He had come upon the other men a mile downstream from the night camp, carrying the robes and bundles. They had already caught the three horses that had panicked and run after the fleeing Crow. He himself was on Bat's mare; she had run into the trees and stopped, and he had been the first to reach her.

"If that feller got away, might be he'll bring his friends," Bat said as he helped lower Blackbird to the ground. Hawk Chaser had brought coals from the old fire and was already feeding twigs to a small blaze.

"He didn't get away." Hardeman had dismounted to shoot the Crow from seven hundred yards away when he saw it was his only chance to save the boy. It wasn't bad for night shooting, but well within the range of the Sharps. When he reached Blackbird he had covered the wounded youth with the dead man's cape and his own coat, and had left him just long enough to catch the horses before starting back. Little Hand took the horses now as Hardeman dismounted; he handed the white man his Winchester, which had been recovered from the third dead Crow.

Standing Eagle looked up from where he knelt by his son. "You just seen the one? No others?"

"No others."

"The others was around, they'd of been on us by now," Bat said. "Them three bucks just couldn't pass up a chance to steal Lakota horses, I reckon."

With all the men helping, a shelter was built in short

order, a crude lean-to facing the fire, which now blazed high. The night air was clear and bitterly cold. The moon had moved to the western part of the sky and in the east the stars shone brightly, revealing no hint of dawn.

Blackbird was placed close to the fire and covered with several robes, leaving only his wounded leg exposed. Hawk Chaser pulled aside the boy's legging, which Hardeman had slit with his knife in his haste to expose the wound and stop the bleeding. He had bound a bandanna over the deep gash, and above the wound he had placed a tourniquet to staunch the bleeding, which had pulsed from a severed artery. Revealed again now, the wound glistened wetly in the firelight. Hawk Chaser looked at Hardeman and nodded his approval of the measures the scout had taken. He loosened the tourniquet cautiously, and retightened it as blood began to surge from the wound.

Bat picked up the lance that Hawk Chaser had laid close at hand and he set the blade in the fire. Standing Eagle bent low to listen to Blackbird's shallow breathing. He placed his ear on his son's chest for a moment, then felt the boy's face and hands, and finally he made a sign, passing his right forefinger under his left hand, which was held on edge in front of him.

"He'll go under for sure if'n we don't do nothin' fer him!" Bat said angrily.

"The boy's gone beaver," Standing Eagle said, and Hardeman marveled at the man's control. He revealed no emotion at all and might as well have been talking about a wounded horse. "His fault anyway. He'd of been lookin' t' the horses like he was supposed to, none o' this would of happened."

"He's your son!" Hardeman said, shocked by the war leader's attitude.

"Takes his chances on the trail, same's any coon."

Hawk Chaser spoke in Lakota then, and Standing Eagle replied in that language. Bat joined the conversation and Little Hand said a word or two, and when the talk died, Bat turned to Hardeman. "Eagle says even if the boy lives he'll slow us down. We'll have to take him on a pony drag and we'll never catch Three Stars. He says the council sent him to deliver a pipe to Three Stars and that's what he aims to do."

"He'll leave the boy here?"

Bat nodded. "Hawk Chaser'll stay with him. Ol' Hawk's a bone setter; he's got some experience with wounds. If'n the boy lives, he'll bring him along."

"If we move out now, we'll catch Crook today, even with the boy on a pony drag," Hardeman said. "The cavalry will have a doctor with them."

Bat told Hawk Chaser what the white man had said, and the warrior replied, plainly disagreeing.

"Hawk won't have it," Bat explained. "He says the white medicine men are nothin' but bone cutters. They'll lop off the boy's leg quicker'n you can spit. Don't know nothin' about healin', he says. Don't know but what I agree with him, but that's neither here ner there. What I do know is, we ain't certain to find Three Stars today, ner tomorrow neither. He's movin' along right quick. Could be marchin' now. Hawk says there's another way. We cross country to the Powder and go downstream till we find a village where they can care for the boy. We move quick's we can, we won't lose much time."

"And if Crook finds a village in the meantime?"

"Tell the truth, we reckon there ain't no villages left on the Tongue. Word is they've all gone to the Powder. We had a news rider not long ago. We go down the Powder, we might find Sittin' Bull. We can give him the pipe, have a parley, then go on to Three Stars, and it's all wrapped up, slick's you please."

While Bat was talking with Hardeman, Hawk Chaser was speaking to Standing Eagle, arguing forcefully, gesturing often at Blackbird, and in the end Standing Eagle nodded his assent, although with apparent reluctance.

Hardeman was not surprised to learn about the news rider. He wondered what else the Sun Band council knew that he didn't. But the change in plan made sense. If there were no villages on the Tongue, Crook was on a wild goose chase for the time being and the pipe carriers might accomplish their goal by a different route. Hardeman had wanted to go to Sitting Bull first, before the council decided against him. It wouldn't be easy to persuade the famous Hunkpapa, who had a reputation as an obstinate foe of the whites, but he didn't have to agree to everything at once. If he would just promise to stay at peace once Crook was gone from the country, that would be enough to take to Crook, and the general's assent would be all the more likely. Still, the thought of soldiers loose in the land made Hardeman uneasy. He had told no one in Putnam's Park or Sun Horse's village about Custer and Gibbon, nor did Johnny know. Hardeman had learned about the other prongs of the expedition from Crook, and he had kept the knowledge to himself. If the Sioux knew that Long Hair was on the move, they would see a chance to avenge themselves on Custer for opening the Black Hills to miners, and there would be no more talk of peace. But to reach the hostile villages the troops coming from Forts Shaw and Abraham Lincoln would have to march twice as far as Crook had come, and they wouldn't cover ground the way he was doing. For now, Crook was the only general in the field. There was a little time to spare. The pipe carriers would need that time, and luck as well.

"We better see to the boy," Hardeman said.

Each man knew what had to be done. They took positions at Blackbird's legs and shoulders, preparing to hold him down. There was only one way to heal such a wound. The tourniquet couldn't be left in place for long or the limb would freeze and gangrene would soon follow, but before the blood could be freed to flow again, the gash would have to be cauterized.

Hawk Chaser took the lance from the fire. The blade glowed a dull red. The men took hold of Blackbird and leaned over his body, placing most of their weight on his limbs. As the hot metal seared his flesh, Blackbird opened his eyes and screamed, but he remained unconscious; he saw nothing and felt only pain.

When the boy was covered again, the men huddled together in the shelter to await the dawn. The wounded youth needed time to recover his strength after the shock of his treatment. If he still breathed in the morning, they would build him a pony drag and set out for the Powder. Bat and Little Hand took the opportunity to curl in their robes and get some sleep, but the others remained awake, looking at the fire, which was heaped high with new wood.

Standing Eagle's expression revealed nothing of his thoughts, but he was secretly pleased. The threat to abandon his wounded son had brought about a change of course, and the idea had not come from him. He had been certain that Hawk Chaser would propose some way to save Blackbird's life without leaving him behind. It was the responsibility of a *hunká* to do everything he could to protect the life of his relative-by-choice, even at the cost of his own. And indeed, everything had worked out exactly as the war leader had expected.

Standing Eagle placed little faith in his father's hopes of finding a way to lasting peace with the whites. Sun Horse was a wise leader but he took too much on himself. It was madness for any one man to think that he could save the entire Lakota nation, no matter how strong a vision he had been given. As it was, the change in the pipe carriers' course made it all the more likely that Three Stars would come upon some group of Lakota and begin the war, and then the warriors would show the bluecoats how to fight! It was true that the news rider had said that many bands were camped on the Powder, but the hunting bands were spread far and wide across the land, each in its preferred place for the winter. They moved or stayed according to the decisions of each band's council, not by any concerted plan. There might be a small village anywhere.

The *washíchun* Hardeman would have to be closely watched now. Even Sun Horse had seen the need for that, and so Hawk Chaser had come along to guard the whiteman. Hardeman knew the location of the Sun Band's village and now he knew more, because Lodgepole had foolishly told him about the villages on the Powder.

"You will watch him carefully," Sun Horse had told

Hawk Chaser in the council. "As long as he is with you and does not betray our trust in him, you will protect him. I wish no harm to come to him. But if he tries to leave you or does anything that might bring danger to the helpless ones of our people or any band of Lakota, you must stop him. If you must kill him to stop him, you will kill him."

CHAPTER NINE

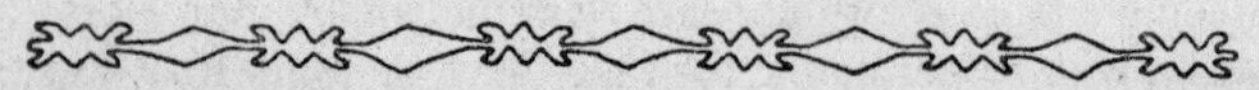

At midday on the fourth day since the attack by the Crows, the pipe carriers smelled smoke. They were in the valley of the Powder, which narrowed ahead of them where a pointed bluff intruded from the left like an outstretched arm of the rugged, wooded hills that lay to the west. Since Blackbird's wounding, travel had been slowed by the pony drag that bore the wounded boy and by the failing strength of the horses, even though the addition of the three Crow horses to the band's mounts allowed the weakest animals to go unburdened much of the time. The travelers had made their way due east from Prairie Dog Creek until they struck the Clear Fork, which they had followed down to the Powder. By Hardeman's guess they had covered less than twenty miles a day, despite clear weather and pleasant sunshine, which had eased their going. They had seen no recent sign of man—Indian or white—since leaving the trail of Crook's cavalry behind.

The little band came to a halt. It was snowing for the

first time since before the night attack, big wet flakes that gathered on their blankets and robes and even clung to Hardeman's oilskin. The wind gusted the smoke smell away, then brought it back stronger.

Hardeman sniffed the air as the others were doing. It was the clean smell of dry wood burning, with a hint of cooking meat.

On his travois Blackbird groaned and opened his eyes. Hawk Chaser was off his horse and beside the youth in an instant, placing a hand gently over Blackbird's mouth and motioning for silence with the other. Blackbird's eyes asked a question and the warrior made quick signs to say they had smelled smoke and must keep quiet until they knew whence it came. The boy tested the air, then signed that he smelled meat cooking. He passed the edge of his hand across his midsection to indicate his hunger, and he smiled.

At first the boy had lain as still as death on the pony drag the men had made for him, but on the second day he had opened his eyes for a time, though he scarcely seemed to know the men who bent low to speak to him. On the third day he had rested comfortably in the warm sunshine, sleeping most of the time, but once, when Hardeman was riding near him, he had spoken to the white man.

"Why did you come with us?" the boy had asked.

Hardeman had not been sure that the boy knew him, or his own whereabouts, but he had answered, "I came because Sun Horse asked me to."

Blackbird had looked at him steadily from his jouncing bed. "Yes, but why did you . . . want . . . to come?"

"There's been enough fighting," Hardeman had said. "It's time for the Sioux and the white men to make peace."

"My father says if we surrender, the whites will take our land," the boy had said. Hardeman made no reply and before long the youth had dropped off to sleep again.

"I'll go have a look," Hardeman said now. It was snowing thickly, although the morning had been bright and sunny. It would be good to investigate the source of the smoke while the weather offered some protection. By now the soldiers could be anywhere; they too might have crossed to the Powder.

Standing Eagle made a sign to Hawk Chaser, motioning him to accompany the white scout. The warrior nodded, rising from Blackbird's pony drag.

Leaving their horses with the others, the two men went forward on foot, Hardeman carrying his Winchester, while those remaining behind moved themselves and the horses to cover in the cottonwoods, which grew densely here. For the most part since reaching the Powder, the pipe carriers had been able to travel its broad valley under cover of the trees, only occasionally being compelled to cross an open space from one stand of cottonwoods to the next.

The two scouts kept to the brush along the bank of the stream and in a short time they were picking their way through dense willows at the end of the pointed bluff, where the river ran close beneath it. Beyond the bluff, the valley broadened considerably, although its boundaries were concealed by the falling snow. From the left, a sloping benchland reached out onto the valley bottom, created by outwash from the hills. The two men moved along the base of this intrusion, making their way among the bushes that grew there. As they went, the snow began to thin, and in a short time it had ceased entirely, leaving the air clear beneath wispy, thinning clouds that moved gently from the northeast. The wind brought the smoke again, stronger still, and Hardeman thought he caught a hint of horse smell too. The smoke heralded something more than a solitary campfire: there was a gathering of men and animals ahead.

They rounded a small point of rocks where the bench extended farthest onto the bottomland; all the valley beyond lay exposed before them, and there they saw the village.

The tipis were set among the cottonwoods where the river swept close to the western side of the valley perhaps a mile away, beneath broken bluffs that rose sharply for hundreds of feet, offering good protection from the winter storms. A few lodges were in full view but most were hidden by the trees, only their peaks visible. There were dozens, perhaps fifty or sixty, Hardeman guessed. Between the village and the two men, hundreds of horses browsed for grass in the few inches of snow that covered the valley bottom.

Hawk Chaser smiled and said a single word. "Shahíyela."

As the pipe carriers drew near they could see the whole camp, closer to a hundred tipis. There was no single camp circle as in the Sun Band village, but clusters of lodges wherever there were open spaces among the trees. While Hardeman had returned to get Bat and the others, Hawk Chaser had gone ahead on foot to announce the pipe carriers' coming and prepare the Cheyenne for the presence of two white men among the emissaries from the Sun Band. The crier was moving through the village, and from the more distant lodges men and women were still emerging, moving toward the center of camp to see the visitors arrive. Children and dogs were everywhere. As the riders emerged from the dense plum bushes that girdled the upstream end of the camp, the children pointed at the white men and stared with mouths agape at Blackbird on his pony drag. The youth was awake and looking about him with interest. There were many fresh hides in evidence and the smell of cooking meat pervaded the camp; apparently the hunting had been good. Hardeman's stomach rumbled. Since the day of Blackbird's wounding, the pipe carriers had killed just two rabbits and otherwise had subsisted on *wasná*.

"Lakota lodges yonder," Standing Eagle observed, motioning toward the downstream end of the village, where newcomers traditionally placed their tipis. "Oglala, I'm thinkin'. Some just out from the reservation." He grinned at Hardeman.

Among the farthest lodges, Hardeman saw some that were bright and new, made from the heavy canvas trade cloth the reservation bands used instead of animal hides. The rumors that agency Indians were coming west to join the hostiles were true.

Hawk Chaser stepped forward to meet the riders as they reached the first grouping of tipis and dismounted. He addressed himself to Standing Eagle, speaking as a scout who had gone ahead of the party, reporting what he had learned to the man in charge.

"Cheyenne, all right," Bat said for Hardeman's benefit. "The old-man chiefs is Old Bear and Little Wolf, but the day-to-day business is took care of by Two Moons. He's a young feller, but good 'n' steady; I've seen him a few times. This bunch was on the Tongue most of the winter. Got the order to go in to the agencies and come this far. They'll go on when the weather gets warm again." He listened for a few moments and then spoke again. "The Lakota lodges is Last Bull's, the new ones. Come out from the agency durin' the thaw. The others belong to He Dog. They're goin' in with Two Moons. He Dog's *hunká*-relative to Crazy Horse. His brother-friend. Them two been through thick and thicker. He Dog's Crazy Horse's best friend in the world." The disappointment was plain in Bat's tones and Hardeman wondered what had caused it. Was it because the Cheyenne and Sioux here were going in without a fight? Bat had never said what he thought the hostiles should do, or the Sun Band either, for that matter.

Hardeman was pleased by the news. The government's order had said only that the free-roaming bands of Sioux must go to Dakota; there had been no mention of the Cheyenne, and yet Two Moons was going in. If a village this large showed such prudence, there might be others, both Sioux and Cheyenne, that felt the same. It would be worth a little time to learn what Two Moons might know of other bands nearby. If he and the other headmen here were willing to join Sun Horse's call for peace, it might be possible to promise Crook a general movement toward the reservation, and more than one chief to speak for an end to hostilities, if only he would give them time until the weather warmed.

The crier approached the pipe carriers now; he was missing one eye and wore no covering to conceal his loss. He invited the newcomers to follow him to Two Moons' lodge, where the headman awaited them. The horses, all but Blackbird's, were led away by young boys to be unsaddled and picketed until it was learned if the strangers would be continuing on their way that day. Hawk Chaser led Blackbird's horse as the pipe carriers moved off behind the crier, and the wounded youth motioned to one small child to sit beside him on the pony drag and ride with him, but the child was too bashful to accept. The curious crowd followed along, and Hardeman tried to estimate how many Indians there might be in Two Moons' village. Usually there were four or five in a lodge, but here there were many small lodges, scarcely more than wickiups, most likely inhabited by single men. Still, there would be upward of four hundred souls in the camp, about a quarter of them warriors.

"That's Two Moons, now," Bat said softly. They were approaching a prominent tipi in the middle of the largest cluster of lodges, set back against the bluffs. The man standing in front of the tipi had taken the time to don his ceremonial headdress; he wore a fresh buffalo robe with a white band of beadwork around the border and in his right hand he held an eagle wing, his badge of office. His face was round, the skin dark, the eyes clear.

If you took a dime-novel picture of an Indian chief, that's what he'd look like, Hardeman thought. Young to be a headman. He stood straight and proud and patient, waiting for his guests to come to him as if he had no curiosity at all and all the time in the world. Around his neck he wore a bone-and-bead choker, the red beads bright against the white bones. His braids were wrapped in what looked to be lynx fur. He could have been a Sioux, for all that his garments and ornaments revealed. The differences between the two peoples had diminished over the years as they received similar goods from white traders and adopted similar styles of beadwork and personal ornamentation. They were different in language and some customs, and a glance at the arrows of either tribe was enough to distinguish one from the other, but both were horse-riding, buffalo-hunting people. The northern Cheyenne had shared many of the victories and defeats as the Sioux came increasingly into conflict with the whites, and many of the southern bands had come north after Black Kettle's death at the Washita, to live in the Powder River country with their more numerous ally.

Even as Hardeman surveyed the people, many eyes were looking at him, and in one pair recognition sparked. A man turned away and went quickly to his lodge, which stood nearby. Moments later he re-emerged, carrying something in his hand.

The pipe carriers halted a few paces in front of Two Moons, and around them the crowd flowed into a half circle before it too came to rest, joined at the last by a contingent of Lakota from the farthest lodges. Two Moons prepared to speak, but there came a sudden movement—one man, his arm raised, cutting through the people like a buffalo through the tall grass, rushing toward the strangers. His quarry was looking the other way, and so the man gave a short cry of warning.

Hardeman felt someone approaching rapidly from behind, heard the cry, and acted without thinking. Only the speed of his reaction saved his life. As he turned, his body dropped into a crouch, the right hand going for the pistol in his waistband and the left raised against something striking down from above. The Cheyenne war club in the hand of the attacker was deflected by Hardeman's arm and it glanced off the white man's head, a blow that left Hardeman stunned and reeling, but still on his feet, his right hand fumbling at the buttons of his coat where it blocked the way to his pistol. Before the Cheyenne could strike again, a man stepped between Hardeman and the attacker. It was Hawk Chaser, his lance held ready.

Bat took Hardeman by the arm to steady him. "I'd leave that six-gun be, hoss," he said softly. "What're ye feelin' like?"

The wound on Hardeman's head was beginning to bleed and his left arm was numb where the club had struck it. He shook his head to clear his vision. Bat wiped the blood from Hardeman's forehead with a finger and Hardeman winced.

The mountain man grinned. "It don't look too bad, but I reckon it'll swell up some."

Two Moons left the front of his lodge and moved through the crowd, which had clustered around the pipe carriers. Men and women made way for him and gathered behind him as he advanced. Two other men stepped forward more quickly and spoke harshly to the attacker. They were Cheyenne *akíchita,* camp marshals charged with keeping the peace. The pipe carriers had not been formally welcomed into the camp but they were guests nevertheless, their identities and purpose known and announced by the crier, and an attack on them was a serious breach of custom.

Hardeman's attacker replied angrily to the marshals, gesturing at Hardeman, drawing aside his blanket to show a scar of twisted skin in the muscle of his shoulder above the collarbone. As they heard his words some of the other Cheyenne grew angry, but none moved toward Hardeman, who was protected by Hawk Chaser.

Hardeman was standing straight now, his composure regained. He neither looked at his attacker nor moved toward him. Instead, all his attention was on Two Moons. He wanted the headman's good will. By choosing to go to Dakota peacefully, Two Moons had become Hardeman's ally, albeit unknowingly.

Two Moons spoke at some length with Hardeman's attacker, and while the two men talked, the pipe carriers were joined by one of the camp marshals, who took a place beside Hawk Chaser, his stance indicating clearly that he too would protect the white man. When the talk was done, the marshal turned to the visitors and addressed them in Lakota, gesturing at the man with the war club.

"This is Kills Fox. He knows this white man." Bat put the translator's words into English as the Cheyenne spoke. "He is one of the scouts who brought the soldier chief Long Hair to the village of Black Kettle at the Washita, eight snows ago. Kills Fox was wounded there; he shows you the scar." Again the attacker drew aside his blanket, his face dark with anger. "The wife of Kills Fox died there, and one of his sons."

Two Moons and the rest of the crowd were waiting for some kind of reply from the pipe carriers.

"It is true," Bat said in Lakota. Many in the crowd understood that language, and for those that did not, he made signs as he talked, translating his own words for all to see. The crowding warriors surged forward like wolves toward a wounded buffalo, but Hawk Chaser raised his lance again and now even Standing Eagle and Little Hand closed ranks in front of Hardeman, together with the Cheyenne marshal. Hardeman remained where he was, showing no fear. He felt blood trickling down his cheek.

"It is true that this man was a scout for Long Hair," Bat said, directing himself to Two Moons. "It is also true that after the Washita battle he left the bluecoats and has not scouted for them since. He came to my father-in-law Sun Horse bearing a message of peace from the soldier chief Three Stars; he travels with us to seek Three Stars now, carrying Sun Horse's reply. Two Moons knows that among those who scout for the bluecoats there are many who were once our friends, men who lived among us, traders' sons with Shahíyela and Lakota mothers. Friends become enemies and enemies become friends. We judge a man by what he does now, by whether he behaves as a friend or an enemy. This whiteman has proved himself our friend. When we were attacked by *Kanghí,* he fought them with us and helped to recover our horses. He saved a young man's life." Here Bat gestured at Blackbird, who lay quietly on the pony drag. There were murmurs of surprise in the crowd and some nods of approval. The anger vanished from many faces to be replaced by a new curiosity and respect. Bat waited for the surprise to subside before he turned back to Two Moons. "We come to you tired and hungry, our horses worn out. We need your help to continue on our way. Will our brothers the Shahíyela refuse help to those who carry pipes of peace?"

Two Moons had listened politely as Bat spoke, showing no reaction. Bat had chosen his words with care, framing his appeal in terms that the headman could not refuse, not if he expected to live up to the traditions of his position.

More than any other people of the plains, the Cheyenne revered the peace men. Keeping the peace had been the first duty of their chiefs ever since those positions of tribal authority had first been created by Sweet Medicine, the legendary hero of the Cheyenne. A Cheyenne chief must be a man of peace before all else, as well as brave, and generous to friend and stranger alike. "When a stranger comes to your tipi asking for something, give it to him," Sweet Medicine had said. Bat had asked for help in a way that reminded Two Moons of his obligations, and he admired the skill with which the young Cheyenne headman concealed his embarrassment.

"You are the son-in-law of Sun Horse?" Two Moons inquired with no more than polite interest.

Bat nodded. "My wife is Otter Skin, daughter of Sun Horse." He indicated Standing Eagle, at his right hand. "My brother Standing Eagle is war leader of Sun Horse's camp. It is he who carries the pipe for Three Stars. My cousin Little Hand carries a pipe for Sitting Bull."

There was a sound from the crowd at the mention of the Hunkpapa war man, but Two Moons pretended not to notice. He turned to Kills Fox and spoke to him quietly for a time. The angry fire had left the warrior's eyes as Bat talked, and his manner had become subdued. He nodded now, submitting to his leader, then turned and spoke briefly, keeping his eyes averted from the pipe carriers.

"Kills Fox offers a horse to Ice, who knows the secrets of healing," Bat said to Hardeman once the man's words had been put into Lakota by the camp marshal. "He asks Ice to treat your wounds. Old Ice, he's about as famous a medicine man as the Cheyenne got."

A white-haired man stepped out of the crowd and joined Kills Fox. With his short nose, round face and dark skin, he might have been a much older version of Two Moons.

Hardeman touched his forehead and found that the blood there was beginning to dry. His head still throbbed and the pain made it difficult for him to organize his thoughts, but he had no wish to place himself under the healer's care and miss the conference with Two Moons.

He made signs to say that the wound was not serious and required no treatment, inclining his head to Kills Fox to acknowledge the courtesy; he was willing to meet the warrior more than halfway if the man wanted to let bygones be bygones.

Kills Fox seemed less than pleased by Hardeman's reply and he spoke again, gesturing now in Blackbird's direction.

"He's offerin' to have Ice look at the boy," Bat explained. "We best accept this time, to let him off the hook."

Bat spoke briefly to Standing Eagle in Lakota and Hardeman inwardly cursed his own stupidity. By refusing to let the healer at least look at his wound, he had denied Kills Fox a chance to atone for his offense against a guest. He would have to find some other way to accept the warrior's apology.

With a show of good will, Standing Eagle agreed to let Ice care for Blackbird's wound. The old healer came forward to kneel beside the pony drag, where he spoke softly to the boy and made signs to inquire about the wound, and Hardeman imagined that he saw a trace of satisfaction on Two Moons' face as the headman welcomed his guests at last.

"All men of peace are welcome in the camps of the *Tsistsístas*. Our brothers the Lakota are always welcome. People of Sun Horse's camp are most welcome, for it is known that Sun Horse is a great man of peace. His sons and their friends are welcome in this village. The whiteman who accompanies them is welcome. Come to my lodge and eat."

The last of the tension dissipated now, evidenced by the soft buzz of conversation in the crowd and the smiles that appeared on many faces. Peace had been restored to the village.

Two Moons motioned his guests toward his lodge, but paused as an ancient man stepped out of the throng and hobbled slowly forward, aided by a younger man who himself was gray-haired and bent. The gathering fell silent. The aged warrior made straight for Hardeman with one arm extended, and when he reached the white man he seized Hardeman's coat and pulled with surprising strength, forcing Hardeman's face down close to his own. He peered through rheumy eyes, blinking often, and Hardeman saw that the man was nearly blind. With a hand as brown and wrinkled as a dried-up leaf he touched Hardeman's face lightly, the fingers brushing the scar on his cheekbone.

The old man spoke a few words, which had to be put into Lakota and then English before Hardeman knew their meaning.

"Where did they give you this scar?"

"I was shot at the Washita battle."

The old man nodded, smiling, and he laughed. His laughter was strong and clean like a young man's. "I am the one who shot you," he said. "I fired from the entrance of my lodge. If you had not moved, I would have killed you." He sounded disappointed that this had not been the case, but then he became very serious and he seized Hardeman's coat again. "You shot into a lodge and then went inside. When you came out you had a boy in your arms." Here the old man held out a hand to indicate the boy's height. "Tell me what became of him."

"The boy is alive," Hardeman said. "He's with Sun Horse now."

"Is this true?" The old man turned to the other pipe carriers, holding out his hands as if he would grab the words from their mouths. "I wish to hear another say this is true! One of you Lakota! Tell me!"

"It is true," said Hawk Chaser, and the old man did not need to hear the words translated into Cheyenne. He raised his face to the sky and held out his arms as he sang his song of power, a high keening wail of joy.

"What is he called, this boy?" Two Moons wished to know, and now it was Bat Putnam who answered.

"He is known by many names among the Lakota. First we called him the White Boy of the Shahíyela, but later we gave him other names. His father was White Smoke, son of Sun Horse, and after his dream we called him the One Who Stands Between the Worlds."

Translations were taking place all through the crowd and now a murmur arose among the onlookers, rapidly growing to an excited buzz of talk as the southern Cheyenne told their northern cousins the meaning of what they had heard. Kills Fox was speaking to Two Moons, explaining what he knew of White Smoke's adopted son. Above it all rose the old man's cry of joy, which stopped suddenly now as he turned again to Hardeman, who was more than a little taken aback by the reaction to his news.

"I thought you took him away to kill him," the old man said. "The bluecoats shot some women and children in a ravine behind the camp and I thought you would take him there. That is why I believed he had died, but I always hoped he might still live." Tears rolled down the old man's wrinkled cheeks, but he smiled as he spoke. "I made his first bow. I was an arrowmaker then. I made his first bow and his arrows. He was a good boy, and he could follow a trail like a wolf. And with horses . . ." The old man shook his head. "He had great power with horses. He was a good boy. I am glad he is alive." Then a new thought occurred to him. "Has he chosen between the worlds?"

Hardeman was considering how to reply to this when Bat answered for him. The old man nodded, apparently satisfied, and started away, led by the second man, who had remained silent all the while.

"Quite a stir it makes whenever folks find out Johnny's alive," Hardeman observed.

"Mmm," Bat nodded, watching the old man move off among the other Cheyenne, who were still talking among themselves with much animation. "Like I said, these folks set a heap o' store by dreams."

Blackbird was lifted from his pony drag by three men, directed with sharp words from Ice, the old healer. As the boy was carried off, the crowd began to disperse and the pipe carriers followed Two Moons to his lodge.

The headman preceded the others into the tipi and took his seat at the back, facing the entrance. He motioned his guests to sit to his left, leaving it to them to work out their positions according to each man's importance. Standing Eagle took the place of honor next to the host and motioned Little Hand to sit beside him. Bat was next, then Hawk Chaser and Hardeman. When they were all seated, another man entered the lodge. It was Kills Fox, who seated himself across the fire from Two Moons, close to the door, in the place of least honor.

The fire was built up high and the tipi was warm and comfortable. The men formed a half circle around the fire, and Hardeman expected that the two women who sat across it in the family's side of the lodge would begin to bring the food at once. The odor of cooking meat filled the tipi, coming from the pot set astraddle of the small cooking fire there. Juices began to flow in Hardeman's mouth, but the women remained where they were, apparently waiting for some sign from Two Moons.

To Hardeman's surprise, the headman began to load a pipe with great care. From the way the smoking mixture was cut and placed in the bowl, Hardeman knew a ceremonial smoke was in the offing, but he could not imagine its purpose. First you fed the guests, then you smoked before the talking began.

Two Moons took a coal from the fire and lit the pipe, and he surprised Hardeman once more by offering it to the directions in the Sioux manner, although the Cheyenne custom differed but little. Honoring his guests, Hardeman thought. When the offering was completed, Two Moons puffed again to be sure the pipe was burning well, and then, partly rising, he passed it with his right hand around the fire to Kills Fox.

At last Hardeman understood the meaning of this smoke. Normally, a ceremonial pipe was passed from right hand to left hand, then to the man on the left, and so around the circle, as the sun traveled around the hoop of the world, as both Lakota and Cheyenne prayed. There was good power in the sun and in the motion it followed through the sky, and men did many things in this way to remind themselves of that power and to partake of it. These things Hardeman knew from his earliest days among the plains peoples, but he had seen the pipe passed in the opposite direction too, on rare occasions. It was a smoke of reconciliation, an apology offered where there had been an argument or open dispute. Here, the village had been dishonored because a visitor had been attacked within the camp; the headman had been embarrassed, although the feeling had to be read from the smallest details in Two Moons' otherwise impassive bearing—a nervous flicking of the eyes, unwilling to meet Hardeman's straight on until the one who had been wronged accepted the pipe.

Kills Fox offered the pipe solemnly and smoked it, and when he passed it to Hardeman his hand trembled slightly.

Hardeman made nothing special of the ceremony. To do so would only call more attention to the wrong and further discomfort his host. He pointed the pipestem to the four directions, then to the sky and the earth, touching it to the ground in front of him before smoking and passing it on. The mixture of red willow bark and trade tobacco went to his head at once and set his wound to throbbing again. His head felt fuzzy, as if he had a fever, and his stomach rumbled.

Kills Fox was smiling as the pipe made its way back to Two Moons. The group was joined in friendship, the apology offered and accepted. Two Moons also was visibly relieved; he became the expansive host now, speaking grandly to the women. At once they served up bowls of hot broth, accompanied by chunks of buffalo rib roast that dripped with juice and blood. It took no awareness of good manners to make the guests fall to with a will.

"These folks been havin' a shinin' winter by the looks of it," Bat observed. He ate noisily, nodding happily at Two Moons. He belched as the food hit his belly and began to calm the giddy feeling the pipe had caused. "Ain't seen so much buffler ner so many hides a-workin' in a heap o' moons."

"Shinin' times," Standing Eagle agreed, his mood improving now that he had a handful of meat in his mouth. With his skinning knife he cut off a piece close to his lips and chewed it vigorously, wiping away the juices on his chin with the back of his sleeve. Bat ate in the same manner, as all the mountain men had eaten, adopting the technique of hands and knife from the Indians. Afterwards, hands were wiped free of grease on leggings, keeping them supple and waterproof.

While the guests were still fully occupied with pieces of roast, the women brought forth an offering that made Bat's eyes light up. *Boudin blanc* the trappers had called this sausage-like creation. It was made by stuffing buffalo intestine with hump meat, tying off the ends and roasting it over hot coals, then finally boiling it for a short time. The trappers had considered it a rare delicacy and Bat ate it now until he belched loudly and could hold no more. "Shinin' times," he sighed contentedly.

When the meal was done at last, another pipe was offered, this one passed sunwise around the lodge and smoked contentedly by all, with a minimum of ceremony, and when Two Moons had set the pipe aside, Standing Eagle told the Cheyenne headman the details of the pipe carriers' mission—the exact nature of Sun Horse's message to Three Stars and why there was a second pipe for Sitting Bull. Two Moons listened attentively. When Standing Eagle was through, he spoke at some length in slow but correct Lakota, to accommodate his guests, who took an immediate interest in his words. At last Bat turned to Hardeman.

"Seems like Sittin' Bull's up by Chalk Buttes, sixty miles or so northeast; more'n a day's ride on a fast horse, anyways. Ol' Two Moons, he's been thinkin' on his feet. Even afore we was in camp, he sent off a couple of young fellers on strong horses to fetch Sit here. Hawk Chaser told him we had a pipe for Sittin' Bull, he jest sent them boys off lickety-split." Bat snapped his fingers and winked at Standing Eagle, who scowled, for he had never been able to master this white man's trick. "Now, Two Moons'll give us fresh horses if'n we're plumb determined to move on, but he says we might's well stay put and rest our horses, get ourselves fattened up. He told Sittin' Bull we've come far and got a man wounded. He reckons Ol' Sit'll be along in two, three days."

Once more, Hardeman totted up the risks of delay. The truth was, he would prefer to council with Sitting Bull here, where Two Moons and He Dog were preparing to go in and there were Oglalas with fresh canvas lodges from the agency, to show that life in that place wasn't so bad. If the pipe carriers pressed on now, they might see Sitting Bull a day sooner, but it was worth waiting an extra day to increase the chance of winning Sitting Bull over to Sun Horse's plan.

Two Moons spoke again, as if adding an afterthought, and Bat smiled. "Two Moons says he'd be just tickled to host a big talkfest. Says he'll speak fer peace, and come spring he'll ride with Sun Horse to talk to the other headmen."

Hardeman's hopes rose like water in a spring, but he revealed nothing. Instead he signed a question to the Cheyenne: *Have your scouts seen Three Stars?*

Two Moons made a sign of negation. *Before the moon was full we saw signals saying the soldiers were coming. Since then we have seen nothing.* He showed little aptitude for the sign talk and he added something in words, speaking to Bat.

"Same time as he sent the boys off to Sittin' Bull, he sent more young men down the Powder to warn the villages to keep their scouts out. It ain't likely the pony soldiers'll catch anyone nappin'."

Hardeman nodded, greatly relieved. "We might as well wait here."

Hawk Chaser spoke to Standing Eagle then, saying that with a few days of rest, Blackbird might be able to sit a horse and go with the men when they left to find Crook. Standing Eagle shrugged and gave his consent to the arrangement with a few words, his expression unreadable.

Bat contained his own satisfaction with difficulty. Events could scarcely have gone more to his liking. He too had seen that there was a better chance of bringing Sitting Bull into the plan if the pipe was presented here, but he had another reason for wishing to remain among the Cheyenne. From the first, he had seen that it would be far safer for

Hardeman to meet Sitting Bull here in a peaceful village of Cheyenne than in Sitting Bull's own camp, with his young warriors howling for war, or even out on the trail, where there were the other pipe carriers to be considered. Standing Eagle and Little Hand were blinded by their stubborn distrust of all *washíchun,* and Hawk Chaser had instructions to kill the scout if he acted in a way that could endanger any Lakota, and so Bat had sought any means to protect the white man from his own foolishness, if it came to that, and to increase the chance that he might live out the next couple of days. Wherever Sitting Bull was met, Hardeman would almost certainly learn the full extent of Sun Horse's message and he would hear of the call for a summer meeting of the bands. Even if Sitting Bull refused the pipe, the Hunkpapa was still asked to join in convoking a great gathering of all the Lakota in summer so the issues of peace and war could be decided there in the hoop of the nation. Hardeman knew nothing of this, and how he might react to the news Bat couldn't guess, but here, at least, the white scout had a measure of protection. The sudden attack by Kills Fox, followed by the revelation of Hardeman's role in saving Johnny Smoker at the Washita and the news that Johnny was even now safe with Sun Horse, could not have happened better if Bat had planned it all himself. And when the old man had asked if Johnny had yet chosen between the worlds, Bat had answered only, "His time to choose is now." Let the people here think that Johnny might still choose the red man's world; it would give them hope, and they would value the miracle of the boy's return even more.

By Bat's reckoning, Hardeman was safer in this village now than Two Moons himself. In a few moments, he had been transformed from a white man viewed with suspicion to an important guest in camp, one who would be talked about and watched wherever he went. In the end that might help to keep him alive. If he acted rashly and perhaps tried to go off by himself to find Crook, he would be stopped, by force if need be, but Bat wanted no harm to come to him, and not just for Johnny Smoker's sake. On the trail up-country from the Sun Band's village his liking for the scout had grown, and he thought he had come to understand the man. As surely as Sun Horse, Hardeman sought peace at any cost between the Lakota and the whites, but with the bullheadedness of a *washíchun* he did not see that his way might cost the Lakota more than they could afford to pay. Still, his heart was good, and if he could only be made to see things from the Lakota viewpoint, he could be of help to the Sun Band. With help, the Sun Band might stay free for a time, and that was what Bat hoped for above all.

CHAPTER TEN

For several days the soldiers had marched in the daytime beneath bright skies. Since the three days of forced marches under cover of storm and night, which had brought them from Crazy Woman's Fork to Prairie Dog Creek, they had seen no Indians, no signals, and no recent sign. It was as if they traveled in an abandoned land. Among the troopers there were confident proclamations that the hostiles had all fled the country, and rumors that General Crook was persisting in his course down the Tongue even though he knew there were no Indians to be found there. The pace of the march was leisurely now, covering only ten or twelve miles a day.

On the fourth day of sunshine, the seventh since leaving

the supply train, the fourteenth of the campaign, John Bourke came to ride in company with his friend Ham Whitcomb for a time. E Troop was at the front of the column today. Whitcomb rode in the lead, flanked by Sergeant Dupré and Corporal McCaslin. Lieutenant Corwin had been summoned forward a short time before and he rode now with Crook and Reynolds and their staffs, and Captain Mills, thirty yards in advance of the troop.

The day was springlike. Greatcoats were open to the breeze and collars were unbuttoned as the men basked in the cheering warmth of the sun. Recent nights had been shockingly cold. More than once the mercury in the surgeon's thermometer had dropped past the lowest reading at twenty-six degrees below zero and continued to fall until the silver liquid had shrunk down into the bowl, where it solidified and remained quiescent until the sun rose the next morning.

"Your beard is making great progress," Bourke greeted Whitcomb, regarding his wispy growth with a smile. Bourke's own beard was in full flower now.

"You must get tired of eating all that hair," Whitcomb replied soberly.

Bourke laughed. "I won't starve on this campaign, Ham. I'm growing my own hay crop."

"I understand our rations are already half gone." Whitcomb hoped by this observation to elicit from Bourke some hint of Crook's plans, but he was disappointed. The general's aide merely shrugged and kept his own counsel. One thing that was clear to Whitcomb without need of confirmation was that the command could not go much farther north if they expected to return to the supply train before their provisions were exhausted.

"Corporal McCaslin tells me that the men think we are here for a look at the country," he told Bourke. "This whole campaign is nothing more than an entertainment for the troops, they claim."

"An extended constitutional, yez moight say, sorr," McCaslin added. "Some of the wagerin' kind—and I add that I never wager, sorr—but some of them as does 're givin' odds that Mr. Lo has taken his wife and kiddies and gone to the reservation, hearin' that we was in the country and all."

"Mr. Lo?" Whitcomb was puzzled.

"From the poet," Bourke explained. " 'Lo, the poor Indian, whose untutored mind sees God in everything, and hears Him in the wind.' " He turned to McCaslin. "And what about you, Corporal? Do you think General Crook has brought us here for our health?"

"No, sorr, I do not."

"Well, then?"

"Well, sorr, I'll not be denyin' that I've benefited from the exercise. I'm proper fit, sorr, and that's a fact. And the lads have color in their cheeks. But for meself, sorr, I believe we are here by the grace of the good general, and not forgettin' the Almighty, for one reason."

"Which is?"

"To smite the haythen, sorr."

"As simple as that?"

"As simple as that. The Bible tells us that our Lord Jaysus said to his disciples, 'Go yez forth and teach the haythen.' And that's why we're here, sorr. To teach them haythen redskins a lesson. And I have no doubt that the Almighty will provide haythens enough for the teachin'."

Whitcomb held back the laughter that rose within him. It wouldn't do to embarrass such a firm and simple faith. But he said, "Are you sure that smiting the heathen is the sort of teaching that Jesus had in mind?"

"We're soldiers, sorr. A soldier teaches by the sword. Of course, we have the modern convanience of the Springfield carbine."

"This is true, Walter," Sergeant Dupré said. "But before we can smite the heathen, we must find him. This is a big country, the Powder River country. As big as *la belle France,* but not so *belle*. Eight hundred thousand Prussian pigs could not occupy France, and we are only six hundred men. If the Indians wish to play cat and rat with us, we never see them."

It startled Whitcomb to think of the Powder River country as France. In a civilized land the little army would have followed roads and passed often through small villages and larger towns, fighting battles every step of the way if the land were hostile, but here they had seen only vast areas of unpopulated wilderness. On the first day after the storm, descending Prairie Dog Creek, they had had frequent views of the country far and wide, dropping gently away in front of them toward the valley of the Tongue; then once they had reached the Tongue itself they had traveled for a time in a deep canyon where they could see nothing at all except the valley floor; they had imagined the land above swarming with Indians just waiting to rain down arrows and rocks on the helpless soldiers, but when they emerged from the canyon they had found the countryside peaceful and unthreatening once more. They had followed the twisting course of the river, crossing the ice repeatedly, traveling at first in a valley much like that of the Clear Fork, with broad bottomland contained by low hills. Today the hills had dropped away on either side, revealing a valley several miles wide with gently sloping terraces composed of fine, arable earth. Off to the west stood majestic red-walled buttes, thoroughly timbered on the top. It was an impressive country, beautiful in its own way, and much more hospitable than the barren land along the Platte. The hills were well wooded with mesquite, juniper, pine and spruce, while the bottomland was thick with plum and cherry bushes, ash and box elder, as well as the ubiquitous cottonwood. Firewood had been plentiful at all the night camps and the horses and mules had been glad to forgo their evening ration of grain while they browsed instead on the thick black grama grass and a plant the scouts called "black sage," which they swore was as nutritious as oats. With each passing day, game had become more plentiful. It was a region that could comfortably support both men and their beasts of burden even in winter, but the many village sites found by the scouts, and both of those through which the column itself had passed in recent days, were deserted. The Indian villages were not permanent like those built by white men of all nationalities. They were movable, and what Dupré said was true: in a country as large as France, how could six hundred men hope to find, much less subdue, the Indians?

Whitcomb was pondering the apparent hopelessness of this task when the head of the column rounded a curve in the river and came upon a dense growth of cottonwoods covering dozens of acres, and he saw that it was yet another place of recent habitation. The village was by far the largest seen by the main body of the command and a halt was called while the scouts went ahead to look for signs that would tell them how long ago the Indians had left. There was widespread devastation in the cottonwoods, many of the trees, some of them huge, having been cut down for firewood and for the tender inner bark of the upper limbs, which the Indians fed to their ponies. By the freshness of the plentiful horse manure as well as the reddish shreds of meat that still clung to the bones of elk, deer and bison that were piled high near the drying racks, even the unpracticed eye could see that the village had been occupied not long before.

Captain Mills and Lieutenant Corwin left the generals and their staffs and as they approached the head of E Troop a rider came trotting from the rear of the column. It was Captain Egan.

"What's it to be, Anson?" he demanded of Mills. "We could make another ten miles today if we push on."

Mills shook his head. "We're going to camp here and wait for the scouts." The day before, a small party of the most experienced scouts had been sent off to the north, to explore the country to the Yellowstone.

The words were scarcely out of his mouth when six shots sounded rapidly from the direction of the village site. The officers looked around in alarm, but they relaxed when they saw General Crook's party halted among the cottonwoods, apparently unconcerned. The general himself had dismounted and was walking among some low bushes. Here and there he bent to pick something up and at last he turned and raised one hand high, holding up six pin-tailed pheasants. In his other hand was his Winchester rifle.

"My God," Egan exclaimed. "I've never seen the like of it. Shooting pheasants with a rifle! Even if they took off in a flock, that's damn good."

Crook's coat with its high collar of wolf fur was unbuttoned and it flapped as he walked back to his horse, revealing the red flannel lining in narrow flashes of bright color. Beneath the coat gleamed a row of forty or fifty brass cartridges in the cartridge belt he habitually wore around his waist. Together with his Kossuth hat, the top of the crown open to the air, and the ragged and burned corduroy trousers that flapped about his field boots, the overall impression was distinctly unmilitary.

"He looks like a bandit on the Mexican trails," Corwin said with a trace of awe.

Egan laughed. "God, Boots, have you had a look at yourself recently?" With his unkempt reddish beard, buffalo coat and fur cap, Corwin might have intimidated any run-of-the-mill border ruffian.

When the scouts had completed their examination of the site, the command was permitted to advance. With camp made in short order and supper not yet ready, the men occupied themselves with the curiosities the Indians had left behind. On many of the cottonwood trunks the savages had drawn varied scenes in bright colors, and on the far side of the river there were a number of Indian "graves" among the trees. Although the Indians did not bury their dead, there was no other term by which to call these final resting places. The bodies were raised six to ten feet above the ground on scaffolds or placed in the branches of the trees, wrapped in the best blankets and robes and, in the case of the warriors, accompanied by their weapons, and there they were left to desiccate slowly in the dry climate. The Irish glanced sideways at these eerie remains and did not linger long among the scaffolds.

Throughout the evening, eyes glanced often to the north and heads were raised whenever a horse stamped or whinnied, but the scouts sent off to the Yellowstone did not return that night.

Nor were they in camp the following morning, and word

was passed from company to company that the command would remain here for a day of rest. Some of the soldiers amused themselves by hacking through the river ice, which was nearly three feet thick, and trying to coax a somnolent trout up to a simple hook baited with a morsel of jerky, but the trout apparently knew the season as well as the men and refused to be lured into this premature sport. Other men were content to find a warm rock and lie in the sun, or to stroll along the banks of the river. In the E Troop bivouac, Corporal Walter McCaslin stayed close to the cookfires whenever his duties did not take him elsewhere. He had noted Whitcomb's remark about the too-rapid depletion of the expedition's provisions. On the march there was no midday meal, but today the cooks offered up a hot dinner at noontime, and McCaslin was among the first in line. The tough buffalo bull meat that had been the steady diet of recent days was enlivened by a welcome addition, a hot gruel of hominy grits and Indian corn that had cooked throughout the morning on beds of coals. McCaslin ate all he was allowed with methodical care. If there were to be even shorter rations later on, he would do his best to prepare himself by building up his reserves.

By mid-afternoon, a solid front of clouds, thin at first but rapidly thickening, blocked off the sun. The mercury began to drop in the thermometer that hung outside Dr. Munn's improvised shelter and an ungentle wind gusted down the river from the north. As the men buttoned their greatcoats and began to move toward the cookfires for warmth, the scouts returned from the Yellowstone.

"Vell, Frank," a grisled sergeant called out, "haff you find vork for de boys, or are ve bound for de poorhouse?"

"Plenty sign, no Injuns," Little Bat Garnier replied.

"We'll find 'em pretty soon," Grouard said, and went on with the others to report to General Crook. At once, rumors began to circulate throught the camp, and if they were to be trusted equally, elements of the command were to strike off in all directions as soon as the horses could be saddled. After an hour or two, when the scouts had left the headquarters fire and gone off to their own mess for a hot meal, one story came to dominate the rest: the command would set out under cover of dark and march all night. The direction of the march was hotly argued and several disputes came close to fisticuffs, but as evening approached there were no orders to break camp.

The guides had brought in the carcasses of six black-tail deer and at supper the remains of the last buffalo were scorned.

"Whaddya think, Corp? Should we be packin' our truck after supper?" Private Dowdy inquired of McCaslin as they left the cookfire with their plates in hand.

"Boyo, when the officers in their wisdom tell me what's to be done, I'll be lettin' yez know. Until then, eat hearty."

He chewed long and hard at his buffalo meat, savoring the flavor so close to beef but indefinably richer. He had traded his share of the deer to Private Dowdy for a much larger serving of buffalo the poor man had received by the chance of the draw. Walter McCaslin was not one to fuss over the quality of his meat so much as the quantity. He was a spare man and had been lean for all his thirty-eight years, and he missed no opportunity to eat his fill against the chance that he might have to do without on short notice. In his youth he had survived the Famine, and it was his most oft-repeated prayer that if ever he were brought close to death again before his natural time, it would not be through starvation.

After supper the long-awaited order came down the chain of command, passed from the headquarters staff to the battalion and company officers and thence to the men, and the rumors were laid to rest at last. Reveille would be at four o'clock in the morning; the command was leaving the Tongue and crossing to the Powder. The scouts had found no recent Indian sign in the open valley of the Yellowstone and no trace of General Terry or Colonel Gibbon. The trails from all the abandoned village sites on the Tongue led to the east, and it was now the consensus among guides and officers alike that if any hostiles remained in the Powder River country they would be found in the sheltered bottoms of the Powder itself.

Lieutenant Corwin found Corporal McCaslin at the cookfire, accepting the last scrapings of the stewpot from the cook. "What do you think, Walter? Is he ready?" Corwin nodded toward Whitcomb, who was brushing aside the remains of his bed-warming fire not far away, preparing his robes for the night.

"Oh, I think so, sorr."

"I hope you're right."

"He looks to his superiors as well as the men, and the soldier's life is in his blood."

"We'll see soon enough."

At dawn the column was already threading its way into the wooded hills east of the river. E Troop was at the front once more, and responsible for flankers to protect the head of the column. As he gave out the assignments that morning Corwin had looked at Whitcomb as if following a routine that had been established for weeks. "Mr. Whitcomb, you will take charge of the flankers. Set them at three hundred yards but tell them to keep in sight of the column as much as possible. There will be no bugle calls today, so warn them to keep an eye on the guidons."

Now, as the column passed over a low hill and left the Tongue behind, Whitcomb struggled to contain his excitement. He had placed two sets of flankers on either side of the column, each in the care of a non-commissioned officer, and then he had ridden a hundred yards beyond the foremost squad on the southern flank, assigning to himself the position of lone outrider, utterly unfettered by restrictions of any kind. Ahead, the first rays of the sun glinted among the trees atop the next hill, and it seemed to him that he had never seen a day or a landscape so beautiful.

Throughout the morning he kept his position, now and then dropping back and drifting closer to the column to check the positions of his flankers. During a brief nooning stop he checked his squads on the northern flank and then rode in to report to Corwin, fully prepared to be relieved of his position and kept once more under close watch, but Corwin merely accepted his report and turned to some other business, and Whitcomb cantered away with joy in his heart. What had caused the sudden change in his commander's behavior he did not know, but he would neither inquire nor complain.

As the command got under way again he resumed his solitary post, even with the head of the line and well behind the scouts, who were fanned out in a broad arc several hundred yards to the front as they had been in the opening days of the campaign. Occasionally a rise or depression would cut off his view of the column, but usually he could see all or part of it and he was struck once more by the ragtag look of the expedition. Only the coloring of the horses by troop and the close order maintained throughout the march revealed the fully trained soldiery beneath the tatterdemalion garb. He swelled with pride at having been chosen to protect such a noble force, so confident and battle-ready, but he reminded himself quickly that the Indians were a capable foe, often rated as the finest light cavalry in the world, and he examined his surroundings minutely, seeking any movement, any trace of color that did not belong among grass, trees, snow and rock. He glanced often at the guidons, watching for any signal of danger or change of direction. These swallow-tailed miniatures of the national flag were carried at the head of each troop, and in hostile countryside, where bugle calls might forewarn an enemy, they could be used to make silent signals up and down the column and to the outriders on either side. As the afternoon grew long, the guidons fluttered in the breeze but said nothing.

Whitcomb was out of sight of the column, riding through a patch of trees, when he saw the two horsemen. They were a hundred yards or more to his right, standing in the light of the lowering sun, and for an instant he thought they might be others like himself, soldiers who relished the danger and solitude of riding beyond the protection of the command, but as he watched them curiously, one man dropped lightly off his horse and knelt to examine something on the ground before him, and by his clothing and movements Whitcomb knew he was an Indian.

His first thought was to alert the column so it might

escape detection. He urged his horse into a trot and made his way toward the top of the low hill that separated him from the command. He reined in before topping the rise, not wanting to present his silhouette against the sky for the Indians to see, and he looked back. The two men were as before, one still examining the ground for tracks or other signs, when suddenly the mounted man extended an arm, pointing to Whitcomb's rear. The brave on the ground leaped to his horse and the two of them were away and into the trees and gone from sight in the twinkling of an eye.

Without waiting to see where the Indians might reappear, Whitcomb spurred his horse over the hill and down the other side at a gallop. "Indians!" he shouted as he passed by Corporal Atherton and his set of four troopers. "Come in to a hundred yards!" To his right he saw another man riding in to report, one of the guides from the front positions. It was Louis Richaud, by the look of him. Whitcomb knew half of the scouts by sight now. He raced for the cluster of officers at the head of the column and he arrived seconds before Richaud. Lieutenant Corwin was there with Crook, Reynolds, Mills, Bourke and several others, and it was to his own troop commander that Whitcomb directed his report. "Indians, sir! Two of them, a quarter mile to the south!" he said as his horse hunched down on its hind legs and skidded to a stop, raising dust on the bare patch of ground.

"Hunters, I make 'em," said Richaud as he drew in beside the young officer. "No war shields." Whitcomb noticed that the laconic frontiersman was breathing easily. His own breathing was loud and rapid, as if he had run the whole distance on foot. The guide's simple confidence in his identification of the two braves, made at a distance of several hundred yards, reminded Whitcomb forcefully of the yawning caverns in his own knowledge.

"Hadn't caught sight of us yet," Richaud added, speaking to Crook, "but they'll make our dust, sure."

"They have already seen it, sir," Whitcomb said, glad he knew something that the scout did not. "When I first saw them one was dismounted. He seemed to be reading sign. Then the other one pointed in our direction and they both rode into the timber."

Crook nodded thoughtfully. "It may be a futile exercise, Mr. Richaud, but you might try to head them off. Take half a dozen men and try to take them alive."

Richaud acknowledged the order with a wave of his hand and he was gone, waving to the other scouts to follow him.

"I think we might bring in the flankers somewhat, if you agree, General," Reynolds said to Crook. "Perhaps Lieutenant—" He hesitated, glancing at Whitcomb.

"Whitcomb, General," Crook said. "Lieutenant Whitcomb. This is our famous Mr. Reb."

"Indeed. Well, Lieutenant Whitcomb, perhaps you would bring the flankers in to a hundred yards. In an orderly fashion, please. We want the hostiles to know we are alert but have nothing to fear."

"Place yourself with the lead set on the southern flank when you're done, Mr. Whitcomb," Corwin added.

Whitcomb snapped a salute. "Yes, sir. I have already brought those men in, sir. I'll notify the others."

As he galloped off to the north, to the lead flankers there, the command resumed its march. He recrossed the column to the south and there, as he had done on the other side, he instructed the flankers to send one man back to bring in the next set; they in turn would send one man to the rear, and so on down the length of the column. In this way all the flankers would be brought in in the least possible time; Whitcomb was pleased with the ingenuity of the plan, which allowed him to rejoin Corporal Atherton and his set of four within a few minutes of receiving his orders. The column was in an open plain among the hills and buttes now, and he could see its full length clearly. One by one the flanking squads were moving in, while the measured progress of the mounted force demonstrated a serene self-confidence, exactly as Reynolds had wished.

Whitcomb kept his eyes on the wooded areas to the south, expecting at any moment to see the scouts return with or without the two Indians, but half an hour passed, and then another, and the column left the open plain to enter a wooded draw between two hills. With each passing moment his impatience for action grew stronger. What could have become of the scouts?

Overhead, the scattered clouds that had sent shadows scudding across the land throughout the day were thickening now, becoming a solid cover, and a little snow was beginning to fall. New snow could help the scouts track the two braves, he realized. How far away might their village be? Richaud had said the men were hunters, and the hunting was good in these regions. Already that day the command had startled twenty or more deer and once they had seen a group of six elk moving off through the trees at a leisurely pace. The abundance of game meant that there was no need for the Indian hunters to range far, no need for them to spend cold nights away from the comfort of their lodges. The village would be within half a day's ride.

This quick analysis of the situation, made without conscious effort, startled him. He examined his conclusions again and found them sound, and he smiled. He was learning! Just two weeks before, such reasoning had been beyond his experience, yet today it came to him as naturally as adjusting himself to the movements of his horse.

"Look there, sir!" Private Dowdy was pointing to a ridge ahead and to the right of the column's line of advance. The expedition was out of the trees now, entering a shallow valley where a creek flowed off to the north. Two riders sat atop the ridge, unmistakably the Indians. Even at the distance, Whitcomb could see the blankets flapping in the wind and the horses' tails blowing. One pony stamped and shook his head.

"Cheeky devils," said Private Gwynn; he was a barrel-chested Irishman and the regiment's champion boxer.

"Countin' our noses, I'll warrant, sir," said Corporal Atherton.

"Come on, y' spalpeens! Man t' man! What d' ye say? Gwynn's the name and boxin's me game!"

"You'll have a chance at them soon enough," Whitcomb

said, but he wished he were as certain as he sounded. What was Crook planning? And where were the scouts?

His consternation deepened as the command reached the frozen creekbed. A bugle call sounded and the head of the column turned left, downstream, away from the silent watchers who sat their horses as immobile as statues.

When the entire command had reached the creek and completed the turn to the north, the bugle sounded the order to halt, the notes clean and clear, whipped down the column by the wind, straight toward the Indian lookouts, and now Whitcomb saw the scouts riding in from the southeast. What had they been doing off there? Couldn't they see the Indians sitting brazenly in plain sight?

The scouts joined the clump of officers at the head of the column and long moments passed while they talked, gesturing to the southeast, at the Indians, and to other points seemingly at random. And then to Whitcomb's astonishment the flankers were ordered in from their posts as the command dismounted and cookfires were started. In a short time the smell of coffee and beans filled the air.

It was a quiet bivouac. Horses were not tethered individually to browse, but were kept on picket lines by troop. The men clustered in bunches around the fires and talked in low tones, glancing often from their officers to the Indians and back again. Was it possible that General Crook was not going to give chase?

Lieutenant Corwin paced nervously by E Troop's fire, drawing near to warm himself for a few moments, then spinning abruptly on his heel and striding off to stare at the headquarters fire and the ranking officers gathered there, breaking this routine only when someone noticed that the Indian sentinels were gone.

"They was there a minute ago!"

"I was watchin', and I swear t' God they didn't move. Just disappeared."

"Dey are nott human," muttered Willy Stiegler, E Troop's Austrian corporal. "Deffils, dot's vot dey are!"

Some of the Irish crossed themselves.

Corwin's pacing increased in tempo now and once he

seemed to start off toward the headquarters fire, but he thought better of it and turned back.

The day darkened, although it was hard to tell if the loss of light was due to the setting of the invisible sun or merely the thickening of the clouds that rolled overhead from the northwest. The wind picked up and snow flurries fell here and there about the landscape, dropping from the clouds like wispy beards and occasionally sending a handful of flakes to sting the faces of the men and melt in the steam from their coffee.

LISA PUTNAM'S JOURNAL

Wednesday, March 15th. 5:40 a.m.

I have been up and about since just after two o'clock and I am already drinking my fourth cup of coffee. Our heifers delight in making a great fuss and commotion just when one thinks all is quiet and there may be a little sleep to be had. Out I go, which requires a thorough job of dressing (it was just below zero at two-thirty), only to find one heifer that had given birth as efficiently as if she had been at it for a number of years, and another that regarded me with her liquid brown eyes quite placidly and waited until an hour ago to produce her calf. Both are healthy and took quickly to nourishing themselves in the proper manner. One bull, one heifer calf. We now have eight bulls and ten heifers. Not quite half done. I discov-

ered yesterday afternoon that my father forgot to order more of the patent remedy for scours last summer; we have a small supply of the medicine left, but if many calves develop scours this spring I will have to fall back on the old folk treatment.

Hutch and Johnny do most of the feeding now, leaving Julius free to hunt. Yesterday we finished the last of the hay in the east meadow, but we have plenty in the cribs in the west meadow to last until the grass is green. Yesterday afternoon we moved the herd across the river.

The friendship between Hutch and Johnny Smoker continues to grow apace. Johnny has been giving Hutch some instruction in roping, and whenever Hutch isn't trying to spend a few moments with Maria Abbruzzi he is roping fenceposts or farm implements or some unlucky calf in the heifer lot. When he and Johnny are together Amanda is often with them, and where Amanda is, there Chatur is sure to be found. He dotes on her, and although he is nearly twice as old as any of them, I cannot help thinking of him as one of "the young people," perhaps because of his short stature and the delight he takes in all things. They are quite a quartet. I fancy that I am beginning to know Amanda well enough to perceive a change in her just in the short time she has been here. As a violinist or clown she is completely in command, yet when she is simply Amanda Spencer she is often somewhat timid and unsure of herself. But it seems to me that since she has been in company with Johnny she has begun to reveal some of that same confidence and spirit she otherwise reserves for her music and clowning. Love (if I can so dignify her youthful infatuation for Johnny) works wonders on one's self-confidence. Clearly the least of her concerns is how soon the road will be clear and the circus free to leave.

The same cannot be said of Mr. Tatum. He and I have dined together twice more (without the luxuries of that first occasion) and he was pleasant company as always, but I can sense his impatience with the pace of his work. Yesterday there was another slide at the avalanche site, some of the recent snow falling down to replace what had already been dug away. Many of the teamsters have experience with blasting powder but they tend to use too much. This is the second time they have created a larger mess than the one they sought to remove. And still Mr. Tatum persists. Each morning he accompanies his men and oversees the start of their work before returning for his daily riding practice. He works with his white stallion for an hour or longer in the tent, then inspects the other animals. For the rest of the morning he watches the clowns or practices his pistol shooting, and after dinner he returns to the avalanche with the men to spend the rest of the day there. By his disciplined work habits, he certainly sets a good example for all those who work for him.

I must get to breakfast and away with Julius into the hills. We promised Mr. Chalmers that we would take him hunting with us and we hope to do better than we have done thus far by going lower into the foothills and moving northward through the valleys there, gradually working around and coming back by way of Sun Horse's village. It will be a long day for me; I feel about all in now, but I imagine I will survive. Mr. Chalmers and the three Waldheims and a few others provide the core of the circus hunting parties. What tales they will have to tell when they leave here, all about being led through the wilds by Sioux guides! I only wish our collective efforts would produce better results. We have been hunting in earnest for a week now, but I am afraid that Sun Horse has made little progress toward preparing himself for a move. There is some improvement in the Indian horses and the hunters are able to range a little farther afield, but what little meat has been brought in is consumed at once and he has put up no jerky at all yet. Still, I have every hope of greater success soon, and that is why I continue to push myself through days like this one. (But how I look forward to my bed tonight!)

Sun Horse has lookouts on the ridges but they have seen no signals in many days. For some time the whereabouts of the soldiers have been unknown.

CHAPTER ELEVEN

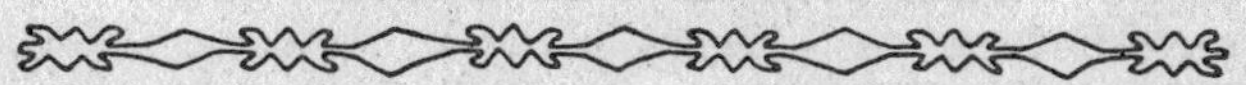

The afternoon was well along when the hunting party reached the Lakota village. After a morning of brisk, chill winds and occasional flurries of snow the day had cleared and now the sun stood bright and alone above the western ridge. Willy Waldheim had joined the hunters at the last moment, bringing their number to four. Lisa and Julius led the way while Alfred Chalmers brought up the rear, looking all around as they entered the camp.

"Extraordinary," he said, and Willy nodded. The younger Waldheim brother was fair of skin and hair, with the same well-muscled build as his brother Johann. His sporting rifle, made by Manton of England, was held tightly in his hands and he had checked his load twice as the riders neared the village. He was prepared for anything—except the apparent indifference that greeted their appearance. Here and there a man or woman made a sign of greeting to Lisa and some glanced curiously at the huge Englishman, but otherwise the whites occasioned no more interest in the village than a returning group of Sioux might have done.

Lisa had noticed that the horses in the herd looked a little sleeker and here among the tipis a few women were working at the hides of deer and elk, but the village still had a listless feeling about it; the hunting had not yet had the revitalizing effect she had hoped for. She caught herself slumping from fatigue and she sat up straight, dreading the long ride home.

They found Sun Horse sitting on a robe in front of his lodge, enjoying the warm sunshine. As they dismounted he rose to greet the hunters. He took Lisa's hands in his own and he smiled, but it seemed to her that he was tired.

"We saw two elk, Grandfather," she said in Lakota. "They were far away and we could not get close enough to shoot."

"The Lakota hunters have found no meat today," he replied. Recent days had been clear and bright, and snowblindness was affecting nearly all the hunters now. For two days Rib Bone had been confined to his lodge with pieces of trade cloth soaked in melted snow water resting on his eyes. Early in the afternoon Sun Horse had seen Crooked Horn return to the village alone, with no meat hangng from his saddle, and now he too kept to the darkness of his lodge. For seven days Lakota and *washíchun* had hunted together, and as the days passed and so little meat hanging from his saddle, and now he too kept to the bright hope fade like the leaves of autumn once the golden glory was past.

"Stay and eat with us," he invited the whites, but Lisa shook her head. Groups of white hunters passed through the village often enough now that they were no longer obliged to observe the courtesies of formal visits, and she had no wish to eat the meat that others needed.

"We cannot stay, Grandfather. We must get home by dark. We came to give you more grain and gunpowder. Tomorrow if you send a few men to the park, we will hunt in the afternoon down below the river canyon."

She turned to take the sacks of grain and powder that Julius had already removed from the saddles, but Sun Horse held up a hand in refusal.

"Already you have given us much and we have given little in return. For a time, both our hunters and our horses will rest. We will make ceremonies to call our four-legged brothers, to remind them that we are hungry and need their help. When the power of the hunters returns, we will hunt again."

Lisa had half expected something like this. Lakotas did not persist in fruitless endeavors, either in war or peace. Instead they sought the reasons for their difficulties, and those reasons lay always in the realm of spirit power. If hunting was bad, the four-leggeds were displeased with the Lakotas; if war went badly, some warrior had broken a taboo or a ceremony had been performed incorrectly or the enemy's medicine was stronger. Seeking spiritual reasons for difficulties and failure was so deeply ingrained in the Lakota way of thinking that she knew there was no use in arguing. She had heard the finality in Sun Horse's tone; he spoke in the manner of one whose mind was made up. It reminded her of the way her own father had spoken when he had reached a difficult decision.

"Take these," Julius said in Lakota, holding out the sacks, and before Sun Horse could refuse again he added, "Our horses tired. Too much to carry back to lodge." He set the sacks beside the entrance to the tipi, on the robe where Sun Horse had been sitting. "We go now," he announced, turning his back on the gifts and remounting his horse. Once he was in the saddle he said, "Your friends ready to hunt again when you say."

Lisa was grateful that Julius had found a way to leave these last offerings. It was little enough, and far less than she had wanted to give. She wished she could find something to say, something to show how disappointed she was that the joint efforts of whites and Lakotas had come to naught, but her fatigue was overwhelming. She could find no way to encourage Sun Horse or brighten his spirits while her own discouragement was so profound, and she knew her exhaustion was mostly at fault. After a good night's rest she might see things differently, but now the future seemed dark and forbidding.

She took Sun Horse's hands in her own once again and met his gaze, trying to say with her eyes what she could not put in words, and as if he understood her thoughts perfectly, he nodded and favored her with another wan smile.

She left him quickly then, remounting her horse and

kicking it into a trot that carried her beyond the village before the others overtook her.

"No sense taking it hard," Julius said gently as his horse fell into step with hers. "We done what we could. He's a sight better off now than before."

"I know," she said. "I just don't like to see him give up."

"I dunno that he has. Seems to me more like he's waitin' on somethin'."

When the whites were gone from the village Sun Horse resumed his seat on his robe. The sun was still some distance above the ridge and the warmth eased his aching joints. In the first days of hunting with the whites the moonlit nights had been so cold that the trees had popped just as they did in the true winter moons. *Waziya,* the winter power, remained strong. The Ancient Ones said that *Okaga,* the life-giving power of the south, battled *Waziya,* in time driving him back to the north so the warmth could return to the land, setting free the spirits of all living things. Many spoke of *Waziya* as a fearsome and evil power because he opposed *Okaga,* but Sun Horse saw the balance between the two. The cold of winter prepared the way for new life, cleansing and healing the earth. In time *Okaga* would return and the balance would be restored. He reviewed in his mind these most basic tenets, seeking something that would show him the way to realize the power of his vision. He had believed the hunt with the whites to be the beginning of that power, but the hunt had failed.

When the women lose their virtue, the buffalo go away, said the Ancient Ones. But no woman of the Sun Band had acted badly or thrown her man away without reason. None had gone to the plum bushes with a man not her husband. These things happened in other bands, the tales told behind raised hands at the summer gatherings, but the Sun Band kept to the old ceremonies and the old ways, and the women in Sun Horse's camp were not responsible for the absence of *pte.*

It had been a fleeting thought, not a serious concern. He knew that he was like a one-eyed wolf circling the herd with his blind eye towards the old sick bull that would be easy prey. He was seeking to avoid the reason that stood so plainly before him: the fault was his own. He had seen a promise of power but the promise had not been fulfilled.

Where had he failed?

He arose from the robe and lifted it from the snow to wrap it around him. Chunks of snow stuck to the coarse hair, making him resemble the old bulls in summer, the fur shedding in patches until mighty *tatanka* looked as ragged as a robe that was cut up to make moccasins after many years of use. The thought amused Sun Horse and he wrapped the robe tighter about him and swung his head low, snuffling like *tatanka* testing the wind. He moved across the camp slowly like an old bull, and the people saw him and wondered why he imitated the buffalo. Perhaps there would be another buffalo dance to summon the four-legged creature that gave so much to man.

Outside the lodge of Sees Beyond, Sun Horse coughed lightly, the *chuff* of the buffalo bull, and he stamped his feet to shake the snow off his moccasins, making the sound of *tatanka* stamping the ground.

"My lodge welcomes a visitor," came the voice of Elk Leggings, Sees Beyond's father. Sun Horse entered.

Sees Beyond and his father were eating. Elk Leggings sat at the place of honor across the fire from the entrance. Sees Beyond sat beside him. Sun Horse moved around the lodge to the left, moving as the sun passed around the sky, stepping behind the men, not coming between them and the fire. A gust of wind shook the lodgeskins and gusted smoke downward from the smoke hole. Elk Leggings' wife stepped outside to adjust the flaps as Sun Horse seated himself in the guest's place at Elk Leggings' left hand.

Sees Beyond had listened carefully to the visitor's progress and now he smiled. "*Hau, tunkáshila,*" he said, and Sun Horse wondered what it was that had allowed the blind man to know him with such certainty. Was it the way he walked? Or perhaps some smell? Or was it simply that Sees Beyond could see his spirit with the inner eye that saw the real world?

"Eat with us," said the old man. Elk Leggings was the band's rememberer and one of the old-man chiefs of the band, the four principal councillors who walked at the head of the village when it was on the move. The old chiefs carried the fire and chose where to smoke and where to camp.

"I have eaten," Sun Horse said. He knew there was little to spare, but when the wife returned she passed him a spoon made from the horn of the mountain sheep and he ate a little, making the polite sounds. When the men had finished eating, a pipe was lit and passed around, and as the bowl cooled, Sun Horse spoke. "I have had a vision. *Wamblí gleshka* has told me of a power that comes from the meeting of two people. It is a power that can bring the Lakota and the *washíchun* together in peace. Hears Twice told me of its coming, before the Strange-Animal People entered the whiteman's valley, before the *washíchun* Hardeman and my grandson, the One Who Stands Between the Worlds, came here. Hears Twice says this is a power that can help the band or destroy us."

"Where does the power of peace come from, Grandfather?" Sees Beyond smiled slightly as he spoke the question. It was a question a *wichasha wakán* might ask a very young man who sought to understand the spirit world, but Sun Horse didn't mind. This was Sees Beyond's way, asking simple questions, and this had become almost a game that the two holy men enjoyed together.

"It comes from the east," Sun Horse replied seriously. "We pray to the morning star, which ushers in the light, and this is the light of true understanding. Without true understanding there can be no peace. Not within a man, not among the people, not between two peoples. The morning light is red and so the color of the east is red, and red is the most sacred color, in part because it symbolizes the peace that comes from true understanding."

Sees Beyond nodded. "And even this is not the whole

truth of the power of the east. The whole truth is more than one man can ever see, but still each man seeks it."

Not so many years ago they had spoken nearly identical words, during Sees Beyond's apprenticeship, but then it had been Sun Horse who taught and Sees Beyond who learned. They did not need to repeat all the words now, for both knew them well. Recognize that what you see is only a part of the whole. No matter how much you see, you cannot see the whole. Do not ask that something be only that which you perceive, for this is to deny the whole, limiting it to a lesser existence.

There was a soft sound from Elk Leggings and they saw that he had allowed his head to drop to his chest and was snoring lightly, his eyes closed. The old man's wife sat in the back of the lodge repairing torn beadwork on a ceremonial shirt, leaving the men to speak alone.

"My father seeks the truth more and more often in dreams," Sees Beyond said, smiling, and then, "You know that Crooked Horn has returned?"

Sun Horse nodded, then grunted his acknowledgment, remembering Sees Beyond's blindness. Crooked Horn was the best hunter in the band, yet after six days of hunting with the whites he had brought no meat to the kettles, not even a snowshoe hare. Yesterday he had gone out alone to the high places to seek the reason for his failure, as a man often did when his power left him. He sought inside himself, to know if he had broken some condition of his power, an agreement with his spirit helper made at the time of his becoming-a-man vision. Sometimes a man forgot these obligations and his power waned. If he found no reason within himself, the man might speak to the spirits, addressing his spirit helper, or even the Great Mystery, to know if the invisible powers might have forgotten their obligations to the two-leggeds.

The Lakota respected the spirits but they did not bow down to them as the *washíchun* did; the spirits too might be at fault, and a good man was not afraid to stand strong before them and remind them of their obligations.

"He spoke to the *pte*," Sees Beyond said, "but they told him nothing."

It was like Sees Beyond to know what was in a man's mind before he had spoken it. Sun Horse had said nothing about the hunt, nothing to show his fear that the hunting was bad because the power he had felt so strongly at the white settlement when the Snowblind Moon was young seemed to have slipped away from him. He had felt the power and he had waited for it to be revealed to him instead of seeking it out. A vision was not a gift but a possibility, something that would come about only if the man to whom it was given fulfilled the promise.

The fault is mine, not Crooked Horn's, Sun Horse thought. I have done nothing. I felt the promise of power and I have waited, doing nothing.

I was so sure! And here in the camp circle I saw the power begin to grow, the *heyoka* of the Lakota joining with the white clown girl, making the people laugh. Lisaputnam and the black whiteman asked that Lakota and *washíchun* hunt together and I saw the power of the white world joined with that of the Lakota; I believed the power I had felt was growing, and I did nothing.

Like Crooked Horn I must look within myself.

"I will make *inipi,*" he said to Sees Beyond. "Will you help me?"

Sees Beyond seemed to think very hard for a time. Finally he nodded and reached for his ceremonial pipe. In his own lodge he knew the place of every object and his hands found the pipe and tobacco pouch and then the smoldering stick placed between the rocks of the fire pit, filling and lighting the pipe as easily as a seeing person might have done. As he passed the pipe to Sun Horse, his sightless eyes found the older man's face and he said "Look beyond the symbol!"

He said it sternly, forcefully, almost like an order.

Sun Horse felt a chill as he in turn offered the pipe to the sacred points and smoked, and he knew he was feeling the strength of this *wichasha wakán* whose power grew so strong, and so different from his own. Sun Horse used his knowledge of the spirit world to guide his people through this life, walking with feet placed on the solid earth, yet always acting with proper awareness of the real world behind the world of solid objects, never losing touch with the great spirit power that was available to all men. Sees Beyond seemed to be a part of that real world ordinary men could not see, keeping just a part of his awareness in the living world of men. Never until now had he spoken to Sun Horse of *wakán* things except in questions, always questions; yet now he said *Look beyond the symbol!*

When the pipe was smoked and the ashes emptied carefully into the fire, the two holy men rose together and left the lodge, Sees Beyond holding Sun Horse's arm at the crook of the elbow. There was no need to make special preparations for the *inipi* ceremony; it was the ceremony that preceded all others, and some members of the band performed it daily merely for relaxation and cleaning the body.

The men went first to Sun Horse's lodge, where they found Elk Calf Woman asleep. She often slept away the short winter afternoons and they left her resting, asking Sings His Daughter to come and assist them. Near the aspen grove by the creek, the young woman helped Sun Horse gather the materials while Sees Beyond supervised the building of the *ini ti*, the house where *ni*, the life force, was to be purified. The whites called it a sweat lodge, but the purpose was to cleanse the inner being. Nearby there were several of the small structures set along the bank of the stream and Sun Horse had used one or another of them at various times, but today only a new *ini ti* would suit his purpose. Today he made a new beginning.

The grove was bright with sunlight and shadows. A few small clouds floated past now, coming from the mountains, and to the north the clouds were thicker, but the winds stayed high above the ground and the valley was quiet. The sounds of the village carried to the grove, where they mingled with the sound of the water running beneath the new ice that had covered the stream during the recent nights of deep cold. Sings His Daughter broke the ice with an iron hand-axe and brought a bowl of water for the ceremony.

Nothing in the preparation of the *ini ti* was overlooked, nothing done carelessly, but from the first, Sun Horse noticed that Sees Beyond did not pause as he would have done on other occasions to remind the participants of the meaning in each step of its construction, nor did he sing the usual prayers, and Sun Horse understood his intention at once: they were both *wichasha wakán* and they had no need to be reminded of the symbols; today they sought the deeper meanings.

Working silently together, they placed four willow poles on each of the four sides, marking the four quarters of the universe, bending the poles toward the center, where they were lashed together by Sees Beyond's quick fingers. The surface of the ground had thawed in the afternoon sun, allowing the men to dig a shallow pit for the hot rocks that would be placed there. They covered the floor of the lodge with sage, and strewed the earth from the rock pit in a straight line from the small entrance, forming a path leading eastward to where they would build *peta owíhankeshni,* the fire that does not go out. As Sun Horse built the fire in the sacred manner, Sees Beyond took the rocks that Sings His Daughter handed him one at a time and he placed them at the four corners of the fireplace to mark the corners of the universe, finding their proper positions with his hands, and all the while the two men were silent. Only when Sun Horse lit the fire did Sees Beyond pray aloud for the first time, calling to *Wakán Tanka,* who gave men fire and all other things. "*Peta owíhankeshni* burns forever," he chanted. "It shall make us pure and bring us close to your powers."

When all the preparations were done, Sun Horse stood at the entrance of the *ini ti*. Here too the ceremony might have been shortened. He and Sees Beyond knew all the meanings of the lodge and the pathway and the fire; they might simply enter the *ini ti* now. But something compelled him to add to the ceremony today.

He removed his ceremonial pouch from the cord that held it around his neck. He opened it with difficulty, for the rawhide thongs that held it closed had not been untied for twenty-five years; he had to use his teeth to loosen the knots, but finally the pouch was open and he reached within. He took out a pinch of dust and dropped it on the pathway, and he prayed to *Unchi,* Grandmother Earth, from whom all generations of man were descended.

"Upon you, O Grandmother, I build a sacred path," he prayed. "I purify myself for the people, that they may walk this path with firm steps. There are four sacred steps on this path, which leads to *Wakán Tanka.* Let me be pure that the people may live!"

He took a step and there he dropped another pinch of dust from the pouch, the dust he had carried for twenty-five winters, the pouch never opened since then. Sees Beyond waited silently as Sun Horse took another step. Another pinch of dust, the prayer said again, and another step, until Sun Horse had placed a pinch of dust on each of the four steps to *peta owíhankeshni* and said the prayer four times, and then he prayed to *Wakán Tanka.* "I place myself on this sacred path for my people. I send my voice to you through the four directions, which we know are but one direction, and that leading always to you. *Ho Tunkáshila, Wakán Tanka,* help my people to live in the sacred manner! Help my people to live!"

A band of clouds dropped a little snow on the grove and Sun Horse breathed deeply of the cool air and tasted the snow of his tongue, clean and pure.

He touched Sees Beyond and together the two *wichasha wakán* removed their robes and entered the *ini ti.* Custom told that the one who led the ceremony should enter alone with the pipe to purify himself and the lodge before those who made the *inipi* ceremony joined him, but here the two holy men combined their powers for the quest that Sun Horse undertook. Over coals that were brought from the fire and placed in the center of the lodge, they burned a dried twist of sweetgrass to purify the little house and invoke the presence of the spirits. After the sweetgrass they burned sage, for all spirits loved the fragrance of sweetgrass but only the most benevolent powers liked sage, and these remained while the others were driven out.

Now pinches of *chanshasha*, the red willow bark smoking mixture, were offered to the four directions and to the sky and the earth, and as each pinch was offered to the sacred points it was placed in Sees Beyond's ceremonial pipe. The men did not pray aloud as was usually done, but each prayed within himself. When the pipe was filled, Sun Horse stooped low and left the *ini ti* to place the pipe on the mound of earth at the end of the pathway to the fire, where he left it with the bowl to the west and the stem pointing east. He re-entered the lodge, closing the entrance flap behind him, and sat across from Sees Beyond.

The inside of the *ini ti* was as dark as night. In the center of the floor, where the rocks would soon be placed, a few coals still glowed. Even the darkness had meaning; it symbolized ignorance, the receptive emptiness that was the proper state of one who sought to purify his inner being.

So many symbols in this and all ceremonies, Sun Horse thought. The people were constantly reminded of the spirit powers and the meaning of each one, all truly part of one spirit, called *Wakán Tanka* and *Taku Wakán, Taku Shkan-shkan,* and other names known only to the holy men. *Wakán,* a mystery, that which is not to be understood. Not by one man, nor by all men. Yet each experienced and understood some part of the mystery, not only holy men but all men and women of the tribe. Grown people constantly reminded children of the meanings of each act that sought to propitiate the powers, until the sight or mention of a symbol brought forth a host of the deeper meanings. And yet even the holy men retained the symbols, and perhaps could never reach a true understanding while the symbols remained.

Look beyond the symbol.

Was this what Sees Beyond meant? Cast the symbols aside as he had done today, making the *ini ti* but leaving out so many rituals, so many pauses for prayer; not to say that prayers were unimportant but to cut through obstacles that impeded understanding, knowing that Sun Horse sought the path to peace. . . . The peace that came only from true understanding.

Over the years Sun Horse had sought to understand so much. Perhaps too much? How could a Lakota understand the essence of the *washíchun* nation? Yet this was the promise of Sun Horse's vision and for twenty-five winters he had sought to fulfill the promise.

The little flap covering the entrance opened now and Sings His Daughter passed in a hot rock held on a forked stick, the first of the rocks from the fire-without-end. Each should be touched by the pipe, each standing for one of the directions, a symbol for the boundaries of the universe, but Sun Horse merely took the forked stick and deposited the rock in the center of the lodge without ceremony, passing the stick back to Sings His Daughter. More rocks were brought until the ground was piled high with rocks that carried the strength of the fire within them, cracking and popping as they touched the cold ground, hissing as Sun Horse sprinkled water over them and filled the little house with steam. He threw sage leaves on the stones and the scent of the sage was carried on the steam and the men tasted it as they breathed and felt it tingle on their skin.

Again Sun Horse opened the sack at his throat and reached within, this time withdrawing a perfectly round stone, which he placed among the hot rocks. *Tunkán*, the stone that has fallen from the sky; *tunkán*, the round stone that represents the earth, the whole universe; *tunkán*, part of the word *Tunkáshila*, Grandfather, the one who encompasses the universe, one of the names of *Wakán Tanka*.

Now the holy pouch hung loosely at Sun Horse's neck, only a little dust left, the symbols gone, made part of the *inipi* ceremony. Today he had thrown away the symbols of his own vision, carried with him for twenty-five years; it was time to look beyond the symbols and realize the full power of what he had been given.

There on the small butte overlooking the Laramie fort all those years ago he had watched the few wagons he could see on the wagon road and he had felt the power of the *washíchun*, like the threat of a storm that was heralded far in advance by a few black clouds on the horizon. He had prayed to *Wakán Tanka* to help him understand these strangers who brought such change, such power, to the lands of the Lakota and their allies, and *Wakán Tanka* had sent him a helper.

One day, two, then three days he had prayed, and in his heart he had feared that he would fail again as he had failed to find a vision in his youth, but on the morning of the fourth day the horse had come, running out of the sun. The sun had just come up and the morning star stood in the sky above it. Stands Alone had been praying to the morning star, asking for the light of understanding, when he heard a horse neigh. At first he thought perhaps a friend had come to seek him but he could see no one on the hilltop, and no horse. Again the horse neighed and he realized then that the sound came from the sky. He turned towards the sun and saw that something was partially blocking the light. The shape grew rapidly, shutting out the fiery disk altogether now, and he saw that it was a horse, galloping in the sky, coming straight toward the hilltop. The horse was black, so sleek and shiny that it reflected the deep blue of the sky. It reminded Stands Alone of his favorite mount, his black hunter, but he knew this was a spirit horse, and not of this world. When the horse drew closer he gasped, for there on the hindquarters were the jagged streaks of lightning and dotted hailstones with which he marked his hunter; the other markings were the same too, all but the eyes, which glowed with an inner light like the shine of the morning star.

Nearer and nearer the horse came, galloping silently on the air, and when it reached the hilltop it raced around him four times, moving sunwise, its feet never touching the grass. When it completed the fourth circle it came to a stop beside him, facing to the south. Stands Alone gazed in wonder at the horse, but suddenly there arose a great commotion from the direction the horse was facing, coming from the Lakota encampment by the soldier fort. There were guns firing and a great cloud of smoke and dust, and then he saw the people, white soldiers and Lakota men, rising through the smoke and dust until they were floating in the air at the level of the hilltop. A chief was standing between the white soldiers and the Lakota warriors, his hands empty, and he was talking to them, pleading that they should not fight, but one of the soldier guns fired and the chief fell and then the soldiers vanished in a cloud of warriors that drifted over them like a thunderstorm moving over the peaks of *Pahá Sapa*. When the dust blew away, the *washíchun* soldiers were gone and only Lakota were left, their lodges falling like leaves in autumn and the people floating off in a long line to the north, until Stands Alone could see them no more.

He looked back to the south and to his surprise he saw that the Lakota camp was as it had been before, peaceful and unchanged. The other camps were peaceful too, all the tribes that had been called there by the whites for the great council that would begin soon, traditional enemies camped side by side in peace.

The horse neighed now and pranced about, inviting Stands Alone to mount. He grabbed a handful of mane and leaped to the horse's back, and the horse soared away from the hilltop into the sky, going north and west toward the Snowy Mountains, which the whites called the Big Horns. The mountains grew quickly and in no time at all the horse was descending, approaching a small valley. Suddenly there was a great crying and shouting, and Stands Alone saw *washíchun* ringing the valley, all angry, and some soldiers among them, but as the horse descended to the valley floor the whites disappeared and their voices grew silent.

Stands Alone dismounted and walked by the clear stream and the small lake among the grasses and flowers of summer. He saw the bushes that would soon be heavy with berries, the straight pines for lodgepoles, the deer and elk tracks and the droppings of buffalo. The horse moved with him, whickering joyfully, prancing in the air just above the tops of the grass. Stands Alone lay in the grass, the sun warm on his face, and he felt a great contentment.

Now the horse nuzzled him, danced away and returned, away and back, and he understood that he should mount again. Grasping the black's mane he swung up onto the strong back and together the horse and rider flew up and away, going south and east now, and Stands Alone laughed to feel the wind as they flew. When they reached the hilltop where the horse had come to him, he was surprised to see someone sitting there waiting for him. As he drew closer, he caught his breath, for the man on the hilltop was himself, sitting cross-legged with eyes closed, as if asleep or dead.

Then his vision clouded and for a moment he was afraid, but the horse whickered near at hand and he opened his eyes to find himself sitting on the hilltop, the black prancing in the air before him. The horse neighed a final time, then turned away and galloped off, disappearing into the sun.

At his feet Stands Alone saw a small round stone; he picked it up together with some of the earth from the hilltop and carried it with him when he returned to the encampment by the Holy Road. There he found a camp at peace; nothing bad had happened while he was gone.

In his lodge he found his father waiting for him. With his father was a blind youth called Sees Beyond, his father's apprentice and already *wichasha wakán*.

"I have had a vision," Stands Alone said, and he told them of his vision in as much detail as he could remember, but he did not ask them to interpret it for him. Instead, he explained his own understanding of the vision, the power it offered him and the obligation it imposed, and when he was done each of the holy men in turn spoke his approval, agreeing that Stands Alone's understanding was complete.

"But is it a true vision?" Stands Alone had asked then, voicing his one doubt. "It is said that in true visions only those four-footeds known to the Ancient Ones appear."

Branched Horn shrugged. "Others have had visions of horses."

"Do we not call them *shunka wakán*?" Sees Beyond asked. "If the *shunka wakán* had appeared to the Ancient Ones, would they not have tamed them as we do? Next to *pte,* what four-legged is a greater helper to the Lakota? Shall he have such power in our lives and none in our visions?"

Reassured by this final confirmation, Stands Alone had sent a crier through the camp to say that he would give a feast the next day, inviting all to come, and when the people gathered on the following day they found the kettles full of meat that Stands Alone had provided, and Stands Alone waiting there with robes and moccasins piled beside him and gift sticks in his hand, each stick representing a horse to be given away. When all had eaten, he stood and spoke to them.

"My friends," he said, "we have come here for a great council with the *washíchun*. They say this council will make peace between the whites and all the peoples of the plains, but I have had a vision. In time there will be trouble between the Lakota and the whites, and a great leader killed. I will stay for the council and I will work always for peace, but when I leave this place I will travel to the Snowy Mountains. In the warm moons I will camp with the hoop of the nation, but in the Moon of Falling Leaves I will return each year to the Snowy Mountains to a place I have seen in my vision. I will no longer go east to the Muddy River and I will not winter near the *washíchun*. I go to live in the old way, the Lakota way, and I will welcome any who choose to go with me, for I no longer stand alone. Today I take a new name. Now I am called *Tashunke Mashté Wi Etan Hínape*." And then his relatives passed among the crowd, giving the gift sticks to those who were poor and had few horses, meat to families that had no one to hunt for them, and robes and moccasins and other things where they were most needed.

When the gift giving was done, Branched Horn surprised the gathering by announcing that he was no longer the headman of the band. "From this day forward my son will lead our people," the old man proclaimed, "and I will follow him, for I believe in the power of his vision. He has been given the power to lead us to peace, and so long as I live I will follow in his footsteps."

And so when the great council was done and the tribes broke camp to return to their own lands, the little band of Hunkpapa had grown, some Oglala and Brulé joining the new leader who seemed so sure of his power.

Tashunke Mashté Wi Etan Hínape. It meant His Horse Comes From the Summer Sun. It was a long name, and the people took to calling him *Tashunke Mashté Wi*—His Horse Is the Summer Sun. Because it had truly been the spirit power of the summer sun that had come to Sun Horse in his vision and taken him on his journey to the Snowy Mountains, the contraction preserved the deeper meaning of the name, and he did not object. It was Lodgepole who christened him Sun Horse in English. The band was known simply as Sun Horse's camp, or band. Among themselves the people sometimes called it the Sun Camp, or Sun Band, but they always used the full name when speaking with other Lakota; it would have been arrogant to imply that they were People of the Sun, for *Wi*, the sun, was one of the most powerful manifestations of *Wakán Tanka*.

The inside of the *ini ti* was black as night, and dense with fragrant steam. Sun Horse was sweating freely. He breathed deeply, tasting the sage, remembering the day of his vision and the early years of his leadership as if he lived through that time again.

He had not told the people of the other things he had felt, the certainty of great changes coming. The soldier fort and the Holy Road were little islands in a river of Lakota, but he knew there would come a time when the numberless whites would become the river and the Lakota bands would be the islands, and the troubles between the two peoples would grow. His vision had given him the power to lead his people and to find peace with the whites, a peace that came from true understanding. He knew he must perceive the nature of the *washíchun* and at the same time preserve the Lakota way, not by retreating far from the whites and imagining they would go away, nor by living close to them where their strange powers could overwhelm the people before they understood how to resist the destructive influences that had made the Loaf-Around-the-Forts less than Lakota.

Keep the Lakota way. Be strong in the old ways and at the same time seek to understand the whites. This was what Sun Horse had set out to do, and before long the strength of his vision had been confirmed. Scarcely a year later the band had been joined by Jed Putnam, the brother of Lodgepole, searching for a home in the mountains. Sun Horse had led him to a valley not far from the band's wintering place and there Jed Putnam had settled with his family. From the two brothers, one living like a *washíchun* and the other like a Lakota, Sun Horse had learned much of the white world, and as two more winters passed peacefully Sun Horse thought perhaps he had already discovered the pathway to peace. But then came a second confirmation of his vision, this one terrible and frightening.

It was summer in the year the whites called 1854. Sun Horse and his people were camped with a few other bands on the Powder when riders on sweating horses found them, bearing news of bad trouble at Fort Laramie. An emigrant's cow had strayed and been killed, and Conquering Bear, the great chief of the Brulé, had been shot by soldiers while trying to preserve the peace. Thirty soldiers had been killed and the Lakota had struck their lodges and fled to the north, just as Sun Horse had seen in his vision.

More lodges joined the Sun Band then, and that winter fifty tipis stood in the camp in the Snowy Mountains.

In the next year the soldiers struck back, a large group of them attacking the Brulé of Little Thunder. Little Thunder worked hard to keep the peace; he smoked with the soldier chief Harney and explained that his was not the same band that had killed the soldiers at Laramie, but Harney was an angry man and hot for revenge. After the smoke he attacked, leaving many women and children dead and a hundred of the people taken off in chains to the whiteman's iron house, where they were kept for more than a year.

From that time the troubles grew, a few years of quiet followed by more fighting and new treaties, and then more fighting. Lakota and whites both had their victories, and white scalps hung from Lakota lances. But something else happened, something Sun Horse had not seen in his vision: the Lakota grew stronger, like the point of a wooden lance held in the fire to make it hard. After the first troubles the whites stopped all trading at Laramie and said the Lakota must trade only at new agencies in Nebraska, farther from the hunting grounds. No traders might enter Lakota lands, they said. These words made the Lakota angry, and fewer and fewer went to the new trading places. Only the weakest of the Loafers stayed, while the others kept to the buffalo country along the Powder and the Tongue and learned to do without many of the trade goods they had depended on for so long, finding instead the strength of the old Lakota way. "We do not need the *washíchun* things," they said proudly. "Let him keep them, and his new trading places. Let him roll his wagons on the Holy Road, but he must not come here. If he comes here, we will fight him!" But still there was some trading with the halfbreed sons of former traders, who brought wagons to the hunting grounds despite the ban. Beneath loads of blankets and trinkets they brought good percussion rifles and powder and lead, for these were things the newly defiant Lakota did not wish to do without.

In the summer the Sun Band joined with the other bands to experience the strength of the Lakota nation and in winter they returned to their valley in the Snowy Mountains, and through the growing troubles they did not fight the whites. "To fight the *washíchun* is to fight the whirlwind," Sun Horse counseled his young men, and all the while he sought the path to peace—a peace without surrender, one that preserved the Lakota way.

As more winters passed, the number of lodges in the circle of the Sun Band declined as young warriors left for the bands that fought the whites. But other good men remained with Sun Horse, for there was fighting here too, with the traditional enemies—the hated Blackfeet, the Crows, the Snakes and the Gros Ventres. The Sun Band had its share of hunters and sharp-eyed scouts, and warriors too, not as many as other bands but just as brave. In the summer camp the Sun Band occupied a place of honor in the circle of the nation, and from their men *akíchita* were chosen to police the camp and the buffalo hunts, and men from the Sun Band sat with those who decided matters of importance for all Lakota. Among the bands Sun Horse was respected as a peace man, and at the great summer gathering of 1857, the Lakota headmen bestowed on him the highest honor they could give: they gave him the shirt-for-life, the symbolic shirt made of mountain sheepskin that recognized the wearer as a man to whom everyone looked up, a man who thought always of the good of the people.

When the fighting was the worst, on the two occasions when the war pipes were sent out and the Lakota and their allies the Shahíyela and Arapaho had fought together, Sun Horse journeyed to the peace councils that were called to stop the fighting and there he listened to the whites and spoke to them. During Red Cloud's War he was unable to keep some of his own young men from riding off to join their brothers who swarmed like hornets around the soldier forts, and when the Laramie treaty was made, Sun Horse touched the pen to this new paper even though he had not approved the fighting and had used all his persuasion to keep his warriors home.

The entrance flap of the *ini ti* was pulled aside, admitting the light, and a hand passed in a bowl of cold water. Sun Horse drank a little and handed the bowl to Sees Beyond. He felt the water cold within him and hot without; it was the same water, hot where it had been dripped on the rocks to hiss and steam, breathing throughout the tiny lodge, cold within his stomach. The same water, flowing from the west, falling from the thunderclouds, bringing the life-giving power to make things grow.

A power is coming. It can help the Sun Band or destroy us, Hears Twice had said. Sun Horse had seen the power joined, or so he thought. His grandson returned from the dead after eight winters, meeting the clown girl of the whites. Johnny's power, like Sun Horse's, touched the worlds of both red men and white. And the clown girl as well had a two-sided power, the *heyoka* power to make life or to destroy. Together, they created a force that could help the Sun Band or destroy it; it was up to Sun Horse to turn that power to the good and to apply it to his larger task: to understand the *washíchun*. He must grasp their essence! How could they be persuaded to make a peace that would leave the Lakota strong?

Peace without surrender.

He shook his head, feeling unequal to the task. For twenty-five years he had sought to understand the whites and through all that time something had eluded him. He could not find the center of the white nation, the core of its spirit. The *washíchun* spoke always with many voices; the more of them in one place, the more voices that spoke. Always they seemed to be scattered. Sun Horse was sure he lacked some insight, something he had not yet seen that would make plain to him the whole. Surely such limitless power could not come from people who were broken and scattered?

The *washíchun,* not at peace with themselves.

The thought came to him as if it had been spoken clearly by someone close at hand. The lodge was dark again. Had Sees Beyond spoken aloud? Sun Horse felt sure the words had not come from the world of man. He felt a chill of power, despite the warmth of the little lodge.

Not at peace with themselves . . . That would explain the turmoil of the spirit Sun Horse had always sensed around whites—except a few, such as Lodgepole, who was Lakota now, and his brother Jed Putnam.

If spiritual calm came from true understanding, how then to make peace with a people who had not reached that understanding, that inner calm?

Sees Beyond moved. He poured the rest of the water in the bowl onto the rocks, which sent up a cloud of steam. Sun Horse felt a wave of new warmth envelop him. Droplets of warm water gathered on the bent willow poles and dripped on Sun Horse's back and shoulders.

"Soon the helper will open the entrance for the last time," Sees Beyond said. "And we will see the light."

Hearing this signal, Sings His Daughter opened the flap and the steam poured forth, carrying away everything that had been cleansed from the two that had participated in the ritual, leaving the men fresh and new, as if reborn. As the steam dispersed and the soft light of evening entered the little hut, Sun Horse saw across the creek to the snow-covered slopes where the last rays of the sun were turning the snow red, a warm red like the first light of a new day.

The light that entered the *ini ti* at the end of the ritual symbolized the light of the east, the light of true understanding, which should be the first thing seen by one who has just purified himself. But here it was truly the light of day's end, coming from the west. Sun Horse felt a chill course along his backbone, but this time it was a chill of fear. Could this be the end of the day for the Lakota? Were they to be swept away by the flood of whites?

Twenty-five winters had passed since his vision and still the whites came, moving always from east to west. In Lakota symbolism there were two roads that ran across the hoop of the world. One began in the east, where all the days of man began, and went to the west, where all the days of man ended, and that road was black, for it was the road of worldly difficulties. But there was another road, one that began in the south, where dwelt the power to grow, and ended in the north, the realm of white hairs and the cold of death, and that was the good red road of spiritual understanding. Only by walking that road could a man grow spiritually throughout his lifetime, and so acquire the wisdom to withstand the difficulties he would surely encounter. But it seemed to Sun Horse that the black road was the only one the *washíchun* knew. Was that what he sensed? Was there some vital part missing from the *washíchun* spirit? Could it be that they did not know the red road at all?

The implications of this troubling thought rose in Sun Horse's mind and swirled around him, confusing him, but he put them aside with an effort of will. Later he would return to them, but now he looked once again out the entrance of the *ini ti* to the sun-red hills across the river. The light had reminded him of the two roads all men must walk; that was enough for now.

Moving out of the cross-legged position he had kept for

so long, Sun Horse left the *ini ti*. Outside he stood up straight. There was no stiffness in his body. He moved like a young man.

He prayed as he walked the path to the fire, feeling the cool air on his naked body. "*Wakán Tanka,* I place my feet on the sacred path. With joy in my heart I walk the sacred earth. For my people I walk in a sacred manner. Let the generations to come also walk in this sacred way. *Waníktelo!*" The word meant "I will live," but in his heart Sun Horse said, I will live that my people may live.

He squatted and rubbed handfuls of snow all over his body, feeling the shock as he rubbed between his legs, but he laughed at the feeling and stood again, rubbing the snow on his face last of all.

Sings His Daughter held out his robe. As he wrapped it around him he wished for a moment that it were a newer robe, thicker, with good winter fur. The air found its way through a small hole and he felt a cool spot on his leg. He slipped into his old moccasins.

He had not found the answers he sought, but *inipi* was not a ceremony for providing answers; it was a beginning, a cleansing, an opening up.

He looked around and saw the smoke from the lodges rising straight into the dark blue that was spotted with slow-moving clouds. The clouds still showed sunlight on their bellies, but the sun had left the eastern ridge now, and even as Sun Horse watched, the fire-glow died in the clouds and one by one they turned gray.

Inipi—a beginning. The real task lay ahead of him. Now the true search began. On his shoulders lay the burden of fulfilling the promise that *wamblí* had given so recently, and the older promise as well, the promise his spirit horse—his sun horse—had given, all those snows past. Still he sought the way to peace, but now the time was short.

Sees Beyond had also come out of the *ini ti* and was standing beside him now, taking his own robe from Sings His Daughter's hands. Sun Horse looked to the ridges surrounding the valley. For the task before him he should seek out a place of solitude, a high place where he could speak to the spirits and look within himself, as Crooked Horn had done. If the answers to his questions lay within his grasp, they were within himself. It was there he would look.

Already the warmth of the *ini ti* had left his body and he could feel the chill air rising from the creek. With the sun gone, the cold grew quickly stronger. He knew he could not spend a cold night on some lonely ridge like a young man seeking a vision.

Sees Beyond laughed. "Look beyond the symbol," he said, chuckling.

Sun Horse wondered why the young holy man repeated these words now, but then he understood. He took Sees Beyond's right hand and shook it once, firmly, and then he smiled. *"Ho hechetu aloh. Lila pilámayayelo!"* he said, thanking the young *wichasha wakán* for making *inipi* with him and for reminding him of this most important lesson. He took Sings His Daughter's arm and they started together for the camp circle.

Look beyond the symbol. The high ridge was a symbol, one very helpful to a young man on his vision quest. The high places are closer to *Wakán Tanka,* the young were taught, and so they sought the solitude of the high lonely places where the winged ones flew with dignity and where it was easy for a man to look inside himself and find his pathway to power.

But the ridge was only a symbol. A man could find his power anywhere, and so Sun Horse and his young wife made their way toward his warm lodge. The woman leaned against him as they walked. He felt the warmth of her body through the robes and something stirred in his loins. He chuckled and shook his head, and she glanced at him, her face asking a question, but he only smiled. He would like to enjoy this young wife tonight. She knew how to move, and how to give a man much pleasure by showing her own. But he would not go to her robes tonight, although he knew that she wanted him. A warrior did not enjoy a woman on the night before a battle, and Sun Horse's task demanded all the strength a man brought to war.

Inside the cheerful lodge Elk Calf awaited them with the fire built up strong and a little soup warmed, but Sun Horse refused the soup and said nothing as he seated himself in front of the fire. He filled his pipe and smoked, once again offering the pipe to the directions, and his wives knew he thought of matters that concerned the spirit world. Sings His Daughter took up an old deerskin to rub between her hands and make soft again while Elk Calf worked slowly with sinew and awl at the goatskin moccasins, and the three sat together in silent peace with Sun Horse's thoughts undisturbed.

Peace. A word used in so many ways—the peace of a few moons between the Lakota and their enemies; the peace among allies of long standing; the peace of a happy lodge; a man at peace with himself.

For a time Sun Horse put aside all thoughts, his mind at rest like the plain under the summer sun, the swaying of the buffalo grass the only movement.

Then he returned to the question at the center of his task and now a certainty came to him: the Lakota must continue to walk the good red spirit road, whatever the form of the final peace with the whites. Few men could walk only the spirit road; Sees Beyond was one who seemed to tread there almost exclusively, but most men walked both the red and the black roads. To walk only the road of worldly troubles meant to be like the *washíchun,* with no inner calm, no understanding. There must be a balance. The Lakota symbols recognized this; where the red road of spiritual understanding crossed the black road of worldly difficulties, there stood the tree of life; its branches were filled with singing birds and it shielded all creatures. There the Lakota nation dwelt, surrounded now by the swirling rivers of *washíchun* that threatened to uproot the tree and sweep the Lakota people away forever.

Washíchun, a people not at peace with themselves. How then to make peace with them?

Lisa Putnam's Journal

Thursday, March 16th. 11:50 a.m.

I am ashamed to admit that I have been up and about for only half an hour, but I do feel greatly improved. Yesterday when we arrived back here just before suppertime I could barely walk, I was so tired. But I thought a bite of supper would do me good and would give me enough strength to help with cleaning up the dishes before going to bed. Ling insisted that I should have a bath and change into fresh clothes before supper, which I see now was part of a conspiracy she hatched with Harry. They had already placed the tub in my room and filled it with hot water, and of course I couldn't resist. I got out of the bath and lay on my bed for what I thought would be only a few moments, and that was the last thing I knew until waking a short time ago to discover that Ling had tucked me in all warm and comfortable and left me to sleep away the night and half of today.

Our dinner this noontime will be quieter than usual. Mr. Tatum has come up with an arrangement which will allow his teamsters even more time at the avalanche. Until now they have been returning here for the midday meal, but beginning today Joe Kitchen's helper Monty will take their dinner to them in a wagon, saving them the time of riding back and forth. Despite the setbacks caused by a too-

liberal use of blasting powder, Mr. Tatum is apparently making some progress and is intent on making more.

After feeding the cows this morning Johnny and Hutch spent another two hours mending fence, and they told me just now that they have inspected and repaired all the fence in the park during the past week. What a pair of workers they are. In recognition of their efforts I gave them the afternoon off, which took them quite by surprise. They looked at each other as if to say "What on earth shall we do with an afternoon free?" but Hutch found the solution at once. "You said I was about ready to learn to rope from horseback," he suggested, and I even agreed that they might cut out a sturdy calf from the herd to practice on, if they don't run him ragged.

They say they observed some scours among the calves in the meadow. Julius and I will ride down this afternoon to see for ourselves, and we may stop at the avalanche to have a look at the work going on there.

Well, try as I may to keep my mind on the ranch and its demands, I cannot escape the discouragement I feel over the end of hunting. Our lack of conspicuous success thus far has apparently convinced Sun Horse that the spirit powers do not view our efforts kindly, and yesterday when Julius and Alfred and Willy Waldheim and I passed through the village on our way home, he informed us of his decision to suspend the hunt. We, of course, can continue our own efforts, but Sun Horse's resignation to an unkind fate fills me once more with a fear that he and his people will ultimately surrender or be taken by soldiers, or be otherwise compelled to go to Dakota. As I thought of the Lakotas and their predicament upon first waking this morning, I grew angry all over again at this clear violation of the Fort Laramie treaty, and then I found cause for a new fear, one that makes me wonder if even the most peaceful delegation of headmen can obtain the right to continue living in the Powder River country, for I believe I know now the true reason for the government's efforts to gather all the Sioux in Dakota. It may not be simply "to keep an eye on them" during the Black Hills troubles, as Mr.

Hardeman suggested. The Laramie treaty says in no uncertain terms that there shall be no further cessions of land unless agreed to by three-fourths of the adult male members of the tribe. In a nation of some thirty thousand souls, close to ten thousand may be grown men, and surely the required degree of consent will never be obtained unless the Sioux are all gathered in one place! As long ago as last summer I recall some mention in the newspapers of needing to have the Sioux come to the agencies <u>to be counted</u>. Once there, confined on the reservation, stripped of their freedom and possessions and hope, they might be coerced into ceding not only the precious Black Hills but the Powder River country as well, thus putting a stamp of legality on the theft after the fact!

How much depends on the pipe carriers! If they succeed, the hunting bands will remain free at least until summer, and the government can never obtain any cession—whether of the Black Hills or this country here—without coming to terms with the bands in the Powder River country. And so the hopes I had placed in the hunting are now vested in Mr. Hardeman and Uncle Bat and the others, and my concerns, which until now have been mainly for the Sun Band, have broadened to embrace the whole Sioux nation, for I see now that the fates of all the bands are inescapably intertwined. Such thoughts make my own efforts on Sun Horse's behalf seem small indeed, and I feel helpless once more. It is my hope that by recording these feelings here I may enable myself to set them aside; here in Putnam's Park life must go on, and we can only await the outcome of the momentous events taking place beyond these hills.

The weather continues to be changeable. It is snowing lightly now, but when I first sat down with my journal the sun was shining. Harry tells me last night was clear, and the mercury was below zero when he went to look at the heifers.

CHAPTER TWELVE

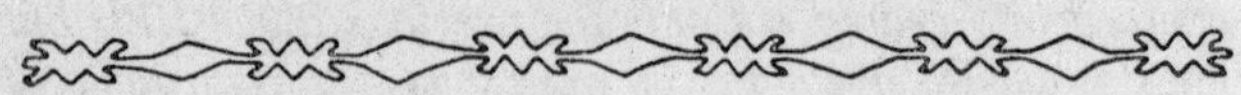

The cow's sides heaved with a final contraction and the calf's hindquarters slipped onto the straw that was scattered six inches deep all along the fence by the barn wall. Lisa and Julius sat atop the fence, watching the birth. Normal births took place here, out of doors; the calving shed was for pulling calves and caring for the sick ones.

"Pretty big calf," Julius ventured.

Lisa nodded, smiling. "She might be a keeper." Each spring her father had surveyed the new calves from the moment of birth, watching for the ones that stood best and sucked soonest, the ones that kept close to their mothers and the mothers that took best care of their offspring, and from these bloodlines he had chosen the heifer calves he would keep when the steers and the rest of the heifers were sold. Now the responsibility for this selection had passed to Lisa and Julius. Together they would decide the fate of each calf born, and already the process was under way.

The two of them had saddled their horses and started off to look over the calves in the meadow when they had noticed that one of the heifers was about to give birth, and they had stopped to watch. The inspection of the young animals was a pressing task if there was scours in the herd. Scours was a form of bovine diarrhea that could weaken a calf and leave it susceptible to pneumonia or some other fatal ailment, and the affected animals, if any, would have to be treated promptly. But the birth of each new calf was important too, and so Lisa and Julius lingered to watch the most recent arrival while their horses shifted about and stamped, impatient to be off.

The new mother rose now and turned to sniff at the wet bundle she had delivered. Streamers of thick mucus and strands of membrane hung from the cow's organs. Tentatively at first and then with growing confidence she began to lick the whitish birth sac off the newborn calf. The calf's eyes were open and its nostrils flared as it grew accustomed to the experience of breathing. After a first small cry it had remained silent.

"Natural mother," Julius said, pleased.

"Smarter than that other one," Lisa agreed sourly, nodding toward a nearby chute where a cow and calf were confined together. Two nights before, the cow had slept on top of her perfectly healthy calf and killed it. Lisa had been so infuriated that she had wanted to slaughter the cow, but Julius had calmed her down and made her see reason. Another cow with an incurably rotten hoof had a good calf that would need a mother to get him through the summer, but his own mother would not last that long. Crippled, barely able to walk, she would not get enough to eat to sustain both herself and the calf. And so the cow with the bad foot had been slaughtered and her calf was now being grafted on the careless cow that had killed her own offspring. The calf had a section of the dead calf's hide tied to its back so it would smell familiar to the mother, but still the cow was not satisfied with the arrangement. She was haltered and tied to limit her movement in the chute, but as the calf tried to nurse she shied away and kicked at it.

"Quit that!" Lisa said sharply. The cow rolled her eyes and sighed and allowed the calf to suck for a time, but when it butted her udder to release more milk, she kicked again.

"That's enough now!" Lisa jumped down from the fence and climbed over into the chute with the cow and calf. When the cow kicked at the calf again, Lisa kneed her sharply in the side. Again the cow kicked and again she was kneed. After a few repetitions it began to penetrate the cow's dim imagination that there might be some connection between the two actions, and she stopped kicking. Lisa stroked her neck and spoke to her softly as the calf sucked and butted at the udder. Pacified by this attention, the cow settled down and continued to allow the eager calf to nurse even when Lisa left the chute and rejoined Julius on the fence.

"There goes Alfred," Julius said. He was looking off past the circus wagons to where two figures with rifles over their shoulders were walking across the meadow toward the woods.

"Who's that with him?"

"One of those acrobat fellers. Not Abbruzzi; that other bunch from Connecticut."

"Alfred enjoys the out-of-doors more than any of them," Lisa said. "He's to the manor born, I guess. They hunted a good deal in his family." She had been surprised to learn that Alfred Chalmers was descended from English gentry. He was the third of three sons and his eldest brother was now the lord of the manor. With no expectation of ever inheriting it himself unless both of his brothers should die before him, Alfred had turned first to the theater and then to circus life for his livelihood. His tale had reminded Lisa of her own father, the eldest of three sons, and the family business he might have managed had he been a less adventuresome man.

"He don't give up easy," Julius said. "Wish I could say the same for old Sun Horse." Neither he nor Lisa had spoken of Sun Horse or the end of hunting since leaving the Sioux village.

"We mustn't give up hope," Lisa said. "We may hunt together again. And meantime we can save some of our cows by bringing in game meat."

Julius nodded, but he felt no enthusiasm for hunting now that the Indians had abandoned the effort. The good feeling that had come over him back when he and Lisa had first offered the cows to Sun Horse along with the powder and grain had grown even stronger as the hunting got under way. Out in the hills with parties of circus men and Indians, Julius had experienced an elation like nothing he had known since the Rebellion, when he was given a uniform and a chance to fight to preserve his own freedom. Could taking a stand for another man's freedom make him feel just as good as fighting for his own? It didn't seem possible. But when Sun Horse had told Lisa that he was quitting the hunt, Julius had felt betrayed.

A light snow was beginning to fall as a band of clouds passed low over the park. There was a sudden clanging from the blacksmith shed and Julius heard the sounds echo off the west side of the valley. Harry had his forge hot and he was getting down to his afternoon's work. He was forging spikes from an old tooth harrow into improvised pick heads, which he would attach to any tool handle he could fashion. All the picks and shovels in the park were already in use at the avalanche and Tatum wanted more. The circus master was digging himself out of his predicament, but Sun Horse was just waiting. For what?

Willy and Johann Waldheim came out of the barn leading two horses apiece, making for the candy-striped tent. The animals all wore brightly colored woolen warming blankets woven in a tartan pattern. Scotch blankets on English thoroughbreds led by Germans who came here with a New York man, Julius thought. The white man isn't sitting around waiting. He's on the move. The Indians best stir themselves or they'll get left in the dust.

"Look at that," Lisa said softly.

In the heifer lot, the newborn calf had its front legs propped on the ground and was trying to get to its feet in a tiny imitation of the peculiar heave an adult cow used to rise from a lying position. The calf jerked upright, nearly overbalanced, then caught itself and remained standing, legs splayed, looking curiously about. It didn't stay still for long. The mother cow was close at hand, sniffing and licking, and now the calf turned its head toward the hindquarters of this large and attentive beast that smelled so familiar. With a few unpracticed lurches and hops it reached its goal, head probing the udder and finding a teat, beginning to suckle.

"That a girl!" Julius encouraged the calf.

"Will you look at her?" Lisa exclaimed. "If they were all like that . . ." She shook her head in wonder. "We can turn them out tomorrow if they keep on like that."

"Good mother, good calf," said Julius. "Looks like a keeper for sure."

"Oh, Johnny, look!" came a voice, and they turned to see Amanda and Johnny Smoker approaching, followed by Hutch and Chatur. The quartet of "young people" had taken the midday meal together, and there had been much animated talk and laughter from their end of the table. By custom, Amanda ate with Hachaliah Tatum, but with her guardian off at the avalanche she had joined her friends today.

Amanda ran to the fence and stared at the mother and calf. "He's beautiful! How old is he?"

"It's a she," Lisa said, smiling, "and she was born about fifteen minutes ago."

Hutch turned to Chatur. "Say, how big is an elephant calf when it's born?"

"Oh, very much bigger than that," Chatur replied. "He is approximately this high"—he held a hand about three feet off the ground—"and he is weighing, I should say, two hundred pounds."

Hutch's eyes opened wide. "Say now, you cross one of those with a shorthorn cow and you'd bring up the weight of your calves pretty quick."

Julius grinned. "What you gonna do with a calf's got a trunk and maybe tusks and horns both?"

"Well, I hadn't thought much about it. You don't reckon it's a good idea?" Hutch gave Julius a wink and glanced quickly at Chatur as if to say the little Indian man was buying the whole thing and let's keep it going a while longer.

Julius swung himself down from the fence and untied his horse. "Oh, I don't know." He looked at Chatur.

"You suppose old Rama'd like to have a go at one of our cows?"

Chatur appeared dubious. "He has had no company of lady elephants for a long time. I will ask him, certainly. If he is willing, I will turn him loose."

"Don't you dare," Lisa said as she got off the fence and took her own horse's reins. "I won't have some foreign creature terrifying my cows."

As Julius mounted up, Hutch could see that the colored man was laughing softly; Johnny and Miss Lisa were smiling and Chatur was grinning like he knew the whole thing was a joke from start to finish, and Hutch wasn't quite sure who the joke was on but he was grinning too. At moments like this he felt that Putnam's Park was a pretty special place and he was a part of it, and the thought of ever leaving made him uncomfortable. Well, who said he had to leave? It wasn't even spring yet and he still had a lot to learn. There was no great rush about it all, was there? Just now he and Johnny had the afternoon off and they would do as they pleased and take their time about it, and he was darned if he was going to worry about what he might or might not do three or four months from now.

The snow kept up for a time and Hutch and Johnny followed Amanda to the barn and lingered to watch the acrobats and the clowns work. Hutch managed to catch a few words with Maria Abbruzzi and she squeezed his hand and gave him a quick kiss when her father wasn't looking. Johnny seemed content just to sit and watch Amanda even when she wasn't doing a thing. When the snow stopped they saddled a couple of horses and went outside to teach Hutch how to rope from horseback. Lisa had said that Hutch could use any horse he wanted and he saddled a nice sorrel he fancied. He had thought of using his own mule but he gave up that idea without a fight. Old Joe, as he called the mule, was willing enough to be saddled and ridden wherever Hutch wanted to go, but that was the extent of it. He wouldn't haul a wagon or tote a pack or do a lick of serious work and today Hutch didn't feel like fighting a stubborn mule that was set in his ways.

They cut a calf out of the herd and drove him into the big pasture where the circus horses and the bulls were kept. It took Hutch the better part of an hour to master the skill of handling the reins and the rope at the same time and not get anything tangled after the loop was thrown, and then it took him a while longer to get the horse right on the calf and place his loop anywhere near the calf's head. The first time the loop sailed neatly into place around the calf's neck Hutch got so excited that he dallied his reins to the saddle horn and dropped the rope and the calf led the two of them a merry chase to get it back. By then the three Waldheim men were done work for the day and they had come to sit on the fence and watch Hutch's lessons, and Amanda came from the barn in her clown suit and buffalo coat, but Hutch was enjoying himself so much that he didn't mind making a bit of a fool of himself in front of his friends. After all, none of them could even rope on foot, and Johnny said Hutch was learning quick and would be a top roper in no time.

But when he finally roped the calf and got the rope dallied right, his sorrel wouldn't hold the rope tight.

"Let me get on him for a minute," Johnny said, and Hutch dismounted and turned the calf loose. Johnny took out after the calf and roped him again before he even had a chance to get up to full speed. Johnny brought the sorrel to a quick stop and showed him how to keep the rope tight. "Back now. Back," he said, pulling gently on the reins whenever the rope slackened for a moment. After a minute or two he got off and moved hand over hand along the rope to the calf to take off the loop.

Julius and Lisa were passing by on their way back from the meadow. "You been ropin' off that horse?" Julius wanted to know.

"Oh, he's all right," Johnny said, "but he ain't never been taught to back right."

Julius laughed. "He ain't never been roped off before. He's doin' pretty good, considerin'."

The Waldheims seemed to think this was one of the funniest things they had heard all day. "Oh, ho!" they exclaimed, and they clapped one another on the back and pointed at Johnny and the sorrel and talked back and forth in German, which Hutch thought sounded like a string of the fanciest cuss words he'd ever heard.

Johnny just said, "He takes to it quick enough. He'll make a good roper if you keep after him." He turned the calf loose and gave the sorrel back to Hutch. "Here, you try him once."

With Julius and Lisa watching, Hutch chased after the calf and dropped the loop as neat as you please and the sorrel hunched down and jerked the calf clean off his feet when he hit the end of the rope, and he kept the rope tight as a string of barb wire while Hutch got off to set the calf free.

"So, you are a cow-boy now!" Papa Waldheim called out to Hutch.

"Oh, I got a ways to go," the youth replied, not wanting to sound too puffed up in front of Julius and Johnny and Miss Lisa, but he was pleased with himself all the same.

"So, ve buy the cow-boy a beer before supper. What do you say?"

"You go on," Johnny told Hutch. "I'll take care of the horses. We better let that calf go find his mama anyway. He's lost a couple of pounds by now. He's gettin' rope shy too."

The day was getting on and it was beginning to snow again. People were leaving the barn by twos and threes and making for the main house.

Amanda followed Johnny to the barn and as he unsaddled his own mount she took on herself the unsaddling of the sorrel. She brushed his back where the hair was matted from the saddle and when she was done Lisa and Julius had unsaddled their horses and gone, and she and Johnny were alone in the barn.

"You seem right at home around horses," Johnny said. Like everything else he said to Amanda it sounded awkward and inappropriate in his ears.

She smiled. "You can't spend your whole life in the

circus without knowing something abour horses. I thought I wanted to be a trick rider once."

They turned the horses out and Johnny said, "I guess it's almost suppertime."

"Will you wait for me while I change?" Amanda did not draw the curtain in the dressing-room stall, where the steamer trunks stood open and overflowing with costumes. She slipped out of her buffalo coat and drew her clown's blouse over her head, followed by the thick woolen jersey she wore beneath it to practice in the cold barn, and Johnny saw her bare back, smooth and white. She held the jersey clutched to her chest, covering her bosom, as she half turned to him. "Would you hand me my petticoat? It's there on the vaulting horse."

He saw the frilled satin garment on the padded top of the wooden vaulting horse and he handed it to her, feeling like an intruder in her dressing room. As she turned away to don the petticoat she dropped the jersey and one small breast was revealed in silhouette. The blood rose to Johnny's face and he walked off to absorb himself in inspecting other parts of the barn, wondering how in the world he would ever be able to express the emotions that were so strange and new to him. For two weeks now he had been searching his past life for some signpost that would point the way he should follow with Amanda, but his knowledge of courting was sharply divided between distant memories of his Cheyenne boyhood and recent years in the cattle towns of Kansas, and neither way seemed suited to his present feelings. Among the Cheyenne, courting procedures, like all other relations between men and women, were circumspect and strictly prescribed by custom. As a small boy, Little Warrior had seen the older boys waiting outside the lodge of a girl who was approaching womanhood. By the lodge or along the trail to wood or water the young man who arrived first was given first chance to speak to the girl when she came along; each made his feelings known and in time the girl did the choosing. As for the physical joining of man and woman, that was no mystery to Cheyenne children. The Cheyenne had a different set of taboos from the white man, and frank discussion of what took place between a man and a woman at night in the warmth of the buffalo robes was not among them. The old women told stories that would have been unthinkable in a St. Louis ladies' sewing circle, and when he entered the white world Johnny had found that he was far better informed in these matters than other boys his age. But although talk had been frank among the Cheyenne, behavior was anything but loose; no women were more respected among the plains people for their chaste comportment than the women of the *Tsistsístas*. A maiden who allowed herself to be seduced was disgraced, and no man would think of marrying her. Courtship was long and young men and women came to know each other well before marrying and starting life together as husband and wife.

It was with this purity of intent that Johnny wished to approach Amanda, but he did not see how such alien customs could have a place here in Putnam's Park. He could not stand outside her bedroom in the Big House and wrap her in his blanket when she came out, or play the courting flute beneath her window. Nor did the courting rituals of the white world provide the answer. It seemed to Johnny that everyone from preachers to stable hands proclaimed their admiration for one sort of woman while chasing after another, and his own experience with both whores and well-bred young ladies had only served to confuse him further.

He had crossed the tracks to McCoy's Addition in Abilene just once, five years ago at the end of his first trail drive. That part of town, which was also called "the Beer Garden," was named for the then-mayor and father of the Kansas cattle trade, Joseph G. McCoy. It housed saloons, gambling dens, houses of ill-repute, and other diversions for the trail hands. Johnny had been in the company of a dozen other young drovers and like them he had been a little drunk, but he hadn't shared their enthusiasm for exploring the fabled pleasures of the brothels. He had almost backed out at the last minute, remembering Sammy Tadich and his refusal to go along. Just a bath and a night's sleep in a real bed was all that Sammy had wanted after two months on the trail. He had met a girl before leaving Texas and he was keeping himself pure for her, although he had set eyes on her just once and for less than an hour. "I met me a girl, Johnny," he had said. "Hair like spun sunbeams." And there had been a look in his eyes that Johnny couldn't fathom. But the other drovers were thirsty for a drink stronger than water and eager to mount something softer than a saddle, and Johnny had no girl back in Texas so he had tagged along. The girl he ended up with was nearly as shy as he was and scarcely older, a sad little thing that had tugged at his heart. He had chosen her more to protect her from the others than to have her for himself, but her shyness hadn't kept her from showing him, gently and expertly, some of the pleasure to be had with a woman. She had instructed him with patience and no trace of condescension, and Johnny liked to think she had shown him more of herself than she did with other men. He had wanted to help her but it seemed that nothing could shake her out of that sadness; she clutched it like it was the only thing anyone had ever let her keep.

There had been another girl too, as different from the first as day from night, just a few months ago in Ellsworth. Johnny had avoided the advances of the whores in Ellsworth, but he had been taken completely by surprise after a proper dance attended only by the town's respectable citizens and their offspring when a very cheerful girl of good family had charmed the pants right off him in the loft of her father's barn. For a time Johnny thought she had her sights set on marrying him and he was giving it some consideration, but she had gently disabused him of the notion. What they had done together seemed to mean about the same thing to her as sharing a beer with a good friend meant to Johnny, and he later found out that she had similarly charmed several of the other boys in town, but never the ones that boasted of their conquests. In late winter her engagement to the son of the town's foremost banking family had been announced, and Johnny had come to see that it wasn't only men who had to sow their wild oats before settling down.

From his two experiences with women, Johnny could draw no useful lessons about courtship in the white world. The stories he heard had led him to believe that it was the whores who were cheerful and gave you a moment's pleasure and sent you on your way with a smile, and the little sad girl that tugged your heart was the one you got in trouble and had to marry with her father's eyes boring hard into your back as you stood up before the preacher. It had happened the other way around with Johnny and he considered himself lucky that things had come out that way, for now at last he figured he knew what Sammy Tadich had felt for the girl back in Texas. Amanda was the girl for him. He would do anything for her, sacrifice anything to win her, but he was walking a trail he had never set foot on before and he felt less sure of himself than a blind man might.

"Johnny? I'm ready." Amanda stepped out of the stall. She had put on a plain gray woolen dress and her feet were clad in small boots with a fringe of fur on the top. She looked altogether as proper as any of the bankers' and stockmen's daughters at that dance in Ellsworth and for the moment at least Johnny was not at a loss. He offered her his arm and she took it, and they left the barn together like any young couple out for a stroll, their bearing measured and correct, only the closeness of their bodies and the bright look in their eyes revealing the pleasure they took from simply walking arm in arm.

A light snow was still falling and down on the wagon road they could see Tatum and the teamsters making for home after a long day's work, the horsemen in a tight bunch and moving briskly, just rounding the turn at the clump of pines. Farther to the rear came the wagons, drawn by mules and oxen. The meal gong broke the silence of the deserted yard and Amanda quickened her pace, hurrying Johnny along. "Come on," she said, holding him tightly against her. "I'm hungry."

But in the saloon they did not find the usual jostling at the serving tables. There was a large group around a table near the stove and a cheer went up as Amanda and Johnny entered. They made their way through the crowd and discovered that an arm-wrestling contest was in progress.

"So, Papa, you think you will do better?" Johann Waldheim rose from the table and ushered his father into the seat opposite Harry Wo.

"I kind of got this deal started," Hutch said as he joined Amanda and Johnny. "I got to wrestling with Johann and Willy and I beat them both, and then Papa Waldheim beat me and I told 'em how nobody'd ever beat Harry, and nothing would do but they all had to have a go at him."

Papa Waldheim set his elbow on the table and clasped Harry's hand and braced himself, smiling confidently, but his expression changed to one of surprise as the signal was given for the contest to start. For a moment the two hands remained motionless and then Papa Waldheim's was borne inexorably backwards. He grunted and frowned and put all his might into stopping the motion, but after a moment it resumed and soon his arm was forced to the tabletop.

"Perhaps you were not ready?" Harry inquired politely, once Papa Waldheim had signaled his surrender.

"Ready? Oh, I vass ready!" He looked up at Julius and Lisa, who stood in the forefront of the crowd. "Ha ha! So you haff a champion? Vell, so do ve! Alfred, a moment of your time, if you please!"

Looking almost reluctant, Alfred Chalmers made his way through the crowd.

"Uh oh, I think I got Harry in trouble," said Hutch.

Harry shrugged and gave Hutch a wink.

As soon as Chalmers seated himself it was apparent to one and all that there was a problem. Chalmers' forearm was nearly twice as long as Harry's and there was no way the squat Chinese could grasp Chalmers' hand.

"Put Harry's arm on a crate," Julius suggested.

"That'd give him an advantage, wouldn't it?" Ben Long protested.

"Oh, I certainly don't object," Chalmers said. "It seems quite the sensible thing to do."

"You don't eat pretty soon, I take the food back," Ling

Wo warned the gathering, but no one moved as Joe Kitchen ran off and returned with an Arbuckles' coffee crate, which he set on the table. Harry stood and propped his elbow on the crate and his hand met Chalmers' perfectly.

"All right now," said Papa Waldheim, appointing himself the referee. "On three you begin. One, two . . . three!"

As had been the case with Papa Waldheim, Chalmers' first reaction was one of surprise, which transformed itself into renewed determination. Harry's face changed very little except for a slight raising of the eyebrows.

"Look at that!" Hutch whispered.

The clasped hands were trembling. The trembling grew in intensity until the table itself shuddered slightly and one leg rattled on the floor. And then the hands moved, swaying first to Harry's side, then to Chalmers', then back to Harry's, and this time the movement was not reversed. At the last, Harry conceded defeat by ceasing his resistance. At once he bowed deeply to the victor as the crowd cheered.

Chalmers rose and bowed just as deeply and then offered his hand, which Harry pumped in vigorous congratulations. When his hand was returned to him, Chalmers flexed his wrist, regarding it as if it were a foreign object. "Extraordinary. Truly extraordinary."

"Never before haff I see Alfred's hand move backwards!" Papa Waldheim exclaimed.

Harry was chuckling. "He got trouble now. He got to stay here until someone beats him. That's the rules. That's what Julius tell me when I come here. Ain't that right?" He looked at Julius and Julius nodded seriously.

"That's the rules."

"Ah. Oh dear." Chalmers was nonplussed. "Perhaps we might have another go? You never know, the first time may have been a fluke."

The onlookers laughed and Harry clapped Chalmers on the back with a blow that staggered the strongman. "You beat me fair and square but maybe we let you go. Come on now, Ling's pretty mad we're late to eat. Lydia!" He waved the Gypsy woman over to join them. "You and Alfred go first." He led the way across the room and there was a general movement toward the serving tables. As Harry loaded a plate with immense portions for Chalmers, the teamsters arrived in a group and hastened to take their places in line. Lisa and Joe Kitchen joined the servers and the line began to move quickly along.

Hachaliah Tatum was the last to enter the saloon. As usual he had stopped in his room to change for supper; his hair was combed and his clothes were as neat as if he had spent the day reading in the library. He spied Amanda near the end of the serving line, chatting with her friends, and he raised a hand to get her attention. He started forward, smiling, but he was intercepted by half a dozen teamsters, headed by Fisk and a man named Tanner.

"We'd like a word with you, Mr. Tatum," Tanner said. He was a bear of a man and the unofficial leader of the Black Hills crowd. He had none of Kinnean's quiet menace but he held a rough authority over the men and he had kept them in line, save for the first night's party and Fisk's bungled attack on Bat Putnam, since Kinnean's injury had rendered the one-armed man's authority impotent. Tanner's voice was deep and resonant and his words were set in place deliberately, like the feet of the oxen he drove.

Tatum waited silently for the man to speak his piece.

"Well now," Tanner said, shifting from one foot to the other and never meeting Tatum's steady gaze for more than a moment. "There's some talk among us, and I'm not sayin' I'm of the same mind, you understand, just to say there's talk. What it is, we signed on to drive wagons, you see. That's what we're paid for, not for all this diggin'. There's some as feels we oughta be gettin' extra for the diggin'."

"I'll drive a team right enough," said Tom Johansen, the lean Minnesota youth who had caused the avalanche by his ill-considered shot, "but I ain't no Paddy to be digging all day with my hands."

"Too proud are yez?" An Irishman named Gimp turned to face Johansen. "We wouldn't be diggin' atall if it wasn't for you and yer shotgun, ye Scandihoovian vagabond! I oughta—'' Gimp raised his fists but Tanner stepped between them and brushed the Irishman aside like a cobweb.

''You two keep shut.''

Tatum remained silent, content to let the teamsters fight among themselves.

''The fact is, Mr. Tatum, we ain't gonna dig no more for you unless you double our wage.'' The speaker was Thaddeus Morton, the gray-haired Ohioan who had run afoul of Hardeman that first night. ''This here trip's takin' a good bit longer than we figured it would, but we're in no hurry, long's we're gettin' fed good. You want to get out of here, you say you'll double our wage and we'll hold you to it when we get to the Salt Lake.''

''You dug quick enough when you thought there was gold at the end of it,'' said a new voice, and the teamsters turned to see Kinnean close behind them.

''You keep out of this, Kinnean,'' said Morton. ''It's no affair of your'n.''

Kinnean stepped closer. ''You want to get paid at all, you'll dig.''

''I ain't afraid of you.''

Kinnean's arm shot out of its sling and the hand seized Morton's wrist, twisting it up behind his back until the driver doubled over with pain. ''You just get on to your dinner, Redeye, like a good fellow, and I'll be along to stand you a glass of whiskey.'' He released the man with a shove, sending him reeling among the tables. Kinnean looked at the rest of the group. ''Go on now, Jack,'' he said to Fisk, and Fisk turned away. The remaining drivers backed off, all except Tanner. ''I've no quarrel with you, Tanner. The sooner we get out of here the sooner we all get paid.''

Tanner hesitated. ''I wasn't much for this deal to start with,'' he said, and he lumbered off, ignoring the other drivers, who looked once more at Kinnean and Tatum, then turned and followed Tanner.

''I'm glad to see your arm is better, Mr. Kinnean,'' Tatum said, pleased with how the matter had been settled.

"This arm does the work of two and it heals quick. I thought it was about time I started earning my keep again."

"Can you hold a gun?"

Kinnean nodded. "I'll be ready for Mr. High-and-Mighty Hardeman when he gets back."

"We may well be gone before he returns."

"You may, but not me. I've a score to settle."

Tatum gave a small shrug. "Suit yourself. Just keep an eye on the men until the road is clear and I'll pay you off before we leave." Kinnean nodded and moved off toward the serving tables. Tatum watched him go. It wouldn't matter if the one-armed man remained behind when the circus left, but Tatum needed him now. There was a week or more of hard work left to clear the road and there might be other quarrels to settle. But once the way was clear the circus would reach the railroad in a week and Salt Lake City the day after that, and he would need Kinnean no longer.

At the serving line Amanda was just receiving her plate from Lisa Putnam. Once again Tatum raised a hand and started forward. Amanda looked in his direction, hesitated, then turned away to follow Johnny Smoker and the Waldheims. Tatum stopped in his tracks, frowning.

The silent exchange had not gone unobserved.

"There is trouble there, you mark my words," Lydia said in a low voice. She and Chalmers were seated alone at an out-of-the-way table.

"He seems to bide his time." Chalmers' tone was noncommittal, but he had seen the almost defiant look Amanda had given Tatum. All the same, he saw no good in raising speculation about what might or might not happen because of the youth's interest in Amanda and hers in him.

Lydia fixed him with her sharp black eyes. "He bides his time like a badger in its hole. Come. We will eat with them so there are no empty chairs at the table. If she wishes to eat without Hachaliah watching over her, that is how she shall eat."

Chalmers made no protest. He gathered up both plates

in his huge hands and followed Lydia to the table where Johnny and Amanda sat with Hutch and Chatur and the Waldheims. The German equestrian family was made complete by the presence of Greta Waldheim, the mother of Johann and Willy. She was as slight as her husband and sons were robust.

"So, you teach tricks to do horses," Papa Waldheim was saying to Johnny.

"Oh, I never had much call to teach a horse tricks," Johnny said. "Not like you do. But a horse'll learn most anything if you treat him right."

"*Ja,* and you know how to treat him right. Ve been vatching you, Johann and Villy and me. What do you say you come vork for us? Ve got some new horses to train. Ve train them, you and me, and Johann and Villy got more time to practice the act."

The unexpected offer took Johnny aback. "Well, I don't know," he said uncertainly. "I got to wait here for Chris to get back."

"Don't vorry about that. Maybe ve are all here when he gets back, maybe not. Maybe you come join us in Salt Lake City. What do you say?"

"I guess I'd have to think about it. What would Mr. Tatum say?"

"Don't you vorry about Hachaliah Tatum." Papa Waldheim lowered his voice as he noticed Tatum standing in the supper line not far away. The circus master was looking at the table. "You vork for me, not him. Ve hire who ve like. So, you think about it. You see San Francisco, plenty of other places. You talk about it to Amanda. Maybe she thinks it's not such a bad idea you should join the show." He gave Amanda a wink.

"Gunther!" Greta Waldheim chided. "Don't tease her."

Amanda blushed and dropped her eyes. Johann and Willy chuckled at her embarrassment. She heard the hard edge in their laughter, not unkind, but knowing. They thought they understood why she had encouraged Johnny's attentions, but they were wrong.

It was true that at first she had led him on for the same

reason she had led many others on, the young men in the cities and towns, the ones who flocked to her like butterflies to a bright flower, for this was how she retained a measure of control over Hachaliah Tatum. If he feared that some young man might whisk her out of his life forever he was more easily swayed, and by the frequent exercise of just this threat Amanda obtained from him whatever favor or gift she wished at the moment. It was a game they played, she and Hachaliah, but she had no doubt which of them held the stronger hand. Hachaliah was her protector and he knew her too well; she could never deceive him for long. He knew how much the circus meant to her, the performing most of all, and he knew she depended on him for guidance.

But here in Putnam's Park something had changed. The understanding that she was approaching a turning point had come to Amanda slowly; only in recent days had she realized what it meant, and what she must do.

Until now Hachaliah had supervised her art together with all other aspects of her life. He never interfered with the details of movement or technique in the clown routines but still he exercised overall control, and Amanda had welcomed his advice, for she shared his dream of blending the best of pantomime with the belly laughs of the slapstick and pratfall. It had shocked her to realize quite suddenly that she had learned all she could from Hachaliah and from now on his continued supervision would only hold her in check. This awareness had begun just a week ago, on the day when she and Sam and Carlos had performed the English gentleman and Spanish cavalier routine for the first time. Hachaliah's first reaction to the new act had infuriated her, and her anger had helped her to see clearly. Later that evening he had taken her aside and he had tried to soothe her with words of praise, but at the same time he had suggested small changes in the act and she had seen that they were meaningless changes, and she had remembered something her father had said to her long ago, when he had been instructing her in clowning for less than a year. Even as a child she had been an apt pupil and her father's delight in her progress had been her greatest reward. One day after she had done some small thing to exceed his expectations he had taken her on his knee and he had said, "Many clowns can learn the old acts and perform them well, but you are one of the rare ones, Amanda. You can dream the new acts. Follow your dreams and never let anyone hold you back." Now at last she had learned how to bring her dreams to life. She and Sam and Carlos had worked out the act together but the vision had been hers, and Hachaliah had tried to change it solely to retain his control over her.

He would never give up that control willingly, of that she was certain, and she had begun to cast about for some means of breaking free. To her astonishment, she had discovered a growing conviction that the key to her freedom lay somewhere within Johnny Smoker.

From the first she had been fascinated by this strange boy who had lived in two worlds, the Indian and the white, if for no other reason than that his life had been so different from her own. She had given him encouragement, using all the small signals she knew how to use to such good effect, thinking only to keep Hachaliah on edge while the circus was trapped in Putnam's Park. Over the past two weeks Johnny had told her the remarkable story of his life bit by bit until she knew it all, and her fascination had grown. He was utterly different from the young men of the cities and towns. Sometimes there in the background, beyond her fawning admirers, she had noticed a shy youth hanging back; she had ignored those, imagining that she could find no attraction in one who lacked the courage to step forward and press his suit. Yet Johnny reminded her of the boys who had watched from a distance. He was hesitant and shy and he did not force his attentions on her, but in him she had discovered another kind of courage and she suspected that she could learn something vital from him, if only there were enough time. He seemed to be without fear. He accepted as natural and right that he should set out on his own, leaving behind the man who had protected him and guided him during all the years since he had been rescued from the Indians. She had felt herself reaching out to him, drawing him closer and closer to her, as if she might absorb his fearlessness along with his tales of adventure on the frontier, and as she saw the willingness, even the eagerness with which he looked forward to his new life, she had realized that she too must make a break with her own protector.

But how? Hachaliah was the circus master; he had the final say about every act of every performer. Could there be a way to remain under his authority and still escape the restraints he would try to impose on her art? Clowning was everything to her; it allowed her to express feelings she could reveal in no other way.

The Waldheims' offer of employment for Johnny had given her sudden hope. It was a possibility she had never considered. If Johnny were a part of the circus, could she use him as a way of controlling Hachaliah and preventing him from interfering in her work? Would Hachaliah stand for it? What if Johnny refused the offer?

He must accept. She would make him accept, and she was glad that she had already taken the first steps to draw him out of his shyness. She had not planned to change her clothes in front of him in the barn, or to defy Hachaliah by sitting with Johnny and the others tonight instead of joining Hachaliah for supper as usual. Both decisions had been made suddenly, on impulse. She was following her instincts and she felt both exhilarated and afraid, sure of only one thing—she must awaken Johnny's desire and bind him to her while the circus was still in Putnam's Park, and she must play on Hachaliah's feelings as she had never done before.

The circus master was leaving the serving table now and as he glanced again in her direction she favored him with a quick smile. It wouldn't do to have him think she was rebelling. She would soothe his suspicions for a time, until she was sure of Johnny; until she was sure of the course she would follow to assert her independence.

After supper Gunther Waldheim took up his accordion and played songs from the mountains of Germany and

Austria, and a few couples danced. Johnny led Amanda through two waltzes, but as the second tune ended, Hachaliah Tatum appeared at his side to cut in politely, and when the next song was done Tatum said he was worn out from the day's work at the avalanche and he offered to escort Amanda to her room if she was ready to retire. She accepted with a small nod and he led her off on his arm.

Lisa had come from the kitchen to hear the music and she saw Johnny's disappointment as Tatum took Amanda away.

He'll have to speak up soon or he'll lose her, Lisa thought. The young never see how much they may lose until it's already gone. I knew no better at that age.

She stayed for a time, listening to the accordion and Papa Waldheim's pleasant tenor, but she found herself nodding and she slipped away to go to her own bed.

In the morning she awoke early. She felt fully rested, but not dulled by too much sleep as she had been the morning before, when she had slept past eleven o'clock. She sat up and stretched, her tousled hair falling over her face. As she brushed it away with a hand she heard the rooster crow faintly two or three times. Outside, the wind was up and snow was falling. She arose from the bed and crossed to the window, walking on tiptoes on the cold floor, and she saw that the fainthearted rooster had announced the day from the shelter of the henhouse door rather than take his accustomed perch on the gable.

There was no one stirring among the circus wagons and tents. The rest of the settlement was still asleep, it seemed. But as she turned from the window to dress, a movement caught her eye. The side door of the barn opened and a head emerged, looking first one way and then the other. The head retreated and the door opened wide as Hutch stepped out, but he turned back as someone took his arm. A glimpse of blond hair and the tilt of the boy's head told Lisa that he was being kissed farewell. Suddenly, Hutch ducked back into the barn and closed the door.

The reason became apparent a moment later as Harry Wo came into Lisa's view carrying a milk pail in one hand

and a bucket of hog slop in the other. He emptied the slop into the trough in the pigpen and moved on to the barn, entering by the same door and closing it behind him. After another moment the door opened yet again and Maria Abbruzzi scampered away toward the wagons, clutching her cape around her.

Lisa smiled, imagining the mutual embarrassment of Harry and the young couple, and she blushed at her own tacit approval of Hutch's early-morning rendezvous. She knew she should scold him, but that would only embarrass him further and it would have no effect on his virtue. And how should she counsel young Hutch on virtue, when she had abandoned her own?

None of her own family, not even her father, knew the truth of her interlude with the cavalry lieutenant. The Emersons would have been scandalized, no doubt, but what did they know about the frontier? It was to escape the genteel restrictions of the East that Lisa's mother had married Jedediah Putnam while she had the opportunity, and Lisa had felt herself acting with the same courage and abandon.

She thought of Chris Hardeman then and wondered what she might dare in order to hold him, if she thought she could succeed.

She crouched by the stove to throw in a few sticks of split pine kindling, and as it began to crackle, ignited by last night's coals, she slipped out of her nightgown and into her underthings. She took her gray dress from the wardrobe, but then she remembered that this was St. Patrick's Day, and she exchanged the gray dress for the dark green one.

She sat at her dressing table and held her head straight and high as she brushed her hair. There was no Irish blood among the Putnams or the Emersons, at least none that those proud families would admit, but in Lisa's childhood the holiday had grown steadily more boisterous as more and more Irish reached the shores of the New World, and it symbolized for her the joyous spirit of the Irish in America, out from under the British yoke. Today she claimed it for her own to assert her freedom from the distant social conventions that condemned any risks a young lady might take to test the paces of her heart before submitting it to a single set of reins. St. Patrick himself might not have approved, but his Catholic judgment held no sway over Lisa Putnam.

With her hair tied at the nape of her neck by a bright ribbon of green satin, Lisa lifted lightly on the handle of the bedroom door and opened it silently. As she stepped into the second-floor hallway, lit only by one window that admitted the soft gray light of early morning from the landing by the stairs, another door opened and Amanda Spencer tiptoed out of a room that was not her own. She wore a flannel dressing gown over her nightdress and she was barefoot. She did not see Lisa. With great care she closed the door behind her, but not before Lisa had seen through the open doorway to the bed where Hachaliah Tatum was sleeping soundly.

CHAPTER THIRTEEN

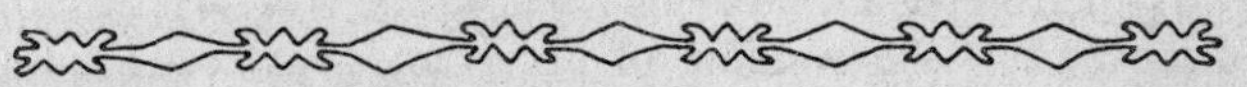

Hardeman awoke. The lodgeskins glowed with daylight and the Cheyenne camp was alive around him. He was warm and comfortable. He allowed his eyes to close again and he lay listening to the sounds of the village and the pleasant crackling of the fire in the lodge. He was in Kills Fox's tipi, where he had slept for two nights. On the day of the pipe carriers' arrival Two Moons had invited them to sleep in his own spacious lodge, once they had decided to wait here for Sitting Bull, but Kills Fox had spoken up quickly to say that while the headman's hospitality was well known, he himself would be proud to have the white scout Hardeman sleep in his lodge, and inasmuch as Blackbird would remain there while he was under Ice's care, would not the war leader of the Sun Band like to sleep by his son? Standing Eagle had accepted the invitation, as had Hardeman, pleased to do anything he could to assure that the hostility between himself and Kills Fox would be completely forgotten.

The Cheyenne warrior had proved himself a generous host. The pipe carriers had been reeling with fatigue when Kills Fox had finally shown them to his lodge, but he had roused his wife and insisted the guests be fed before he would hear of sleeping, and so they had eaten together again and conversed, and Kills Fox had asked to hear of the pipe carriers' journey. Nothing in his manner then or since suggested that there had ever been anything but the greatest good will between himself and Hardeman. Now, lying in the comforting warmth of two of Kills Fox's buffalo robes, Hardeman reflected on the way hostility was allowed to linger like a festering sore between white men who had fought for any reason, or no reason at all. Here it had been erased. Kills Fox had had every reason to attack him, seeing his enemy delivered providentially into his hands after so many years, but when the error of his ways was made plain to him, he put his anger away as if it had never existed and banished any thought of revenge.

Hardeman put a hand to his forehead and was surprised to discover that the swelling of his wound was reduced to almost nothing and the skin there was much less tender to the touch. On the day before, the effects of the head wound had grown worse. He had had no appetite in the morning and had suffered from recurring bouts of dizziness. When Kills Fox had insisted that Ice should treat the wound, Hardeman submitted gladly. The old healer had placed an odd-smelling poultice on Hardeman's forehead and instructed him to spend the afternoon flat on his back without moving. Since then, he had spent most of the time asleep.

He heard a small noise and opened his eyes. He was on one of the sleeping pallets in the family's portion of the lodge to the left of the entrance, behind the backrests that surrounded the fire. Not far away, Ice knelt beside the still form of Blackbird, and Hardeman saw that the boy's leg was exposed once more to the old man's ministrations. Even by the soft daylight filtering through the lodgeskins, it was obvious that the wound was healing.

Hardeman swung his feet off the pallet and sat up, feeling more stupefied than refreshed by the long night's rest. Ice turned at the sound and nodded. No one else was in the lodge. Kills Fox had a comely daughter and a young son; they had been instructed to make themselves scarce while the wounded boy was recovering.

The boy is sleeping, Ice made in signs, putting a finger to his lips. Blackbird had remained unconscious throughout the previous day and Hawk Chaser had expressed renewed concern for his *hunká*-relative, but Ice said he had given the boy a potion to help him rest and he assured the pipe carriers that all was well. The medicine man made more signs now, inquiring about Hardeman's head, and Hardeman indicated that he was much improved. Ice smiled with satisfaction before returning to his work over the boy.

Hardeman stretched and looked about the lodge. The weapons and medicine bundles hanging behind the host's seat, and the skin hangings that lined the inside of the tipi from the ground cloth to a point above the height of a standing man, these decorated with many paintings of the owner's deeds, showed that Kills Fox was a prominent man among the Cheyenne. Two nights ago, entering the lodge for the first time, Hardeman had noticed none of this. It was careless to get so tired that you missed things like that.

Ice began a soft chanting. He took a clump of moss with earth still clinging to the roots and applied it to Blackbird's leg with hands as gentle as a mother's, pressing it carefully into place until no part of the wound showed. With a few motions over the wound he ended the chant, and began to wrap the boy's leg with fresh strips of hide to hold the moss in place.

The entrance flap was pulled aside and Bat Putnam's head appeared. Seeing Hardeman awake he stepped into the lodge, followed by Standing Eagle and Hawk Chaser. "'Bout time you decided to jine the livin'," Bat said. "I reckoned you to sleep plumb through to supper. What're ye feelin' like?"

Hardeman shook his head. "Can't wake up."

At the sounds of the voices, Blackbird's eyes opened.

"*Hau, chinkshí,*" Bat said. Hello, son. Among the Lakota, the use of a kinship term closer than that warranted by the actual relationship was a deliberate way of expressing affinity and friendship. Bat did it now to show his concern for Blackbird.

"*Hau, até,*" the boy replied. Hello, father. His gaze moved from Bat to Standing Eagle, then on to Hawk Chaser and Hardeman, recognizing each in turn. His face was flushed and his eyes were feverish. He struggled to sit up but Ice held him down with a firm hand. Blackbird asked a question and Standing Eagle replied at some length, saying where he was and how long he had been there. Blackbird said something else then, and Bat laughed.

"He says he's only sorry he didn't take the scalp off'n that Crow feller you shot," he explained to Hardeman.

"Was his fault the horses got took," Standing Eagle said. "His job to fetch 'em back too, not lollagag about to count coup and lift topknots." But he was smiling at his son, who lay back now while Ice finished wrapping the wound.

Kills Fox's wife put her head into the tipi and her mouth dropped open to see Hardeman awake and the other men there too. She vanished, and returned a moment later with her daughter, carrying a steaming pot. The woman spoke rapidly in Cheyenne and motioned the men to sit. In no time at all they were provided with bowls of broth and chunks of meat, elk this time, and Ice joined them in the meal while Kills Fox's wife spooned broth to Blackbird, who swallowed the first bowl without saying a word, and then asked for more, causing the men to laugh.

Hardeman found that the meal acted like a tonic. It restored his strength and sent him out to walk about the camp under blustery skies with small patches of blue, feeling immune to the cold. Children played on the snowy banks and ice of the river and the dogs ran between their legs and bowled them over. Despite the freezing temperatures and gusting winds, men and women were everywhere about the camp, the women hard at their daily tasks. Several of the men beckoned to Hardeman and invited him with signs to eat in their lodges, but he declined these invitations, saying that he had only recently eaten and that the Cheyenne cared for their guests as no other people did, remembering the polite refusals Jed Putnam had taught him as the only defense against being compelled to pass the entire day in eating when visiting friendly Indians.

Before long, he noticed Hawk Chaser walking among the lodges, stopping here and there to exchange a word or two, seemingly concerned only with his own affairs and moving at his own pace, but somehow always within sight of Hardeman. Hardeman hadn't missed the protective stance the warrior had taken on the day they arrived; he had put himself in danger to protect the white man, and it occurred to Hardeman now that perhaps this was why the extra man had been sent along: it might be Sun Horse's way of safeguarding Johnny Smoker's longtime protector and companion.

He motioned to the Sioux and made signs to say that he had a mind to climb up the bluffs and have a look at the countryside. Would Hawk Chaser like to come along?

The warrior agreed willingly and together the two men found a trail that climbed to the benchland close behind the village and wound its way along the base of the massive bluffs that overlooked the camp. The men left the trail to climb a small butte whose slopes were strewn with slabs of reddish rock. With some difficulty they scrambled to the top, which, like the rim of the bluffs that stood more than twice as high above the valley floor, was fringed with small pine trees.

The little butte afforded a good view of the village and the valley beyond. A few flakes of snow were falling now but the clouds remained high and there were still some small patches of blue. Bright shafts of sunlight touched the valley here and there, glowing pillars that supported the clouds above. The white landscape was touched with brown and yellow and red where grass and earth and rock showed through the thin mantle of snow. To the east, the hills were covered with trees.

It's a good land, Hardeman thought. Good for elk and deer and buffalo. Good for the Indians. Small wonder they don't want to leave it.

He felt no impatience today, no urge to rush on to find Sitting Bull and then Crook and set matters to rest one way or the other. These things would take place in good time; there was just so much a man could do to force the pace of events.

He looked at the village below him. No one there was in a hurry either. There was a great deal being done among the clustered lodges—robes and clothing made and repaired, arrows straightened and fitted with new heads, torn lodgeskins replaced, wood cut for fires and bark stripped for the horses, meat butchered and cooked and fat rendered and a hundred other things all done every day—but none of it forced or rushed. In a white settlement it seemed that half the people were forever hurrying from one place to another as if each moment were their last one on earth. The scene Hardeman saw from his vantage point was so full of life, yet so calm and peaceful, it was hard to imagine that Crook's column was anywhere within a hundred miles, hard to feel any danger at all.

"*Le anpetu lila washté,*" Hawk Chaser said. He made signs to say, *this day is good,* and then he made a gesture that took in the Cheyenne village below, the river and the country beyond, everything between earth and heaven. "*Iyuha washtéyelo.*" It is all good.

"*Washté,*" Hardeman agreed. "*Lila washté.*" It is very

good. He had expended half his vocabulary of Sioux words. To an onlooker it might seem like a conversation of the feeble minded, the two of them standing there and agreeing that the day was good, the village was good, it was good to be alive, but each knew what the other meant, despite the differences between them.

"*Washtéyelo,*" Hawk Chaser repeated. He opened his blanket and drew aside his loin cover and began to urinate, urging the steaming stream into a high arc, to fall as far as possible down the face of the butte. Hardeman realized that he had not relieved himself since awakening. He unbuttoned his buckskin trousers and joined the Indian, the two streams competing for height and distance, dispersing in the air and mingling as a fine rain of drops that showered the reddish rocks and melted the snow. The flow of Hawk Chaser's urine began to jerk and shake and Hardeman saw that the Indian was laughing. He didn't know what was so funny, but his own laughter rose inside him and the two men laughed together as they finished, urging out the final drops, and they kept on laughing as they rearranged their clothing and stood once more side by side atop the butte.

Hardeman felt the pleasure of an empty bladder and a new surge of hope. Surely there must be a chance for these unhurried people, living at peace in their own country, to keep that peace in some way other than the one laid down by the white man—a way they chose for themselves. If Crook should chance to come near this place, Hardeman would go out to meet him. He would take Bat and Standing Eagle with him and they would give Crook Sun Horse's pipe. Hardeman would explain that the village was peaceful and Two Moons was only waiting for the weather to warm again before moving to take his people to the reservation. He would tell Crook that Two Moons was willing to join Sun Horse in speaking to the hostile headmen, and Crook would understand. He would let these people remain here, glad of a Cheyenne ally in his quest for a peaceful settlement.

"*Wan!*" Hawk Chaser let out a sudden exclamation of

surprise, pointing to the north, downstream. A dozen riders were approaching along the west bank of the river, now reining their horses in to a walk to let them breathe and collect themselves before they reached the village. Already children at the edge of the stream had seen the approaching riders and were running to spread the news.

Hardeman could see that the riders were Indian, but Hawk Chaser was trying to discern something more. The warrior shaded his eyes with one hand and peered long and hard, and his face split in a broad grin. He spoke rapidly in Lakota, and then in response to Hardeman's blank look he made the signs for a buffalo bull, the curved index fingers raised beside the head to evoke the horns of a buffalo, then the right hand held close to the waist with the index finger extended to signify the male organ. Finally he raised his right hand in a fist before him and brought it sharply down for a short distance in the sign for sitting or stopping.

Now it was Hardeman's turn to be surprised. "Sitting Bull?" Two Moons' messengers had been sent off less than two full days ago; it seemed impossible that they could return so soon with the famous war leader.

"*Tatanka Iyotake.*" Hawk Chaser nodded enthusiastically. "*Tatanka Iyotake.* Sit-ting Bull." He began to look for a way down off the little butte, but he paused and offered his hand to Hardeman. They shook hands firmly, sealing some unspoken compact they had made by coming here to enjoy the day together, and then they helped each other down over the sheer lip of the butte and made their way quickly to the village.

Once more the Cheyenne turned out to welcome important visitors. Already, several women were moving off among the cottonwoods to gather wood for the council lodge, where the men would meet once Sitting Bull had been properly greeted and fed by Two Moons.

Bat spied Hawk Chaser and Hardeman approaching, and he moved quickly through the crowd to meet them. "Piece o' good luck here," he said. "Ol' Sit was already on his way, comin' to see Last Bull and get the news from the reservation. Two Moons' boys met him on the trail and brought him along quick.''

As the riders drew near it was plain to see that their horses had been ridden hard. The animals were streaked with sweat, which steamed in the cold air. A group of men on foot accompanied the newcomers as they moved through the camp, Oglala from the downstream lodges, led by He Dog and Last Bull, the one muscular and tall, the other shorter and older but also walking straight and proud, honored by this visit from the great Hunkpapa. The day before, Bat and Standing Eagle and Little Hand had visited with the Oglala headmen to speak with them and hear their news.

Only the eagle-wing fan in Sitting Bull's hand showed that it was he who led this band. His hair was combed straight and he wore no feathers, no paint. He was barrel-chested and thick-legged and his eyes were piercing, his face round and sharply lined at the corners of the eyes and mouth. He rode a palomino horse that stood several hands above the shorter Indian mounts. With him were three of his councillors and six younger men, and the two Cheyenne messengers that had ridden to bring him here.

''Well I'll be,'' Bat exclaimed suddenly. ''That's my boy there. Hey, Bear!''

One of Sitting Bull's young men turned at the shout and, spying Bat in the crowd, leaped off his horse and ran to greet his father. The two men embraced, and then Bat's son slapped his father on the back in a gesture remarkably like a white man's.

''Howdy, Pop,'' he said. ''Didn't look to find you here.'' His English was more heavily accented than Standing Eagle's.

''Big doin's,'' Bat explained, growing serious. ''We got pipes for Sittin' Bull and Three Stars. You know Three Stars is in the country?''

The younger man nodded. ''We heerd tell. Ain't seen hide ner hair of him.''

Bat turned to Hardeman. ''Christopher, shake hands with my boy, Bear. Full moniker's Bear Doesn't Sleep, but you can call him Bear. This here's Christopher Hardeman. Used to scout for the bluecoats but he seen the error of his ways." Bat flashed a grin. "He come along to help us out."

Bear was about thirty, Hardeman judged. He was shorter than Bat and he had the black hair, roundish face and prominent cheekbones of his mother, but his skin was lighter than the average Sioux's and his eyes were gray. As the eyes appraised Hardeman, the scout was reminded of Jed Putnam, and Lisa, and the way they looked a man over when meeting him for the first time.

"Glad to know you, Christopher," Bear said, and then he recognized Hawk Chaser. His face broadened in a smile of pleasure and without pause he switched to voluble Lakota and moved on to the warrior, offering Hawk Chaser both his hands, the forearms crossed in a handshake of special respect.

As they talked, the men moved along with Sitting Bull and his escort, who were being conducted to the village headman's lodge. For these visitors, Two Moons did not delay his appearance. Already he was standing in front of his tipi and he raised a hand in greeting as the riders came to a halt before him. Young boys gathered around the newcomers as they dismounted, vying for the honor of unsaddling the horses and leading them to water. Sitting Bull dismounted with the movements of a man glad to quit his saddle after a long ride. He handed his braided rein to one of the boys and stepped forward to meet Two Moons, walking with a pronounced limp. There was a soft rustle of comments from the onlookers, like a breeze passing through a grove of trees. Those who had not recognized the Lakota holy man at first were sure now, for the tale of this limp was well known. It came from a wound received on the Hunkpapa's first war party, made in his fourteenth year. He had been shot in the foot by a Crow, but that evening Sitting Bull had danced the Crow's scalp around the victory fire.

Hardeman watched the solid, rolling gait, and he was reminded of another limp, also caused by a wound. He took in the Springfield carbine in Sitting Bull's hand, the stock decorated with brass studs, but only four of the others in the war man's party carried rifles and all of those were muzzle-loaders, no two alike. Hardeman had noted a similar shortage of modern weapons in Two Moons' village, belying the rumors that the hostiles were equipped with repeating arms.

Like any visitors to a friendly camp, Sitting Bull and his men were invited to eat, but it seemed to Hardeman that he detected an almost imperceptible urgency behind the brief but courteous greeting Two Moons extended and the promptness with which he ushered his guests into his lodge. The pipe carriers retired to Kills Fox's tipi while Sitting Bull ate, and Bear accompanied his father, taking this opportunity to exchange news of relatives and friends; Hardeman was uncomfortable at being shut away from the sight of the camp and he stepped outside after a short time to wander among the lodges, always keeping an eye on the headman's tipi. Not far from Two Moons' lodge was the council lodge, standing nearly twice as tall. A fire was burning there now, the thick plume of smoke rising into the air that never stopped moving today. A hush had descended on the camp and the calm that had pervaded the scene earlier that morning was gone. Conversations were conducted in lowered tones and many eyes kept watch on the entrance of Two Moons' tipi. Great matters would be decided here today; the village was waiting, anxious for the council to begin.

Long before he expected it, Hardeman saw Sitting Bull and his men emerge from the headman's lodge with Two Moons in their midst. They moved slowly toward the council lodge, giving all that were summoned there time to gather. For Indians, the brevity of the newcomers' welcoming meal amounted to bolting a bite of *wasná* on the run. It seemed that Sitting Bull himself was impatient to hear Three Stars' message to Sun Horse, and the peace man's reply.

Each of the Sun Band pipe carriers had received a stick of specially marked ashwood from the camp marshals, a formal summons to the council. Even Blackbird was carried from Kills Fox's lodge with Ice walking close by his side to see that he was made comfortable in the council lodge and placed close to the fire. The boy was speechless with pride at this honor done him, for he had never sat in council before, but the details of the pipe carriers' fight with the *Kanghí* had been told throughout the village and none doubted that the youth had earned the right to sit with his companions and face the great war leader and holy man of the Hunkpapa. Blackbird had eaten for a second time that morning, a piece of liver from a deer killed the day before, offered to Ice by the wife of Kills Fox. The boy felt new strength in his body and his heart and he had wanted to walk to the council lodge, but Ice insisted that he be carried.

In full regalia the councillors came. Those who were entitled to wear them had donned their feathered headdresses, all except Sitting Bull, and each man had chosen his best robe or blanket for the occasion. They wore breastplates of bone and shell, armbands of silver and copper and bronze. Their cheeks and foreheads were daubed with symbolic paint and around their necks hung necklaces and silver crosses, and presidential medallions presented in Washington by the Great Father of the whites. Beneath fringed leggings they wore brightly beaded moccasins, some hung with little silver bells that jingled as the men walked in stately parade to the council lodge.

The old-man chiefs of the Cheyenne village entered the lodge first. Old Bear was as venerable as his title implied, but Little Wolf was a much younger man, in his forties, his position of trust earned by a combination of selfless concern for his people and great courage in war. Three years before, he had been to Washington, and only his eloquent plea had prevented the northern Cheyenne from being ordered south to the Indian Territory with the remnants of the southern bands. In the fall of 1875 he had attended the council at the Red Cloud Agency, where the Lakota had refused to sell the Black Hills. Little Wolf knew the whites and his words would carry much weight here today. It was he who sat in the place the Lakota called *chatkú,* the place of honor across the fire from the entrance, with Old Bear at his right hand and Two Moons at his left.

The Lakota pipe carriers were seated to the right of Old Bear, Standing Eagle and Little Hand first, then Bat Putnam and Hardeman and Hawk Chaser. Standing Eagle had the feathers of his namesake bound in his hair and Little Hand was similarly adorned. Blackbird was brought to the last place among them, but Hawk Chaser moved, indicating that those carrying the litter should place it between himself and Hardeman. The boy flushed with embarrassment at this new honor done him by the warrior he so admired. Standing Eagle smiled at his son and Little Hand greeted him warmly, "*Hau, misúnkala.*" Greetings, little brother.

Sitting Bull and his three councillors sat at Two Moons' left, completing the circle closest to the fire. Outside this one a second circle was begun by the other councillors of Two Moons' band and the leaders of the warrior societies. Warriors always had a place in council, more so than ever when matters of war and peace were to be discussed, but the *Tsistsístas* were merely hosts here and had no real part to play in what would take place, and so the men of Two Moons' village had yielded the seats of greatest importance to their Lakota guests. Others came, Sitting Bull's young men and more Cheyenne, until more than fifty men were seated in three concentric rings within the lodge that stood higher than any other in the Cheyenne camp. In summer, the lodgeskins would have been rolled up so the villagers might gather outside to hear the deliberations, but today, because of the cold, the coverings were lashed to the ground; despite this, many men and women grouped around the entrance once the councillors had entered, to hear what they might.

As Sitting Bull took his place he spoke briefly with Standing Eagle and greeted Little Hand formally. Sun Horse and his descendants were Hunkpapa, as were others of the Sun Band, and although the band contained many

Oglala, even some Brulé and Minneconjou, when the Lakota nation gathered together in summer the Sun Band camped with the Hunkpapa council fire. Little Hand was related to Sitting Bull through Hears Twice's bloodline, and it had been Sitting Bull who interpreted the vision Hears Twice received late in life, and confirmed his status as a prophet.

The Hunkpapa looked at each of the pipe carriers in turn and Hardeman met his gaze calmly, feeling equal measures of curiosity and caution in the man's expression. Sitting Bull's distrust of the whites was legendary. He looked away then, and only the frequency with which his glance returned briefly to Hardeman revealed his interest in the white man who sat with the Sun Band's messengers.

Strips of fat were placed on the fire and as they melted they sent the flames leaping high, filling the lodge with bright light and reminding the pipe carriers of the richness of the northern bands; in the Sun Band village all the fat was added to soups for extra nourishment or used in the making of *wasná*. There was no surplus for brightening lodge fires.

As always, the council began with a ceremonial pipe, which Two Moons filled and offered in the Cheyenne manner—to sky and earth, to east, south, west and north—before lighting it and passing it sunwise to Sitting Bull. The Hunkpapa offered the pipe and raised it to his lips slowly and deliberately, as he seemed to do everything in life, even the most ordinary actions. As a child his name had been Slow, for even when offered fresh berries he would always consider them gravely before reaching out.

The pipe was filled and offered and passed again and again until every man in the lodge had smoked it, uniting them in one spirit, and when the last man had smoked and the ashes had been emptied carefully into the fire, Two Moons was the first to speak. He welcomed all the visitors once again and briefly stated the pipe carriers' purpose in coming. The measured tones of his oratory signaled to those present that the formal talk of the council had begun and that the truth of his words was guaranteed by his honor, an obligation that would be binding on every man who spoke after him. His words were translated into Lakota by a man who sat directly behind him, the same camp marshal that had translated for the pipe carriers on the day they arrived.

After the short welcoming speech, Two Moons nodded to Standing Eagle, who turned to Little Hand. From within his buffalo robe Little Hand drew a beaverskin sack that contained the pipe he had carried ever since it was handed to him by Sun Horse. Sees Beyond had prepared the pipe with Sun Horse, lending his power to Sun Horse's plea for peace. Little Hand opened the sack and withdrew the pipe and a small pouch containing shredded inner bark from the red willow. With careful movements he fueled the pipe and then, holding it in both hands, he offered it to Sitting Bull.

The elongated bowl of red pipestone gleamed in the firelight. It had been shaped and polished patiently and given a final rubbing with buffalo tallow to seal the porous stone. The stem was a straight shaft of ashwood as long as a man's forearm, split in half and hollowed out and bound back together again, the mouthpiece wrapped in the raw hide of buffalo, which had been allowed to shrink and dry there until it was as hard as wood. Near the bowl four strips of colored buffalo hide hung from the stem, black, white, red and yellow, the colors of the four directions. Tied near the mouthpiece were braided strands of horsehair, also dyed in the sacred colors. A stripe of red paint ran along the top of the stem, following the path of smoke from the bowl to the mouthpiece, symbolizing the good red road of spiritual understanding that was sought by all who smoked the pipe. Around the stem was a small circle of black, and a green spot where the black line crossed the red one, green for the tree of life, which flowered where the road of worldly cares met the path of true understanding.

The lodge was silent. In his slow, methodical way, Sitting Bull leaned forward and took the pipe from the outstretched hands, and there was a slight rustling among the councillors as they relaxed. By accepting the pipe, Sitting Bull agreed to hear Sun Horse's request; if he lit it and smoked, that would mean he undertook the obligation that was requested of him.

Now Standing Eagle spoke and Bat talked low in Hardeman's ear, conveying the essence of the war leader's words as he told Sitting Bull how Hardeman had come to the Sun Band, and of the message from Crook and Sun Horse's reply to the soldier chief. The message to Sitting Bull would not be put forth just yet; first the surrounding circumstances would be explained so the origins of the request were fully known.

Standing Eagle turned to Bat, and now there was no one to translate for Hardeman as Bat spoke in Lakota, but he saw new interest on Sitting Bull's face, and obvious surprise when Bat spoke the name Hardeman had heard for the first time in Lisa Putnam's kitchen and often since then when he was among the Sun Band—*Oyate Tokcha Ichọkab' Najin*—He Stands Between the Worlds.

When Bat was done, Sitting Bull fixed Hardeman with his gaze and spoke to him for the first time, his voice strong and rough, yet almost melodious.

"The White Boy of the Shahíyela lives . . ." Bat translated as soon as Sitting Bull began to speak, and then he paused as the squat warrior paused. "He is in the lodge of my cousin Sun Horse, and my cousin believes that a power has come to him with the return of his grandson. A power to make peace with the whitemen. A just peace for both Lakota and whites . . ." Again the words trailed off and Hardeman felt a certainty that the news of Johnny Smoker's return to Sun Horse had put the Hunkpapa off-balance. Which was just as well, for he himself was brought up short by the war man's words. *My cousin believes that a power has come to him with the return of his grandson,* he had said. A *power to make peace with the whitemen*. What had Bat told Sitting Bull? Did Sun Horse still believe that Johnny had brought him some miraculous power even though the boy had chosen the white world? Was the old man grasping at straws?

Sitting Bull spoke again. "Since the Washita the boy has lived among the whites?"

Hardeman nodded, offering nothing.

"And still he remembers his dream?"

There it was again, always the talk of the dream and a strange power it gave the boy, these things as remote from Hardeman's understanding as the particular beliefs of the white man's many religions. Hadn't Bat told the Hunkpapa that Johnny had at long last chosen between the worlds, that he brought no new hope for the Sioux? Hardeman had no answers for the questions that came to his mind and no time to ponder them. He saw one chance to strengthen his hand and he took it. "The boy has returned as Sun Horse told him he should, because of his dream."

He Dog spoke now, directing a question at Sitting Bull. Sitting Bull seemed to gather his thoughts for a moment and then he replied, obviously intending to speak for some time. Bat listened for a while and then turned to Hardeman. "He Dog wants to know about the dream. Ol' Sit's tellin' him, but he'll make it short. Short's he's able. He was in the summer camp the year young Johnny come a-visitin' with his folks. Sun Horse and Sittin' Bull had themselves quite a talk about that dream."

The Cheyenne knew of the dream and He Dog had heard of it briefly when the pipe carriers arrived, but he and his men listened thoughtfully to the tale Sitting Bull told, some blowing softly through the smoking pipes they had lit after the passing of the ceremonial pipe, the sound conveying wonder and concern at this thing they heard.

Hardeman no longer tried to imagine what was passing through the minds of the Indians. To him the whole thing was unreal. In Washington City, senators and congressmen and the President's ministers decided not only the fate of these bands but of all the western tribes with strokes of pen and ink on pieces of paper, motivated by gold and railroads and land and visions of a union that stretched from Canada to Mexico and sea to sea, while the headmen of the Sioux and Cheyenne sat here as sober as a bunch of Mormon judges pondering a dream a white boy had a dozen years ago, as if the fate of their people hung in the balance.

But if the dream made it more likely that the men assembled here would agree to Sun Horse's plan for peace, so much the better.

When Sitting Bull was done no one spoke right away. The Hunkpapa fanned himself slowly with his eagle wing, dispersing a puff of smoke that had drifted his way from the fire, and after a short while it was he that broke the silence, turning once more to Hardeman.

"You have scouted for the bluecoats. You have led men to war. They say you come here now to speak for peace. Why does the soldier scout wish an end to war?"

Hardeman framed his reply with care. "When I was a young man I traveled the Holy Road, guiding the wagons, and often I stopped in the camps of the Sioux and Cheyenne. I rode with one you call the Truthful Whiteman, the brother of my friend Lodgepole. He taught me the ways of the plains people. Much of what he knew, he had learned from you, and he taught these things to me." He paused, looking around the circle of faces that revealed so little. "One year in the Moon of Changing Seasons I returned from the great water in the west and I found the Sioux gone from Fort Laramie. I learned there had been trouble, a great chief killed and some white soldiers killed too. Since then I have fought for my people as you have fought for yours. But there has been too much fighting. I would like to see our people live side by side as we did before the trouble began."

Sitting Bull sucked on his own pipe thoughtfully for a time before looking up again at Hardeman. "And Three Stars, what does he want?"

"He wants peace."

"Yet he comes to our country with soldiers, and he says we must surrender or fight!" Sitting Bull spoke sharply now, and there were sounds of agreement from around the lodge.

"I believe there is another way," Hardeman said, keeping his tone even and firm. "If he will accept the pipe Sun Horse offers."

Sitting Bull was noncommittal. "I would hear what our friends the Shahíyela will do."

The eyes of the Cheyenne found Little Wolf now, and the man who sat in the place of most honor prepared to speak for the first time. He drew himself up and looked around the lodge, the firelight shining off the bright streaks of vermilion that lined his cheekbones, and then he addressed the Lakotas.

"My friends," he said, "I have heard the white scout's words. I too wish peace with the whiteman, so our people may live side by side again. In my village there are many who have seen the bluecoats come to make war on us, at Sand Creek and the Washita, and on the Platte and the Arkansas. The women are frightened by this talk of soldiers in our land. They cry out in the night, seeing the soldiers again while they sleep. The *Tsistsístas* are at peace with the whites, and yet the messengers came to us in the Moon of Strong Cold and said that we too must go to the agency. Old Bear said perhaps it was only the white traders who sent this message, wanting us to come and buy their blankets and whiskey." He glanced at the gray-haired man by his side and Old Bear nodded. "When Last Bull came, he told us that soldiers were coming soon to make us all go to the reservation, and some say the whites will take our country here and never let us return. I do not know what the whites truly want; it is hard to know the heart of a whiteman." He looked at Hardeman and then his eyes moved to Sitting Bull. "If Sitting Bull will accept the pipe from Sun Horse, I will wait to hear what the soldier chief says. If he will leave us in peace, we will stay here. But if Three Stars says we must surrender, we will go to Dakota, for the sake of the helpless ones."

Sitting Bull waited a decent interval to be sure Little Wolf was finished; when he spoke again he looked at Hardeman. "In the time you speak of," the Hunkpapa said, "when there was peace between us, the whites were few in this country, surrounded by the lodges of Lakota and Shahíyela. You came to our land and you learned our ways, and we accepted you among us." There were a few soft *hau*'s from the Sioux, and the Cheyenne made their own sounds of agreement. Sitting Bull kept his eyes on Hardeman, and as he continued, Hardeman felt the rising rhythms draw the listeners along.

"At the great council in the year the whites call 1851, you asked only that we should permit the Holy Road through our lands. We are going to the great water in the west, you said, and we will not return. Each year more whites went along the road and soon the soldiers came to the Laramie fort. Why do you need soldiers here? we asked. To protect our people, you said. Protect them from whom? we asked; we are at peace with the whites. Why do you need soldiers? The whites did not answer and soon we saw that the soldiers were like *akíchita*, but not good like our *akíchita*. They came to speak loudly to the people and tell them what they may and may not do."

The sounds of agreement were stronger now. Hardeman kept his eyes on Sitting Bull's, unwilling to be the first to break the contact.

"And so there was trouble. Men on both sides died and the Lakota moved away from the Holy Road. Still we wished to live at peace with the *washíchun*, but General Harney came; he smoked the pipe with Little Thunder, and then he killed Little Thunder's women and children and took the men away to the iron house." An angry sound filled the lodge. Sitting Bull waited for it to die away and then he continued, guiding the emotions of his listeners as easily as a Lakota warrior controlled his best war horse.

"Before long, some of the wagons did not follow the setting sun, but stopped in our lands. A few of our people wish to stay here, you said. The land is good. The Lakota and Shahíyela agreed to share the land, and some signed the new treaty you made to stop the fighting that you yourselves had begun."

At last his eyes left Hardeman and he addressed himself to the council at large. "Tell me, my friends, which of the treaties have the Lakota broken?" He paused just for a moment and then answered his own question. "Not one. Always the whites broke them first. I signed none of them and yet I kept each one until the *washíchun* broke it!"

"*Hau, hau!*" the Lakota chorused, and the swell of assent from the Cheyenne lagged only a moment behind as the running translations caught up with Sitting Bull's words.

"Each time the whites want a new treaty, and then before long they want more land. Always we give more and each time they promise that what remains is ours forever." Sitting Bull looked once around the circle and then back at Hardeman. "I have signed no treaties. The land is already mine. It was given to my people by *Wakán Tanka*. The whiteman cannot give me that which is already mine." Here the sounds of approval filled the lodge again. "Once before the bluecoats came to this country. They built forts and they said the wagons of the whites would pass along the road to the lands of the *Kanghí*." He looked around him. "My friends, we fought those soldiers and we whipped them! The forts are like the black stumps that remain after a forest fire. Now the soldiers come again and they want even more than before. They want this country here. They want the *Paha Sapa*. They want all the Lakota living at the agencies. They want to count us, they say. But we are not the spotted *pte* of the whiteman, to be counted and placed in pens! We are men!"

Now the *hau*'s were deafening, and outside the lodge the voices of the men and women gathered there to listen in the cold joined those in the council lodge. Sitting Bull waited until the approving sounds died away and then he drew something from within his robe and unfolded it. He held it up and Hardeman was surprised to see that it was an edition of the Denver *Rocky Mountain News*.

"My friends," Sitting Bull said, "Last Bull has brought me the whiteman's talking leaves from the agency. It is called a *newspaper*." He used the English word, and Hardeman was even more surprised when the Hunkpapa held the paper to catch the light from the fire and began to read aloud in English from the front page. He read slowly, pausing before the longer words and then pronouncing them with precision, all in a flat tone that made Hardeman wonder if he understood what he read.

"Lying north and northwest of Fort Fetterman is a vast scope of country, known as the 'unceded lands,' to which the Indians have no right or title, but in which the most warlike of them have sought refuge, ever since the general abandonment of that region during the massacre of 1866. Since that date, those bands of Sioux who bid defiance to all attempts at reconciliation have marauded north, south and east from this, their natural stronghold, and then, with the swiftness of an Indian in retreat, have plunged back and regaled themselves on their plunder, thoughts of their isolation, and plans for future incursions."

Sitting Bull lowered the paper and spoke once more in Lakota. "My friends, it says that this land does not belong to us. It says we raid the whites and then come here to hide, and it says we do not want peace. But it is the whites who make this war!" He raised the paper and shook it. "The talking leaves say much more. They speak of opening the land to whites the way a man opens the entrance to his lodge, and they speak of opening it with guns. They call us *heathens* and *savages*." Here he spoke the English words. "We do not have words for these things, but they are bad things. A *heathen* is one who does not believe in the *Christian* spirit called *God*, and a *savage* is less than a man."

There was a buzz of disapproval, and angry scowls on many faces, and Sitting Bull waited for the silence to return. When all attention was on him once more, he held the newspaper out before him and allowed it to drop at the edge of the fire, within the ring of stones that lined the pit. The pages curled and turned black and burst suddenly into flame. He waited until the whole sheaf of pages was burning brightly before he spoke, and now his voice was low, almost soft.

"My friends, the whites see only the wrongs another man does to them, never the wrongs they have done themselves, and so they are strong for revenge. They want to fight us, and I believe if they do not fight us now, they will fight us soon. The treaty they made at Fort Laramie says this land is ours, yet now they would deny their own treaty as they have done before. They want this land and if we do not give it to them they will try to take it.'' He drew himself up and his voice grew stronger. ''We have given enough. We can give no more. The game is almost gone from the lands along the Muddy River, the one the whites call Missouri, but this country is still strong. Here there is meat for our kettles. Perhaps the buffalo will stay here with us, their two-legged brothers, when the whites have killed the buffalo everywhere else.'' The firelight reflected brightly in his eyes as they moved about the lodge, sweeping the faces there, making sure he had their full attention. ''This country is our home. I will not give it away nor will I share it with the whites. I have fought them for a long time and I have killed many *washíchun*. They will never let me live beside them in peace.'' Here he turned to Little Wolf. ''I too worry for the helpless ones, but I cannot take them to Dakota. Others may live at the agencies if they wish. Each man must choose for himself. I will stay here. When friends wish to visit me, my village will welcome them, but if the white soldiers come to steal my land, I will fight!''

Sounds of approval swept the gathering, almost every man there adding his voice. After a time the chorus waned, then swelled again as it became clear that Sitting Bull was done speaking for now. When the sounds of assent died out, they were replaced by a soft hum of conversation that gradually came to an end as all waited to see who would speak next.

To Hardeman it seemed that the council might as well end then and there. As long as Sitting Bull held the gathering in the palm of his hand, there would be no dealing with Crook, no chance to delay until summer so the Indians could talk among themselves and agree to the white man's terms. The stumbling block had been reached: if the Indians insisted on keeping the Powder River country, there could be no peace without fighting. But the Hunkpapa had not refused Sun Horse's pipe outright. He still held it in his hand. And he had not said what he would do if Crook left the country now and managed to delay the campaign. Could there still be a chance?

The silence deepened. No one wanted to follow the spellbinding oratory of Sitting Bull. From outside the lodge there was a rustle of movement and a few words exchanged, and then a soft cough at the entrance, followed by a polite scratching on the lodgeskin.

Two Moons spoke a few curt words, wishing to know who it was that would interrupt the council.

The entrance flap was pulled aside and a man entered. He was slender and not very tall, and his hair was much lighter than an Indian's—almost sandy at the ends. His nose was straight and thin, and a dark scar at the corner of one nostril spread a little onto the cheek.

Hardeman's first thought was that the newcomer must be a trader's son, one of the halfbreeds who moved between the northern bands and the agencies, offspring of the men who used to trade with the Sioux along the Holy Road and in their camps, bringing wagonloads of goods to trade for furs. In recent years the army had limited trade to the government agencies, where no guns or powder would be included with the goods. As long as the Indians could get the things that enabled them to lead a nomadic life, they would remain free, but once their supplies came only from the official agency post, that, together with the diminishing numbers of the buffalo, would soon compel them to live where the white man wished them to be. Denied the occupation of their fathers and mostly raised among their mothers' people, many of the traders' sons now rode with the hostile bands.

Hardeman looked at the man's eyes, seeking the trace of blue or gray that would tell him he was right, but the eyes were soft and brown, and in his dress the newcomer was Sioux from the fringes of his winter moccasins to the mountain lion fur that wrapped his braids. He wore blue leggings and a red breechcloth, beaded modestly with a single stripe along the lower edge. His blanket too, which he now folded and placed over his left arm, was bordered with a band of beadwork, but otherwise his clothing lacked the ornamentations the young men of the Sioux loved so well; no copper or silver disks hung from his hair, no quill or beadwork adorned his simple buckskin shirt; he wore no paint or feathers.

The man's eyes moved around the lodge, pausing on the white men, and Hardeman felt as if the eyes looked right through him.

Two Moons spoke, his voice utterly changed, all cordial welcome now and revealing a trace of deference. To Hardeman's astonishment the Cheyenne chief moved a little to one side, making room for this strange man between himself and Sitting Bull, who offered no objection. The man moved through the outer rings of the council, those seated there moving with alacrity to permit his passage, but he made a sign of polite negation and seated himself in a vacant spot next to Hawk Chaser, close to the bottom of the inner circle.

Hawk Chaser shifted himself slightly to make more room for the newcomer, and by a slight inclination of his head and a small movement of his hand he indicated both welcome and respect. "*Hau,*" he greeted the slim man as he settled himself.

"*Hau,*" the stranger replied, his eyes taking in the warrior's erect bearing, quiet dignity, and the single eagle feather bound in the graying hair.

"*Tashunka Witko,*" one of Sitting Bull's young men whispered to his neighbor. Hardeman caught the words and it seemed there was something familiar there, but he couldn't put his finger on it. Was it the man's name? He cursed his own ineptness at languages. Who was this stranger that caught everyone's attention so completely? Since he had entered the council lodge all eyes had followed him. The councillors didn't stare, which would have been impolite, but if the light-haired man had turned his head or raised a finger, every man in the lodge would have been aware of the motion.

Hardeman forced himself to hear the words again in his mind and search them for some hint of meaning. *Tashunka Witko*. That was it! *Shunka* meant a dog, or a horse. The full name for horse in Lakota was *shunka wakán;* it meant sacred dog, but horses were sometimes just called *shunka* if the meaning was clear. *Tashunka* would be "his horse" or "his dog," but what was the rest of it? *Witko?* It seemed he had heard the word before, if he could just . . .

A chill enveloped his body so completely that he had to struggle to keep from shuddering. The hair on the back of his neck felt like crawling insects. Was there so much power in a name? Realizing at last who it was nearly paralyzed him. He feared that his efforts to regain control of himself would be noticed, but he saw that all the others were looking from the newcomer to Two Moons and Sitting Bull, waiting for one of them to speak. On Hardeman's left, Bat Putnam was smiling.

Bat needed no one to tell him the identity of the stranger. He had first met Crazy Horse when the young man was just twenty-two, in the Lakota summer camp the same year Johnny Smoker and White Smoke and Grass Woman had come to visit Sun Horse, and he had seen him occasionally since then when the bands gathered together. The people spoke of Crazy Horse as they spoke of no other, and Bat felt the man's power now, grown so strong in the intervening years. He might sit at the bottom of the lodge or go about with no feathers in his hair, but he would never just melt into the people and be one of them as it often seemed he wished to do.

Our Strange Man, the Oglala called him. As a child his hair had been almost yellow and the other children had teased him. His people had been among those that camped at Fort Laramie until the death of Conquering Bear, and white women traveling along the Holy Road had often asked if he was a white child held captive by the Sioux, but Crazy Horse's parentage was known beyond a doubt, his mother a Brulé, the sister of Spotted Tail, and his father an Oglala of the northern band called Hunkpátila.

Bat had heard nothing of a messenger sent to find Crazy Horse, but he was not surprised that the warrior should show up like this. He was always sent for whenever Lakotas met to discuss important matters, although he held no formal position that entitled him to sit in high councils. Probably He Dog had sent a rider. His arrival here just two days after the pipe carriers meant that he was camped not far away.

Once again Two Moons prepared the ceremonial pipe and once again it was passed, just around the inner circle now, to include Crazy Horse in the proceedings. When the pipe had returned to Two Moons' hands and was emptied and set aside, Crazy Horse took out his own smoking pipe and loaded it in an unhurried way from his pouch, seemingly intent on this little task as the silence deepened around him. Many noticed this pipe and knew what it meant. It was the short pipe of a man who had been brought down from high position. Crazy Horse had once been a shirt wearer of the Oglala, one of just four young men chosen for this honor when the ceremony was revived a dozen years before. The shirt wearers were named by the Big Bellies, the chiefs' society, and the giving of the special shirt meant that the ones chosen were men of the people, placed above the *akíchita* in camp and on the trail, men who guarded all the people, great and small, and set aside their own passions even when wronged. But Crazy Horse's shirt had been taken away in bad trouble over a woman. A Lakota woman had the right to leave her husband and go with another man if she chose, and Black Buffalo Woman had gone with Crazy Horse openly, in the light of day, but the husband had chased the couple and had shot Crazy Horse in the face, the scar still plain to see, and because Crazy Horse was a shirt man, he had sent the woman back to her husband to prevent trouble among the people. He wanted the woman and she wanted him, but he thought of the people before his own happiness and in the quiet of the lodges the people praised him. But then one day, weakened by another grief, the death of his younger brother at the hands of the Snakes, Crazy Horse had spied the woman's husband and in a fit of rage and sorrow he had taken a gun and chased the man all the way to the Yellowstone, and for this the Big Bellies had taken away his shirt.

The chiefs had the right to do this thing, but the people did not approve the act. Crazy Horse is still a man of the people, they said; always he counsels the young men to think of the people in war, not to spoil an ambush or let the enemy escape because a foolish warrior could not wait to count coup; he does not sing his own deeds, they said, and always he thinks of the people first. But Crazy Horse accepted the Big Bellies' judgment without protest. The people said that taking the shirt was a shameful act that had broken the power of the Big Bellies. The chiefs' society had never met again and now its members were scattered among the agencies, holding out their bowls for the white man's rotten meat and wormy flour, while Crazy Horse, although no longer a shirt man, was honored still, for the people believed in his power and they looked to him for guidance. In his becoming-a-man vision he had seen his horse floating above the ground, carrying him safely through the ranks of his enemies and leading his people to victory. The name he was given after this vision did not mean his horse was crazy, as a white man understood the word. It meant something closer to enchanted. In the vision the horse had behaved strangely because it was a creature of the spirit world, bringing him a promise of power. As long as the power stayed with him, Crazy Horse could not be hurt by his enemies, and that was strong medicine in the eyes of the people. In the years since the taking of the shirt, he had been made lance carrier for the Raven Owners warrior society and more recently lance carrier for all the Oglala, this honor not given to anyone for many years.

"Well, my friends," Crazy Horse said when the pipe was lit and going, "they say that pipe carriers have come from Sun Horse, and they say a whiteman brings a message from the soldier chief Three Stars."

As if these few words had broken a beaver dam and released the waters of a stream, the silence of the lodge was broken and one voice followed another, first Two Moons and then Standing Eagle and then Bat Putnam, telling why the pipe carriers came and what had been said up to now, and when Bat spoke of Hardeman and Johnny Smoker, Sitting Bull joined in, and he and Bat between them, aided by the southern Cheyenne, told of the boy and his dream. The name He Stands Between the Worlds was mentioned often, along with the word *wakán,* to touch on the mysterious powers of dreams and prophecies.

At length a silence fell as Crazy Horse absorbed what he had heard, rocking slowly back and forth as he sucked on the pipe that had grown cold in his hand.

He looked up at Bat Putnam and he smiled. "Perhaps my friend Lodgepole carries the pipe to Three Stars?"

Bat motioned to Standing Eagle. "My brother-in-law carries the pipe. I will go with him to Three Stars and I too will speak with him."

"Then Three Stars will hear the words of Sun Horse as if they came from his own lips."

There were a few soft *hau*'s from the Lakotas. Bat was embarrassed by this quiet expression of praise and trust from the great Oglala. He had translated Crazy Horse's words for Hardeman automatically, before he absorbed their meaning.

The soft brown eyes of the light-haired man shifted to Hardeman. "They say Three Stars keeps his promises. If he takes the pipe will he go in peace?"

Hardeman knew it was time to talk straight; there would be no deceiving this gathering. "Three Stars is a soldier," he said. "If he has to, he'll make peace in the way a soldier knows best, but he's a man who thinks for himself, like the men of the Sioux and Cheyenne. Show him a way to a lasting peace without fighting and he'll listen. If he takes the pipe, he'll keep his word."

"They say Three Stars sent you to Sun Horse," Crazy Horse said, and here he made a gesture that took in the lodge and all he had been told. "They say you told Sun Horse he must surrender or there will be war."

"Three Stars didn't send me," Hardeman said, meeting the steady gaze. "I went on my own. Johnny Smoker, the one you call He Stands Between the Worlds, wanted to see his grandfather. He told me about Sun Horse and I saw a way to make peace. We found Three Stars and talked with him and then we found Sun Horse. Three Stars gets his orders from Washington. They think the only way to make peace is to get all the Sioux onto the Dakota reservation now. But if you show Three Stars a new way, one he can believe in, he'll take it.'' He didn't say that both he and Crook had planned on Sun Horse's surrender as the first step to peace, or that both of them believed the hostiles would have to give up the Powder River country. If there were many as stubborn as Sitting Bull, unwilling even to consider leaving these pleasant, wooded hills, there would be fighting in the end, despite all the efforts of the peacemakers.

Hardeman fought off a chill of foreboding. Sitting Bull had fired up the council with his carefully chosen words, but still Two Moons and Little Wolf intended to take their people to Dakota unless a deal could be struck with Crook, and it remained to be seen where Crazy Horse stood.

''It is said that Three Stars is a quiet man who listens,'' Two Moons said now. ''Perhaps if the soldier chief hears words of peace from the war leader of Sun Horse's people, he will—''

''It is my father who speaks of peace!'' Standing Eagle burst out. ''His words are not mine! I would fight Three Stars now and leave his bones for the wolves to chew! I would carry the pipe of war, not peace! Let us fight him now, any who are brave enough. Let others run away like the camp dogs before the sticks of the old women! I will not run away! If Three Stars must fight, I will fight him!''

There was a heavy quiet in the lodge. Many of the men covered their mouths and looked away, everyone there embarrassed by this shocking breach of good manners. Several of the Cheyenne glared angrily at Standing Eagle and one man put his hand on his skinning knife. Standing Eagle reddened, but he continued to sit straight. He had spoken against his own father and come near to calling his host a coward, but to show weakness now would only bring more scorn on him.

From the head of the second circle of councillors, He Dog spoke to Standing Eagle, his voice heavy with sarcasm.

''Has the camp of Sun Horse enough guns and powder

to fight the soldier chief now? It is well known that Sun Horse's people do not trade with the whites often. It is said they have few guns. The pipe carriers say that the people are hungry and the horses weak. Would the war leader fight the bluecoats even before the new grass is up?" He paused for effect and then continued. "The winter has been hard. My own horses are well. They found good grass on the Tongue and the Rosebud and we gave them much cottonwood bark, but still I would not entrust them with the safety of my helpless ones if the soldiers came to chase us day and night as they like to do. Are your horses so much stronger than mine?" After another pause he looked across the inner circle at Crazy Horse. "My brother-friend has fought the bluecoats often. He tells of many guns, all of them the back-loading kind now, and some the many-shooting kind. Let my brother-friend say if he believes we can fight the bluecoats in the Snowblind Moon."

Once again the eyes in the lodge turned to the light-haired man. He Dog had stated the risks of fighting, but it seemed he was asking Crazy Horse if there might be hope in such a course. There were others here who might permit themselves to be swayed if the great Oglala encouraged them.

It was a moment before Crazy Horse replied. "It is true the soldiers have many guns," he said, and his eyes moved to Standing Eagle. "Some will go to Dakota rather than fight and they do this because of concern for the helpless ones." He glanced at Sitting Bull, who held himself aloof from the proceedings. "Sitting Bull says he will not go. He will stay here and fight the bluecoats if he must, and he too does what he thinks is best for the people. Each man must choose for himself. Standing Eagle carries pipes from Sun Horse, a true peace man. Sun Horse wears the shirt-for-life and always he thinks of the helpless ones. The war leader of Sun Horse's people knows this and perhaps that is why he bears a pipe of peace instead of war."

There was an easing of tension. Anger faded from the Cheyenne faces. Crazy Horse had offered Standing Eagle a way to atone for his outburst if he would acknowledge his responsibility for the helpless ones. And by emphasizing that each man must choose for himself, the Hunkpátila had told He Dog to follow his own conscience.

Hardeman felt a glimmer of hope. If Crazy Horse came out on the side of peace, that might bring Sitting Bull around.

Standing Eagle kept his head high. His face was set and hard, and he did not meet Crazy Horse's eyes. "The hunting has not been good for my people. It is true our ponies are weak, but no weaker than the whitemen who live in wooden houses and hide away from the coldest days of winter. Who has known the bluecoats to remain for long where snow covers the ground and the wind blows cold? Even on weak horses we can fight them and send them running with their tails between their legs."

"It is said that Three Stars rides always at the head of his men," Crazy Horse said evenly. "They say he sleeps on the ground, under the stars, like the war men of the Lakota. They say he is at the front of battle, never the rear. They say his men fight hard for him and will follow where he leads them."

Standing Eagle saw that bravado would not get him through this moment; he would have to yield. "Perhaps Three Stars is not like the others. When a leader is strong, the warriors fight harder." He turned to Crazy Horse as he said this and those present knew he was acknowledging the Hunkpátila's great skill as a war leader. Standing Eagle's head was no longer held so high and his voice had softened. "If Three Stars comes to fight the camp of Sun Horse, I will fight him, but the helpless ones will suffer. To save the helpless ones, our councillors would have us go to Dakota if there is no other way, but my father hopes to make a peace with the whites that will let us keep our country here. A peace not only for Sun Horse's people but for all the Lakota. It is for this reason that he sends pipes to Sitting Bull and Three Stars, so there will be no fighting now; so he may have time to find another way. I will take the pipe to Three Stars and with my brother-in-law and the white scout I will tell him my father's words.'' Here he gestured at Bat and Hardeman, sitting near him.

The last of the tension dissipated. Standing Eagle had retreated from his angry call for war and had restated his responsibility as a pipe carrier. Within the customs of a Lakota council, he had apologized for forgetting himself.

Hardeman was struggling with the realization that Sun Horse had tricked him. From the start, the old man had said he would speak for peace, but he had never said outright that he would take his people to Dakota or encourage others to do so. All along Sun Horse had been just like the others, intent on keeping the Powder River country! Was it possible that the whole business with the pipes was nothing more than a trick? Hardeman couldn't believe that. Sun Horse's desire for peace was real, he was sure of it. But how could there be a settlement if the hostiles wouldn't go in? Like the men in Washington, Hardeman had always believed that giving up the unceded lands was a precondition for peace. Until now. Suddenly he felt that belief weakening. Could there be another way? Only this morning, looking down on the tranquil Cheyenne village, he had felt that the Indians might find peace on their own terms, but then he had imagined only a short delay in submitting, not counter proposals that flew in the face of everything the white men wanted.

One of Two Moons' councillors broke the silence, and his eyes were sad. ''The whites are more numerous than the buffalo,'' he said. ''More numerous than the blades of grass on the prairie, so they say. To speak of fighting them is useless. Perhaps we should take the whiteman's hand and accept what he offers us, rather than fight him and risk losing everything.''

''They *want* everything!'' Crazy Horse snapped, his eyes flashing with sudden anger, and Hardeman felt the shock of this change in the light-haired man like a slap in the face. ''They always want more! They want the *Paha Sapa;* they want this country here; they want everything! We can give no more!'' And then as suddenly as it had come, Crazy Horse's anger was gone and the fire left his eyes. He looked at the Cheyenne councillor kindly. "Each man must choose for himself what to do," he repeated, and for a time he seemed lost in thought. Finally he drew himself up and looked around him.

"My friends," he said, and his voice was calm now, "the Lakota and the whiteman walk different trails. Each man is good in the sight of *Wakán Tanka,* but the *washíchun* do not see this. They wish to make us like them, only poor and weak beside them. They call us wild and they do not like wild things. They kill the buffalo and bring the tame spotted kind in his place. They wish to tame us as well. They do not like to stand beside one who is strong in a way different from their own." His eyes looked around the inner circle. "They even seek to tame the earth, the mother who gives them life. They claim the land for their own and fence their neighbors away, and love of possessions is a sickness among them."

There were some *hau*'s and other sounds of approval, but a few men looked away in embarrassment. Like the whites, the Lakota and the Cheyenne sometimes measured a man by his possessions, by the number of horses he had or the hides he brought in as a hunter, hides his women made into robes and shirts and leggings he wore with perhaps too much pride. Crazy Horse spoke often against these things, giving his own horses away to the needy and wearing none of the finery some men admired. "Do not become like the whites," he often said, "seeking power and possessions."

"My friends," he said now, "we cannot live beside the whites. I do not wish to make the *washíchun* into a Lakota, nor will I let him make me into a *washíchun*. We have given them some land and they have taken more. They are all around us now, as once we were around them. Let them keep the land they have and live there in their own manner, but I will not live beside them."

As Sitting Bull had done earlier, Crazy Horse held the gathering in his hands, but unlike the Hunkpapa he did not dominate them with fiery rhetoric; instead he showed them his reasoning, revealing the workings of his heart. He glanced at Sitting Bull now, and the war leader nodded, revealing just a trace of a smile.

"If I must choose between surrender and fighting" —Crazy Horse paused, and he gave a little sigh before he said the next words—"I will fight. I will not go to Dakota. I will stay here. If the soldiers come, I will fight them."

He picked up a handful of earth from the edge of the fire pit, where it was dry and warm from the heat of the fire, and let the sandy soil trickle from one hand into the palm of the other; he reversed the position of his hands and repeated the action as he spoke again.

"I have signed none of the whiteman's treaties, but after we whipped them when they built forts in our country, I kept that treaty and I have fought them only when they broke it."

There were murmurs of assent now, for all knew the deeds of Crazy Horse. Since Red Cloud's War he had fought the soldiers when they came along the Yellowstone to find a way for an iron road there, and he had fought in the Black Hills when the miners came to dig for gold. Each one present knew the truth of these things.

"The Ancient Ones say that a young man must know war so he can understand peace. I have seen much fighting, and I will fight again if the whites try to take what is mine. But I do not wish to fight forever. I like to see the little children play unafraid and I like to hear the women sing with happy hearts. Sun Horse is *wichasha wakán;* he has great power for the good of the people and now he seeks the path to a lasting peace. If the soldiers will go away now, I will stay at peace until the grass is tall, and when Sun Horse comes to speak to us, I will listen." The sounds of approval were strong now, and Crazy Horse turned to Hardeman. "Tell this to Three Stars. Tell him he must leave our country now. Tell him to speak to the Great Father in *Washing-ton* and say that the Lakota want peace. But we cannot live side by side with the whites. If there is to be peace, we must each live in our own country, in our own way."

Hardeman allowed himself to betray no reaction to the

Oglala's words, but his mind was working furiously. The lines were clearly drawn now: on one side were Crazy Horse, Sitting Bull and Sun Horse, all determined to keep the Powder River country, and on the other was mustered the limitless power of the white nation. Sun Horse might not fight to keep his land, but Crazy Horse and Sitting Bull would, and between them they could sway the majority of the hostiles. If there were any way left to avoid war, it would have to be found now.

From the start, Hardeman's own goal had been to prevent fighting by any means, but he had not planned to help the Indians defy the government's order, and yet if they remained adamant about keeping the Powder River country, there would be war . . . unless there were some way for them to remain here and still satisfy the white man's demands. It seemed a futile hope. Crazy Horse was willing to hold in his warriors if Crook would leave the country now, and that was a start, but the hostiles would have to give up much more. If the whites didn't get what they wanted, they would fight for it. . . . But what if the hostiles yielded everything the whites truly wanted? What if they appeared to surrender? Whites were often shortsighted. If they believed they had won, the hostiles might secure for themselves the one thing they demanded without conditions—a part of the Powder River country to keep forever! Not all of it, for there too they must yield, but they might keep a part!

But as quickly as they had risen, his hopes fell again as he realized the whites would never strike such a bargain. In their minds, the Powder River country represented a hiding place for the "warlike" bands, those that defied "all attempts at reconciliation," in the newspaper's words. Such views were widespread on the frontier, where the unceded lands were seen as a place where the hostiles could perpetuate their wild way of life and gird themselves for repeated outbreaks, and that was what the whites feared most, failing as they did to see their own role in maintaining the hostilities.

Hardeman looked at the rings of seated figures around

him. Say the word "Indian," and most whites imagined just such men as these—the painted and befeathered warriors of the Sioux and Cheyenne. Illustrations in dime novels and magazines and newspapers alike depicted all Indians in a similar manner, whether they were plains Indians or not, and they were usually shown brandishing tomahawks and rifles, threatening peaceful settlers. And always there were white women cowering in terror in the foreground; that was how the fear was kept alive.

Hardeman looked at Crazy Horse and Sitting Bull, leaders who shunned the finery for which their people were famous across the land. Newspapers imagined them plotting rapine and bloodshed; their names were spoken with fear in the taprooms of Custer City in the Black Hills; mothers invoked them to frighten children into nightmares. Yet here they sat before him, giving no orders, commanding no legions except by respect, strong personalities and greatly admired by their own kind, but so different from the popular notion among the whites. Men of the people, the Lakotas called them, and it was true; they were natural leaders who had risen from the people. As the words spoken here made plain, they were not afraid to fight, even against superior weapons and bad odds, but they fought for their people. They were portrayed as constantly seeking war, yet here they sat discussing ways to end it forever, willing to fight only if war came to them. And in that they were no different from other men. What man would not fight if his home were attacked?

If only the whites could be made to see these men as they truly were. . . .

There were soft conversations going on here and there about the lodge, but Little Wolf cleared his throat now and the others fell silent. The Cheyenne chief glanced at Sitting Bull, who remained as expressionless as a chunk of rock, and then moved his gaze to Hardeman.

"If the pipes Sun Horse sends are accepted, and if Three Stars goes from our lands, when will he come again to speak with the headmen of the Lakota?"

It was Crazy Horse who answered, before Hardeman could frame a reply.

"In the first moon of summer, when the wild turnips are ripe," the Oglala said. "But we will not meet him at the Laramie fort or the one called Fetterman. Too often in the past our headmen have gone to the forts when the whites called them. They sat under the guns of the soldiers and they signed the talking leaves full of promises the whites never kept. This time the bluecoat chief must come to sit among the Lakota, to be heard by our women, our men and our children."

"He must not bring his horse soldiers," one of Sitting Bull's councillors put in, his eyes flashing. "He must come alone."

The idea came to Hardeman then in a rush. He began to speak even before he was certain what he would say, but he knew he could not yield on the first specific demand or he would win nothing. It was important for Crook's prestige that he have an escort. Of course, no one yet knew if Crook would agree to the plan at all, but when the pipe carriers met with him they must know all of the Indians' demands. First secure Crook's escort, then broach the new thought that Hardeman felt would surely burst him at the seams if he did not voice it soon.

"When the Lakotas go to council with the whites, they always take their young men," he said. "Red Cloud took his young men to Laramie, so did Spotted Tail. Every chief who has gone to council with the whites took his young men. Three Stars must bring his young men when he comes to council with the Lakotas, but he needn't bring them all. One company. Forty or fifty men."

Crazy Horse nodded. "It is true that our headmen take young warriors to council. Three Stars may bring one *troop*." He used the English word, surprising Hardeman, but the scout merely nodded and was careful to keep his face calm and his voice even when he spoke again, as if bringing up a matter of only passing interest.

"It may be that Three Stars will want to bring other men with him, some white men who are not soldiers. You know that much trouble has been made when the men who sit in the Great Father's council in Washington don't understand what the soldiers and the Lakotas have agreed. If some men from Washington come with Three Stars, you'll know that they hear you with their own ears and will take your words truthfully to the Great Father. They will come here and they will see that you want peace." Then, as if it were only an afterthought, he added, "And perhaps some of the men who write for the talking leaves will come, so they will write the truth about Crazy Horse and Sitting Bull."

Sitting Bull gave a small shrug and attempted to conceal his interest, but Hardeman knew he had the Hunkpapa's attention.

Two Moons spoke briefly with Little Wolf and then exchanged a word or two with Crazy Horse before he turned to Hardeman. "Three Stars may bring some men from *Washing-ton.* The Great Father may come himself if he wishes, but at least he must send some of his advisers to hear our words."

Crazy Horse nodded. "They say that Three Stars speaks the truth. It may be that he would carry our words truthfully to the Great Father, but it is good that his advisers should come here to see us at peace in our own country."

"Let Three Stars bring the men who make the talking leaves," one of Sitting Bull's councillors added, his voice edged with sarcasm. "Perhaps then they will tell no more lies about us."

There was a chorus of agreement from the gathering and even a little laughter, and Hardeman felt hope growing strong within him. In a moment he had changed the very nature of the summer meeting. No longer would Crook come alone, accompanied only by soldiers; instead he would bring a peace commission to treat with the hostiles. The Indians believed Crook was trustworthy and as long as he led the commission they would not object. Alone, Crook might have reached an agreement with the hostile bands, but a full peace commission might achieve something far more important. Received here, in the hostile camps, the officials and the newspapermen could see the true state of affairs for themselves. They would see that Crazy Horse and Sitting Bull were defenders, not attackers, and that could be the start of changing white opinion on the frontier and beyond. Such a change was vital if these brave men were to keep some portion of their hunting grounds.

There was a chance it might work. If Sitting Bull would agree, the chance became almost a certainty. With a pipe from Sun Horse and the agreement not only of Sitting Bull and the Cheyenne, but also of Crazy Horse, the most feared warrior of all, and an invitation to bring a new peace commission in summer, Crook might be willing to order the army from the field and take the part of the Sioux against the likes of Phil Sheridan. "It is preposterous to speak of keeping faith with the Sioux," Sheridan had once said, but Crook knew the value of bargaining with the Indians in good faith, and for the sake of a real peace that gave the whites what they wanted, cooler heads than Phil Sheridan's might make a pact and keep it.

As if he sensed Hardeman's hopes and wished to caution the white man, Crazy Horse turned to him now. "Tell Three Stars one thing more," he said. "Tell him we will hear no more talk of selling *Paha Sapa* or leaving our country here. He must know this, so he will understand what is in our hearts."

Hardeman took a deep breath. If the whites were denied the Black Hills gold there would be no peace commission, no new treaty. But here in this council the speeches were done and the bargaining had started, and as long as there was room to bargain there was still hope.

"The whites don't want the hills," he said, new ideas coming fast to him now. "They want the gold. Do the Lakota and Cheyenne want the gold too?"

Sitting Bull broke his long silence. "We have no use for the soft shining metal. Sometimes we cast it into bullets." He smiled, but the expression was out of place beneath the eyes that were as hard as ever.

"Let the whites have the gold, then," Hardeman suggested as if this were nothing more than good sense. "Say they can go to the Black Hills and mine the gold, and when the gold is gone the hills will be yours. In a few years the miners will be gone, just as they have gone from the diggings in Colorado, and over in South Pass in the land of the Snakes."

"The whites say they want the land," Crazy Horse said. "They do not give up what they want without a fight."

"How do you get a bone away from a dog?" Hardeman asked. "Offer him another bone, one he might like better."

Crazy Horse's expression revealed a new interest. "What bone should we offer the whites instead of *Paha Sapa*?"

"The whites want an iron road along the Yellowstone. Let them build it, but not in your country. Say they can build it north of the river in the land of the Crows."

Crazy Horse pondered this for a moment, then nodded. "If it is north of the river, that is not our country, so we give away nothing. Will the dog let go of *Paha Sapa* for that?"

For this too Hardeman had an answer. "Give him more. Offer him the land north of the Platte up to the place where the Dry Fork joins the Powder, at old Fort Reno." It was the last card he had conjured out of his sleeve in recent moments. His whole hand was on the table now. If there were ways around the obstacles that remained, others would have to find them.

There were rumblings of discontent when the white scout's words were translated, but Old Bear leaned forward, fixing Hardeman with his gaze. "What will the whites do with the land?"

Hardeman shrugged. "They'll farm, or raise cattle."

Old Bear shook his head. "The land there is dry. The water is bitter. There are no trees and little grass."

Hardeman didn't argue the facts. "You've seen in other places how the whites dig ditches to bring water to dry land. Let them do that along the Platte. There are men who will bring cattle or try to farm anywhere they feel safe from attack by Indians. Give them the land along the Holy

Road so they feel safe there. This country here is better for the Lakota and Cheyenne."

Little Wolf nodded. "And when the country there is full of whites, they will look here and they will say, 'That land looks good to me,' and they will wish to take it away."

There it was. Someone had seen the weakness. How could even a new treaty erase that fear?

"They'll do that right enough," Bat observed in English, and Hardeman was surprised to hear the mountain man speak for himself. For what seemed like hours, Bat had said nothing except to translate the words of others; his voice had been the voices of Crazy Horse and Little Wolf and Sitting Bull and each of the others, conveying both their words and emotions; now there was a triumphant spark in his eye as he added his own thoughts to the council for the first time. "Leastways if it's still 'unceded Injun territory' like it is now, they'll try to get it for sure. To a white man, 'unceded' means he ain't got 'round to takin' it yet." He stroked his beard thoughtfully. " 'Course now, it'd be a mite harder to steal if'n it was reservation land all official and proper. Say it was called the Western Sioux Reservation, and say in exchange for what you reckon we oughta give the white man, he give us one thing a heap o' folks been wantin' fer a long time. Say they build us an agency in this country, a reservation post where we can trade peaceful-like without goin' off to the Red Cloud Agency or clear to the Missouri."

Without waiting for a reply from Hardeman, Bat repeated his proposal in Lakota to the councillors, who received it with a rising buzz of approval. Men spoke to their neighbors, nodding, and in the inner circle Hawk Chaser smiled and said a few words to Blackbird, who had followed the proceedings raptly with eyes and ears, never making a sound. Even Standing Eagle looked pleased.

When quiet returned, Crazy Horse spoke to Hardeman, and it seemed he might be suppressing a new excitement. "Many times we have asked for an agency here, but it must not be on the Powder River or anywhere in the middle of our country. Always before, when the *washíchun* build a trader fort, soon the bluecoats come with their guns. If there is to be an agency for us, it must be on the Yellowstone. The whites may bring their fireboats with goods to trade, but the agency must be there, at the edge of our land, not in the middle."

The council expressed approval of these conditions and Hardeman fought to remain outwardly calm. Why not? An agency might be just what was needed to seal the bargain and make it stick with both sides. The whites would know that the former hostiles were being closely watched, and with the northern part of the Powder River country a proper reservation, the western bands might keep some of the land they cherished most. Crook could make it work! He would see where the road to peace lay: not in demanding that all the hostiles go to Dakota, to give up the Black Hills and everything else they held dear, but by offering the one thing the Indians wanted above all else—part of the Powder River country—and getting in return not only the Black Hills gold but an end of opposition to the Yellowstone railroad and a gift of land along the Platte into the bargain! Such an exchange might appear lopsided enough to please even the greediest whites.

One by one each pair of eyes in the lodge came to rest on the solid figure of Sitting Bull. It was time for his decision. The bargaining had gone ahead as if the Hunkpapa had already smoked Sun Horse's pipe, which still rested cold in his hands; Crazy Horse had agreed to the peace man's request, although there was no pipe for him, but without the cooperation of Sitting Bull, all the talk might be for naught.

With deliberate slowness, Sitting Bull turned to look at Standing Eagle. "Sun Horse asks me to hold back my young men and stay at peace if Three Stars will leave our country now. Is that all he asks?" Before binding himself to grant a favor that was asked by the sending of a pipe, a man naturally wished to know the exact nature of the terms.

Standing Eagle cast a short glance at Bat Putnam before answering, but as the war leader began to talk, Bat put his words faithfully into English for Hardeman. There could be no question of keeping back anything now. Hardeman had contributed as much as anyone to the success of the council. He had brought Crazy Horse into the bargain, and if anything would convince Sitting Bull, that would do it. The scout deserved to know the whole truth of what was going on.

"Sun Horse asks that the seven council fires of the Lakota meet in the Moon of Fat Calves, together with our friends the Shahíyela and Arapaho. He asks Sitting Bull to join in calling for this great gathering, where my father will speak to the headmen of all the bands."

"What will Sun Horse say to the council?" Sitting Bull asked softly.

"He will speak for peace between white and Lakota," Standing Eagle replied. "Surely, my father says, all the Lakota gathered together are strong enough to make a peace with the *washíchun,* one that includes our country here." He hesitated for a moment and then continued. "If Three Stars will take my father's pipe and agree to return in summer to talk of peace, I too will speak to the council. I will ask them to give the whites the gold from *Paha Sapa* and the land along the Platte, and to let them make their iron road on the Yellowstone in the land of the *Kanghí.*"

Throughout the lodge there were murmurs of approval. If the terms reached here today could win over the angry war leader of the Sun Band, they were fair indeed.

Silence returned, and once again all attention was on Sitting Bull, but he did not acknowledge it. For a long time he sat staring into the fire. Just when it seemed that Little Wolf might speak to the Hunkpapa, Sitting Bull moved. In his careful way he reached out and took a burning stick from the fire. He blew out the flame and touched the glowing end to the bowl of the pipe that he had held for so long in his hands. He puffed once, twice, then drew in a little smoke and let it out at once, watching it as it rose up and dispersed in the updraft from the fire. The others watched it too, for they knew that the smoke taken through this pipe, or any pipe so consecrated, had the force of a prayer.

The quiet in the lodge was complete but for the sounds of the fire. With the measured movements of ceremony, Sitting Bull offered the pipe to the west, the north, the east and the south; he raised it high toward the heavens, then touched it to the earth. "My friends," he said, "I accept the pipe sent by Sun Horse. If Three Stars takes his soldiers and goes out of our country I will keep the peace until the great council. I will send a pipe among the bands and ask that all come together in the Moon of Fat Calves, which the whites call *June* and my people call the Prairie-Turnip Moon." He looked at the faces around him, wishing none to misunderstand. "I do this because my cousin Sun Horse is a man to respect, a man of peace. It may be that by sending this pipe here today he has already set us on the path to a peace that will last. It may be that the whites will take what we offer and leave us alone, here in our own country. I too want peace, but I will not sell our country here. The bones of my fathers lie among these hills, and before I give this country to the whites, my own bones will join them." The sounds of agreement filled the lodge again and Two Moons and Little Wolf and He Dog gave their own approval to Sitting Bull's words of defiance. It seemed that the councillors had found not only the terms to present to Crook, but a new strength as well, born of this gathering. When the voices died away, Sitting Bull continued. "In the hoop of the nation I will make the Sun Dance to ask for power to help my people. After the Sun Dance the great council will meet, and when it has ended, then we will meet with Three Stars and the men from *Washing-ton*."

Once more the Hunkpapa holy man touched the glowing brand to the pipe and puffed, and then he handed it to the man on his left, sending it sunwise around the inner circle. As the pipe was passed, the smoke rose into the air, mixing with the smoke of the council fire and finally wafting out the smoke hole at the peak of the lodge. It rose into the sky to signify that each man who smoked was witness to what had been said, joined in a spiritual commitment to the promises made here today.

CHAPTER FOURTEEN

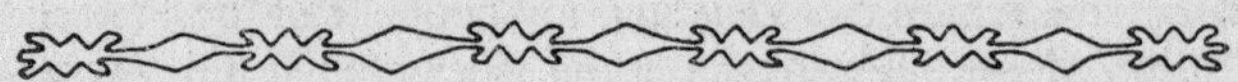

The council had taken up the greater part of the day. When it ended at last, some men remained around the large fire, talking among themselves, but finally even they left the lodge and stepped into the bleak light of late afternoon. The clouds were breaking and the air was turning colder, but there was no promise of a general improvement of the weather. The winds still gusted fitfully and to the west a new bank of clouds loomed high, cutting off the light of the sinking sun.

Here and there about the village, men and women were grouped around individual councillors to hear what had been said and decided in the long meeting. Beyond the central cluster of lodges, Sitting Bull and his men were already mounted on fresh horses given them by Two Moons. Ordinarily the visitors would have accepted the hospitality of a friendly camp; as it was, they would travel in the dark of what promised to be a bitter cold night. Sitting Bull wished to return to his own band without delay. When he left the Powder to make for Chalk Buttes, his young men would continue down the river to spread the news of today's council and to warn the villages there to keep watch for Three Stars and his soldiers. No one wanted to risk war now, just as the hope of a strong peace was born.

Crazy Horse too would leave soon. He had lingered for

a time in the council lodge, talking to He Dog, but now he was at the bottom of the camp among the Oglala lodges, changing his saddle over to the horse He Dog had given him in exchange for his own tired mount. Soon he would be gone off to the southeast, riding alone.

There was a clatter of hooves as Sitting Bull and his party set off. Bat Putnam waved a last farewell to his son and watched until the riders were across the river and on their way; then he turned and rejoined the rest of the pipe carriers, who stood in a group near Two Moons' tipi.

"You reckon Three Stars will talk turkey?" Standing Eagle asked Hardeman.

"Not all white men are fools," Hardeman replied, trying to sound hopeful. He couldn't let the others suspect what he was thinking. Stay hopeful and keep calm, that was his best chance now. "They're bullheaded, but not all fools. There was strong talk here this afternoon. He'll listen."

"Mebbe," Bat said. "Most white folks don't put much stock in Injun talk. They'll just go on to get what they want, regardless."

"Crook wants peace. If the whites stick to that order pushing all the hunting bands to Dakota, there'll be a war."

"That's truth." Standing Eagle grinned. "This coon smells the war paint." He seemed to think it was a pretty good smell.

Two Moons passed by and stopped to say a few words to Standing Eagle before going on towards his lodge.

"He invites us to come eat," Bat said.

Hardeman smiled in spite of himself. "I could have guessed that. They don't let a person work up much of a hunger."

"A man gets honor by feeding his guests." Bat grinned.

"Do this child good to fill his belly," Standing Eagle said. "We'll have a long day tomorrow, I'm thinkin'." He started off after Two Moons and the others followed along; you ate when the opportunity presented itself, for you could never be sure when you might eat again.

The pipe carriers would not leave the Cheyenne village

until morning. Darkness was only an hour or two away and there was no reasonable cause to rush off into the gathering night, not when the whole countryside would be alive with sharp eyes by morning, all watching for Crook and his cavalry. The pipe carriers would be accompanied by Cheyenne riders and some of He Dog's Oglalas, to keep them in touch with the scouts from the Powder River villages and bring word to the messengers as soon as Three Stars was found.

Hardeman couldn't wait until morning, but as the daylight waned and the night gathered force, the snow creaking beneath the feet of those who moved about the camp, it seemed to him that not only Hawk Chaser but Standing Eagle and Little Hand and even Bat Putnam watched his every move. When they had all eaten their fill and smoked and talked for a time with their host, Hardeman stretched and yawned and said he guessed he would turn in, and at this Standing Eagle was suddenly very tired and he rose to accompany Hardeman to Kills Fox's lodge, where Blackbird was already asleep and the Cheyenne were preparing to go to their robes. As the fire burned down and the lodge darkened, Hardeman let his breathing become deep and long as he listened for Standing Eagle's familiar snoring, but it didn't come. He waited for what he thought was an hour or more and then he raised himself on one elbow.

By the dull red glow of the fire he saw Standing Eagle's eyes open. Hardeman nodded and smiled, as if he couldn't sleep, and remained for a time with his head propped on one arm, watching the glowing coals. Finally he lay back and pretended to sleep, but he sensed Standing Eagle's wakefulness. He decided that there would be no getting away tonight and he tried to doze off, but his mind would grant him no rest and in the middle of the night, long before dawn, he heard the sounds of horsemen entering camp.

In moments there was movement in the lodge. Kills Fox put a few sticks on the fire to make light and Hardeman wondered if the Cheyenne too had been feigning sleep. Kills Fox's family was awake, and only Blackbird remained unaware of the movements both inside the lodge and without.

"Big party, sounds like," Hardeman said softly, pulling on his boots.

"Twenty horses or more, I make it," Standing Eagle said as he threw back his robes and sat up. "Hunters comin' home, I reckon. They had a party out."

There was an undercurrent of excitement in the voices that could be heard from beyond the lodge. Kills Fox slipped into his winter moccasins and pulled a heavy robe around him, then stepped through the entrance with Hardeman and Standing Eagle close on his heels.

In the center of camp, women were already bringing fire from their lodges and adding new sticks to make a blaze. The men from Kills Fox's lodge encountered Bat, Hawk Chaser and Little Hand in company with Two Moons, all moving toward the fire. Bat glanced at the dark sky overhead.

"Solid cloud," he said. "Dark's a white man's soul. 'Scuse the expression." He smiled, and Hardeman could see the mountain man's teeth in the gloom.

Men from many lodges were gathered around a group of Cheyenne horsemen near the growing bonfire. A rime of ice coated the hairs of the horses' noses and the sweat was frozen to their flanks. They had been ridden hard. Already, young men were leading some of the horses away to be unsaddled and turned out with the rest. Some cuts of buffalo and the carcasses of three deer were unpacked from behind the saddles and carried off.

"They been huntin' the land between the Tongue and the Powder," Bat said when he had listened to the talk for a time. "Two o' their boys seen Crook."

"Where?!" Hardeman was buttoning his St. Paul coat against the cutting cold and now he slipped his hands quickly back into his heavy fleece-lined gloves, flexing fingers that had grown stiff from the chill in a few short moments.

"There ain't no rush. They was headed east, then hit a crick at sundown and turned north to the Yellowstone.

Otter Crick, I make it. Thirty miles off and headed the wrong way. There ain't no villages up there."

"What time do you make it?" Hardeman asked.

"Oh, 'bout a good snooze to first light, Injun time. White man time, some past midnight, I reckon."

"We put out at first light, we'll find 'em by 'n' by," Standing Eagle said.

"Suits me." Hardeman wrapped his arms around himself and shivered. "Too cold to put out now." He turned back toward Kills Fox's lodge. His shoulders were hunched against the cold and he shuffled along like a man still half asleep and anxious to get back to bed. He did not look back until he reached the lodge. As he hoped, Bat and the others had remained with the hunters to hear more of what they had to say. With luck the talk would go on for some time, in one lodge or another. They might even sit down with Two Moons and make a formal report on the hunt and what the scouts had seen. Half the camp was awake now.

Hardeman's guns were inside the tipi, all except his Colt, which he had stuck into his waistband when he arose. He had slept fully clothed and had put on his hat and jacket and St. Paul coat before stepping outside, but his saddlebags were in the lodge with his rifles. The cardigan and extra cartridges and other odds and ends would have to be left behind. He couldn't risk going inside, where Kills Fox's wife and children were awake.

He moved around the lodge and slipped into the cottonwoods that surrounded the cluster of tipis. Some light came from the cloudy sky now, brighter when the clouds thinned in the east, and once he caught a brief glimpse of the waning moon rising there over the hills across the river. He had no trouble making his way among the trees to the horses. The pipe carriers' mounts had been cut out of the herd the evening before, and were tethered close to camp. The saddles were in an unoccupied lodge nearby, used to store bales of buffalo hides and dried meat and kegs of gunpowder placed atop the hides so the powder would stay dry.

In moments he had his roan bridled and saddled. Before

mounting, he turned the other horses loose and watched them amble off toward the river. After drinking they would drift upstream to the main herd.

Once on his own horse's back, Hardeman leaned low and guided the animal downriver at a slow walk. To a casual observer, the horse might seem to be moving at random, looking for forage.

His chance had come along and he had taken it. He might not get much of a lead, but a man traveling alone at night was hard to find. If he got clear of the village safely, he could be anywhere by morning.

The clouds were thickening now and the way was dark and difficult. Hardeman gave the roan his head and kept the river on his right. While he was still within hearing of the village he strained to catch any alarm, but none came. On a night as cold as this even the sentries stayed close to the warmth of the lodge fires.

When he judged it safe, Hardeman straightened in the saddle and urged the horse into a trot. Bat had said there was a trail that left the Powder some miles north of the Cheyenne camp, one that avoided the roughest land due west of the village. The going was faster that way, Bat said, and the pipe carriers had planned to take that route in the morning. The cross-country trail went straight to Otter Creek, heading west and a little north. Even if Crook broke camp an hour after dawn, Hardeman would be nearly upon him by then.

When he had ridden for perhaps an hour he saw a fork to the left and took it, following the new trail up a long shallow ravine and into the hills beyond. Once up out of the confinement of the Powder River bottom and alone in the open country, his fear of pursuit diminished and he gave most of his attention to what lay before him. His senses were fully alert, his eyes seeking anything the gray-shrouded night would reveal. He was glad to be on the move again, using old familiar skills to find the way and follow it. As the moon rose higher above the clouds the night brightened somewhat, allowing him to move faster, alternating between a trot and a lope, and the country fell away behind him.

At the moment when Standing Eagle had told Sitting Bull of the call for a great summer council, Hardeman's brief surge of hope had died like a lone candle blown out by a storm wind and he had known at once what he must do. Why hadn't they told him, Sun Horse or Bat or one of the others?! If he had known, he could have tried to make them see the fatal folly of the notion, and maybe talked them out of it.

It was plain why they had kept the knowledge from him. They knew the whites feared any gathering of the tribes, but they didn't see just how strong and deep that fear ran. In the camps of the Sioux and their allies, counting the reservation bands and those scattered across the Powder River country, there might be as many as ten thousand men of fighting age, while the entire army of the United States, stretched thin across a vast continent, numbered only twenty-five thousand. After a generation of bloodshed, the whites saw in any massing of the tribes but one possible consequence: the long-feared uprising that might overwhelm the sparsely garrisoned frontier posts and set back a final peace for years. Hardeman had heard these fears voiced during the long winter months in Kansas by townspeople and farmers, citizens and soldiers. Now, with such a gathering in the offing, the whites would howl for war, and any talk of new peace negotiations would be swept away like thistledown in a thunderstorm.

And on the Indian side it was far from certain that the terms agreed upon at the council in Two Moons' camp would survive once the bands were assembled in all their strength. The council had foreshadowed the change that might come about then—the defiance growing stronger and stronger as one man after another recalled the history of injustice at the hands of the whites and stated his willingness to fight before he would yield anything more. Sun Horse would speak for peace and some like Two Moons might support him, but others would speak as well, men who were hot for war, and in the end it might not be the words in council that would decide them, but the sight of hundreds, maybe thousands of lodges arrayed along some stream, the grass tall for the pony herds and the young men feeling the flow of new life and courage that all young men felt in springtime. They would imagine themselves invincible. "Let the *washíchun* come," they would say. "Let them bring as many soldiers as they wish. We will fight them!" The terms from yesterday's council would grow in proportion to the Indians' confidence until the demands were as unreasonable as those of the whites; until there was nothing left to say and only war remained.

Even if by some miracle the great union of the tribes did not result in war, the whites would never accept any new treaty that sprang from such a gathering. It would seem that the Indians were dictating terms from a position of overwhelming strength, and no matter how reasonable the terms might be, the white man's pride would make him refuse any settlement offered in such conditions.

No, there could be no summer council for the Sioux. If fighting were to be prevented, the peace must come now, swiftly and with no further talk, and Hardeman could see only one way to bring it about, using the same tactics by which he had originally planned to force a bloodless surrender on Sun Horse if all else failed, only now the prize would be the most famous of the hostile chiefs. With Sitting Bull taken to Dakota unharmed, there might be no summer gathering after all, and then there was a chance to salvage some of the good from the council at Two Moons' village. White politicians had been known to listen to a general who brought peace to a troubled region. If Crook could force a peace on the north plains while the country was still in the grip of winter, there was a chance that the things Crook believed in could be implemented here as they had been in the deserts of Apachería—justice for the Indian; promises made and promises kept. It would mean night marches and great caution if Crook's column were to reach Chalk Buttes and locate Sitting Bull's camp without being discovered by the hostile scouts. There was much risk in the plan, but nothing was gained without risk. On the way, Hardeman would tell Crook what had taken place at Two Moons' council, what had been said by Sitting Bull and Crazy Horse and the others. Without new fighting and bloodshed to arouse a new wave of hostility, Crook might persuade the men in Washington to be magnanimous in victory by granting some of what the Sioux asked, including a western Sioux reservation and an agency on the Yellowstone. With luck, and with white fears calmed by a victory, the terms reached in the council still might come to pass, although at the point of a gun.

The trail was following down the bed of a frozen creek and now the curving swale widened abruptly and ended, opening into the valley of a larger stream, which Hardeman guessed must be Otter Creek. Here the trail left the little rivulet and made straight for the larger watercourse. The wind had dropped and a few patches of moonlight shone through the clouds. As he neared the banks of the creek, Hardeman saw that the trail met a larger pathway there and he reined in sharply, looking to left and right at a swath of fresh tracks in the shallow snow.

He dismounted and led his horse along, his eyes on the ground, until he found what he sought. He squatted beside a dark clump on the trail and with his gloved hand he picked up a round ball of frozen horse manure. It seemed solid enough, but as he applied more force it suddenly broke and fell apart in his hand. He removed a glove and tested the road apple with his bare finger to be sure. The center was not frozen.

How long would it take horse dung to freeze solid on a night like this? One hour? Two? Not more than that. The clumps of droppings were scattered over a distance of fifteen or twenty feet. The horse was ridden. A horse on its own would stop to move its bowels.

Someone had passed this way recently. The Cheyenne hunting party? They had been only thirty; this group was larger, fifty or a hundred or more. It was hard to say how many, after a certain number of horses had passed along in a narrow row. It might have been a band of Sioux—Hunkpapas or Oglalas returning to another camp after a day of hunting. . . .

The new snow had been scattered by the many hooves and the older snow beneath had been broken up until it was as soft as sand; it shifted about underfoot and did not hold tracks well, but here and there on the edges of the trail were a few clear imprints. Hardeman took from the pocket of his jacket the tin box that contained his sulphur matches. He struck a light and saw the sharp outline of a shod hoof. Captured American horses?

A sudden fear chilled him. He returned to the dung and broke open another partially frozen dropping. He lit a second match and his fear was confirmed. The dung was not composed solely of digested grass. In the soft center of the road apple were the hulls of oats.

CHAPTER FIFTEEN

A weary soldier leaned against his horse to rest. Gradually his body relaxed and he dropped into the snow at the animal's feet, but the fall did not wake him. A form appeared out of the gloom of the ravine and leaned over the exhausted trooper.

"Luttner! Get up, man! You'll freeze to death!" Lieutenant Whitcomb shook the sleeping private harshly and hauled him to his feet. "Luttner? Do you hear me? You've got to stay awake! Here, Private Gray, Donnelly, keep an eye on him."

"We'll watch him, Mr. Reb," Gray said softly. "Come on, Heinie, snap out of it. There's a good fellow."

"Quietly, Mr. Reb, we don't want to advertise our presence." Whitcomb heard Corwin's voice before he saw his commander coming along the line. Somewhere above the clouds a half-moon shone down, but little of its light managed to penetrate the frozen gulch where the expedition had halted an hour before to allow the scouts to survey the land in front. Whitcomb thought the warning ridiculous. The horses were making enough noise to wake the dead, stamping and snorting from thirst. They had had nothing to drink since the previous afternoon. All the water encountered on the night march had been locked away under thick ice, and the axes were back with the cooks and the pack train.

"I'll be at the head of the column for a few moments," Corwin said. "See that the men are kept awake, but do it quietly."

"Yes, sir." Whitcomb continued on his way along the length of the troop, encountering first Dupré and then McCaslin. Sergeants Polachek and Duggan were on the move too. It seemed that a man fell to the ground every few moments only to be hauled to his feet by his comrades or one of his superiors.

After what had seemed an interminable delay at the stopping place of the afternoon before, the company officers had finally been summoned to the headquarters fire and there were given their instructions by General Crook. Colonel Reynolds and six companies had been detailed to leave at once on a forced march through the night. The scouts had discovered the back trail of the two Indian braves and were confident they could follow it to the hostile village. Fifteen scouts led by Big Bat, Little Bat and Frank Grouard had been sent along to guide the expedition.

They had marched for nine hours up the drainage of the winding creek, through rugged hill country frozen as solid as glass and just as treacherous under foot. The night had been pitch-dark until the waning moon rose at last; the clouds were broken for a time but then they regathered to drop new showers of snow on the soldiers, and even with the dim light afforded by the moon the going had been slow. The ground was cut everywhere with ravines, each of which had to be scouted on foot before a crossing was attempted. The men had traveled under the constant threat of being thrown when they were mounted or of losing their own footing when they led their horses over the worst obstacles. Miraculously, neither man nor horse had been seriously injured, but there had been many falls.

As the night lengthened, the temperature had plunged, and now, in the frigid arroyo, the waiting was almost unendurable, but few of the men complained. The entire campaign up to this moment, the sixteen days of marching through storms and sleeping through sub-zero nights, had had but a single goal—to launch a striking force against the hostiles. And now that force was on its way, following a recent trail, ready to do battle at a moment's notice. They were unencumbered by packers or mules or extra equipment. Each man carried the clothing he wore and a lunch, nothing more. Even the pistols had been left with the companies that remained behind. Only Captain Egan's Company K still had their Army Colts, for they would lead the charge when the Indian village was found.

Whitcomb thanked his lucky stars that E Troop had been one of the companies chosen for the night march. The four companies that had stayed with General Crook would start in the morning by a direct route for the juncture of the Powder and Lodgepole Creek, where the command would reunite within twenty-four hours, it was hoped. If there was to be a battle, they would miss it.

He stumbled on the rough ground and nearly fell, but someone caught his arm.

"Good God, Ham, have a care." It was John Bourke.

"Thanks, John. I haven't much feeling left in my feet, I'm afraid." He hopped from one foot to the other, hoping to stimulate the circulation.

"We're all having tough going. You'll see it through."

"I should say both horses and men are doing very well," said another voice, and Whitcomb made out Strahorn, the newspaperman, behind Bourke. Crook's aide was unattached, sent along on the march at his own request, free to go where he wished; he and Strahorn and Hospital Steward Bryan had formed a compact to stay close to one another and to be in the thick of the action if a fight came about. Throughout the night they had traveled in company with E Troop. "This is a difficult march under difficult circumstances," Strahorn said. "Your first campaign is turning out to be more than you bargained for, Mr. Reb."

"Not at all, Mr. Strahorn," Whitcomb replied with what he hoped was a convincing nonchalance. "It's everything I expected."

"Perhaps Mr. Bourke has seen worse?"

"I have marched about Arizona on nights just as dark, Robert, but none as cold as this."

From the head of the ravine a general rustling of equipment and a renewed stamping from the horses revealed that the waiting was over at last and the command was getting under way. The three men lost no time in reaching the head of the troop, where Steward Bryan was holding Bourke's and Strahorn's mounts. As they rose out of the ravine, following Company K, they found Captain Egan waiting there beside Lieutenant Corwin, and the two troop commanders fell in beside them. There had been no order to mount and the men were glad to walk for a time to stir some warmth into their limbs.

Egan was swinging his arms and bouncing about as he walked, and his teeth chattered as he spoke. "This is it, John," he said to Bourke. "A village, the scouts say."

"Where?! How far?"

"Oh, they haven't found it yet, but they will. Those two bucks we've been tracking are ahead of us now. Fresh tracks came in on their back trail and they joined up with some of their friends. Twenty or thirty of them, Grouard says, a big hunting party, all heading for home. 'Are you sure, Frank?' Reynolds asks. He's a cautious bastard, John, and you can tell Crook that for me when you see him. I wish old George was here. Anyway, Big Bat spits in the snow and he says 'You bet on it, General. Huntin' party goes out, they split up in threes and fours. When they come back together, they're makin' fer the lodge fires.' " Egan's mimicry of the scout's speech was close to perfect.

Being on the move once again quieted the horses, although they continued to shake their heads and snort, both from excitement and thirst. The gray horses of K Troop looked like ghostly shadows in the darkness, while E Troop's bays were all but invisible. Whitcomb's senses were sharpened by the anticipation of battle and the fear of premature discovery, and the rattle of the bridles and the whispered soothings of the troopers seemed to him a cacophony that could not fail to alert the hostiles, if any were near.

The attack force appeared to be on the apex of the entire region, having reached the headwaters of the creek they had followed all night and passed at last into another drainage that sloped away to the east. If anything, the land ahead of them was rougher than that behind. For an hour they stumbled along in silence and then Corwin raised a hand and pointed to the front. "Look there, Teddy. That's the bluffs of the Powder. I'll bet four bits."

"No, I think you're right. Damn, it's getting light already."

Not far ahead there was a perceptible bulging of the horizon. Between the land and the cloud bank above, a thin band of sky was visible, and it seemed to glow. The moon was high overhead and it could not account for the hint of brightness in the east. Dawn was approaching, and Whitcomb imagined that he knew what the two troop commanders must be thinking. If the scouts failed to find the end of the hunters' trail soon, the chance for a dawn attack would be lost. There could be no thought of a daylight assault unless conditions were perfect for achieving surprise; lacking that, the column would have to go to ground. Could the six companies of cavalry still fight effectively after a cold day in hiding with nothing but jerky and hardtack to eat? The horses needed water badly, and heavy demands had been put on them since the ration of grain they had received before parting company with Crook and the others. They had no large reserves of strength. Water and a day of rest might change that, but no fires could be made to melt snow and ice for drinking water, not this close to the hostiles.

Whitcomb could feel his heart pounding in his chest and he breathed deeply of the cold air to calm himself. There was nothing he could do to speed the column along, nothing to conjure an Indian village up out of the frozen ground.

But if there were a camp anywhere along the stretch of the Powder that lay just ahead, shouldn't there be a sign of smoke against the first light in the east? . . . Yes!

"John! Look there!" He nudged Bourke, who was walking beside him.

Bourke had been half asleep on his feet but now he jolted fully awake. Directly ahead, where Whitcomb was pointing, there was a dense column of smoke that had been hidden until now by a dark cloud far on the horizon. Others had seen it too, for the column halted now and Bourke and Whitcomb could make out the horseborne figures of several scouts moving off to investigate.

While the expedition waited once more, excited whispers flew up and down the column, but Bourke held himself apart from the others, watching the place where the scouts had disappeared, praying that they would find a village so General Crook's hopes for the attack force might be realized.

"Gentlemen," Crook had said once the company officers were gathered around him the afternoon before on the banks of the icebound creek. "I hope those Indians have taken the bait and believe we are proceeding towards the Yellowstone with no interest in pursuing them. But pursuing them is precisely my intention. The scouts have found their back trail and Frank is confident he can follow it in the dark." Here he had looked at the swarthy scout and Grouard had nodded, a little cautiously it had seemed to Bourke.

"The expedition will consist of the First, Third and Fifth Battalions," Crook had continued. "General Reynolds will be in command."

Bourke had been stunned. In each department where he had been stationed, George Crook was known as a commander who led his men into battle personally. He was always in the front, never in the rear. In Arizona he had eaten as much trail dust and smelled as much powder burned in anger as any man in the department. There could be only one explanation, Bourke had decided: Crook was giving Colonel J. J. Reynolds a chance to vindicate himself and burnish his reputation by making a good showing here. And it was not as if Crook himself would be safely in the rear; with only Hawley's and Dewees' four companies left to him he would have to protect the pack train, which would be a great temptation to any other hostiles who might happen upon the reduced command. He would have to make his way with that small force across some fifty miles of broken country to the appointed rendezvous with the attack force. But for Reynolds' sake he had given up the chance to be in at the kill.

When the officers' council was done, Bourke had asked Crook's permission to go with Reynolds and it had been granted at once. No doubt the general would be glad to hear a detailed report on the action, if any, and how Reynolds conducted himself throughout, although no such request had been made. Crook did not use Bourke as so many lesser men employed their aides, to follow them about like servants, awaiting any indication of their masters' pleasure. Bourke served as an extra pair of eyes and ears, an extension of his general, to be where he could not and to learn what the presence of a general officer would have prevented learning.

Already he had seen that Crook's faith in his scouts was justified. More than once during the night Grouard and the others had had to get down on their hands and knees to follow the faint signs, and more than once the trail had been lost, but never for long. They had proved themselves the equals of any scouts Bourke had known in Arizona, and the smoke rising so plainly in the east gave every indication that they had led Reynolds to the long-hoped-for goal: an unsuspecting village of hostiles.

Like those around him, Bourke was bitterly disappointed when the scouts returned.

"Coal measure!" came the whispered word. "Burning coal!"

The disappointment was general as the column got under way once more. They mounted their horses now and set off at a faster pace.

"I don't know if I can stand another false alarm like that," Whitcomb muttered.

"It's going to ruin my story if the whole campaign turns out to be a false alarm," said Strahorn.

They passed near the burning coal deposit and regarded the thick black smoke with hostile glances. It was not the first one they had seen and they felt they should have known better than to be taken in. They smelled the burning lignite and there seemed to be a sulphurous taint to the smoke, like a suggestion of hellfire. The Montana and Wyoming countryside abounded with such outcroppings, a surprising number of them on fire, set alight by some savage's campfire or by lightning. How long did they burn? Bourke wondered idly. Until they consumed the coal, or enough of it to deny air to the fire. The scouts said that one bed they had passed had burned for more than forty years.

The cloudy skies were brightening now and it was apparent that dawn was not far off, but scarcely a quarter of an hour later the alarm came again, "Smoke ahead!" and once again the cavalrymen came fully alert in an instant, all their senses straining to gather whatever they might have missed in a moment's inattention. The column halted and the three rearmost troops were brought up beside those in front so they stood in a double column, and all the officers were ordered to join Colonel Reynolds as he waited for the scouts to return.

"I think we will not be disappointed this time, gentlemen," he said. "Smell the air."

They did, and it was not the burning of coal they recognized, but woodsmoke. When the scouts returned, appearing silently out of the misty air, Frank Grouard was grinning.

"Big village, Colonel! Plenty horses! Down in the bottom. We find a way down, one here, one there."

He pointed, and aided by the other scouts, he conveyed what they had learned. Two rocky gorges led down to the river, hundreds of feet below. One emerged south of the village, they believed, and the other to the north. The village was west of the Powder, between the frozen stream and the mesa on which the command now stood. Its location had had to be judged by the situation of the large pony herds on the bottomland, but there was no doubt that a village was there and that it was a large one.

"We shall have to move without delay, gentlemen," Reynolds said after hearing the scouts out, and he gave his orders quickly. Captain Henry Noyes's Third Battalion, composed of his Company I and Egan's K Troop, would descend the southern gorge, led by Big and Little Bat and three other scouts. They would attack from that side as soon as they reached the bottom, with Egan's gray-horse company charging the village while Noyes himself secured the horse herd and drove it away upstream. Capturing the Indian horses and leaving the warriors afoot was a vital part of the scheme. Meanwhile, Captain Moore's Fifth Battalion, after being led to the valley floor by Frank Grouard and Louis Richaud, would advance from the bottom of the northern ravine to prevent escape in that direction; thus Moore would be the anvil against which Egan's hammer would strike. Mills's and Corwin's companies, the First Battalion, were to follow behind Moore and be kept in reserve, to be used as needed as the battle developed. Both of these battalions would lead their horses as far as possible and leave them in a safe location, going the rest of the way on foot. Reynolds was to accompany Moore and Mills; he wished Noyes and Egan Godspeed with a firm handshake to each one.

"Well, Ham old fellow, this is where we part company, I'm afraid," Bourke said to Whitcomb. "Mr. Strahorn, Steward Bryan, I propose we accompany Captain Egan."

"You lucky bastard!" said Whitcomb, but he was grinning and he shook Bourke's hand fervently.

"It's the luck of the Irish, boyo. Happy Saint Paddy's Day!" With a farewell wave, Bourke moved to join Egan, whose soldiers were already starting off behind Noyes's company. With Strahorn and Bryan close on his heels he joined Egan at the head of K Troop and in a short time the other elements of the attack force were left behind.

When the two companies reached the boulder-strewn defile that the guides had chosen for the descent, Bourke was aghast. It seemed impossible that men, let alone horses, could make their way down the eroded gorge, which was cluttered with fallen trees and undergrowth. Leading their mounts, the battalion entered the gorge in single file and immediately their progress was marked by the snapping of twigs and limbs as the guides forced a way through the brush. Saddles creaked in the cold and the men cursed as their horses stumbled repeatedly. Bourke winced at each stone overturned, every clatter of hoof against rock or frozen ground, but he soon ceased worrying about the noise and concentrated instead on getting himself to the bottom in one piece. There were frequent halts as one horse at a time was helped past the worst obstacles, and when the column emerged at last into a gentle vale that sloped away to the valley floor, the sky was bright overhead. The descent had taken more than an hour.

The vale was bordered on the left by an uneven ridge that intruded into the valley like an arm. Ahead, in the narrow width of valley bottom that was all they could see, there was no sign either of an Indian village or the expected horse herd.

"Is this where we're supposed to be?" Noyes wondered aloud. Neither four years at West Point nor fifteen years of army service since then had erased his strong Maine accent.

Egan nodded to Big and Little Bat. "You boys have a look-see over that ridge."

The two scouts mounted their horses and raced off to a low saddle that was fringed with pines. They were out of sight for only a few moments and when they returned they brought shocking news. "We ain't nowhere close to the village, Cap'n," Big Bat said to Noyes. "You best see for yourself. We can cross the ridge up yonder."

The battalion mounted and followed the scouts over the saddle and into the much broader valley beyond, where they halted again. To their right was the Powder. Ahead of them lay a wide benchland divided roughly in two by a small creek that flowed from the west. Beyond the benchland, over a mile away, where the river swept close to steep, rugged bluffs that overlooked the valley, the peaks of many tipis were visible in a sizable stand of cottonwoods. Nearer at hand in the valley bottom, which was ten or twenty feet lower than the edge of the benchland, hundreds of ponies were grazing in plain view.

"My God, we've botched it!" Noyes exclaimed.

"Couldn't be helped, Cap'n," Big Bat said. "Frank, he reckoned the village was down about there." He pointed to the foot of the ridge behind them. "It was there, we'd be sittin' pretty."

"Look!" cried Bourke, pointing across the benchland. There, on the southern end of the bluffs, was a line of men on foot advancing toward the slopes overlooking the village. Below and behind these small figures was another group, probably Mills's command, descending the edge of the benchland beyond the creek. Noyes's battalion, which had confidently expected to be the first into battle, was in danger now of being the last.

"That must be Moore up on the bluff," Egan said. "It looks like he's trying to work his way along to the north end of the village. He might still cut off their retreat."

"But the Indians will see him!" Strahorn objected.

"They can't yet but they will soon enough," said Egan. "The quicker we get into the village, the better." This last remark was directed at Noyes.

"You don't think the mix-up calls for any change of plan?" Noyes seemed perplexed by the discovery that Reynolds' plan of attack could not be executed as originally given.

"Good God, Henry!" Egan exploded. "We're the only ones who still have a chance to do what we're supposed to! Let's get on with it!" He yanked his horse around and started off with his troop following behind, placing Noyes in the awkward position of hastening to overtake his nominal subordinate.

"These animals don't have much spunk left," Egan said to Bourke, reining in from a trot to a fast walk. "Damn the luck, anyway! I just pray to God we get close to that village before some young buck decides it's time for a look around the countryside."

In a double column the battalion crossed the benchland. Once down off the low ridge they were out of sight of the village, and the danger of sudden discovery lessened for a time. As they crossed the little creek they saw Mills's battalion emerge from a gully not far ahead, and Egan sent one of the scouts to tell Mills to hold back until the attack began, then to come in and support him from behind.

"I can't see Moore," said Bourke, searching the bluff that now rose close above them.

"I hope to hell he keeps out of sight until we get into the village," Egan muttered. "If the Indians see us now and set up a defense, we'll be in hot water."

The battalion was approaching the northern edge of the benchland, and once more the peaks of tipis could be seen among the cottonwoods on the river plain below. The scouts, who had been moving ahead of the column to watch for gullies that might impede its advance, now returned.

"Injuns wakin' up, Cap'n," said Little Bat. "Boys 're takin' the horses to water."

"Better yet," said Egan, pleased. "The ponies will be that much farther from the village. Where do we get down off this bench?"

"Go down here," Little Bat replied, gesturing to a gully nearby. "Ain't many trails good for horses up ahead."

"Dismount. Pass it back," Noyes called out in a soft voice as he swung out of his own saddle.

Like dominoes toppling in a row, the mounted men leaned over one by one and stepped to the ground. Overhead, two ravens floated on motionless wings and one of the birds croaked twice; otherwise the valley was silent but for the soft rush of the wind and the small stampings and whuffings of the horses.

Egan glanced at Noyes, who nodded. "You go ahead, Teddy. We'll follow you. I'll separate to the right when you form into line."

Egan moved part-way down the short column of troopers and addressed his company in a tone just loud enough for all to hear. "Once we're down below, mount up when I do. Forward by twos and left front into line on my signal. Trot until we're seen. Buglers will then sound the charge, and forward at the gallop." He grinned. "From then on it's Murphy's saloon, boys. Don't be afraid to let them hear you coming."

As they descended the gully the soldiers were hidden from the village and when they gathered on the bottomland only a few tipis were visible at the edge of the cottonwoods. There was no movement there.

The scouts drew aside as the soldiers formed up by company. The attack was up to the troopers. For now, the scouts' job was done. Together with the men who had guided the other companies to the valley floor, they would join Colonels Stanton and Reynolds, to be reassigned as needed during the fighting.

"Good luck, John," Egan said to Bourke as he set his foot in his stirrup. As one the troop mounted behind him and the riders moved out two by two, straight toward the river. Bourke rode beside Egan, with Strahorn and Bryan right behind. When the company was formed in a straight column, Egan raised his arm and swung it to the left. In the space of a few heartbeats the troop had executed a letter-perfect left front into line, and the forty-seven horses and riders advanced in a company front, breaking into a trot. Behind them, Noyes's black-horse troop moved away from the gully in a column and swung off to the right, toward the pony herd. K Troop's grays strutted as they advanced, sensing the repressed excitement of their riders, but the line remained as straight as if they were on parade, and still, ahead of them, the village was silent.

CHAPTER SIXTEEN

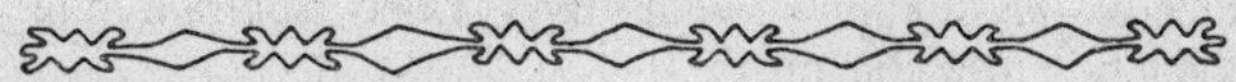

Blackbird came awake with a start. Daylight showed through the lodgeskins; the winds were gentle and the camp was quiet. It was early then, if the women were not yet up and about.

The fits of sweating that had kept him in a feverish haze for most of the day before were gone now and his leg no longer throbbed beneath the tight wrappings the Shahíyela *wapíye* had placed around the wound. He felt much better, and unusually alert.

What had wakened him? It was as if he had heard a distant calling or a strange sound, but everything was quiet; unnaturally so, it seemed.

That was it! He raised himself on his elbows to see the pallet where his father had slept each night since they had been in the Shahíyela camp. His father was gone! And so was his uncle Lodgepole and the *washíchun* Hardeman! All his life Blackbird had slept with his father's soft snoring close at hand. He had been awakened not by a sound but by the absence of one so familiar he scarcely noticed it until it was gone.

He sat up and reached for his moccasins, grunting slightly as the movements awakened a pain deep in his leg. Ignoring the pain he struggled into the tall winter moccasins and laced them tightly.

A voice said something in Shahíyela and he saw that Kills Fox was awake.

"Where is my father?" Blackbird asked.

"The *washíchun* scout runs away," Kills Fox replied in crude Lakota. "He go to bring the horse soldiers, your father say. Your father, your *washíchun* uncle, Hawk Chaser, they go after him. They find him, they kill him."

The *washíchun* Hardeman a traitor? His father and Lodgepole gone? They had left him here! Blackbird struggled to his feet, but he fell back as pain shot through his leg.

"They come back for you!" Kills Fox said, motioning Blackbird to stay. "Stay here. Get better. They come back."

"I am the moccasin carrier!" Blackbird protested. He looked about desperately and saw the poles that had been used to carry his makeshift litter to the council lodge. He seized one and used it as a crutch to heave himself to his feet. If he could only get to his horse he might be able to ride. He threw his lionskin cape over his shoulders and struggled awkwardly to belt his robe around him.

Kills Fox's wife and children were awake now. The woman spoke to her husband, and although Blackbird could not understand her words, he knew by her tone and the concerned expression on her face that she was urging Kills Fox to make him stay.

Kills Fox merely shrugged in reply. The boy was not his son, nor even of his tribe. He was moccasin carrier to the Lakota messengers and he had his own responsibilities. It was not for Kills Fox to tell him what to do. He made a gesture wishing the boy well.

Blackbird smiled gratefully and with a few words of thanks he slipped out of the lodge.

It was well past sunrise but still the village slept. In winter there was no rush to leave the warmth of the buffalo robes. The day was cloudy and cold and there was a thin mist in the valley bottom. Blackbird shivered. He wondered how he would ever find his horse and then he remembered that the pipe carriers' horses had been taken to the bottom of the camp after the council of the day before, so the little band could leave early in the morning. He started hobbling in that direction, but even with the help of his makeshift crutch, pain shot through his wounded leg at every step. If the wound began to bleed he would grow weak, and what use would he be to his father then?

He saw a fur-clad youth riding among the tipis and he recognized him as Lakota, a nephew of He Dog. He waved to get the boy's attention.

"*Hau*, cousin! Will you take me to my horse? I have to go after my father and the other pipe carriers."

"You're Standing Eagle's son, aren't you? I'm glad your wound is better. Does it hurt much?"

"Not much," Blackbird lied. "Will you take me to my horse?"

"Come, I'll help you." The youth held out a hand and hoisted Blackbird up behind him. At once some of the pain left Blackbird's leg. Sitting on the horse was much better than walking.

"I'm going after our horses now," the youth said. "Many scouts are going out to watch for the bluecoats. My uncle He Dog is going with them."

"Bluecoats? Where are the bluecoats? Has someone seen them?"

"The hunters saw them. Didn't you hear?"

"I've been asleep since yesterday after the council."

"Shahíyela hunters came back in the night. They saw the bluecoats half a day's ride to the north, going toward the Yellowstone."

"Wait, you're going the wrong way! Our horses are over there." Blackbird pointed toward the downstream end of camp but the boy shook his head.

"The *washíchun* turned them loose. Your father and the others found their horses with the herd. I hope they catch the *washíchun* and come back with his scalp." The youth kicked the pony into a trot and Blackbird held on to the other boy, bouncing painfully. He felt an increased sense of urgency now. If the soldiers were going toward the Yellowstone there might be no immediate danger, but why had Hardeman gone off alone? Why hadn't he waited so the pipe carriers could all go together and take the pipe to Three Stars? Had the white scout really gone to betray them? Hardeman was his uncle Lodgepole's friend. "Not all white men are bad," Lodgepole had said to Blackbird one afternoon on the trail north, before the attack by the *Kanghí*. "This one has been like a *hunká*-father to your cousin, the One Who Stands Between the Worlds. He is a good man and he speaks the truth." But Blackbird remembered other words as well, words his father often said: "Do not go to the hilltop for water nor to a white man for the truth." It seemed his father was right.

There were a few other boys among the trees, gathering the horses to drive them to water, and Blackbird looked everywhere for the familiar coloring and three white moccasins of his own horse. The ponies moved among the plum bushes and cottonwoods, appearing and disappearing, and he began to fear that it would take all morning to find the sturdy pinto when suddenly he saw the half-white, half-black face that he knew so well.

"There he is! That one!"

"I see him. You go on foot and I'll bring him to you."

Blackbird slipped to the ground, forgetting his wound in his excitement and grunting as a jolt of pain reminded him. The Lakota youth trotted off, placing himself between Blackbird's horse and the others, guiding him out of the trees and away from the river.

As the pinto drew near Blackbird he caught the boy's scent and whickered softly. Blackbird said a few words to calm the animal and he stood still as the pinto stepped close to sniff his outstretched hand to see if it held some sweetgrass or perhaps some dried buffaloberries. The rawhide rein slipped easily over the pony's lower jaw and Blackbird fastened his braided war rope around the horse's middle. His injured leg would not grip the horse properly, but the war rope would hold him in place.

"Thank you, cousin," he said to the Lakota youth. He realized he didn't know the young man's name.

"Ride quickly!" the youth encouraged him. "Maybe

you can count coup on the whiteman's body!" He trotted off after the other boys.

Blackbird tried to jump to his pony's back but his wounded leg buckled and he nearly fell. He needed something to stand on. He was in a wide, flat-bottomed wash that led from the base of the bluff to the river. It was deeper than the height of a man and twenty or thirty paces across. Not far away there was a short stump. He started toward it, supporting himself with one hand on the pony's withers. He realized now that he was thirsty and very hungry. In the village, smoke was puffing up from a few lodges as the women built up the fires. He thought of stopping to get a little *wasná* or jerky from Kills Fox's wife. But someone might ask where he was going. The scouting party might want him to wait and go with them, and he didn't want to wait for anyone. He was moccasin carrier for the Sun Band's pipe carriers and it was his duty to catch up with them as soon as he could. Worse yet, someone not as understanding as Kills Fox might insist that he remain in camp and not go out at all. The *akíchita* could keep a young man in camp if a scouting party was planned.

No, he would not risk stopping in the village. He would follow the broad channel to the bluff and ride around the back of the camp to the downstream end. He would find the pipe carriers' tracks and start out on their trail at once.

The thought of setting out alone frightened him a little, but he had been given another chance to prove himself a man and he must take every opportunity he got. Besides, there was really no reason to be afraid. Hadn't he saved the pipe carriers' horses? Hadn't he counted coup on a *Kanghí* enemy? And hadn't he sat in council with Sitting Bull and Little Wolf and Crazy Horse? The recollection of his recent deeds and the honors they had won him bolstered his courage and he felt himself well along the path to manhood.

He had nearly reached the stump when a fluttering in the corner of his eye caught his attention. He turned to see that the branches of an old cottonwood not far away were filled with black specks; here and there a head cocked or a wing flashed, revealing a bright red patch. The tree was alive with blackbirds. They were the first he had seen since autumn and their arrival was a sure sign of spring.

He felt a chill, and tightened the thong that held his robe belted at the waist. There was nothing springlike about the day. Riding would warm him. He climbed atop the stump and was about to mount his pony when he felt the chill again, not truly a chill of the body but more of the senses.

Taku shkanshkan. Something is moving.

It was as if he heard his grandfather's voice. How often had the old man told him to be aware of the motion of spirit power, of *shkán*, the life force that pervaded all things?

Taku shkanshkan, Sun Horse said whenever Blackbird tried to explain some inexplicable feeling he had had, some sense of the mysterious powers that moved invisibly through the world. Something sacred is moving, the old man would say, as if that explained anything to a boy of fifteen winters.

With a shock of recognition he realized that this was the feeling that had awakened him that morning, not simply the absence of his father's snoring but this sense of power moving about him, calling him from sleep. The feeling had brought him out of the lodge and here to this place, where he found a tree full of blackbirds, his spirit helpers, the messengers from the vision that had given him his young man's name.

Had they come here today as messengers? He watched them intently, as if they might tell him something of great import, when suddenly they took to the air as one, clucking a *chk, chk, chk* of alarm, and flew off in a tight cloud down the river.

And now Blackbird felt the hair on the back of his neck rise as he made out other sounds that seemed to come from all around him. He heard the sound of many feet stepping in the cold snow and something like the bells on the sticks the Lakota horse dancers carried in their ceremonies, but not so sharp and clear; it was the clink of metal on metal;

he heard leather creaking, and beneath these noises he heard breathing, tens of mouths breathing, the spirit world breathing in his ear.

He could not move. His skin seemed to have become rigid, as if he were encased in a coating of ice.

His eyes saw motion on his left and suddenly all the sounds came from there. Fur hats were the first thing he saw, rising above the bank of the wide channel all in a row. Then faces came in sight, eyes almost hidden beneath the fur caps pulled low. The faces were covered with hair.

The heads rose higher, supported on shoulders and bodies that sat, that did not move, but still they jogged up and down and drew nearer, looming above him all in a row. The men were cloaked in furs and dark colors. They were whitemen. Now he saw the horses, all gray. Every horse a gray horse but for three on the near end of the line. Eyes swung in Blackbird's direction and found him.

No man made a sound and each held a pistol in his hand. All in a line on their gray horses they reached the edge of the bank and rode down into the wash.

The behavior of the riders was otherworldly. Were they spirit riders or men?

It didn't matter. They were upon him now. The end of the line would pass within ten paces of his stump. The breath puffed from the horses' nostrils and steam rose from their coats. He could see the breathing of the men too.

Blackbird inhaled deeply, noticing the clean taste of the air. It filled him until he felt light enough to rise up and float away. He would fly away like the blackbirds.

The second man from the end of the line pointed his pistol at Blackbird and the boy heard a *chk* as the hammer was drawn back. The sound was unnaturally loud and seemed to echo in the wide ravine. *Chk, chk, chk, chk.* All along the line came the sounds now, like the warning of the blackbirds.

CHAPTER SEVENTEEN

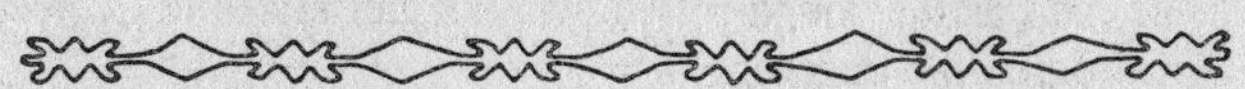

"Let him alone, John."

Bourke lowered his Colt, grateful that Egan had spoken. He hadn't really wanted to shoot the boy, whose courage in the face of certain death was impressive. He had aimed instinctively to prevent the boy from giving an alarm but then he had realized that a shot would wake the village just as surely.

Keeping to its steady, unhurried trot, the company was across the wash and up the far bank in a few moments. Bourke looked back. The boy stood as before, motionless atop the stump, but as Bourke watched he leaped to his pony's back, giving a whoop that sounded almost joyful, and galloped away toward the river where he disappeared among the trees. Bourke saw another rider there, then two more, youths pushing a few horses to the river to drink. They looked up, startled by the cry, and saw the cavalry. It was a miracle that they had not seen the soldiers before now. The first boy's exultant whoop sounded again from among the trees.

"Easy now," Egan said calmly. The troop was nearing the plum bushes that girdled the near end of the village. Egan slipped out of his greatcoat and let it drop to the ground, and along the line others followed his example, freeing themselves for action. In the village, dogs began to bark.

The riders threaded their way among the bushes and emerged in a ragged but unbroken line on the far side just as the entrance flap of the nearest lodge was raised from within. A woman looked out and her eyes and mouth opened wide. For a moment she made no sound; then she took a sharp breath that Bourke could hear from thirty feet away and she let out a frightened cry. Her head vanished and the flap fell closed, and for a heartbeat the village was as it had been before. Then came a shot from the far end of the line, answered at once by the distinctive report of a cavalry carbine; the two shots echoed off the face of the bluff, and as the sound rolled away, Egan raised his voice and ordered the charge.

The K Troop bugler had been holding his instrument to his lips for several moments, nervously awaiting the order. His first notes overlapped Egan's shout and the line broke into a gallop, splitting into fragments as it reached the lodges. Some of the men fired at random into the tipis and then suddenly the camp erupted in chaos. Men, women and children poured from the lodges like sparks from a hundred fires and running figures were everywhere, many lightly clothed or partially naked, as they had slept. The men had weapons and they began to use them at once as others ushered the women and children toward the brush and boulders at the base of the bluffs.

The troop was in the midst of the thickest grouping of tipis now, and they began to hear the sound of bullets ripping the air around them. A horse screamed and went down, blood and intestines pouring from its stomach as if from a burst balloon. The troop farrier called out "Help me, boys, I'm stuck!" as he struggled to free his leg from the weight of the writhing animal. The stark panic in the cry of the mortally wounded horse sent a chill through Bourke. He raised his pistol, looking for a target, but he seemed to see nothing but women and children running every which way around him, all glancing at the soldiers as if they were devils incarnate.

"There's something wrong with my horse," Hospital Steward Bryan said, and Bourke looked over to see only a wet bulge of bloody flesh where the animal's right eye should have been. The horse pitched forward, throwing Bryan clear. A single shot had pierced both of the animal's eyes, killing it so suddenly that its heart continued to pump, its muscles to work, carrying it a dozen paces beyond where it had been struck before it finally fell.

"Are you all right?" Bourke reined in beside Bryan and he realized that he had shouted at the top of his lungs although the stunned youth was only an arm's length away. The din of battle was growing around them, shouts of anger and fear making more noise than the scattering of shots exchanged between the soldiers and the fleeing Indians.

"That's the one!" Bryan shouted suddenly, pointing at a warrior kneeling behind a nearby lodge, hastening to reload his flintlock. "He killed my horse!" He leaped to his feet and raced toward the Indian, holding his pistol aloft as if he intended to bash the murderer over the head with it. The Indian ran off toward the bluffs with Bryan hot on his heels. Realizing that he was in danger of running straight into the arms of the hostiles, Bryan suddenly reversed direction and scampered back as quickly as he had gone.

"That boy can run," Egan observed. "I'd like to have him on my team for the regimental foot races. Oh, look out, John!" He swerved his mount as a brave jumped from a tipi and fired in their direction. Bourke's horse jerked his head as the right rein fell loose, cut neatly by the bullet just inches from the bit. The animal reared and Bourke nearly lost his seat. He brought the horse under control with pressure from his legs, leaning forward in the saddle and pulling on the left rein, wheeling the frightened beast in a tight circle until it came to a stop, panting, and allowed Bourke to dismount. Egan leveled his Colt at the now defenseless brave, but the Indian flung his ancient musket at Egan, and as the troop commander ducked to avoid it, the brave sprinted off, leaping a fallen cavalry horse as lithely as a deer and vanishing into the brush.

"I wish Mills would get in here!" Egan reined his horse around, trying to make some sense of the sporadic action around him. The advance had stalled in the center of the village. With their women and children shepherded to safety, some of the warriors were working their way back among the lodges.

"We'd better—" As Egan started to speak, a ball struck his horse in the neck and the animal dropped dead in its tracks, barely giving Egan time to throw a leg out of the stirrup to avoid being pinned, as the farrier had been. The fall knocked the wind out of him and he was gasping for breath as Bourke helped him up from the ground.

"They're not stupid, you know," Egan said when he could speak again. "They're shooting at the horses."

The handful of troopers who had overrun their commanding officer and advanced farther into the village were falling back now, firing as they retreated. Bourke realized that he was panting as if from hard physical exertion. He forced himself to breathe slowly as he sighted at an Indian darting among the lodges, working his way towards the soldiers, but his shot went wild as a horseman galloped up, causing Bourke's own horse to shy and jostle him. The rider was the bugler from Noyes's company. He jerked back on his reins, dropping the horse to his haunches; the skidding hooves sprayed dirt and snow around Egan's feet.

"Major Noyes's compliments, sir, and he begs to inform the captain that he is having some difficulty gathering all the Indian horses. Major Corwin has gone to help us and Major Noyes expects to have them in hand soon enough. He inquires to know what your situation is."

"He'll have them in hand, will he? I wish to Christ I had something in hand. Do me a favor, will you? Sound dismount. I haven't seen my bugler since we started the charge."

As the call to dismount sounded through the village it was picked up by another bugle not far away, and K Troop's bugler came riding to rejoin his captain.

"You stick by me, dammit!" Egan barked, and he turned back to Noyes's man. "You can tell Major Noyes I am holding my ground but I would appreciate some reinforcement as soon as possible. If you see Captain Mills on your way back, give him my compliments and tell him to get his ass in here!"

Noyes's bugler saluted and rode away. The men of the troop were grouping on Egan now, leading their horses. One man held a shattered elbow. Another cried out suddenly and fell to the ground spewing blood, shot through the neck.

"Someone help that man, and follow me!" Egan called out. "Sergeant McGregor! Defensive line along the river!" He led the way toward the thick growth of trees and bushes along the river, on the east side of the village. A riderless horse galloped past, stirrups pounding its flanks, reins trailing.

Once among the brush, Egan and his non-commissioned officers dispersed the company in a line facing the village and the bluffs beyond. One man in eight gathered the horses and led them away to a cluster of cottonwoods at the southern edge of the village. The cavalry bridle included a link-strap, a fifteen-inch piece of leather clipped to the bit ring and throatlatch. Whenever the troop dismounted, the horse handler in each set of four unclipped the link-straps from the throatlatches and hooked them to the bit ring of the next horse until he had four horses on a single lead. In battle, one man in eight held the horses, freeing all the rest to fight without concerning themselves for the safety of their mounts.

"It's a big village," Bourke observed when Egan was satisfied with the placement of his men and returned to take a position between Bourke and Strahorn. Nearby, Steward Bryan was tending the unhorsed farrier, who had been shot through the shoulder.

Egan nodded. "Bigger than it looked at first. There must be a hundred lodges here."

"We still outnumber the braves two to one, I should think."

"Not with this troop on its own, we don't. Reynolds has got five other companies out there and I'd like to know what in Christ's name he's doing with them." He turned to Steward Bryan. "Do you know how many wounded we have?"

"Three at least, sir, probably more. Your Private Schneider isn't likely to make it. Another man is shot through the stomach but he may survive."

"There are six horses dead too, sir." A sergeant threw himself to the ground beside Egan as bullets clipped the brush above his head. "Three more wounded. As best I can make out, the wounded men are not the ones whose horses are shot, with Private Goings the only exception."

"Which means a quarter of the troop is either wounded or unhorsed," Egan said dryly. "That's a hell of a score for— How long would you say, John? I looked at my watch when we came through the bushes."

Bourke thought for a moment. In battle, time was notoriously hard to judge, but he had some experience. "Thirty minutes," he guessed. "Thirty-five."

"Well, which is it? Thirty or thirty-five. A dollar if you're within five minutes."

"Thirty-five."

Egan rolled on his side to reach through his blanket coat and withdraw a pocket Waltham. "Forty minutes even! You lucky so-and-so. Another minute and I'd have won. I owe you, if we get out of here alive." He grinned.

"You're not serious, are you, Captain?" They were the first words Strahorn had spoken since the battle began, although he had never strayed more than a few yards from Bourke and Bryan.

"Oh, we'll try to get you out of here in one piece, Mr. Strahorn," Egan said good-naturedly. "But just so your notes are accurate, I should point out that the attack is not going exactly according to plan."

"Where the hell is Moore, that's what I want to know," Bourke said. He rose to his feet in a crouch and fired three quick shots with his Colt.

"Find a target, John," Egan cautioned. Several bullets cut the brush nearby, forcing the men to duck down. Egan raised his head slowly. "Look at that, dammit!" he exclaimed. "The red bastards are all up and down the bluffs!" He pointed at the rugged slopes, where puffs of smoke came from concealed positions that commanded excellent views of the village. In addition, fire came from warriors who were moving among the lodges, threatening to retake the ground K Troop had abandoned as it withdrew to cover along the river.

Egan aimed his carbine at a brave climbing the bluff face and he fired. A puff of dust to the Indian's right showed where he had missed. "Son of a bitch. I'll tell you one place Moore isn't. He isn't where he ought to be. What in Christ's name is so hard about moving along those bluffs and getting in position to cover us?"

"Good God!" Bourke exclaimed suddenly. "Look there! You don't suppose that's him over there?" He pointed to a place low on the southern flank of the bluffs, where a few clouds of white smoke revealed an uncertain fire from a more removed position.

"He can't even see the Indians from there! He's shooting at us! Jesus!"

"It's a good thing he's too far away to do much damage," Bourke observed. He reloaded his pistol and holstered it, then looked to the load of his carbine. Unlike the officers that preferred to purchase their own side arms, he had always kept the cavalry's standard issue. He fired a round at an Indian high on the bluff.

"Here's some help, sir," said the sergeant, pointing through the trees. "It must be Captain Mills."

Off to the left, where K Troop had first entered the village, men on foot were advancing close to the base of the bluffs, pushing the Indians before them as they came.

"It's about time," said Egan. "Sergeant Fisher, I want you to go down the line and instruct the men to concentrate their fire on the Indians on the hillside. Mills will need some cover."

The sergeant disappeared in the brush and a moment later the rate of fire from Egan's troopers increased.

Hoofbeats sounded to the front. A lone warrior raced through the village straight at the advancing soldiers, shooting with a revolver. When the gun was empty he threw it at them, then wheeled and galloped back the way he had come, hanging on the side of his horse. Shots from Mills's men chased him and K Troop set up a deafening fusillade, but as the Indian disappeared from sight in the trees he raised himself upright and shouted his triumph.

"By God, they've got courage, you have to give them that." It was Strahorn who spoke, standing to get a last look at the horseman. A ball snapped twigs a handsbreadth from his shoulder and he dropped to the ground.

"Some of them can shoot, too, Robert." Bourke grinned.

"Here's some more o' the boys, sorr." Private Goings, the wounded farrier, had joined the officers, together with Steward Bryan. Goings gestured with a pistol. Another line of men on foot was coming along behind Mills, this one extending from the middle of the village almost to the river. Their advance would bring them close in front of K Troop.

"This is more like it," Egan said. "I wonder who it is."

"It's Boots Corwin!" cried Bourke. "I know that red beard. And there's Ham Whitcomb."

"All right, boys!" Egan shouted down the line. "We'll move out when they reach us. This time we're going to clear the camp. Covering fire!" He fired at the hillside and flipped up the trapdoor in the carbine's breech as he dropped it to his waist to reload. Around him the bushes sprouted fire and smoke as the men of Company K peppered the face of the bluffs.

The firing continued for several minutes and there were cheers from Corwin's men as they advanced. The Indians in the village were falling back, firing hastily and then dashing to a new hiding place before they stopped to reload. With repeating rifles they'd be a match for us, Bourke thought. His fingers were almost too cold to hold his carbine firmly and he thought wistfully of his greatcoat, discarded with the others back at the southern end of the village.

E Troop's line was coming on fast. They had passed by Mills's men and were nearly at Egan's position. Egan fired a last time and stepped out of the brush, struggling with his carbine.

"Someday I'm going to meet the man who designed this extractor," he said to no one in particular. He pulled out a pocketknife and pried at the base of the jammed cartridge with the blade until at last it popped free. "Boots! Over here!" He waved to Corwin.

"John!" Ham Whitcomb came running up to Bourke and seized him by the hand. "My gosh it's good to see you! What a morning we've had! We brought the horses all the way down and I'm damn glad we did. Mills's are still up on top of the mesa. First we got sent off to help Noyes and I thought we'd never get to see any fighting, but then Reynolds heard you wanted reinforcements and here we are! Our horses are back there with yours now."

As the words gushed out of him he was pumping Bourke's hand all the while and now he noticed that Bourke was wincing in pain.

"What's the matter, John? You're not hurt?"

"No, nothing like that. But there's something not right with my hand." He slipped off his right glove. The tips of three of his fingers were a stark, lifeless white.

Steward Bryan appeared at Bourke's side. "Here, let me have a look, sir." He took the hand and inspected it. "That's frostbite, sir. You'll have to come along with me." He led Bourke off toward the river holding him by the arm, and Bourke raised his carbine in farewell to Whitcomb.

"I'll see you later, Ham! We'll catch up with you."

"Mr. Whitcomb!"

Whitcomb turned to see Corwin beckoning him. Captain Egan and his men were moving off toward the center of the village, joining up with Mills's line. There seemed to be a lull in the firing.

"You will be responsible for this end of the line," Corwin said when Whitcomb joined him. "I want you to take twenty men and get to the far end of the village as quickly as you can. You shouldn't find any resistance there just now. Take Polachek and McCaslin and Stiegler. Put the men in cover and watch out the Indians don't try to flank us by moving up across the river. I'll join up on your left as soon as I can."

"Major Corwin!" First Sergeant Dupré came running up at a lumbering trot, breathing hard. As he ran, the waxed points of his mustache bounced like curls of wire spring. "General Reynolds, sair, he has given orders to burn the village. In my opinion this is a mistake. We 'ave found meat, sair, a great deal of meat. And robes, and much gunpower in kegs, enough to supply us until summertime. If we can hold the village and send a *courier* to General Crook, I think maybe he will wish to use this as a base camp."

Corwin nodded. "I'll have a word with Captain Mills. Maybe we can both speak to Reynolds. Lieutenant Whitcomb, you will take your position and hold it until you hear further from me, understood?"

"Understood, sir." Whitcomb saluted and they parted, Corwin going off with Dupré and Whitcomb trotting to overtake the troop, which was still in a line but advancing more slowly now, as the sergeants and corporals awaited further orders.

"Polachek! McCaslin!" The two men turned at the sound of their names and waited for Whitcomb to overtake them. A few troopers drew near to hear what was in store. "We're to establish a perimeter at the far edge of the village and prevent the Indians from flanking us on the right." He gave the orders crisply. It had taken him a moment to understand that Corwin had given him command of nearly half the troop. There would be no hesitation here, no reason to find fault now or later. Orders would be obeyed at once and to the letter. When the battle was done Boots Corwin might invent some reprimand if he wished, but there would be no good cause for one.

There was a sound like a ripe melon breaking on the ground, and something wet spattered Whitcomb's face and coat. A few feet away, Private Peter Dowdy slumped to the ground. A bullet had struck him in the head.

Whitcomb wiped his face and saw blood on his glove. He stared dumbly at the body. Dowdy looked up at him with eyes that no longer saw. The youth was sprawled awkwardly, half twisted on his side.

During the war Whitcomb had seen dead men in Petersburg, some of them stacked like firewood, but they had been stiff impersonal things. He had never seen the spark of life snuffed out before. Already the frigid air was glazing over Dowdy's eyeballs, making them dull and lifeless, while the grisly wound continued to ooze blood. Whitcomb knelt by the corpse and closed the eyes. He looked up at Corporal McCaslin. "It would seem the heathen does some smiting of his own." He rolled the body onto its back and arranged the limbs, folding the arms on the chest. "Do we just leave him here?" he asked.

"There isn't much else we can do, sorr," said McCaslin. "He won't mind."

Whitcomb became aware that Polachek and the others were watching him. He saw his own shock mirrored in the troopers' faces, but the expression of Private John Gray revealed only a sad acceptance.

"You have your orders, Sergeant. Quickly, now."

"Yes, sir. Chentlemen, if you please." Polachek addressed the soldiers like a schoolmaster. He herded them away from the body and they spread out in a line once more, but McCaslin remained with Whitcomb.

Whitcomb got to his feet. "I'll be all right, Walter."

"Yes, sorr. I'm sure of that."

McCaslin left him then. Whitcomb felt a little dizzy, although whether from hunger or fatigue or the shock of Dowdy's death, he wasn't sure. He bent over and removed Dowdy's cartridge belt and then he started after his men.

The village immediately around him was quiet, although there was some firing farther away. Once the village was securely in the hands of the cavalry, the hostiles would no doubt melt into the hills.

He had gone perhaps fifty yards when he came on Private Donnelly kneeling beside a fallen Indian. As Whitcomb drew near, the Indian screamed and his legs jerked.

"What are you doing?" Whitcomb demanded.

"None o' your affair, friend," Donnelly replied without

looking up. "I done for this one meself and he's all mine."

"I asked what you were doing, Private."

Now Donnelly glanced up. "Oh, sorry, sir. Just getting a souvenir." He held up the Indian's penis and testicles, dripping blood.

"God damn it!" Whitcomb leveled his carbine at Donnelly. "God damn you! If I ever see you doing this again, if I even hear you have mutilated another Indian, I'll kill you myself! Now get away from me!"

Donnelly fled, but he kept hold of his souvenir. Whitcomb looked down at the dying Indian. The man's loin cover was raised and the bloody damage between his legs had made a pool of blood on the snow. The man had his hands clutched to his stomach, where Whitcomb could see intestines and more blood between the fingers. The Indian was looking steadily at Whitcomb. His breathing was shallow and rasping.

"Damn you too," Whitcomb gasped. He shot the Indian in the heart and turned away, swallowing hard, fighting to choke back his rising gorge.

I will not be sick, he told himself. In the space of a few minutes he had seen the first of his own men die and he had killed his first man, but it was not an honorable victory, not as if he had faced an equal foe in open combat. His mouth tasted of bile. He paused to lean against a tree, breathing deeply, hoping that the chill air would cleanse him.

A bullet struck the ground five yards away but he did not move. He would live or he would die. He would do what he could to survive, but he no longer felt a trembling fear like the one that had come over him after he had chased the beef herd and been pursued by the lone Indian. What he felt now was a sickness in the heart; it was deep within him, leaving him free to think and act, but he knew it had changed him forever. He would never be the same.

He became aware of hoofbeats approaching rapidly and he was surprised to see a white man on horseback coming from the north end of the village. The rider held no weapon in his hands and the rifle scabbard that hung on the near side of his saddle was empty. Whitcomb was sure he was not one of the expedition's scouts, although he wore buckskins and a long brown oilskin slicker whose tails flapped behind him as he leaned low over his horse's neck and darted among the trees, apparently making for a group of horsemen near a central cluster of tipis. Whitcomb recognized Colonel Reynolds among them.

"Get the renegade!" came a cry of alarm from among the men of K Troop.

"He's after General Reynolds!" another voice shouted.

A volley of shots chased the rider and he seemed suddenly to lose interest in his goal. The reins dropped from his hands and he slumped in the saddle; the horse slowed and veered toward the base of the cliffs. Two troopers sprinted after him. The rider rolled from the saddle and fell to the ground.

"Lookit, will yez! The sonofabitch is wearin' army boots!" The first trooper knelt by the fallen man and pulled off one of the man's boots, then struggled with the other.

"Look out, Liam!" the second man cried out, stopping in his tracks and starting to back away. "The sonofabitch is still alive!"

The second boot came off in the trooper's hands and he fell back hard on the frozen ground, looking into the muzzle of a revolver as the renegade heaved himself up on his elbow. "God damn it, this is a peaceful village!" the man shouted, blinking to clear his vision. Blood dripped from a wound on his scalp.

An arrow sprouted suddenly from the trooper's shoulder and he regarded it with mild curiosity for a moment before he let out a howl of pain and leaped to his feet. As he ran pell-mell for safety, still clutching the renegade's boot, two Indians darted from the brush at the base of the bluff and helped the wounded white man to his feet. Half carrying, half dragging him, they took the man away amidst a scattering of shots that failed to stop them from regaining the cover of the brush.

Whitcomb had watched the entire scene distractedly, like a spectator at some curious entertainment, but his attention was seized now by a thunderous detonation behind him. He turned to see that several lodges at the southern end of the village had been set afire and one of these had exploded. The force of the blast had sent lodgepoles into the air like jackstraws, some spinning end over end, others arcing up cleanly for a hundred feet or more before they plummeted back to earth. Close on the heels of the first explosion came a second, sending the troopers among the burning tipis running for cover.

What the Indians' reaction to this destruction would be, Whitcomb did not know, but he knew that he had been away from his men for too long. He set out at a jog trot in the direction Polachek and the others had taken. He could see no Indians remaining among the lodges now. Faced with the advancing troops of Egan's, Mills's and Corwin's companies, they had withdrawn to regroup at the base of the bluffs, but with none of their number remaining in the village, the hostiles on the slope had no further need to be careful with their aim, and fire from that quarter had resumed, heavier than before. As he ran, Whitcomb surveyed the positions there. The pace of firing from individual Indians revealed that most of their weapons were muzzle-loading pieces but here and there a single weapon spoke more rapidly—one of the trapdoor Springfields or perhaps a lever gun used carefully. It was plain that the Indians had no shortage of powder, and it was equally plain that as long as they held their elevated positions, the soldiers in the village were in danger. Why hadn't Moore dislodged them? Before the attack began, Whitcomb had seen Moore start off along the bluffs.

When he reached the bottom of the camp he was relieved to find that most of the fighting seemed to be concentrated elsewhere. His platoon was in good cover in a dense stand of trees and brush that faced a narrow stretch of uneven bottomland lying between the river and the base of the bluffs north of the village. Without the cover of the bushes, some of which stood three or four feet above a man's head, the position would have been untenable. For the moment, the Indians on the slopes above the village were directing most of their fire at Egan's and Mills's men, but an occasional ball reminded the men of E Troop that they must keep well concealed. On the right, across the icebound river, there were more trees, willows and brush, and Whitcomb saw that the danger of being flanked on that side was very real.

"Corporal Stiegler!" he called out, spying the man nearby. "I want three or four men on this end of the line to devote their full attention to the brush across the river. If they see any movement there, I want to be notified at once."

"Yes, sir." Stiegler moved off and vanished.

"Leftenant!"

Whitcomb turned to see Polachek waving to catch his attention, pointing down the line to the left, where Dupré was bringing more of E Troop forward and extending the line in that direction. Dupré saw Whitcomb and waved.

"Step this way, if you please, sir." Polachek joined Whitcomb and led him forward to a concealed vantage point from which they could see across the open ground beyond. "The savages haff a stronghold there." Polachek pointed to a place where the river had scooped out a section of the hillside long ago. The little cove was protected by a fringe of brush and boulders. "I haff no idea how many savages are there, sir. We haff been keeping them pinned down."

"Well, with Dupré and the rest of the men on the line now, we shouldn't have any trouble with them."

"Even so, sir, there is a considerable gap on our left. We are not in contact with any of the other companies."

"There should be someone along soon enough up above, to push the Indians off the hillside. One of the other companies will join up with us then, I imagine."

"Perhaps, Leftenant. I hope so." Polachek sounded uncertain.

"Don't worry, Sergeant. We'll do all right until someone comes along. Carry on."

As Polachek disappeared among the bushes, Whitcomb tried to envision his present position as if it were drawn on a blackboard at West Point. There was an enemy strongpoint to the front, strength unknown. No danger from the rear, no sign of any on the right. Men posted to watch for any flanking movement. But there was a gap on the left and the enemy held the high ground. What could go wrong? One of Whitcomb's instructors in tactics had asked that question repeatedly. "Try to imagine what may go wrong before it does, gentlemen," the major had said. "Because it almost certainly will." Whitcomb was trying to determine what might go wrong here when Steward Bryan appeared suddenly at his side.

"How many of your men have frostbite, sir?"

"Frostbite? I have no idea."

"You had better find out quickly. Many of the men in the other troops are affected because they left their coats behind. The sooner it's treated, the less likely the tissue will be permanently damaged. Find an air hole in the river ice and put the frozen part in the water if you can—if it's a hand or a foot. Then rub it hard with some rough cloth; a piece of saddle blanket or gunnysack or anything like that. Then bathe it with this—it's iodine. Bandage it cleanly if you can and for God's sake try to keep the man warm." He handed Whitcomb a small bottle.

Whitcomb was glad he had kept his own buffalo coat, despite the occasional inconvenience of moving in such a heavy garment. Lieutenant Corwin had called out harshly as some of the men had thrown their outer garments to the ground when the troop prepared to enter the village, and there had been a brief delay as all the discarded coats were made fast to the saddles before the horses were led away to be held with K Troop's. Whitcomb had thought the delay foolish then; he had thought the Indians would be quickly vanquished and the garments could be easily recovered while the mopping up was under way. Now he saw the order in a different light. If the present stalemate continued for long at least E Troop knew where their greatcoats were to be found; he remembered that none of Captain Mills's men had been wearing coats as they advanced into the village. All their coats had been left up on the mesa.

"Thanks," he managed to reply as Bryan hurried away. "McCaslin!" he called out, and was relieved to see the hatchetfaced Irishman scramble through the brush a moment later. "How much frostbite have we got?" He noticed that McCaslin too had chosen to keep his coat.

"Fingers and toes, sorr, and Gwynn's ears."

"Get the affected men to the river." He handed McCaslin the bottle and repeated Steward Bryan's instructions, adding, "Two or three men at a time, mind you, and don't leave a hole in the line."

"Understood, sorr." McCaslin nodded, and was gone.

There was a sudden outbreak of shooting on Whitcomb's left, and a curse.

"Watch out! The bastards are behind that bank!"

Whitcomb ducked out of the brush to the rear and ran along the line to where the firing was heaviest. He made his way forward there and came suddenly upon Lieutenant Corwin and Sergeant Dupré. Dupré was reloading a smoking carbine. He fired again across the open ground to the front. Fifty yards away the Indians had advanced to a natural breastwork, a ridge of earth and rocks and driftwood left behind by the river in spring flood. Behind the warriors, among the trees at the base of the hillside, women and children were fleeing on foot along a trail that led off downstream.

Corwin glanced up at Whitcomb. "No cause for alarm, Mr. Reb. They're just covering the retreat of their women. They're going to slip out of the trap, it would seem."

"Should we fire on them, sir?" inquired Corporal Atherton from his position to Corwin's right.

"Fire on the women, Corporal?" Corwin's tone was edged with contempt. "No, I think not. We've done our job. It's Captain Moore who failed to do his. Report, Mr. Whitcomb."

"There are no new injuries, sir. No wounds, at least. Several of the men have minor frostbite. Corporal McCaslin is taking them to the river a few at a time for treatment as instructed by Hospital Steward Bryan. We're in position to the bank of the river."

"All right. If there's enough cover, I want you to bring the right flank forward and have them increase their firing to hold these Indians down. Twenty of our men were requisitioned to help burn the lodges. If the Indians suspect how few of us are holding this line they'll attack for real."

As he said the last words there was a deafening explosion from quite nearby, and another tipi disintegrated in smoke and flames and flying debris. A lodgepole crashed into the brush ten yards away, causing one soldier to jump for his life.

"It's the powder kegs going up," Corwin explained. "They've got enough powder for an army."

"I take it you had no luck with General Reynolds?" Whitcomb ventured.

"Luck? You'll need more than luck to get a sound decision out of old Muttonchop. God, he's a pompous ass! 'We must deny these supplies to the savages,' he says, but he doesn't think we might need them ourselves. Do you know how much meat these people have got? Tons of it. I mean that literally. All nicely jerked and baled. And there are hundreds of buffalo robes. We could all eat well and sleep warm tonight, if we ever manage to chase the bastards off. Noyes took seven hundred horses and I hope to God he holds on to them, because it looks like Reynolds is going to burn everything else. He's a damned fool."

"I'll move the men, sir," Whitcomb said, and he moved off, deeply shocked by this blasphemous indictment of a superior officer. Surely Reynolds knew the overall situation better than Corwin. He must know what he was doing.

Whitcomb found Stiegler and McCaslin and passed on Corwin's orders, and as he made his way back along the line he inspected each man briefly for frostbite. He found it often, but none was serious. One man was struggling with a jammed carbine with his bare hands. The extractor had ripped the base off a spent round and the soldier was prying at the remains of the casing with a knife.

"Keep your gloves on, Private!" Whitcomb said sharply. "You're no good to me with frozen hands."

"Sorry, Mr. Reb. I'm sorry, sir, I mean Mr. Whitcomb."

As he moved to rejoin Corwin and Dupré, it seemed to Whitcomb that the firing from the bluffs had increased, but when he paused to listen more closely there was a new outbreak of shooting from E Troop's front and someone shouted, "Here they come!"

Whitcomb darted through the brush in time to see several Indians running forward shooting as they came, and more still leaping from behind the breastwork. He dropped to his knee and fired once, twice, and brought down a brave who had almost reached the soldiers' line. Two of the others met similar fates and the remaining Indians turned and ran for cover, carrying away their wounded comrades.

"Major Corwin! You are hurt?"

Dupré's voice came from close at hand and Whitcomb turned to see Corwin cutting his uniform trouser and woolen underwear with a pocketknife. Dupré removed his commander's overboot and peeled back the flexible upper of the buckskin moccasin. With the layers of clothing drawn aside, a fresh wound was revealed in Corwin's calf. Bright blood spurted from the injury. "Put a tourniquet on it, Sergeant, if you will." Corwin's voice was strained and his face was pale.

Dupré pulled a large bandanna from his pocket and quickly wrapped it around Corwin's leg above the wound. As he was breaking a stick to use in tightening the tourniquet, Lieutenant Paul, from Mills's company, appeared through the brush with three men behind him.

"Lieutenant Corwin? Captain Mills's compliments. He sent us to make contact with you. He regrets he has been unable to advance to join up with you, but half our troop is burning the lodges and the rest of them are trying to make the hostiles on the slope keep their heads down. Captain Mills is in contact with Captain Moore, but Moore refuses to come up and support our left flank."

"He's in contact with Moore! Where in hell is Moore?"

"On the benchland just at the upper end of the village. He was driven off the slope by the Indians. They're up top now, on the summit. I have to get back fairly soon, Boots, but I can lend you a hand for a little while if you need it."

"Damn Moore anyhow! Yes, by God, I can use your help. Mr. Whitcomb, find Sergeant Polachek, tell him to grab fifteen men, and bring them all back with you."

When Whitcomb returned a few minutes later with Polachek, Corwin's trouser was tied back in place and Dupré was pushing the buffalo overboot back over the moccasin. Corwin grunted as the movement in his ankle flexed the wounded calf muscle.

"What in hell's Rawolle doing?" he demanded of Lieutenant Paul. Lieutenant W. W. Rawolle commanded the other company in Moore's battalion. "Moore may be chicken-hearted but that Prussian bastard is always spoiling for a fight. Can't Reynolds find something useful for him and his men to do?"

"There's some movement to the rear, but I couldn't make it out. Our company's horses are being brought down off the mesa. That's all I know. I've got no idea what Reynolds has in mind."

"Let's see if we can't at least push those Indians back from that breastwork. I'd like them to think there's half a regiment on this line. Sergeant Polachek, you go with Mr. Paul and see if you can't work far enough to the left to smoke the hostiles out. Watch out for Mr. Reb here; he's going to be on the opposite flank. Mr. Reb, take a dozen men across the ice and move up under the cover of that brush. Smoke those bastards out and then get back here quick. The center of the line will support you when you open fire."

As Whitcomb and Paul moved off in opposite directions, another lodge exploded nearby and strips of dried buffalo meat rained from the sky like confetti.

Corwin looked at Dupré. "Well, Sergeant, what do you think?"

Dupré arched his eyebrows, shrugged, and waggled one hand in a gesture of uncertainty.

Corwin smiled. "That's what I thought you thought."

"I get the men ready, sair." Dupré disappeared.

A few moments later a steady firing began from the left and right as Paul and Whitcomb reached their positions. "Supporting fire!" Sergeant Dupré's voice shouted, and the brush on either side of Corwin came alive. The Indians saw at once that they were outflanked; they abandoned their breastwork and retreated to the rocks and brush closer to the hillside, where their comrades set up a brief but fierce covering fire. When the last of the retreating Indians was out of sight, the din of gunfire lessened, but it remained strong from off to the left. Judging by the sound, Corwin guessed that the Indians on the slope had seen Lieutenant Paul and Sergeant Polachek's new position and were doing their best to drive the soldiers back. Polachek would have the sense to withdraw slowly so the hostiles wouldn't think the line was weak. The illusion of a strong force on this side of the village would last a while longer, with luck.

Sergeant Dupré came through the bushes and squatted once more beside Corwin. He pointed off to the right across the river. Only by watching very closely was it possible to discern Whitcomb's men moving in ones and twos from cover to cover, retreating toward the company's line. Occasional fire came from several positions along the riverbank, giving the impression that at least a full platoon was in position there.

"He is doing well, sair," said Dupré.

Corwin grunted noncommittally. "I want you to take two men and bring up the horses. Bring them along the river ice and stay out of sight of the bluffs, if you can. And tell McCaslin to have some men gather up as much of that jerked meat as they can find."

When Dupré was gone Corwin let out a long sigh that was almost a moan. He tried to shift himself about to favor his wounded leg. He was certain the ball had struck the bone, but he had said nothing of this to Dupré. There was nothing more Dupré could do for him now. He wanted to lie down and rest, but he knew that once he closed his eyes he would think only of the pain in his leg, so he propped himself against a tree trunk and threw a shot at the bluffs so the Indians wouldn't think this part of the line was deserted. He reached out to gather up a few cartridges that had dropped from his belt when he fell to the ground after being shot. The belt was new. He had had the post saddler at D. A. Russell make it for him to replace his old one, which had finally worn out. Almost every man on the campaign and a great majority of the soldiers up and down the frontier wore similar belts, which they made for themselves or had made by saddlers. The leather loop cartridge belt had been invented by Anson Mills ten years before and it was a great improvement on the standard cartridge box worn at the waist, which allowed the metal cartridges to clatter about in a manner that was always annoying and could be dangerous in the presence of the enemy, but in cold weather the leather loops of the Mills belts were too stiff to hold the cartridges properly. It occurred to Corwin that canvas loops might do better. He would speak to Mills about it.

Another tipi exploded nearby and Corwin jerked his head up. He had been drifting off. He would have to watch that.

He straightened to a more upright position and peered through the brush around him. He could make out McCaslin and another man gathering pieces of jerky not far away. To the rear there was no sign of Dupré or the horses.

CHAPTER EIGHTEEN

Hardeman was half conscious, struggling to comprehend where he was and what had happened to him. Someone touched his feet. He shook his head to clear his vision and the sudden pain reminded him that he had been shot. The bullet had creased his forehead almost exactly where Kills Fox had hit him with the war club three days earlier. He held his head in his hands to steady it, pressing hard. The pain diminished somewhat and he could make out his surroundings.

He was in some sort of cove at the base of the bluffs. The cove was close to the northern end of the Cheyenne camp; it was screened from the village by a strip of brush and rocks. An old woman knelt by Hardeman's side. She had hold of his stockinged feet and was rubbing them vigorously, causing him to feel a dull pain there as well. That was good. If he could still feel anything at all, his feet were not completely frozen. There was a small fire nearby. Apparently someone had placed him by the fire to warm his feet. Around him, two dozen or more Indian women were busy reloading the motley collection of muzzle-loading rifles that were the Indians' only defense against the steady fire from the cavalry carbines. What was holding the soldiers back?

He let go of his head and his vision remained clear, but

any movement caused it to reel before it steadied again. He moved his head cautiously and looked around him. Above, he saw that there were warriors in protected positions on the face of the bluffs, firing down into the village. Closer at hand there were men behind the rocks and brush, facing the troopers who had advanced to the near end of the camp. The redoubt was well protected by warriors and was a fair defensive position, so long as the cavalry didn't gain the heights above. Hardeman seemed to remember that there had been more women here a short while ago, and some children too; they were gone now but he didn't know where.

Under the old woman's steady massaging he could feel warmth beginning to return to his toes. He made signs that his feet were all right, and the woman spoke soothingly in words he did not understand. He saw now that she had a pair of high winter moccasins which she clearly intended for him. He helped her to pull them on one foot and then the other, but his fingers were numb, so he left for her the job of lacing them tight and tying them. His feet might be all right, he supposed. It really didn't matter. His head ached and it was difficult to think clearly, but the understanding of his failure was sharp and finely drawn in his mind. Once again he had arrived too late.

In his mind's eye he could see the scene as it must have been just a few hours earlier—cavalry approaching the still-sleeping village, warriors roused by the bugles, leaping out to defend their women and children with no time to put on their paint, no time to dance for courage and spirit power, no time to dress properly; no time to do all the things an Indian usually did before he went to war. Hardeman had seen it all seven years ago, on the banks of another stream far away. And now it had happened again, just as before, down to his own belated entry into the battle and his failure to stop it. The one thing he had tried above all to prevent had happened; the war had begun and where it would end he could not imagine.

From the moment he had seen the oats in the horse droppings, he had known in his heart where the soldiers were going. He had pushed his horse as fast as he dared through the cold night, hoping against hope that the cavalry tracks would turn aside to aim anywhere but at Two Moons' village. But they had kept on, straight as an arrow. They led through country that was rugged and broken, much rougher than the way he had come, and finally, when he grew certain that the army scouts must be following the tracks of the returning Cheyenne hunting party, Hardeman had left the trail and struck off to the east, back to the Powder, praying that he would reach the village before Crook's cavalry.

But when he was still a mile or two distant he had heard the firing. Yet even then he had hoped by some miracle to stop the attack and restore the broken peace. As he entered the village he had looked frantically for gray horses—buglers always rode grays and kept close to the ranking officer in each troop—but as luck would have it he saw a cluster of grays off to the cavalry's rear and realized that an entire troop of grays must be present. He looked for the tall form of General Crook, mounted or on foot, but he saw him nowhere, and then at last he had seen a man he knew. It was Louis Richaud, who had scouted for General Smith in '67 together with Hardeman and Hickok. He and some other men were sitting their horses near Two Moons' lodge. One man with muttonchop whiskers wore an officer's Kossuth hat. "Louis!" Hardeman had shouted. "Louis Richaud!" But his words were drowned in the din of battle. He had ridden pell-mell for the horsemen but a trooper's bullet had knocked him from his roan and he remembered little of what had taken place between that time and this. He didn't know what had become of his boots.

The old woman was done lacing the moccasins. His feet were still cold but he could feel his toes when he wiggled them and already the warmth of the fire was beginning to penetrate the thick rawhide soles. He made signs to thank her, and she answered with signs of her own, saying that soon the warriors would drive the bluecoats away and he would come eat in her husband's lodge. Hardeman nodded and smiled as she turned away, but he thought the outcome would be very different. He had heard the explosions from the village and had guessed what they meant. The soldiers were burning the lodges and the kegs of powder were blowing up as the flames reached them. How much powder had the Indians managed to bring away with them as they fled? Probably not enough.

He listened to the sounds of fighting beyond the cove. He judged the battle to be fairly even now, but it couldn't stay even for long. Soon the Indians would begin to run low on powder or lead and then the soldiers would move in and surround them, and finally they would have to surrender. And what would Crook say to find Hardeman in their midst, wounded and wearing moccasins? Would he believe the improbable tale of the scout's travels and the events that had brought him here? If he would listen, Hardeman would do what he could. He would see what terms he could make for the vanquished tribesmen.

His thoughts were interrupted by a hand that knocked his hat off his head and jerked him up by the hair, making his head throb with excruciating pain. He was helpless to resist.

The Cheyenne who held Hardeman's head raised a knife in his other hand, but he hesitated when the old woman who had given the white man the moccasins shouted from across the fire. A few men came running up, Kills Fox and He Dog among them.

"He led the bluecoats to us!" Hardeman's attacker said, preparing to take the white man's scalp.

"He came from that way!" Kills Fox pointed downstream. "He came after the soldiers attacked us."

"It is true," said another Cheyenne. "I saw him come from the north. We were already fighting the soldiers."

He Dog demanded to know what the Cheyenne were saying, and when one man explained to him in Lakota, he held out a warning hand to Hardeman's attacker. "I did not see the *washíchun* come into the fight, but I have seen the man who led the bluecoats here. He is the Grabber, the one the whites call *Grouard*. He came with the second group of soldiers, the ones on foot. I tried to get near him to kill him, but he saw me, and now he stays behind the soldiers, hiding."

"Ahhhhh!" Some of the women were Lakota and they made a sound of wonder and understanding. They remembered the Grabber. When he was just a boy he had been found, naked and alone, by a hunting party of Lakota. When the Lakota approached him, he had held his arms in the air, as if trying to grab something above his head. He spoke a little Lakota, and said his father was a halfbreed trader and his mother an Oglala who lived among the whites. He was given shelter in Sitting Bull's camp and lived there for some years, but when he was a young man he got in trouble with the Hunkpapas and came to live with He Dog, in Crazy Horse's camp. But it seemed that he caused trouble and fighting wherever he went, and in time he had gone back to the whites to live with them. Now he led the soldiers against the Lakota and Shahíyela. Was this how he repaid them for the kindness they had shown him when he was in need?

The Lakota women told the Cheyenne about the Grabber, and one of the Cheyenne nodded. "I have seen him before, in the camp of Sitting Bull long ago, and I saw him here today. This one tried to stop the fighting." Here he gestured at Hardeman, whose hair was still gripped by the other Cheyenne warrior. "I know some of the whiteman's words. He told the bluecoat who shot him that we were at peace."

"He came with the pipe carriers from Sun Horse," said another. "He is a guest in our village."

"We should kill him anyway," said the angry man, but he let go of Hardeman's hair and accepted a loaded rifle from one of the women. He trotted away, back to the fighting.

Hardeman had understood none of what was said, but he gathered that he had Kills Fox and He Dog to thank for saving his life. He wondered what they would have done if they knew that he had run off to find Crook and lead him to Sitting Bull.

"Thought that was you," said a familiar voice, and he turned to see Bat Putnam approaching him with his Leman rifle in his hands. Bat saw the wound on Hardeman's head. "Who done that? Injun or white man?"

"White man. I got into the village but not in time. Couldn't stop the fighting." Hardeman told it in as few words as possible.

"I reckoned you'd try. Glad I was right. Eagle, he didn't believe it, but the tracks told the story. You was on the soldier boys' trail to stop 'em, I said. Bet a horse on it, not that it makes any difference now. 'Course I didn't reckon that's what you had in mind to do when you first lit out. Took us some time to take up yer tracks, what with havin' to catch the horses, and all."

So the other pipe carriers had noticed his absence after all, and they had set out on his trail. How close had they been behind him? If they had caught him they might have killed him, but that wouldn't have changed a thing. The soldiers would still be fighting the Cheyenne and the Sioux and the only thing that would be different was that he would be dead. One man more or less wouldn't matter much. He still might die before the day was done.

"You should have told me about the summer council," he said.

"Sun Horse reckoned you wouldn't come with us if'n you knew. He figgered when you heard about it up here, you might see things our way by then. Guess he was wrong."

Hardeman shrugged. It didn't matter now.

Bat retrieved Hardeman's hat and handed it to him, then brushed aside the hair on his forehead to inspect the wound. He wiped away some fresh blood brought out by the Cheyenne's manhandling, and Hardeman winced. "Hmmp. Looks like you was lucky," Bat said. " 'Bout a whisker closer and we'd be buildin' you a scaffold. Well here's somethin' to make you set up and take notice: we got 'em stopped up above." He pointed to the tops of the bluffs. "Two Moons is up there now with some of his boys. Me'n the fellers, we seen where you turned off the soldier boys' trail, 'n' we figgered like you did—take the quick way back to camp 'n' see could we head 'em off. When we seen the fat was in the fire, we made fer the tops of the bluffs on foot. Eagle and Little Hand, they got a good position and slowed down one bunch of soldiers till some of the Cheyenne come up to help 'em. There's a bunch o' Cheyenne and Lakotas in good cover now, got them bluecoats pushed down off the hill and held to the south end of camp. Hawk 'n' me come down to see could we help some here. He's off yonder.'' Bat pointed and Hardeman saw Hawk Chaser among the warriors in the brush nearby. The Lakota fired an old musket and passed it to a woman to reload.

Hardeman was surprised to discover that he took encouragement from Bat's words. For good or bad he was on the side of the Indians now, and their fate might be his own. With a helping hand from Bat he got to his feet and found that his head was somewhat improved. It felt peculiarly swollen and his hat seemed too small; his hearing was muffled and strange and his eyes worked best when he kept his head still, but his strength was returning.

''Dunno how much longer we'll hold out here,'' Bat said. ''Might be we'll have to skedaddle. Women and kids're mostly off and gone.'' He pointed at the trail that led downstream. ''They'll circle 'round and head for Crazy Horse. He's the closest. I don't guess I should tell you that. Wouldn't do if the soldier boys should hear where the helpless ones've gone to.''

Hardeman didn't resent the suspicion. He deserved it. He had tried to fool them all to make peace at any cost. He had kept his cards close to his vest, and in the end, Fate had dealt from the bottom of the deck and walked off with the winnings.

''Horses are coming!'' a woman cried, and some men rushed to face the trail from downriver in case soldiers were attacking from this new direction, but they saw the horses now, a bunch of ten or fifteen driven by two Lakota boys and a Cheyenne, and they fell back to open a way into the cove.

Blackbird was the first boy to enter the redoubt, leading the way for the horses. He saw Bat Putnam and cried out joyfully, "*Hau,* Uncle! I am glad to see you! We have brought horses!"

"We bring horses for the helpless ones!" the Cheyenne youth called out in that language, and the women set up a trilling sound, praising this bravery on the part of those so young. The men caught the horses as they slowed and milled about. The last youth paused on a section of old riverbank in full view of the soldiers and made a defiant gesture at the whites, smiling proudly. A bullet struck him square in the breastbone and hurled him from his horse like a rag doll. His body fell on the near side of the brush, behind the warriors crouching there.

Blackbird jumped off his horse and knelt beside the young Lakota. It was the youth who had helped him catch his horse that morning. He had found the boy again when he was crying the alarm, fleeing from the soldiers, although he knew that they could not hurt him. From the moment when the *washíchun* had looked down his pistol at him and lowered it without shooting, Blackbird had known that he would survive the day. His spirit helpers, the blackbirds, had warned him of the soldiers' coming and had shown him the way to safety. Feeling brave and confident, knowing his spirit helpers were watching over him, Blackbird had flown away to the river as they had done, crying the alarm, warning the horse guards to save the horses. But already another group of soldiers, these on black horses, were cutting off the herd and the horse guards were riding for their lives. Blackbird had found the Lakota boy and together they had rounded up a few horses the soldiers had missed and drove them downstream, below the camp.

A Cheyenne boy had found them there and together the three youths had waited until they could see where their small bunch of good horses would be needed the most. They had seen the warriors climbing the bluffs to keep back the soldiers, and they had seen the women and children streaming away to the north on the river trail.

Finally they had decided to take the horses to the protected cove at the near end of the village, where the last of the women remained. If the soldiers attacked, at least the women would be able to get safely away.

And now Blackbird's new friend was dead. He reached out to touch the face of the one who had been so happy just moments before, so proud to be doing something brave for his people, and the feeling of the flesh told Blackbird that the spirit was gone.

The father of the dead boy, one of He Dog's men, stared incredulously at the twisted body. His joy at seeing his son, who had been missing since the start of the fighting, had been turned to grief in the blink of an eye. "*Hókahe,* Lakotas!" he cried out suddenly, freeing himself from his shock. "Let us show the bluecoats we know how to fight!" He ran to the exposed piece of old riverbank and fired his rifle at the soldiers' positions. With bullets striking all around him, he began to reload. He poured powder from a flask down the barrel, then dropped in a bullet from a pouch at his waist, and was drawing out the ramrod to tamp the load home when two bullets struck him at once. The rusty flintlock flew into the air as the Lakota threw up his arms and dropped back, badly wounded. Two warriors pulled the man to safety while all along the front of the redoubt other men moved forward through the rocks and brush and set up a brisk return fire, Bat Putnam among them. He sighted his plains rifle carefully and fired, and a cry of pain answered his shot.

Behind the line of defenders, Blackbird was astride his horse once more, the tears already drying on his cheeks. "*Hókahe!*" he shouted. "Come, my brothers, it is a good day to die!" He kicked the pony into a gallop and raced through the brush, making straight for the soldiers' lines.

"Come back, little brother!" Bat cried out when he saw Blackbird, but it was too late. A flurry of shots came from the troopers and Blackbird fell.

Within the cove, a Cheyenne dropped the jaw rein of the horse he was holding and seized a musket from one of the women. Without thinking, Hardeman grabbed the startled pony and swung himself onto the bare back, praying that the animal would respond to knees and heels without the control of a bit. Leaning close to the pony's neck he kicked it into a run and out across the open ground beyond the brush, heading for Blackbird's motionless form.

Bullets flew around him and one nipped at the shoulder of his slicker. His hat flew off his head and he felt the wind in his hair. And now Blackbird moved. Good boy! Playing possum all that time! An arm was raised and Blackbird managed to lift himself high enough so Hardeman would be able to take the arm. He hoped he could lift the boy up behind him. His head still throbbed and his vision blurred, causing him to blink hard and shake his head to clear his eyes.

He was almost there. Careful now, don't want to fall off the damn horse . . . Reach down . . . It's going to work . . . Oh, God! . . .

A searing pain like the touch of a firebrand exploded in his left shoulder. He was knocked backward, off-balance and unable to see his surroundings through a red haze of pain that rose before him. He struggled to stay on the horse's back. His ears were filled with the pounding of his heart and a roaring cry of anger that he realized came from his own throat as he looked about for his attacker. He felt rather than saw his pistol in his hand, and felt the recoil as he fired aimlessly. The horse wheeled in a tight turn, then shied and reared, and Hardeman fell.

He fought off a black cloud that threatened to envelop him and he saw the Indian pony galloping away. Blackbird was nearby, crawling slowly toward him, one arm outstretched. The boy's wounded leg trailed behind him, and there was a new wound in his side, where the shirt and cape were soaked with blood. A bullet ricocheted off the ground between them, throwing shards of rock in Blackbird's face and making him duck back and cling to the earth.

Hardeman's vision was strangely clear, but fragmentary, as if he saw through the eyes of a dream. He and the boy were in a shallow depression, sheltered somewhat from the troopers' fire. Perhaps if they didn't move . . . He let his head drop back and he looked up at the gray sky. In a moment he would do something, but right now he needed to rest. His whole left side was numb and he could feel a wetness soaking his shirt. Where was he wounded? . . . He heard a bugle sound in the village, and horses neighing. The soldiers would advance on horseback now, and that would be that. . . . Nearby, the gunfire had increased . . .

He became aware of hoofbeats close at hand, approaching fast. He looked up and saw two mounted men bearing down on him, soldiers on large cavalry horses, one chestnut and one dapple-gray. He saw every movement of the men and horses, the wide eyes and heaving chests of the animals, the open mouths of the men, shouting wordlessly. One brandished a revolver; the other held a carbine.

And now there were more hoofbeats, from behind. Hardeman managed to turn his head, although the effort seemed enormous. From the base of the bluffs, Hawk Chaser was riding to meet the troopers, carrying only a lance.

Hardeman returned his attention to the soldiers and he saw now that his own pistol was still in his hand. How many shots had he fired? It could have been just one or half a dozen. He wasn't sure. Too much effort to check his load, and not enough time. The ground trembled from the hoofbeats of the approaching horses. He rolled on his right side and raised the Colt, supporting his elbow on the ground. His thumb brought the hammer back and he watched it as if it belonged to someone else. Force of habit. . . . Good habit too. . . . He sighted on the gray horse. . . .

There was a deafening explosion that seemed to come from everywhere around him and his arm jerked from the recoil. Through the smoke he saw the gray buckle at the knees and fall head over heels, throwing the rider clear. The man sprang to his feet and scurried off, favoring one leg. Hardeman sighted at the other horse but the soldier swerved and the shot missed, and the soldier's Springfield boomed harmlessly in reply. Against Hardeman's will, the arm holding the Colt dropped to the ground. He saw the trooper rein in sharply and leap from the horse; the man was going to shoot from the ground this time. Hardeman tried to raise the Colt again but his arm refused to move. He was condemned to watch, unable to interfere.

The soldier gauged the time left to him. Up went the trapdoor at the carbine's breech. The partially extracted cartridge was stuck, but the trooper yanked it free and found a new cartridge at his belt. In went the cartridge, down went the trapdoor. The man sighted, and suddenly Hawk Chaser was upon him, charging into Hardeman's vision like an avenging apparition, his lance raised high, now starting downward as the arm launched it.

The soldier ducked sideways, but not quickly enough. The lance struck his shoulder and glanced off, leaving a deep gash. The trooper cried out in rage and pain and he fired the carbine one-handed at the retreating Indian. Hawk Chaser seemed to sway in the saddle but his horse carried him out of Hardeman's vision and Hardeman could see only the soldier, who had one foot in his stirrup now. With a lurch he was up and away, managing to haul himself into the saddle only after the chestnut had reached a gallop. Cheers came from the watching troopers, accompaned by a ragged volley to keep the Indians pinned down.

Hardeman found the strength to move his head. Blackbird lay where he had been before, unmoving, his eyes closed. From the direction of the village the bugle call sounded again. Hardeman heaved himself up with his good arm and managed to hold himself in a sitting position. There was much activity among the tipis, horses moving about and men mounting. The troopers were preparing to advance.

But they were not advancing! There was no firing from the village now, while from the Indian positions came a renewed barrage of fire and a few triumphant shouts. Three huge explosions drowned out the other sounds for a time, coming one on top of the other as the fires found more powder, and then through the echoes of the blasts came the notes of the bugle once more, repeated over and over, from farther away now. With a shock, Hardeman recognized the rallying call. The soldiers were withdrawing! He couldn't believe his ears, but it was true. The mounted cavalry were milling about beyond the burning lodges, forming up, and now they were off, moving out of the village to the south, upstream, away from the Indians, who swarmed out of the rocks shouting jubilantly.

Hardeman saw movement in the corner of his eye and he looked to the dense brush at the bottom of camp, beyond where the Oglala lodges stood abandoned. There. A man on foot crouched low. Another behind him was helping a third man with a wounded leg, and he caught a glimpse of a horse being led downstream. There were still some troopers there. If they didn't move quickly they would be cut off. Did the Indians see them? It didn't seem so.

A sudden dizziness made Hardeman drop his head until the spinning sensation slowed and stopped. Something was nagging at him. There was something he wanted to do. He raised his head and looked around. The wounded trooper had dropped his Springfield when he fled. Hardeman crawled over to the carbine and used it for a crutch as he struggled to his feet. His left arm hung useless at his side. Nearby, the village burned. No more than a handful of lodges had escaped the torch. Where the kegs of powder had exploded there were smoking craters, as if the Indian camp had been bombarded by artillery. Upstream, the cavalry were streaming across the open land of the valley bottom. Some riders were driving the huge pony herd along behind the column of troopers. A handful of Cheyenne started off on foot after the cavalry. Scouts. They would keep an eye on the soldiers and report back.

Hardeman shook his head. What was it he had meant to do? There was something he needed to know. Someone . . . He looked around seeking some reminder, and then he saw Hawk Chaser.

That was it.

The Indian lay sprawled on his side not far away. Hardeman moved unsteadily across the intervening space, aiding himself with the carbine. When he reached Hawk Chaser he touched the man with the Springfield and rolled him onto his back, and then he saw the wound. Half of the warrior's head was blown away, yet on what remained of his face there was no anger or fear. Just peace.

Men had reached Hardeman's side now. Nearby, one helped Blackbird to his feet. The boy was conscious, but unable to stand on his own. Hardeman looked back down at Hawk Chaser, then turned and stumbled away, searching the ground.

"Easy, Christopher." Bat Putnam put an arm around his waist to help support him.

"It's over here," Hardeman muttered. He pulled the mountain man along, driven by a need he couldn't put words to. He saw what he wanted; he bent over and nearly fell, held up only by the surprising strength in Bat's skinny arms. His hand closed around the feathered shaft of Hawk Chaser's lance.

He shook Bat off and started back, clutching both the lance and carbine in his good hand and using them to help himself along until he stood once again beside the fallen warrior. He dropped the carbine next to the body and then with most of his remaining strength he raised the lance and planted it in the ground. The Indians might not understand, but he knew what it meant. A lance against a Springfield carbine, model 1873. An iron blade made from the rim of some emigrant's wagon wheel against four hundred grains of lead propelled by fifty-five grains of powder. But Hawk Chaser hadn't seen the inequity. Hawk Chaser was a warrior. To him it was just one man against another.

Bat had followed Hardeman closely, ready to catch him if he keeled over. Hardeman turned to him now, searching for something to say, needing an explanation.

"It's good to die for the people," Bat said.

Yes, it's good to die for the people. Hawk Chaser had believed that. And he did a good job of dying. Hardeman wondered if he would die as well when his time came. He had no people to die for. His parents were gone and he had never stayed long enough in one place to acquire a family.

Except for Johnny. And now Johnny was on his own and free to fight for himself.

He saw Blackbird watching him. The boy was leaning on Standing Eagle, who had appeared from somewhere. Blood was oozing from the wrapping on Blackbird's leg and from the new wound in his side. His lionskin cape had fallen from one shoulder and the shirt was torn there. Hardeman could see the fresh scar from the small wound the boy had received in Putnam's Park, from Tatum's shot. More wounds in a few weeks than most men received in a lifetime.

A peculiar sound came from the village. Men and women were moving among the shattered lodges, picking up the few items that might still be of some use. In the center of camp a knot of women were gathered around something that moved along the ground. They followed it, arms lifting and falling. It was a man. He rolled onto his back and for a moment Hardeman saw the dark-blue field blouse and bearded face, and then the women closed in on him again and there was a muffled scream. After a time one woman stood and raised a severed arm above her head, making the high trilling sound of joy.

Hardeman looked away. He removed his St. Paul coat with difficulty and some pain on account of his useless left arm. Using Hawk Chaser's lance to steady himself, he dropped to his knees and sat down beside the body. He covered it with the oilskin to hide the horrible wound and the expression of peaceful acceptance, which was no less unsettling.

"I'll stay here with him," he said to no one in particular. "You fix up something to carry him on."

The wind was stretching its legs again, whipping the willows this way and that, but Hardeman no longer felt the cold. A gust brought smoke from the village and he smelled the odor of destruction. He shrugged off the attempts of one man and then another to see to his wound. Men and women spoke to him in Indian tongues and hands touched his shoulder in attempts to comfort him, but he paid them no mind and soon they left him alone. Before Bat and the other men returned with a pony drag to bear Hawk Chaser's body away, Hardeman had lain down beside the body and gone fast to sleep.

When he awoke, he did not know where he was. It was dark, and there was firelight coming from somewhere out of sight. An Indian bent over him, a man he didn't know. The man's face was painted white and his hands and arms were red. He was dressing the wound in Hardeman's shoulder.

Why was the Indian helping him? He had led the soldiers here. . . . No, that was another time. This time he had tried to make peace and he had failed. . . .

He was in a small shelter made from scraps of old tipi coverings. The smell of smoke, heavy and fresh, came from the hides. The pieces of lodgeskin must have been salvaged from the village. There was another smell as well, one more pleasant, though pungent and strong, and he saw now that the floor of the shelter was covered with small branches of sagebrush. Next to him, so close he could have reached out and touched him, Blackbird lay asleep, with new bindings of cloth and hide around his leg and midsection. Once again the two of them were sheltered together while their wounds were treated. But where were they? . . . Hardeman felt at his waist and relaxed a little when he found his Colt there where it belonged.

There was a loud gasp outside the shelter, a sound not quite human, and then the murmuring of several voices, followed by a hideous scream.

Hardeman tried to get up on his elbows. The medicine man said something and pushed him back down, tying a ragged piece of buckskin in place. Hardeman realized that his left arm was bound against his chest as a white doctor might have positioned it for a sling. There was an ache deep in his shoulder that throbbed in time with his heartbeat. With his good hand he touched his left shoulder cautiously, probing to test the extent of the wound. No broken bones? That was a piece of luck. And the bullet had missed his lung. Maybe God was merciful after all.

He laughed, and the medicine man smiled. Hardeman shook his head, trying to make the Indian understand that there was nothing to smile about. "God isn't merciful," he said. "He's a cruel son of a bitch who lets his children maim and kill each other. He sends young boys to war and lets good men die for no reason."

The medicine man nodded, still smiling, and picked up a small round drum. He began to sing a song, drumming a steady accompaniment. From somewhere outside the little lodge came a short screech, followed by a liquid blubbering sound, and then a few words, "Please! Oh, God, please don't kill me!"

Hardeman rolled off his low pallet of robes and crawled to the entrance of the shelter, ignoring the medicine man's efforts to stop him. He pulled aside the crude flap and looked out.

He stared at the scene before him, unbelieving. They were skinning a young soldier.

"Best you go back and lay down, Christopher." Bat Putnam was seated just outside the shelter, taking no part, just watching. There was no trace of his habitual humor in his expression.

Hardeman crawled out of the shelter and sat on the ground beside Bat. A large fire was burning nearby and he could feel its warmth. On the other side of the fire stood a second shelter; Hardeman could see the wide-eyed faces of three young children peering from the entrance. Beyond the firelight the night was dark, and there was no hint of moon in the cloudy sky. The little camp was close below the benchland at the edge of the Cheyenne village, which was now utterly abandoned but for the small group here. Besides Standing Eagle and Little Hand and Bat there were six others, two men and four women, all presently watching the unfortunate soldier. Just at the edge of the firelight, ten or a dozen horses were tethered and hobbled. Closer to the Indians, a few dogs sat watching the spectacle.

The trooper was made fast to a young cottonwood near the fire. He was naked. His lips had been cut away, and his eyelids too, so he could not close his eyes. Little Hand was working on the soldier with a skinning knife, trying to separate the skin from the chest muscles, but the young white man was writhing and moaning continually, making the work difficult.

"Found him in the willows," Bat said curtly. "His soldier-boy friends run off without him."

"You can stop it."

"It ain't my place." He motioned at the watching men. "That there's the uncle of Blackbird's friend, the boy that got hisself killed bringing the horses. He's brother to the feller got shot just after. The women are relatives too. They're all He Dog's folk, Oglalas. They're goin' with us. Reckon to put in with the peace man after what happened today."

"What's Little Hand's stake in this?"

"He's good at it."

The soldier's eyes met Hardeman's and his ghastly lipless mouth made a sound halfway between a sigh and a groan; it rose in pitch to become a wail of agony as Little Hand attempted to peel off a section of skin.

Standing Eagle barked a few words at Little Hand, his voice full of disgust. Little Hand shrugged and moved away from the captive. Standing Eagle spoke again, this time to the women who stood near the fire. Two of the women had their hair cut short and their arms gashed in mourning. They were the first to move, pulling short butchering knives as they ran toward the soldier.

He saw them coming and he screamed. The women reached him and for a moment he was hidden from view. There was another scream, laden with terror and new pain.

A woman threw something small and red to the dogs, where it quickly disappeared. The women drew back, considering what to do next, taunting the soldier, and Hardeman saw that one of the man's testicles had been cut from its sack, which now dripped blood steadily. New gashes crisscrossed the man's chest.

One of the mourning women swung a length of wood as stout as a man's arm against the soldier's chest and there was a cracking sound. The soldier gasped and coughed, and blood trickled from his mouth. One woman shouted her approval, but the others pushed the woman with the stick away and spoke harshly, gesturing at the soldier, apparently arguing for a slower death.

The men were no longer paying any attention to the white captive. They sat in a small group smoking their pipes, discussing the best way to return to the Sun Band's village, and so they did not notice as Hardeman got unsteadily to his feet and began to walk slowly across the clearing toward the soldier.

Standing Eagle was the first to see the scout's advance and he jumped up to place himself between Hardeman and the trooper. Hardeman met the war leader's gaze and looked at the Indian's hand where it rested on his knife, and then he pushed Standing Eagle aside and walked past him. The Lakota moved to stop the white man, but Bat Putnam said a word and Standing Eagle hesitated.

Hardeman reached the soldier, moving through the women as if they weren't there. They protested but drew back, waiting to see what he would do.

The soldier's head was bowed, and saliva and blood drooled from his disfigured mouth. "Oh God," he moaned. "Oh God, help me!"

"You've got to help yourself," Hardeman said, and the trooper looked up with incomprehension in his eyes. "You'll die quicker at the hands of the women, but it's death without honor. The men torture you to let you die bravely. If you cry out, you're not a worthy enemy. You're a coward and you don't deserve their respect."

He watched closely and saw understanding in the miserable man's eyes. The soldier straightened slightly and the tongue licked what was left of the lips to stop the drooling.

"It's up to you," Hardeman went on. "The women'll do it quick but messy. Stand up to the men and they'll see what you're made of. You'll pass out soon enough." He wanted to say more, to give the man some hope, but Bat and Standing Eagle understood English and so he left it there, hoping the soldier would trust him.

He felt himself waver. A haze obscured his vision for a

moment and he was afraid he might faint. He took a deep breath and his vision cleared.

Slowly, the soldier nodded. He drew himself up against his bonds and raised his head. He looked beyond Hardeman, at his captors, and from the small group of Lakota came a few approving *hau*'s.

Hardeman turned away and the women moved forward, but they stopped at a command from Bat. The mountain man spoke in Lakota to Standing Eagle and the other men, and Little Hand nodded and said something, gesturing at the soldier, who now waited quietly, breathing deeply, shuddering once with a chill or a spasm of pain, but his head remained high and his eyes met those of his tormentors.

One of the other men spoke and the women drew back to the fire. Little Hand drew his knife and approached the soldier, his face solemn.

The soldier's breathing grew more rapid. Slowly, Little Hand extended the shallow incision in the man's chest. The soldier looked away and tried to close his lidless eyes. Little Hand stopped his work and looked up. The soldier's eyes returned to meet the Indian's.

Little Hand smiled and with a quick slice he removed the loose flap of skin, leaving a new patch of raw flesh that bled freely. The soldier drew a sharp breath but made no other sound, and he kept his eyes on Little Hand.

Little Hand stepped back, holding up the skin, and now from the onlookers came a chorus of approving sounds, loud and strong, which stopped suddenly at the report of a single shot.

The soldier slumped dead against his bonds. There was a hole in his chest over the heart. Hardeman returned the Colt to his waistband even as the Indians jumped to their feet, knives and war clubs raised. Standing Eagle leveled his carbine at the white man.

Hardeman saw the weapons poised and he saw the anger and hatred in the eyes, and the disappointment at being robbed of the barbaric sport, and he didn't care. If they could do this to another human being they were less than human themselves, and to hell with their notion of honor and giving a captive the chance to die bravely. How did they expect a man to be brave when he didn't know their customs? That was why Hardeman had spoken to the boy, so he would understand, and so he might regain his courage. And he had done well. The Indians had seen that the soldier could be as brave as one of their own youths, once he knew what was expected of him. Hardeman had given them just enough time to see that, and no more, before he had ended the boy's suffering.

The Indians were drawing nearer now, closing in on him, and Bat Putnam was with them, his face set and hard. The mountain man had sat and watched the torture, and he had done nothing. The growing friendship Hardeman had once felt for Bat was gone now, and with it any trace of sympathy for the Sioux. The newspapers and the terrified whites who had never even seen an Indian were right: they were savages. They claimed to want peace, but once the fighting began they were as eager for it as the soldiers and they gloried in the chaos of battle; he had seen it in their faces today. Well, they would get plenty of fighting now. The soldiers would come again and again until both sides had had enough of fighting, and then the Indians would be penned in and watched over like wild animals and that was right too. He would do nothing to stop it even if he could. It was out of his hands now and he was glad.

He was clinging to consciousness by a thread, but he strove to remain upright, looking at each dark pair of eyes in turn so they could see his small victory. But the haze rose before him again like sunlight filtered through the yellow leaves of autumn. He swayed, and felt hands take hold of him.

The Conclusion of

THE SNOWBLIND MOON PART THREE: HOOP OF THE NATION

is coming from Tor Books
in September

What lies ahead . . .

Sun Horse's stomach rumbled loudly and he became aware of the smells of the welcoming feast, which still lingered in the lodge. There was meat in the pot over the cooking fire. He felt the juices flow in his mouth and he struggled to turn his thoughts away from his hunger. Why had it returned to him now to distract him from his quest for power? His search was no closer to its goal than when he started. . . . Or was it? When he was curing the clown girl he had thrown away the last specks of dust from his vision-hill in an effort to look beyond the symbols of his power, trying to grasp its essence . . . and the clown girl had recovered. His curing power was still strong. What of his power to lead? Perhaps it too was as strong as ever, lacking only the understanding of how to use it. . . .

Even his grandson spoke of power and understanding. It seemed that a power had truly come to Blackbird on the morning of the battle. The helper from his becoming-a-man vision had returned to give him a warning. *Fly away from the whites!* the birds said, *and you will survive the day*. The boy had charged the bluecoats' guns, but his first thoughts had been of the people. Only after he had called a warning to the sleeping village, only after he had taken the horses to a place where they were needed most, did he fling himself into the fight to avenge a fallen comrade. And despite being wounded again, he had survived.

Twice on his journey the boy had been badly wounded. He had been close to death, and he was changed by the experience. He wished to learn the true meaning of manhood now; he wished to learn responsibility for the people. . . .

Sun Horse felt his hopes rise.

Two men had ridden to save the boy from the soldiers. One Lakota and one white, united in a common purpose. . . . Why?

Hawk Chaser had died because he was the boy's *hunká*-father, and one *hunká* would do anything to save another.

And what of the other who rode to save him? Hardeman had risked his life twice in a single day. He had tried to stop the fighting and he had failed, but he had been successful in saving Blackbird. And he had saved another boy, long ago. It was in his nature to save a boy in trouble just as it was in his nature to try to make peace. He knew war and he understood the need for peace. He had been willing to do anything to achieve it, even betray the trust that Sun Horse had put in him when he sent him with the pipe carriers. . . .

But it was not only Sun Horse he would have betrayed if he had led the soldiers to Sitting Bull! That was plain from his words here in the council today. He was ashamed of what he had thought to do. *He would have betrayed himself!* The action went against his nature. It was not his nature to betray a trust.

He would have betrayed himself, and of course he had failed, for a man could not go against his own nature.

It was not in Standing Eagle's nature to make peace with the whites, and so he had failed when he carried a pipe of peace. . . .

Sun Horse trembled with the force of the chill that took him now. Outside, the wind gained force; around him the lodge trembled; beneath him the earth trembled; the universe was pregnant with power.

A man cannot go against his nature, neither Lakota nor *washíchun*. . . .

Three Stars won't give up, Hardeman had told the council. *That's not his way of making war and it's not the whiteman's way. When the whiteman starts fighting, he keeps on until his enemy surrenders.*

Could it be that Hardeman was right after all and the only possible end was surrender? In the end the whites would be true to their nature; if only conquest would satisfy them, then they would destroy the hoop of the Lakota nation forever and there would be no accommodation, no joining, no living together protected by the sacred tree that stood at the center of the world, where the red and black roads came together.

If this were true, then Sun Horse's quest, his days and nights of searching for the path to peace, had been in vain. If this were true, then *wamblí*'s promise was false, Hears Twice's prophecy was false, his own vision from the butte overlooking the Laramie fort was false, and that could not be! Had not his vision led the people here? Had they not lived in peace for twenty-five snows? Had not Hears Twice's prophecy come true, with the life-giving power of *pte* returned to the band?

The visions and the signs could not be false! They must be true, and they must have a purpose! Had not Blackbird been saved by his vision, his spirit helpers coming to guide him safely through the battle? The boy had nearly died and yet he lived. He had grown a great deal in a short time and his thoughts turned to the good of the people. Why?!

Sun Horse looked at the sleeping youth beside him and he recalled his own words—*You are the future of the people*. . . .

He gasped, and his eyes opened wide in astonishment. For a long moment he remained motionless and then he covered his eyes with his hands and bowed forward where he sat.

He had been blind. As surely as the clown girl, he had been snowblind, made sightless from casting about on all sides, even when the *pte* were found, even when the answer to his search came into his very lodge.

He straightened and opened his eyes, and it seemed to him that he saw for the first time. The sleeping forms around him, the furnishings of the lodge, the fire, even the most familiar objects, appeared newly created and full of hope.

He inhaled deeply, tasting the odor of cooked meat that filled the lodge, the flesh of *pte,* the most sacred of the four-leggeds, and then he began to laugh silently. He shook until he had to hold his sides and he laughed until the tears ran down his cheeks. Except for his broad smile, he might have been crying. His stomach growled and he laughed harder.

Finally the quiet shaking stopped and Sun Horse wiped the tears from his leathery cheeks. He sat looking at Blackbird, smiling still, wishing he could wake the boy to share his good spirits, but his grandson needed to rest and grow strong. When Blackbird awoke in the morning, he would be hungry. Sun Horse would see that he ate well. He would need all his strength for what lay ahead of him.

Blackbird shifted position slightly and began to snore softly, as Standing Eagle had snored when he was a boy, and Sun Horse finally stirred himself. He moved around the fire on his hands and knees, pausing when he reached the sleeping forms of Johnny Smoker and Amanda. He dropped his head low and pawed the ground with one hand, and a new fit of silent laughing overtook him, but he quelled his laughter and grew serious. "Oh, *Tatanka,* thank you for leading my grandson to the clown girl," he whispered. "Truly they have brought a power to help the Sun Band!"

He moved on to where Elk Calf slept and he sat back on his thin shanks when he reached her side. With one wrinkled hand he stroked her face until she opened her eyes. "I will have some broth," he said, smiling, and she looked at him in surprise, coming fully awake in an instant. Tomorrow he would have some roasted meat, but for now just the broth, the life force of *pte*. "And a little liver," he added as Elk Calf sat up. "With gall."

Filled with wonder at the sudden change in her husband, Elk Calf moved the kettle to the center fire and soon the broth was hot. Sun Horse drank one bowl slowly, until his rumbling stomach subsided, and then another, more quickly. With his skinning knife he cut small bites off the liver and dipped them in gall. The yellow gall dripped on his chin and he wiped it away and licked the finger clean. All the time he smiled and said nothing to Elk Calf, but she asked for no explanations. She watched him eat as if she had never seen such a thing before, and when his bowl was placed to show that he wanted nothing more, she returned to her robes. Just as she fell asleep again, she was aware that Sun Horse had left the fire and was slipping beneath Sings His Daughter's robes. Elk Calf smiled. Truly, he was himself once more. When he was ready, he would tell her what he had learned when he was beyond his body and its demands.

Sun Horse fitted himself closely to Sings His Daughter's sleeping form and he felt the smoothness of her skin. His manhood stirred and grew strong and it was this movement that awakened her. She made a sigh of pleasure and moved her buttocks against him, making a place for him between her legs, but he did not take her right away. For a long time he lay close to her, his hands moving very slowly over her body, showing her the peace he felt within him. Finally, when she had nearly gone back to sleep, he enjoyed her gently from the rear and dropped asleep himself, still inside her.

* * *

Johnny dismounted and moved forward on foot, leading his horse across an expanse of windswept ground that was strewn with pieces of shale. From the moment the little band started out on Tatum's trail, Johnny had placed himself in front of the others and no one had questioned his right to lead the chase. Through the dark hours before dawn he had pushed ahead as fast as he dared, close-mouthed and grim all the while. Sometimes he had dismounted to feel the trail with his bare hands, but he had made good time, especially at the start, knowing Tatum and his men would have to keep to the river trail at least until it reached the foothills. At first light Johnny had lost the tracks where the wind had wiped them away, and only then had he turned to Hardeman for help. Together they had cast about as the light brightened, but it was Johnny who found the trail again and since then he had not lost it. Hardeman judged that he himself could not have made better progress if he had followed the tracks alone.

"There." Johnny pointed, finding the scrape made by a shod hoof on frozen ground almost as soon as Hardeman's eyes had settled on the faint mark. The youth remounted and rode forward, bending low in the saddle. His pace quickened as he looked to the front and saw where recent tracks crossed a small drift of snow. Beyond, the ground was covered in white once more and the trail was plainly visible.

Johnny urged his horse into a trot and Hardeman kept pace with him, wondering at the boy's control. Despite his anguished concern for Amanda, Johnny had never once panicked, nor had he forgotten that a man who kept his horse to a steady pace all day would soon overtake another who had gotten off to a faster start.

Hoofbeats came from behind them and Hardeman turned to see the rest of the pursuers, Indians and whites, strung out in a long line behind Sun Horse and Walks Bent Over. As the old chief drew abreast of him, Hardeman made a sign of greeting.

"*Hau*, Christopher," said Sun Horse, and he reined in beside the white man.

Walks Bent Over moved ahead of them but he saw the intensity with which Johnny followed the trail and he kept behind the young man. Like Hardeman, he watched for any signs Johnny might miss and allowed the youth to keep the lead. Ahead, the land fell away toward the Middle Fork.

Lisa and Bat Putnam made their way to the front of the pack, followed closely by Julius. Behind them came the quartet of circus men. Chalmers rode a dapple-gray Shire gelding of enormous proportions and Papa Waldheim was mounted on a sturdy bay stallion. By now even the impulsive Waldheims knew that they must adjust their pace to that of the tracker.

Chalmers was heartened by the new strength of the band. Until now the pursuers had numbered only nine, the number kept small so they would not be hindered by men unfamiliar with the demands of what could be a long and arduous ride, but through the night and into the chill grayness of the stormy morning, Chalmers had grown increasingly concerned about what might happen when the fugitives were overtaken. The outcome of a gun battle between the two groups, so evenly matched, was far from certain, and Amanda would be put in danger if it came to an armed confrontation. Now, with the Indians along, Tatum might see that his situation was hopeless and surrender without a fight.

The riders plunged down a slope to the riverbank. Even unpracticed eyes could follow the trail here.

"If he keeps to the Middle Fork he'll come out of the foothills soon," Lisa said. "He could make good time on the old wagon road."

"So could we," said Julius. "We'd catch him in a couple of hours out there. Even a dude like Tatum won't make that kind of mistake."

"They turn south, they'll come on the South Fork," said Bat. "She twists like a snake but she'll lead 'em stright to the Oregon road. It's a fair little valley too. Give 'em some cover for quite a ways."

Ahead of them, where the river passed through a narrow cut and the trail climbed a rise, Johnny halted by a cluster of tracks and motioned those behind him to stay back. He rode in a broad arc until he found where the fugitives had turned off the main trail. His eyes met Hardeman's. "They've seen us." He set off again, following the tracks with new urgency now. Hardeman had to kick his horse into a fast trot to keep up. Within moments Lisa Putnam overtook him and fell in beside him, where she had been throughout most of the night.

Back in the settlement she had reached the barn before Hardeman had finished saddling the horse he had picked at random from the horse pasture, a chestnut gelding. He had taken one look at her riding garb and the Winchester in her hand, and he had tried to dissuade her from coming along. "Lisa, you can't—" was all he got out before she had cut him off. "Can you ride all day and night if you have to?" she demanded. "Can you shoot a rifle with that bad arm? I can do both, Mr. Hardeman!" A quarter of an hour later the nine riders were on the trail and making for the river canyon. Hardeman and Lisa had spoken only rarely since then. Once or twice he had addressed her as Lisa, but each time she had called him Mr. Hardeman in reply and he had fallen back on his former habit of using her surname. Her manner toward him was the same as it might have been if their intimacy of three nights before had never happened, but still she kept close to him.

The band of pursuers rode in silence, slowing where Johnny had to search out the tracks on bare, frozen ground, increasing their pace where the trail was preserved in patches of snow. The tracks were fresher now.

The snow thinned and stopped and the clouds parted to admit a few rays of sunshine to the country below. Just beyond the last of the foothills the trail turned suddenly again, crossing the Middle Fork to its south bank. Hereabouts the stream flowed for the most part in a narrow channel with banks eight or ten feet high, but the fugitives had found a crossing where the banks were crumbled and low. As the pursuers gained the far bank they scanned the countryside, but nothing moved.

"They're runnin' lickety-split along here," Julius observed with his eyes on the tracks. "Must of spooked when they seen us comin'. I cain't see why they'd keep on like this. They'd do better back in the foothill country.

They ever shook us off the trail back there, they could go to ground and lose us for good."

For more than half a mile the tracks led straight as an arrow along the bank of the stream, the fugitives' horses running in line, and then suddenly the trail doubled back, descended a steep bank to the river, and vanished in the water. Johnny crossed the stream and searched the far side, but he found nothing.

Walks Bent Over made signs to indicate horsemen going downstream, hiding their tracks in the water. Johnny understood at once and started off along the far shore, while the hunchbacked Indian advanced on the southern bank. Sooner or later Tatum and his men would have to leave the water.

Sun Horse glanced at Standing Eagle and Little Hand and he made a few signs, motioning them forward along the banks. They obeyed him at once, Little Hand crossing the stream and gaining the top of the bank there, while Standing Eagle galloped off on the near side. Together they would move out in advance of the trackers to see if swift riders might find an obvious trail leaving the river.

The main body of pursuers advanced more slowly behind Johnny Smoker and Walks Bent Over, who watched for signs a man traveling fast on horseback might miss, but before they had gone another half mile Standing Eagle came back in sight, riding like the wind. He made broad signs as he approached and then he swung off toward the southeast, beckoning the others to follow him. In an instant the warriors were off, with Walks Bent Over in the lead and the whites close on their heels. To the rear, Johnny Smoker was already across the river and gaining rapidly on the pack.

"I knew it!" Bat exulted. He had guessed right. Somewhere up ahead Tatum's bunch had left the water and made a run for the South Fork and the shelter of the river bottom there, hoping to throw the pursuers off the scent, but they had failed.

Bat reveled in the thrill of the chase and the sight of the riders around him, whites and Indians together, just like the old days. They were all racing hell-for-leather, eager to close the gap. Standing Eagle led them over one rise and then another, and there was Little Hand waiting for them. He had followed the fugitives' trail from the Middle Fork and now he pointed to the south and led the way. When Bat reached the trail he saw that once more the fugitives had ridden in line, one man leading and the rest following. Why did they take such care to keep in single file? It was an Indian trick, not a white man's, and everyone knew how many men had run off with Tatum, so what was the point?

"How far to the South Fork?" Hardeman called to Bat as he and Johnny Smoker drew abreast of the mountain man.

"A few miles, I reckon. I ain't much of a one fer white man's distance. But I'll tell you what. We'll be there in a jiffy." Bat grinned. " 'Bout the time that hits us." He jerked a thumb back over his shoulder. A gray wall of clouds was bearing down on the pursuers from behind, pushed along by the wind, which howled past their ears and whipped the horses' tails about their haunches even as they tried to outrun it. To the west, the mountains were completely hidden. The storm was coming on fast. Even so, the trail was fresh and they wouldn't lose it now. Soon Silk-Hat Tatum and his bunch would be brought to bay and all the questions would be answered, and until then the chase was the thing. It brought Bat to mind of other pursuits long past, like the one on the Green when a large party of trappers and friendly Snakes had wakened one morning to find all their horses gone; it had taken four days, but they had got the horses back and taught the thieving Crows a lesson too.

"Shinin' times!" he said to himself, and he began to tell himself the story under his breath.

"Where in hell have they got to?" Julius wondered aloud, riding nearby. "We oughta catch sight of 'em 'long about now."

"Gone to ground, mebbe," Bat offered, and he put his memories aside to concentrate on the fresh tracks before him. He was a woolly-headed old coot, never content to take what the moment had to offer, always mooning about some time gone by, one he remembered as better. They hadn't all been good times, and that was truth. He knew what it meant to be cold and hungry and a whisker away from death. But he had lived each day and gone on to the next, and that was what he would do now, just get through the day and take it as it came. By the look of things there would be some doin's before nightfall.

He reined his horse back to a trot and drew aside from the pack, looking around warily. When your quarry disappeared, you might be the quarry before you knew it.

Ahead, the trail followed a shallow gully down to the bottom of a dry wash. Beyond the wash the land rolled away to the southeast where the tops of a few trees revealed the course of the Powder's southern fork a mile or two distant. It was a bleak landscape, almost devoid of vegetation, and Bat recalled with longing the pleasant, wooded hills and the lush grass of the lower Powder valley where he had been so recently. Even in winter the northern country seemed rich and fertile compared with this. Let the *washíchun* have the country here if he wanted it. It was little enough to give away if there could be a chance for peace.

Fifty yards ahead of Bat, Hardeman and Johnny were in the forefront as the pursuers entered the dry wash. Hardeman kept his eyes on the tracks, still in a narrow file like those of a party of Indians, who rode that way when they wished to conceal their true numbers. In the bottom of the wash there was a bare patch of sand and a hoofprint clean and sharp, one of the horses showing a cleat much like an army winter shoe . . .

He looked up suddenly. To the right, the wash curved and twisted away into higher ground, and there was movement along its rim.

"Look out!" he cried, too late.

A crashing volley of gunfire came from up the gentle slope, where clouds of gray-white smoke puffed out along the lip of the wash to reveal the ambushers' position. A horse screamed and in that same moment Little Hand flew backward off his mount, arms flung wide and the rifle falling from his hand; he was dead before he hit the ground.

ACKNOWLEDGMENTS

I am indebted to the following people, who generously contributed their time and expertise and thereby did much to assure the historical accuracy of *The Snowblind Moon:* Marie T. Capps, Map and Manuscript Librarian at the United States Military Academy Library, West Point, New York; Catherine T. Engel, Reference Librarian, Colorado Historical Society, Denver, Colorado; Neil Mangum, Historian, Custer Battlefield National Monument, Montana. Special thanks are due to B. Byron Price, Director of the Panhandle-Plains Historical Museum, Canyon, Texas, who read the sections concerning the frontier army and made many valuable suggestions, and to my friends John and Elaine Barlow and Melody Harding of the Bar Cross Ranch, Cora, Wyoming, and Pete and Holly Cameron of Game Hill Ranch, Bondurant, Wyoming, without whose kindness and hospitality I would know even less about the care and raising of beef cattle.

I am particularly grateful to Dr. Bernard A. Hoehner of San Francisco State University, San Francisco, California, for his invaluable advice in matters pertaining to Lakota language and culture as they appear in the novel. (A *Siháсapa*-Lakota, Dr. Hoehner was given the named Jerked With Arrow in his youth, and is now also known as Grass among his people.)

In including some Lakota words and phrases in a work intended for a general readership I have chosen to disregard certain conventions commonly employed in writing Lakota; I have used no linguistic symbols other than the acute accent and have adopted spellings intended to make something close to proper pronunciation as easy as possible for those with no previous knowledge of the language. These decisions were mine alone. I hope persons familiar with Lakota will forgive these simplifications.

Naturally, any remaining historical errors in *The Snowblind Moon*, whether of fact or interpretation, are my sole responsibility.

John Byrne Cooke
Jackson Hole, Wyoming

ABOUT THE AUTHOR

John Byrne Cooke was born in New York City in 1940. He was graduated from Harvard College and has worked as a musician, filmmaker, rock and roll road-manager, screenwriter and amateur cowboy. He has lived on both the East and West coasts and now resides in Jackson Hole, Wyoming. *The Snowblind Moon* is his first novel.